D0122614

Keep my Heart in San Francisco

Keep my Heart in San Francisco

AMELIA DIANE COOMBS

Simon Pulse

NEW YORK   LONDON   TORONTO   SYDNEY   NEW DELHI

To Mom and Dad, for your unwavering support—also for trying to hand-sell this book to everyone you know, and if we're being honest, some strangers on the street too

SIMON PULSE

An imprint of Simon & Schuster Children's Publishing Division

1230 Avenue of the Americas, New York, New York 10020

First Simon Pulse hardcover edition July 2020

Text copyright © 2020 by Amelia Diane Coombs

Jacket flap texture by sorrapong/iStock

For information about special discounts for bulk purchases, please contact Simon & Schuster Special Sales at 1-866-506-1949 or business@simonandschuster.com.

The Simon & Schuster Speakers Bureau can bring authors to your live event. For more information or to book an event contact the Simon & Schuster Speakers Bureau at 1-866-248-3049 or visit our website at www.simonspeakers.com.

Jacket designed by Tiara Iandiorio

Interior designed by Mike Rosamilia

The text of this book was set in Candida.

Manufactured in the United States of America

2 4 6 8 10 9 7 5 3 1

Library of Congress Cataloging-in-Publication Data

Names: Coombs, Amelia Diane, author.

Title: Keep my heart in San Francisco / by Amelia Diane Coombs.

Description: First Simon Pulse hardcover edition. | New York: Simon Pulse, 2020. | Audience: Ages 14 up | Summary: Caroline "Chuck" Wilson must join forces with her ex–best friend Beckett to try to save her family's failing bowling alley and stay in San Francisco, but his plan is not strictly business—or legal.

Identifiers: LCCN 2019026163 (print) | LCCN 2019026164 (eBook) | ISBN 9781534452978 (hardcover) | ISBN 9781534452992 (eBook)

Subjects: CYAC: Bowling alleys—Fiction. | Swindlers and swindling—Fiction. | Best friends—Fiction. | Friendship—Fiction. | Family life—California—San Francisco—Fiction. | San Francisco (Calif.)—Fiction.

Classification: LCC PZ7.1.C64759 Kee 2020 (print) | LCC PZ7.1.C64759 (eBook) | DDC [Fic]—dc23

LC record available at https://lccn.loc.gov/2019026163

LC eBook record available at https://lccn.loc.gov/2019026164

Please be aware that *Keep My Heart in San Francisco* includes the following content:

Mental illness (bipolar disorder)
Conversations surrounding suicide

Stay afraid, but do it anyway.

—Carrie Fisher

THURSDAY, APRIL 19
DAYS UNTIL
SPRING BREAK: 1

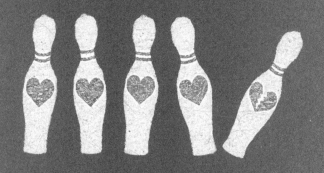

One

I'M ELBOW-DEEP IN some dead lady's clothes when a customer bowls a perfect game.

Hidden from view, I'm kneeling behind the register as I finish cataloging my latest estate-sale finds, but I can hear the players whoop and holler. I take a deep breath, and the smell of Chanel No. 5 mixed with lavender-scented mothballs tickles my nostrils.

My shift ends in five minutes, but now I have to run interference with a cocky high scorer asking for a free game and his name on the wall of fame. Okay, *fame* is pushing it, but people love having their name displayed for the world to see. Normally not an issue, right? Except a bowling alley like Bigmouth's can't go comping games. I sweep the vintage threads into the garbage bag and pop up just as the winner, a regular named Marty, saunters over from the lanes.

I drop-kick the bag beneath the counter. "Congrats on the three hundred."

"Thanks. Sign says perfect games are on the house." He slaps down the scored transparency. Three feet of counter stretch between us, yet my eyes water from Marty's stale nicotine breath and criminal lack of deodorant. Ah, the aroma of Bigmouth's remaining patrons.

I side-eye the sign hanging crooked on the wall beside me. We really should've taken that down *years* ago, because Marty isn't wrong. The refund is for the winning player's entire group, which is a problem. My brain churns for another option because there's not enough in the register to cover the sixty-two dollars the men paid for their games and shoes.

Thursdays are league night at Bigmouth's, but they're only the second group of customers we've had all day. Before his break, Dad grabbed money from the register's drawer for dinner. A lowly twenty-dollar bill remains in the drawer.

Bigmouth's is hemorrhaging cash.

"We can give you a voucher for a free game next time," I offer, grinding my molars. Technically, a voucher *is* an option. Not the most lucrative one. But Marty's a regular, and I cross my fingers that he'll just take the voucher.

"That's not what the sign says. Look, can you comp our game or not?"

Well, at least I tried. To buy time, I rustle through a stack of forms. "Sure thing. Why don't you fill this out with your info so your name can be added to the wall?"

This occupies Marty long enough for me to duck to the floor and grab my wallet from my carpetbag purse. I only have forty dollars, which I crumple into my sweaty fist. *Goddammit, Dad.* When I unload the register, I slip my four tens in with the lone twenty.

"Here you go." I fork over sixty dollars even.

Marty doesn't count the bills. Doesn't notice the missing two dollars.

"Thanks, Chuck," he replies, pocketing the money.

When they leave, I rip the sign off its hook and toss it in the trash. I kick the trash can, my big toe throbbing through my patent-leather flats, and press my fingertips against my eyelids. I take a scrambled, aching breath, itching for a sense of calm. What would've happened if I hadn't had cash on me? Beyond the sheer embarrassment factor, we can't afford to upset or lose our dwindling customer base.

Thankfully, tonight is my last shift before spring break, a week of glorious freedom and fashion. Dad promised me a bowling-free vacation. No clunky register or used shoes or the clang of pins hitting oiled alleys. I've jam-packed my break with estate sales—they're a treasure trove of history and cheaper than the overpriced thrift stores in the city. Plus a vintage showcase and a college tour of San Francisco's Fashion Institute of Design and Merchandising on Saturday.

The bell above the door jingles and Dad walks in, carrying a sweating take-out bag. "Caroline! Did I miss the rush?" he jokes, and I find his cheerfulness grating. Our lack of customers isn't a laughing matter.

"Nope," I reply, flinching the way I always do when Dad

uses my full name, "but Marty bowled a three hundred after you left."

Dad fails to hide his grimace. The to-go bag of food swings against his legs. "Ah, I see. You comp him?"

"Yep. He wants his name up there," I add, jerking my thumb to the stretch of wall above the lanes where we've immortalized our high-scoring customers. Benjamin O'Neill, my maternal grandfather, who opened Bigmouth's, is the first name on the leaderboard.

"How'd you refund him?" Dad slides the form off the counter and pockets it without a glance.

I fixate on a drooping cobweb hanging from the ceiling. "I used some of my money. It's fine."

"I'll pay you back, Caroline. I promise."

The sentiment is nice, but I sincerely doubt I'll see that forty bucks again. Annoyance flares, lightning quick, before I can tamp it down. Why is it up to me? Why am I helping Bigmouth's stay afloat? I work for free—running the register and hosing off bowling shoes with disinfectant. Now I'm comping games with the money in my purse?

The stress lines around Dad's mouth ease somewhat. Bigmouth's is struggling, but his pride would take a serious hit if the customers found out just how badly we're doing.

"Don't worry about it." Annoyed as I am, it's a small price to pay for my dad to be happy. Unstressed. "Hey, did you order wontons?"

He sets the food down and attempts a smile. "Want one?"

I pluck a wonton from the Styrofoam container and

pop it in my mouth. "Do you still need me around? My shift ended fifteen minutes ago." I nudge the trash bag of clothes from underneath the counter, ready to dart toward my freedom. A week far from Bigmouth's.

"Honey," Dad says. "I heard from Pete and he, um, he quit."

That small slice of freedom slips from my grasp. "He what?"

"I'm sorry—"

I groan and drop my forehead to the counter for a dramatic moment before looking up and saying, "But you *promised*."

Dad tucks his hands into the pockets of his knee-length cargo shorts. "I know, I know, but I don't have many options. Help your old man out."

All my weight rests on my elbows as I slouch against the countertop. Helping him out is all I do. "So I'm working spring break after all."

"Until I get the shifts figured out." His fingers tap and twitch. I swear there's an air of relief over Pete quitting—one less salary we can't afford to pay. Other than me—child labor laws be damned—he was our only employee.

The tension webbed between my shoulder blades refuses to relax, and my throat aches. Resigned, I slouch on my stool. "Sucks Pete quit."

"Ah, it'll be okay. Thanks for your help, hon." He slides his phone from his pocket, glancing at the time. "Can you stay until seven? Jesset's coming by, and I need someone manning the front desk."

A visit from the landlord is never good. "Sure thing, boss," I say, unable to bite back my sarcasm.

Dad winces his smile. "Things are gonna change, Caroline. I promise." Before I can respond, he takes his dinner and disappears down the hallway toward his office.

Change. The word turns and tumbles in my head. What kind of change?

The comment—and its implications—rattle me. I don't love working here, but Bigmouth's is a family business, and I'd do anything to help Dad. But the annoyance lingers over having my spring break hijacked. Not to mention losing my forty dollars. When Dad's office door clicks shut, I grab my headphones and plug them into my phone.

Goodbye, spring break; hello, Hellmouth.

No estate sales. No vintage showcases. And the worst part? No FIDM college tour. I'm missing out because of Dad. Because of Bigmouth's. Because of *bowling*. There will be other tours, other chances to explore my future in fashion design, but spring break is turning into a serious bust. And it hasn't even started yet.

The city, with its dour skies and chilly air, beckons me from outside the tinted glass doors. Every April is the same; I don't know why I'm surprised anymore. Spring is disappointing, the fog soupy and the sky weeping well into June. This is my city, and I thrive in it. The hipsters. The hippies. Our not-so-golden bridge. San Francisco may house eight hundred thousand people, but it's *mine*.

I haul the trash bag onto my lap and unearth the vintage James Galanos I scored at my last estate sale. Break might be beyond saving, but at least I have my music and my endless sewing projects. There's something soothing and methodical about mending ruined clothes. The Galanos dress's hem is ragged, so I pull out my travel sewing kit to mend whatever disaster befell the once-glorious yellow silk creation.

Carefully angling the needle along the original seam, I tuck my bottom lip between my teeth in concentration. My time with a needle and thread began in middle school, when I worked on costumes for the theater department. I'm no talented thespian, but once I taught myself how to sew, I became an asset behind the scenes. Over the past few years, I've become addicted to renovating old clothing, mining gold from estate sales and reinventing them.

My mother also had an affinity for vintage, but I prefer to avoid the psychological implications of our overlapping interests.

Something heavy slams onto the countertop and my hand slips, the needle piercing my forefinger. Blood wells. I pop my finger in my mouth and glance at the cardboard box of food—our weekly delivery. But when I peer around the box, whatever semblance of a smile I might've had slips away.

Beckett Porter stares at me expectantly from the opposite side of the register behind a curtain of soft brown curls.

I blink once, twice, three times. How much blood did I lose from that needle prick? I must've passed out because there's no way this is reality. A hallucination is more likely, because Beckett hasn't stepped foot in Bigmouth's since sophomore year.

When I make no move to acknowledge him, he mimes headphone removal, eyebrows raised in expectation. And that's all it takes for my surprise to morph into annoyance. More than anything, I want to return to my dress as if I never laid eyes on him. But Dad expects a certain level of *professionalism* at work.

"Beckett." I say his name lightly, but those two syllables are laced with distaste. "I'd say I'm happy to see you, but we both know that'd be a lie."

"Always a pleasure, Chuck." He points to the Schulman's Delivery logo on his polo's breast pocket. "Schulman's put me on your route." Since I've lost the ability to read him, I can't tell *what* he's thinking right now. Or what he's doing here.

Until this very moment, there was only one place I had to avoid Beckett Porter. With a school as large as Castelli High, it was no problem. But Bigmouth's? What am I supposed to do? Duck and cover beneath the counter whenever he has a delivery?

Schulman's has delivered Bigmouth's food supplies since before I was born, and I had no idea he worked for them. How—and why—he finagled his way into this situation is beyond me. We're not friends anymore. We don't talk. And we certainly aren't going to interact on a weekly basis when he drops off deliveries.

Beckett taps the cardboard box with a pen. "So, yeah, I have a delivery. Can you sign?"

"Nope." Only Dad can sign off. I've been forbidden from signing off on any deliveries after being held responsible for a missing shipment years ago. My free hand is full of sunshine-colored gossamer, and I flick my fingers toward the office.

Beckett sighs and his cinnamony coffee breath hits me in the face. "Mind walking me back? I don't want to get lost."

Lost? Yeah right.

I roll my eyes so hard my ocular muscles cramp. In another life, he used to spend as much time here as I did. What is this? A weird attempt at inconveniencing me? I round the register and snatch the signature clipboard from him.

He trails behind me as I stroll across Bigmouth's lobby. Our feet smack on the red-and-white checkered flooring, and the air is heavy with Febreze and stale fried food. We pass framed photos of my grandpa on opening day in the seventies, stills from tournaments and parties: days when, you know, bowling was a sport.

Beckett smacks his gum between his teeth. "Excited for spring break?"

I glance sideways at him. What's up with the small talk? "No. Working."

Roughly a hundred things bother me about Beckett Porter, but one of my top annoyances is how he's never, ever upset or disgruntled. Once, I liked this about him. He was mellow and easygoing. The direct opposite of my reactive personality. You could force the guy to greet the

Queen of England in the nude, and he'd grin the entire time.

Mental face-palm. *Do not think of Beckett Porter naked.* Because unfortunately, while Beckett's a pain in my ass, he's a mildly attractive pain in my ass. Except I'm not attracted to him. I've forced myself to become immune to Beckett Dylan Porter. But the heat in my cheeks begs to differ.

Beckett wears a delivery uniform—short-sleeved collared shirt, faded jeans, loafers—and his tawny-brown curls hit his narrow shoulders. I hate to admit it, even in my head, but since he grew his curls out, he has ridiculously nice hair. My hair isn't that nice, and I maintain it. He probably rolls out of bed looking like that.

When he's not watching, I discreetly flare my nostrils, sniffing for a familiar drugstore brand. Something to prove Beckett doesn't come by luscious curls naturally. Nothing. A year ago, he never used conditioner, and it's unlikely things have changed. I doubt he knows what conditioner is, let alone applies weekly keratin masks.

I rap my knuckles against the door with the metal nameplate marked OFFICE and lean my hip against the wall.

Beckett clicks and unclicks the pen over and over. "What were you working on back there?"

I look him in his steel-gray eyes and lift an eyebrow.

"Just trying to be polite." He sighs audibly and shoves the pen into his pocket. Huh. Maybe he's not so unflappable after all.

"Well, knock it off." I push open the office door, but

Dad's nowhere to be seen. The accounting books are splayed across the desk. "He's probably out back."

When Dad meets with Art Jesset, Bigmouth's landlord, it's usually in his office. But judging from Dad's twitching hands, he was dying for a cigarette. I ease the hallway's emergency exit open and stick my head into the alley-way alongside Bigmouth's. Whatever sunlight we had this afternoon is gone. The fog this city is so famous for hangs heavy in the air. If you watch closely, it moves across the pavement, disembodied and a little ghostly.

"There he—" I stop. Dad's talking to a slender guy with smooth blond hair. Jesset. From their gestures and spiking voices, I can tell the conversation is heated. I rock onto my heels. Do I interrupt? Walk away? Eavesdrop?

Beckett pauses behind me, the heat of his body narrowing the half foot of space between us. He drops his voice to a whisper. "Are we spying on your dad?"

"Shut up." I inch outside, if only to get away from him.

"Okay, fine, but I didn't dress for spying."

The dumpster is large enough to hide me from view. To my horror, Beckett follows, and I grab him by the collar, pulling us both into a crouch behind the dumpster before Dad or Jesset notice. It's dark out, but a huge light glows above the exit. Moths bounce and burn against the glass.

Jesset's car is parked in the alley's entrance, and he leans against the hood as my dad paces. If I listen hard enough, I can overhear their words slipping through the mist.

"I thought we had an arrangement," Dad's saying, his voice thin and watery.

"Jack," the landlord replies, "I'm sorry, but I already gave you extra time. If you can get me that eight grand in back rent before the lease ends on the thirtieth, then we can talk. . . ."

Eight *thousand* dollars? I glance at Beckett, and from his face I can tell I heard Jesset right.

"I understand," Dad says, but his hands worry through his hair.

"I hate doing this, but I have no other choice." From the tone of Jesset's voice, this doesn't sound hard for him at all. In fact, it's *effortless*, like he could be placing his morning-coffee order. Jesset's breezy tone makes me want to punch him; there's nothing casual about this conversation.

Deep down I know we've been struggling with Bigmouth's rent, but Dad never gave me a reason to doubt that we were square with the landlord. From this conversation, it's obvious he hasn't been paying the whole rent for the last few months if we owe an extra eight grand. That's an entire month's rent.

"Asshole," I say, and shift forward to get a better view.

"What'd I do this time?" Beckett jokes, knees folded awkwardly to his chest as he balances on his heels.

I almost smile, but catch myself. "I meant Jesset, but now that you mention it, yes, you're an asshole."

"That's a bold claim."

"Well, I have a lot of evidence to back me up."

"Do you hear yourself talk?" His tone has hardened, and he brings a hand to his mouth, exhaling harshly

14

between his fingers. "You are such a *hypocrite*, Chuck Wilson."

I'm the hypocrite? If we weren't hiding, I'd push him on his ass. Instead, I ignore him and focus solely on my dad. Because that's why I'm out here: figuring out what's going on with Dad. Not making hostile small talk with Beckett Porter.

Dad's shoulders slump forward and his hand shakes as it brings a cigarette to his lips. Jesset looks at his phone, like he has better places to be. All I want is to give Dad a hug, comfort him, but I stay hidden.

"Sorry, bud," Jesset says, and pats my dad on the shoulder. "You're my favorite tenant, but if you can't come up with the money, take this as an official notice of your eviction."

Dad mumbles something too quiet for me to hear, and Jesset dismissively shakes his hand before ducking into the car and driving off. Dad stands there for a second, sucking on his cigarette, head tilted backward as if he's praying to the foggy skies or trying not to cry. Maybe both.

When he turns and walks toward Bigmouth's back door, Beckett tugs on my arm and snaps me into motion. I smack his hand away, but we hurry inside, and I slump onto the stool, all my energy zapped. My headphones sit on the counter, the music still playing.

Beckett hovers, his face a mash-up of confusion and pity.

"Don't you dare say anything. To anyone."

The menace in my voice does the trick, because Beckett's eyes widen and he holds both hands up in surrender. "I won't say a word."

I nod, even though I don't trust him, not one bit. Beckett doesn't have the best record when it comes to keeping my secrets. "I can't believe this is happening," I mutter to myself, my mind spiraling to the worst possible scenarios. Lingering on Dad's comment earlier about *change*.

"I'm sure it'll be fine. Besides, I never thought you liked it here."

"If Bigmouth's closes"—I wave my hands to encompass the bowling alley—"then we leave San Francisco. So pardon me for panicking."

Beckett just stares at me, but before he can respond, the back door closes with a creak and a slam. I school my expression before Dad enters the lobby. His despondence is gone. The Wilsons are masters at faking it until we make it.

"Wow, it's brisk out there," Dad says, rubbing his arms. "Makes a man long for warmer climates. Wouldn't that be a nice change of pace, Caroline?"

I press my lips together, tethering the haphazard swirl of panic brewing behind my sternum. Like I was explaining to Beckett, if Bigmouth's finally kicks the bucket, Dad will move us to Arizona. Hell, also known as Arizona, will have to freeze over before I leave San Francisco.

Then Dad spots Beckett, and a megawatt smile lights up his face. "Beckett Porter! What're you doing here?"

"Beckett's works for Schulman's now. Isn't that just *great*?"

"It's wonderful!" Dad replies, not picking up on my sarcasm. "We've missed you around here."

"Thanks, Mr. Porter," Beckett says with a super-annoying grin.

"You've missed him," I clarify, handing the clipboard to Dad, "not me."

Beckett's smile droops, and he clears his throat. "Where do you need these?" He gestures to the boxes of—I tilt my head to read the label—nacho cheese. Yuck.

Dad signs the clipboard and then claps his hands together. "Storage room should suffice. Not like this stuff needs refrigeration," he adds with a laugh, and leads Beckett down the hall.

He's so smiley that if I hadn't witnessed him with Jesset, I'd suspect nothing was wrong. Here's the thing—if we can't comp a game, there's no way we can afford eight grand in back rent. Dad knows it. I know it. Hell, even Beckett Porter knows it.

Bigmouth's is like an ancient relative you never want to visit because they smell like death and pinch your cheeks until your face bruises, but that doesn't mean you'd be happy if they died. I practically grew up here, and memories are layered into the dust that's settled over the ancient trophies and wobbly-legged ball racks. But with every passing birthday, the bowling alley lost its fanciful charm. I finally see Bigmouth's for what it truly is: our family's failure. The problem is, Bigmouth's Bowl is all Dad has left. And without it, we won't stay in San Francisco.

I pick up the yellow silk dress and needle and try losing myself in the mindless work of fixing the hem. With each stitch, I can't help but think: *We're screwed.*

FRIDAY, APRIL 20
DAYS UNTIL BIGMOUTH'S
EVICTION: 10

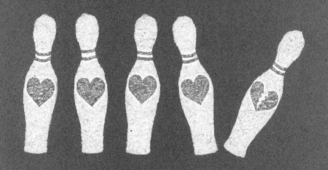

Two

THE QUAD BUZZES in anticipation of spring break, but after yesterday's accidental discovery and the glum realization I'm working all week, I can't muster the smallest bit of excitement.

Castelli High is one of the largest schools in San Francisco, and getting lost in the crowd is easy. The campus is made up of hulking white-and-tan buildings with burnt-clay tile roofs and fancy arches, spanning several city blocks. My classmates spread out on blankets during our lunch period, despite the gray fog. I'm not hungry, but I take my food to the quietest part of campus.

A picnic table shades itself in the observatory's shadow, and I park myself on the bench. Castelli lacks your stereotypical social groups—we don't even have cheerleaders—but this picnic bench is prime loner real estate. At the start of the school year, it draws a few freshmen, but after a month they peel off to sit with their new friends. I took over the bench late last year and have been eating here ever since.

Aunt Fiona packed me a sandwich, but I can't touch it. My stomach is too twisty for food, so I push the bag aside and put on my headphones. I'm grateful to be alone, because I'm anxious and all out of sorts. We have ten measly days to come up with an extra eight grand, money we definitely don't have. Money we *need* to find. Fast.

Yesterday I tried tricking Dad into telling me what happened with Jesset, but his facade never wavered. He smiled, he joked, but when he thought I wasn't looking, worry formed in the crease between his brows.

No surprise there. Us Wilsons? We're not the talking type.

Without Bigmouth's there will be no reason to stay in San Francisco, no money to pay the mortgage on our house. Dad's parents live in a retirement community in Arizona, and that's where we'd end up. No more Pacific Ocean mornings doused in fog or dreams of vintage and FIDM. Every remaining vestige of what makes me who I am *gone*.

Bigmouth's circling the drain is bad enough, but the fact that Beckett Porter is privy to our financial woes makes a crappy situation crappier. Our falling out happened last year, but I have perfectly valid reasons to avoid him and pretend like our friendship never happened.

Beckett and I originally became best friends when he sat with me during lunch in the third grade. He liked my *Princess Bride* lunch box. We clicked instantly; I thought it would be forever. We shared the same brand of weird and understood each other. The more time passed, the closer we became. We took advantage of the whole "friends and family bowl for free" rule at Bigmouth's, we got lost riding BART together, we went swing dancing every Sunday at Lindy in the Park. And Beckett never found out, but I liked him. As more than a friend. He was everything to me.

Then Beckett betrayed our friendship. Not only did he tell a secret that wasn't his to tell, but he robbed me of the thing I cherished most—my trust in my best friend. Since then I've done everything in my power to rid my life of Beckett Porter. I've sworn him off.

Until yesterday, that was going pretty damn well.

Beckett's reappearance really threw me, and I barely slept last night. But I'm not as tired as I should be. Instead, I'm hyped up on nerves and coffee, researching tips on my phone about how to sell vintage clothes on eBay and Etsy. Because I have to do *something* to help Dad. Most of my finds are cheap for a reason—stained, torn, missing buttons, shrunk in the dryer—but maybe I can flip a small profit if I sell my nicer items. Something to help supplement whatever Dad's saved.

Lunch is almost over by the time I've filled a page with various tips on how to drive online auctions higher, ideas on displaying items attractively, and proper listing etiquette. I doodle dress designs in the margins of my notebook, turning up my music until Frightened Rabbit sears my eardrums. My fingers tap along with "I Wish I Was Sober" as it soars, plucky and sorrowful, through my headphones.

As if I didn't already have enough going on, tomorrow

is the FIDM tour, and I haven't canceled—yet. I scheduled the tour during spring break because I was supposed to have the week off. I could slip away without informing my dad what I was up to, but now? If I decide to go, I have to ask my dad, and considering I haven't even told him about FIDM, I'm thinking of skipping.

Telling Dad means admitting I'm serious about fashion design. I'm better off canceling the tour and using that time to save Bigmouth's. Because frankly, I'd rather sell cans at the recycling center than have that conversation.

A prickle of unease runs down my spine, and I glance up from the notebook. Someone is walking straight toward me; there's nothing else in this corner of the quad. Probably a lost-soul freshman. Unusual this late into the year, but not unheard of. But as the figure draws closer, my stomach dips lower. Those messy soft brown curls, the hunched, poor posture, a wrinkled band T-shirt.

Beckett Porter.

I cannot escape the guy.

Beckett lifts his hand in a wave, and I'm trapped with an achy, confused sensation tightening my throat as he draws nearer. People talk about fight or flight, but few talk about freeze. Stuck and unable to react. Yeah, I'm in freeze mode. I'm frozen long enough for him to drop on the bench opposite me.

"Chuck?"

I pretend not to hear him when he says my name and force my attention to my journal, the lines blurring beneath my intense gaze.

Beckett repeats himself and taps me on the shoulder—a quick poke.

Since the sophomore-year betrayal, I've implemented a strict no-touching rule with Beckett. And it didn't stop with him; he single-handedly increased my general personal bubble by three feet with everyone.

I take off my headphones, fighting for the proper response to this huge violation of privacy, and say, "Fancy seeing you here." Sarcasm is a safe choice because it's a language he understands. "I thought being a truant meant never stepping foot on campus."

True to his nature, Beckett is unflappable. "Nah, being a truant means I'm *occasionally* on campus." The way the smug smile lifts at the corners shows me he's pleased I've been paying attention.

Ugh. Rookie mistake. I shouldn't have said anything.

Embarrassment flushes my neck, and I look away, biting into my apple for something to do. If I can't talk him away, I'll ignore him out of existence. He might not be on campus frequently, but he hangs out with theater kids. So that begs the question: What is he doing at my loner table?

Beckett swipes my bag of potato chips and pops them open.

"Dude. Leave. This is my bench"—I lean forward to grab the chips—"and that's my lunch."

He forfeits the bag and then tilts his head. "Are you okay?"

"In general, or in an existential sense?" I ask, expecting sass in response.

"I'm worried about you," he says with strange sincerity. "After the thing with your dad? I thought you'd want to talk."

Dropping my gaze to the table, I say, "I'm fine." Actually, I'm the opposite, but Beckett's the last person I want to talk to. A year ago, he would've never taken "fine" as an acceptable answer. For a fleeting moment, I wish he'd press further, to be relentless and pry open my feelings. In that brief, heartbeat-length moment, I miss my best friend.

Thankfully, that yearning loneliness disappears, replaced by suspicion and a heaping dose of annoyance.

"And if I wanted to talk about it with anyone, it wouldn't be you." The words cause a flicker of pain to cross his face. I crumple up the chips and shove them into the brown lunch bag. "What's your deal? Trying to make amends before I'm gone for good?"

"C'mon, don't say that. You're not leaving."

I sigh so hard the hair sticking to my cheeks fluffs out in front of me. "I might be."

"If that's the case, I want to help," he says plainly, factually. He folds his arms on the table, leaning forward. As if the table between us is an obstacle, not a shield.

"How would *you* help *me*?" I ask. The bigger question remains unsaid—*why?* Beckett should be relieved, or at the very least, indifferent about my departure from San Francisco.

"You need eight grand by next week, right?"

"You were never supposed to hear that conversation."

"Neither were you," he points out.

"Whatever it is, I'm not interested. And you shouldn't be poking your nose into other people's business. Bigmouth's is all my dad has left."

"Which is why I'd like to help," Beckett says, brandishing a notebook from his backpack. "I have an idea."

Is this guy for real? We don't speak for a year and because of one seriously misguided eavesdropping experience he thinks, what, we're friends again? Not happening.

"Chuck?" He slides the notebook into view.

I forgot that ignoring Beckett only makes his powers of annoyance stronger. I switch tactics, hoping he'll leave me alone if I humor him. "What's this? Your diary?"

Beckett laughs, and I make the mistake of looking up. His face is earnest and hopeful. It's all kinds of wrong. "Sorry to disappoint, but nope. This," he says, and Vanna Whites the journal, "is your ticket to staying in San Francisco."

"How is your diary going to keep me in San Francisco?"

"It's not a diary! Just—*look*." He folds back the front cover and turns the journal so I can read it. "Last year I started betting to make some extra cash, just a few hundred bucks. There are these underground bowling games in the Bay Area and some allowed betting. This is where I kept track of those games, different players, and my winnings."

"What about your losses?" I ask, digesting this new piece of information. I'm not surprised—Beckett was all about hijinks when we were friends, constantly getting me into trouble—but discomforted. Not like I made a habit

27

of thinking about Beckett the past year, but I imagined his life as business as usual. It's unsettling to think of him experiencing new things without me.

He grins. "Oh, I rarely lost."

"Your modesty overwhelms me." I don't want to care—and I definitely don't—but I can't fight my curiosity. My eyes scan the notebook, columns of names and stats. "Get to the point. The bell rings in three minutes, and unlike you, I care about getting to class on time."

"Okay, just hear me out. When I was betting on these underground games, I saw players hustle their opponents out of *thousands* of dollars. Hustling was popular in the sixties. It still happens, but it's seedy shit."

"You want to hustle these guys? *Con* them?"

Beckett nods. "You're still good? At bowling?"

Just because I don't love bowling doesn't mean I'm not any good. Growing up in a bowling alley meant I had access to the lanes whenever I wanted. But *never* with bumpers because "Wilsons don't use bumpers."

Beckett and I used to bowl together. I've always had an uncanny talent, but I rarely play anymore. I'm good—not as good as our regulars like Marty, but I have a mean left hook.

"Sure, I guess." The heft of his gaze is making me uneasy. "Hold up, you want *me* to hustle?" Beckett always joked that my comfort zone would kill me, but this isn't just outside my comfort zone. It's in another state—a different freaking country.

He drags his fingers through his curls before tucking

them behind his ears. "I'd coach you, and we could work as a team."

"What do you get out of this?" I ask, wishing I wasn't secretly dying for his answer. Wishing my heartstrings would stop aching with the sincerity of his words. Because everything about this conversation is making me more confused and conflicted than ever.

"We split the winnings fifty-fifty. I could use extra cash, and I know the ins and outs of the illegal side. We could win big." He bites his bottom lip and looks at me. "What do you think?"

"That you've lost your goddamn mind."

Unfazed, he presses forward. "Your talent plus the element of surprise? Priceless. Half of any successful hustle is lowering expectations. No one will expect you to be good."

"What? You can't hustle people with your shitty bowling skills?" I ask, retreating to my safe space: sarcasm.

"I know I suck, okay? And you're right—you can't hustle someone when you're not a decent player. But you're good. Deceivingly so."

I stare at him. I've never broken the law. As far as teenage acts of rebellion go, hustling underground *bowlers* is ludicrous. Beckett must be messing with me because we can't win that much money in a week. It's impossible.

"Not interested," I reply. I shovel the rest of my forgotten food into my backpack, close my notebook, and get up. Showing Beckett how unnerving I find his presence does me zero favors, but I can't sit near him anymore.

"Chuck, wait." Beckett trails me across the quad, stopping me outside the library.

I pivot on my heel. "I said no."

"Why not?" Beckett's face twists in what I can only guess is confusion, and he shakes his head. "C'mon, I . . . I promised Willa I'd help pay for her summer camp, and being a part-time delivery boy doesn't pay well. We both need the cash."

Willa's his little sister, and if he's trying to play the sympathy card, it's not working. "Life is full of disappointments. Willa should learn that now."

"What about Bigmouth's?"

I tuck my jacket tight against my ribs, glaring at him. "What about it?"

"Is it worth losing over being so fucking stubborn?" Beckett's cold gray gaze is hot and itchy, but I can't look away.

"I can save Bigmouth's on my own, thank you very much."

"Yeah? How?" He nods to the notebook tucked beneath my arm, full of my scribbled online-auction notes. "By selling some clothes online? Do you really think that's going to make a difference?"

I open and close my mouth, fists clenching in frustration. "You are such an ass."

"If you change your mind, text or e-mail me, or send me a carrier pigeon."

With an exasperated huff, I walk away, lifting my hand high to flip Beckett a different species of bird.

Three

AFTER SCHOOL, I declare my spring break DOA and head to Bigmouth's.

I'm not sad; rather, my brain has kicked into high-gear panic problem-solving mode. Because there has to be a way out of this mess, a logical one. One that doesn't include accepting help from Beckett and/or breaking the law. I'm hopeful I can make a few hundred dollars selling my nicer vintage items online. It won't be much—and it'll suck to part with the finer items I've saved the past few years—but I hope it'll be worth it. I mean, it has to be worth something. I don't have any other moneymaking schemes hidden up my sleeves.

If we can't come up with the money? I shudder at the only other outcome. In my head, the next few months play out like dominoes falling. Bigmouth's closes. Dad lets me finish junior year at Castelli's. We move to Arizona over the summer, probably before the Fourth of July. Full stop.

Because I can't picture myself existing outside of San Francisco.

When the clock strikes eight, my shift is over, and we've only had one group of customers in the past four hours. The register is more accustomed to cobwebs than dollar bills. This does not bode well. Tonight's the first night of vacation for several local high schools, and Dad hoped for more action.

Dad's holed up in his office, has been for most of my shift. I wish he'd talk to me. Confide in me what I already know. Asking Dad outright is a waste because, knowing him, he'd lie. That's what he does when he's trying to protect me. Good-natured? Questionable. But the truth always surfaces.

Call me a coward, but I don't want to hear that we're leaving. I don't want to hear that this crappy little bowling alley is closing, taking with it my life in San Francisco. The last time we talked about moving was in January, when Dad went over the quarterly losses. Back then, the prospect of change, of leaving our foggy city, excited him. But I didn't really think we'd come this close to letting it all go.

The bowling alley isn't anything extraordinary. Tall ceilings, airy, with a decent twenty-four lanes. Any opulence is long gone. Two or three decades ago, the pinewood might've been glossy, but now it reflects a dull shine. The lanes are oiled, slick, and the walls are gray brick. Above our heads, a maze of rafters with exposed beams and wiring stretches from wall to wall. Outside, in front of the entry, *Bigmouth's Bowl* glows half-heartedly in blue neon script. The second *B* always flickers.

Each lane has a small cracked vinyl couch with the stuffing peeking out and an old-school projector with transparencies to fill in scores with dry-erase pens. The area above each pit is painted like a colorful gap-toothed mouth, the ten pins representing teeth. Get it? This bowling alley is filled with *big mouths*. It's downright creepy with a vintage flair.

The nicest thing in this joint is the jukebox in the corner. Kitschy, vaguely sexist signs like you'd find in a fifties throwback diner decorate the otherwise plain walls. I'm not Bigmouth's biggest fan, but the space is kind of cool. In a funky, well-loved way. But no one wants funky anymore.

The thriving local bowling alleys are trendy, renovated, and you have to reserve a lane days in advance. They serve gourmet food and fancy cocktails in mason jars. Ever since Billy Goat Bowl opened last year, Bigmouth's has struggled to stay afloat. That ten-lane bowling alley is only a mile away, stealing our business with its hipster charm. But if Dad *tried*, if he got a liquor license and fixed this place up, we could turn a profit.

Fat chance. Liquor licenses and renovations cost money.

I abandon my post behind the counter and drag my fingers along a couch. Next month all of this could be gone. The little café/snack stand where we serve French fries and nachos and soda. The three perpetually broken pinball machines, dust layered over the glass tables—*Monster Bash*, *Hercules*, and *Creature from the Black Lagoon*. The sock vending machines and the bowling ball cleaner that hasn't worked in my lifetime. Gone.

Bigmouth's might not be my favorite place, but it's the last thing anchoring us to San Francisco, the city of my heart. If we leave . . .

Maybe if we earn enough money for the back rent and escape eviction, Dad will try harder to keep Bigmouth's afloat.

My arms fall limp to my sides, the possibility far-fetched.

"You heading out?" Dad calls, emerging from his office.

Heart pounding—from him scaring me, from contemplating my darkest timeline—I grab my belongings from behind the register. "That's the plan, unless you need me?"

"Nah, you're good to go. But first . . ." Dad digs into his pockets, pulling out his wallet. "Here," he offers, holding out two twenties, creased but fresh from the ATM.

Guilt twinges, a muscle spasm in my gut, as I take the money. Even if he's paying me back.

We don't speak. The exchange is awkward enough without words. I fold the bills and slip them into my purse. "Thanks." Before I lose my courage, I ask once more, "Is everything okay?"

My father is a sweet man—too sweet—and he lets life and people like Art Jesset waltz over him. Dad's combed-over black hair, a shade richer than my own, is particularly pathetic today, and he has a mustard stain on his shirt. He grabs a rag and runs it over the framed pictures of Bigmouth's more prominent history.

Photographs of Grandpa O'Neill, my mother's father, who opened Bigmouth's, and Grandma O'Neill. Pictures of my mother, which simultaneously hurt and confuse. I understand why Dad doesn't keep any in the house.

"Ah, Caroline, the money thing yesterday was just a mishap, a mistake. Won't happen again, I promise," he says. "And why wouldn't everything be okay? It's a beautiful day."

Every day is beautiful to Dad, a quality I simultaneously admire and hate. On one hand that much optimism must be nice. On the other? I'd rather acknowledge that danger's coming and act than get bowled over.

No pun intended.

I sigh as I readjust my backpack. This is why we're getting evicted. Dad can't admit when the going gets rough.

"I don't know; it's just really quiet for a Friday night." I study his face for any flicker of emotion.

Dad's smile wobbles, imperceptibly, and he glances at his shoes, twisting the rag between his hands. When he looks back up, his smile is steady. "Sure, it's a little slow, but that's none of your concern. You're seventeen, Caroline! Act like it."

"I'll get right on that," I say dryly, and lean into Dad's embrace, hugging him against my shoulder. It's hard to be mad when he has mustard on his shirt. "Wanna watch *Antiques Roadshow* after you close up?"

Dad perks up at this. I have more in common with

strangers on the Internet than I do with my own dad, but watching people turn junk into treasure is a mutual pastime we both enjoy. Shame he has no desire to turn our junky bowling alley into something worth treasuring.

"I'll try. Will you let Fiona know I had dinner at work? She always tries to save me leftovers." He grimaces comically because his sister is the world's worst, yet most ambitious, cook.

Aunt Fee moved in once it became clear Dad couldn't raise me alone. She is my maternal stand-in figure, laughable considering the woman doesn't have a maternal bone in her body.

I smile as my mind spirals with an anxious brand of panic. "See you at home."

Halfway to the door, I hesitate. Tomorrow is the FIDM tour, and I still haven't canceled my spot. If Bigmouth's goes belly-up, is there a point in going? Bigmouth's closes, and we'll be out of San Francisco before I can even apply to be a student at FIDM. Besides, my mom attended fashion school. The parallels are too strong for me to ignore.

A shake of my head clears my mind, and I leave the bowling alley. If, for some miraculous reason, Bigmouth's pulls through, there will be other opportunities.

Relief fills me now that I've resolved to skip the tour. But it doesn't take long—actually, it takes just until the Glen Park BART sign looms—before it disappears.

Because I'm no closer to conjuring up eight grand than I was this morning.

The stairway into the Bay Area Rapid Transit resembles

a descent into hell. The underground station is busy, being early on a Friday night. I shuffle with the mass of pedestrians to the turnstiles, where I swipe my electric-blue Clipper card.

With my headphones on, I avoid eye contact and elbow my way to a seat. I've used BART for years and it still skeeves me out. You always, and I mean *always*, get the creepy leering guys who stare at you for a second too long. Muni is better because you're usually aboveground, but it's all public transportation. Which is why I carry Mace.

The doors slide shut, and the train takes off, bumpy at first, then slick and fast. The smudged windows expose the cement underground tunnel flying past. My reflection is a dark and pale blur, marred by red lipstick that lasted the entire day.

Dad's in denial about the thousands of dollars in back rent, or he plans on letting Jesset terminate Bigmouth's lease. Evict us. Fortunately, I'm made of tougher stuff than Dad. Or that's what I tell myself as the train lurches to a stop and I move on autopilot, taking the stairs up to ground level.

San Francisco is a contradiction of hills and valleys, but I've lived here my whole life. According to the story, I was conceived in the bathroom on a ferry to an Alcatraz Island tour. Amusing, but super gross. Point being, San Francisco is my blood, it's my oxygen, and when I die, I'll have an urn at the Columbarium or my ashes scattered illegally across the city.

I start up a hill and pass pastel-colored houses, narrow

and campy, on either side of the one-way street. With each pounding step, I try reassuring myself Bigmouth's can survive Art Jesset. While I want to help my father—he's the only parent I have left—I want to save Bigmouth's more. Not for Bigmouth's sake, but the bowling alley and San Francisco are linked. If we lose one, we lose the other. We can't afford to live here, and our house belongs to the bank.

When I spot our yellow Victorian on the hill, the thought of moving from San Francisco to the barren desert wasteland of Arizona makes me want to scream. My grandfather bought the property in the sixties, the only reason our struggling middle-class family snagged such fine real estate in one of the most expensive cities in the United States. Even if it sold, and it'd go for over a million, we'd never be able to afford another house in the city until the bubble bursts. Thanks, housing crisis.

Nestled in the colorful Hayes Valley, our home belongs on a postcard, or at the least, in the opening credits of *Full House*. There's no lawn, only a strip of sidewalk with flowering weeds, a single-car garage, and a small staircase leading to two stories of old-timey Victorian charm painted daffodil yellow. The front door is cherry red, the shutters white.

My mom died fourteen years ago, when I was three. I don't remember how bad it was before Aunt Fee stepped in two years later. But I do remember my aunt's face when she arrived at the yellow house, soaking in the wreckage, the disorganized chaos, and wondering if an earthquake had rolled through San Francisco and hit only our house.

We were a mess, inside and out. Yet we scraped by. We persevered. And there has to be a way to keep my family in San Francisco. Where we belong.

Four

AUNT FIONA CAN'T cook. The woman tries, and I'm thankful. But my stomach always does this inverted hunger growl whenever she gets innovative in the kitchen. My aunt loves Pinterest, and when she's not writing articles for local magazines and various online platforms, she's pinning ideas for meals. Recipes for experienced cooks with refined palates. Aunt Fee is not a chef; nor does she have a palate, let alone a refined one.

The smell of her dish mutating—I mean, *cooking*—downstairs is pungent in my attic bedroom. Like most ancient Victorian homes in San Francisco, the yellow house is narrow and tall, and my bedroom is a converted attic space. The ceiling slopes with the roof—peaked in some areas and feet from the floor in others—and the walls are unpainted. A twin-size bed rests in the center, and an ancient knotted rug covers most of the hardwood in nubby fabric and exotic designs. Aunt Fiona helped me decorate the plain walls with fairy lights, the delicate strands looped around nails in patterned swirls.

Along the dusty top of my bookshelf is the collection of wigs on mannequin heads I inherited from my mother. There are five in total—medium-length honey curls with a side bang, messy center-parted blond locks, French-chic black bob, super-long brown waves, and a peroxide-blond cut with blunt bangs. The mannequin's faces are ancient, some pink and painted with eyes and makeup, others blank. All creepy, which is half of why I love them so much.

My cat, Jean Paul Gaultier, is curled into a bun on the edge of my mattress. For years I resisted the urge to adopt, because Beckett was highly allergic. Losing Beckett's friendship allowed me to take in JP, and he became my new feline partner in crime. I kiss him on the head, and he opens his eyes only to glare at me.

I hang my coat on the rack and settle on the floor with my clunky old MacBook. First things first—I cancel my spot on the FIDM tour. Then I piece through one of my bags of vintage clothes, tossing the nicer items beside me. In the end, I find several high-quality pieces worth selling.

My heart aches as I style them on my dress form with jewelry, using an unpainted wall as a background, and snap stylized photographs with my phone. I had plans for these items—sewing them into something new, deconstructing them and harvesting the materials—and I hate parting with them like this. But it's not like I'm swimming in options, so I suck it up. I list the less-fancy ones on my new eBay account with the auction closing in seventy-two hours. The nicer items go on Etsy.

There's no way I'll make eight grand, but it's better than nothing. If I earn some money and turn it over to Dad, it'll show him how much I care. How badly I want to stay in this city.

Dinner's not ready yet, so I play a record on my second-hand Pioneer and slouch onto my bed with my phone, pulling open Instagram. After my friendship breakup with Beckett, I told myself I'd have four years of college to form real friendships. You know, with people who won't betray my trust. But I'm not immune to loneliness.

Thank God for the Internet.

My fashion-centric Instagram account has amassed a small following. There, and on several vintage fashion forums, I've forged a few friendships. But the only person I've truly connected with is Mila—or MavenMody95. We met on an international vintage clothing forum last summer, and we co-run the Instagram account M&C Vintage. Our account has 10K followers, which is small compared to others, but it's enough to keep my heart happy on my lonelier days.

While I post pictures of San Francisco and the truly unique items I find or sew, Mila—who lives in Poland—models clothes and makeup. Mila's supposed to visit the States this summer, and we might meet in real life. Hopefully she's online, because I need to vent about the bowling alley and Beckett Porter.

I switch from checking on our Instagram to WhatsApp, where Mila and I trade messages. But she's not online. Not surprising; it's early in Warsaw. With a sigh, I close the app and rest my phone on my chest. Sometimes it sucks when your only friend lives time zones away.

As hard as I try, my mind keeps circling back to Beckett. Usually, the Internet is a decent distraction, but not today. It's impossible to forget what happened during lunch. Beckett's outrageously weird offer has me on edge, but the sudden appearance of him is even more disconcerting. Why now? Because he feels *bad* for my dad?

When we were friends, Beckett was the son Dad never had. And yeah, he apologized. But he still hurt me, and trying to help save Bigmouth's won't repair the rift in our friendship. I press the heels of my palms to my eyes, forcing myself to forget about Beckett Porter and his super-illegal plan to earn eight grand.

Except I can't.

My brain is running a treacherous marathon right now, and I sit up, searching bowling hustlers on my phone. A handful of articles from the *New York Times* explain the dangerous form of betting popular decades ago. There have been several movies, including one from the sixties with Paul Newman—who was apparently a serious babe—on hustling, but they focus on pool or poker.

Even my *worst* options are outdated. Great. That's just great.

I adjust my search, adding San Francisco to the query, but nothing concrete surfaces.

A banner notification flashes at the top of the screen, alerting me that MavenMody95 is online, and I hop onto WhatsApp.

> VINTAGE_ALLEY415: Did you know Paul Newman was seriously attractive?

> MAVENMODY95: I did actually. My mom's obsessed with him! What's up, other than ogling hot old movie stars?

> VINTAGE_ALLEY415: I've had the weirdest few days.

> MAVENMODY95: What's going on?

I sink deeper into my pile of pillows and tell Mila all about Bigmouth's financial troubles, Beckett Porter's unsettling reappearance, and how I'm missing out on my spring break of fashion to man the register at a failing bowling alley.

> MAVENMODY95: Do you miss Beckett? Sounds like he's trying to mend your relationship.

The question catches me off guard. I haven't really allowed myself to miss Beckett. The hurt is too painful. Blinking, my dry eyes stinging, I type out a response.

VINTAGE_ALLEY415: I don't know. No. UGH. Stop asking the important questions, Mila.

MAVENMODY95: Sorry, sorry. Fuck him (is that better?)

VINTAGE_ALLEY415: Yes. Thank you. He's probably messing with me, anyway. He can't be serious.

MAVENMODY95: What if he's serious? Maybe he's offering a solution? Aren't you the tiniest bit curious?

VINTAGE_ALLEY415: I'm nowhere near a good enough bowler to con people. Dude's lost his mind. New topic?

We chat about fashion until Mila has to sign off. I'm left alone with dangerous thoughts. Such as, is it possible to earn eight thousand dollars in ten days? Not legally, but could I pull off such a stunt? The thought is oddly enticing—the ability to earn more than enough money to stay in San Francisco. But I check myself, forcing it from the forefront of my mind. It's not an option.

Aunt Fee's too lazy to walk up two flights of stairs, so she texts me that dinner is ready. My insides roil with guilt and frustration as I head to the first floor. I hate not being able to solve a problem, but Bigmouth's closure may be beyond my grasp. Because discounting Beckett's offer, I'm out of ideas.

Jean Paul Gaultier stalks me downstairs like a shadow. When we reach the kitchen, he nudges my ankles before disappearing into the darkened hallway. Off to raise hell with the other neighborhood cats, no doubt.

"Buffalo chicken chili," Aunt Fiona announces the second I enter the kitchen.

I wrinkle my nose. "What?"

She taps a spoon on the glass top to our slow cooker. "*Bon appétit.* Amazing, right?"

Suspiciously, I sniff the air and settle at the table. "Let's hope so."

"What'd you say?" Aunt Fee grins and pulls a bowl from the cupboard.

"Nothing." She slides the floral-patterned bowl in front of me, and the oily yellow broth makes me gag. "Thanks." I dip my spoon into the cluster of—vegetables?—in the center, figuring they're safe to eat.

Aunt Fiona is a punk rock Rosie the Riveter, especially when she has a bandanna in her waist-length black hair. Then there are the tattoos and piercings and her infamous sailor mouth. She's my dad's only sibling, younger by fifteen years; she acts like my older sister. With expectant green eyes, she watches me take a tentative sip of chili. "Delicious?"

Nope. *God. Awful.* Lips puckering, I give her a thumbs-up.

I love Aunt Fiona, even if she's the world's worst cook

and shittiest mom figure. When I first got my period, Fee left a box of supermax tampons in my bathroom. Didn't tell me how to use them or bring me less-frightening options.

Embarrassed, I wadded toilet paper in my underwear for six months. Aunt Fee means well, but again, zero maternal instincts. When I finally figured out how to use those tampons, I flushed them down the toilet because I didn't know any better. Needless to say, our ancient house and its aged pipes suffered.

"How was school?" she asks, sipping her kombucha.

I manage a mouthful and chase it with water to clear my throat. No way I'm telling her about my run-in with Beckett, so I shrug. "Fine. Hey, has my dad said anything about Bigmouth's being in trouble?"

"Nope, but business has been on a pretty steady decline since your grandfather retired. And I wouldn't be surprised if it's suffering with all the tech bros moving into the city," my aunt says with an eye roll. "Why? What's up?"

I stir my gruel. How would the grandfather I never knew handle our situation? Not like he had to deal with the Silicon Valley tech boom and watch as it warped the San Franciscan landscape.

Is it worth telling Aunt Fiona what I saw at the alley yesterday? If something were wrong, Dad would confide in her. I think. After all, Bigmouth's Bowl is the tacky glue holding our family together.

"I thought there'd be more customers with the start of spring break, that's all," I say, frowning at my soup.

Aunt Fee shrugs, switching topics and telling me about

her latest article, featuring an heiress who died and left her fortune to her cat. A woman after my own heart. My aunt studied journalism, and her true passion lies in reporting, but she's had trouble finding work as a local reporter. Until then, she writes fluffy human-interest pieces and beauty-product reviews for BuzzFeed and Refinery29. The only upside? Fee gets tons of free makeup and skin-care products to review, most of which she gives to me after she's submitted her write-ups.

Later, once Aunt Fiona sets up camp on the couch with her laptop, I return to my room. Jean Paul Gaultier is off with our neighborhood's alley cats, so it's particularly lonely up here. JP's adoption was somewhat spite fueled, but it was surprising how much comfort a cat brought into my life.

Cats don't love as easily as dogs, but once you win their affection, you have it for life. Wouldn't it be nice if people were the same? No judgment, no ability to let you down? Just love. Stubborn and unconditional love.

I curl up on my comforter with my laptop. My cursor hovers over my iMessage app, and I click it. I type Beckett's name into the search bar, not expecting his phone number to pop up. I swear I deleted and blocked him into obscurity, but there it is. His number. I open a new message and type.

ME: Were you serious today? What you said in the quad?

Beckett has no chill because his reply dings in my in-box not a full minute later.

BECKETT PORTER: As a heart attack. Did you change your mind?

Not willing to give him the satisfaction of knowing I'm considering it, I lie.

ME: Nope.

BECKETT PORTER: Put your misaligned hatred of me aside for one second and consider my idea.

ME: I'm unable to put my perfectly aligned hatred of you aside. So sorry.

BECKETT PORTER: Why can't you let this go?

My fingers hover over the keyboard. Is this a conversation to have over text? Or at all?

ME: Seriously?

BECKETT PORTER: Yes, seriously! We both hurt each other, but you don't see me holding a grudge a year later, do you?

When I don't reply, another message pings.

BECKETT PORTER: Unlike you, I apologized. Are you gonna turn down an opportunity to save your family's business because of a grudge?

Dad's tense shoulders hunched over the books flicker to mind. When he thinks I'm not watching, he wears his pain. All I want is to make him happy—make *us* happy—and failing feels as if I'm being torn in two.

If we paid the back rent in full, Dad could manage the monthly payments, especially if he renovated. But working with Beckett? Breaking the law with him? I can't be considering this.

Can I?

I am.

God help me, I am.

ME: 75-25.

BECKETT PORTER: ???

ME: We split the money 75 (me) and 25 (you).

I swallow, my throat parched and itchy. This is a test. If he says yes, I'll do it. But I expect a rebuttal. Negotiations. A reason for me to call him irrational and back out.

BECKETT PORTER: Fair enough. You free tomorrow?

I frown at the words. I can't believe I'm doing this, but what's my alternative? Oh right. There isn't one. At least if I fail, Dad will be none the wiser. If I have to put up with Beckett for a week in exchange for saving Bigmouth's, then I'll deal.

ME: I'm at work until 6.

BECKETT PORTER: Cool. See you tomorrow.

No explanation about what we're doing or when he'll show up.

Standing, I go in circles—physically and mentally. I do the math. We'll need to bring in more than ten thousand dollars to split it seventy-five twenty-five. I have two hundred dollars in savings, and we'll need cash to start with if we're betting. Or hustling. Breaking the law.

If Aunt Fee or Dad finds out, well, it won't be pretty.

Ever since I hit puberty and fell heart-first into a nasty depressive episode, my family's been on alert. That initial episode in the winter of sophomore year earned me twice-monthly therapy appointments until the end of last summer. After six months of therapy with Sarah, Dad agreed when I asked if I could stop going. The sessions were expensive and they made me uncomfortable. All that opening up and talking about my feelings? Hard pass.

During our initial session, Sarah reviewed my family history and instilled a devastating fear: the disorder responsible for ruining my mom might be lurking in my brain.

Sarah told me it's not my fault.

Faulty wiring. Misfiring neurotransmitters. Losing the genetic lottery.

Whatever you want to call it, it's shitty. And unfair.

During one of our sessions, Sarah mentioned wanting to send me to a psychiatrist, to nail down a solid diagnosis and dose me with antidepressants or mood stabilizers, but I've been doing a lot better. Somehow I've avoided ever having to make that appointment. I get out of bed. I eat and sleep a reasonable amount. I'm doing well at school. I'm introverted, but I have my hobbies.

I might not be happy, not in the traditional sense, but that's okay.

Emotions have always scared me—I can't control them. But somehow that dark lack of emotion while I was depressed was even scarier. Now I just want to find a steady balance between the affectless and the uncontrollable. Against my best efforts, I feel everything too strongly when I'm not depressed, and it's overwhelming.

But more than anything, I never want to feel the way I did that winter. Back then everything was great. Beckett and I were best friends. High school hadn't lost its novelty yet. My life was fantastic, but the joy never reached me, which made me feel even shittier. I woke up only looking forward to crawling back beneath the covers. My eyes would glaze as I tried to read or watch TV, the sinking in my chest threatening to collapse me. I emotionally flatlined.

Wondering if I'd ever feel better.

Worried I wouldn't.

Scared I'd stop trying.

Eating well, therapy, sleeping enough, and exercising—yoga and hiking the Presidio—balance the scales pretty well. I've experienced only a few blips of depression since last year, but I'm constantly on guard. There's nothing worse than waiting for something you can't control to derail your life. Despite my ups and downs, I've managed okay, but my recent decision to break the law might prove otherwise.

Beckett's plan makes me sick to my stomach, because until now my fear of spinning out of control has kept me from taking part in normal teenage experiences. Not like this plan is anywhere near normal, but I fear if anyone looked at what I'm doing, they'd worry.

Isn't this the definition of engaging in "uncharacteristic impulsive behavior"?

In my small adjoining bathroom, I splash water on my face. Hoping to silence the little niggling voice in the back of my head warning me to reel myself in. To behave.

While my mother and I share a name—why I refuse to go by Caroline—our similarities end there. I brace myself against the sink, repeating my comforting phrase, those six little words, until my heartbeat steadies and slows.

You are not your mother's child.

SATURDAY, APRIL 21
DAYS UNTIL BIGMOUTH'S
EVICTION: 9

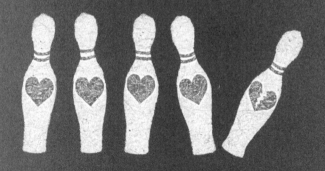

Five

I SPEND THE first Saturday of spring break at Bigmouth's, greatly regretting my recent life choices. What was I thinking last night? Beckett's plan is so many layers of wrong, I don't know where to start. And yet, even though this idea is the most reckless thing I have ever agreed to, my blood is warmer. My heart faster. My hopes lifted.

I've thought this through. Something can't be impulsive if I've thought it through, right? And besides, Beckett has a plan. I'll be safe, I'll earn the money, and everything will return to normal.

Despite telling myself this, over and over, my nerves jangle.

When I arrived this morning, Dad was busy working on the accounting books, and he waved me away from his office when I said hello. I've been manning the register since ten. Unsurprisingly, the alley is dead, and for once I wish we had more customers.

Maybe it's in my best interest we don't, because I'm bombing today. I mess up giving our only two groups their change. I rip the stitching on my sewing project, a Biba head scarf. My body's so energized I smack my kneecap into the counter—*twice*.

After lunch, the tinted glass doors open and Beckett Porter strolls into Bigmouth's, hands tucked into his front pockets. I lower my headphones. He's earlier than I expected. Surely Beckett's not loitering around here for my entire shift. We can't exactly talk Hustling 101 or whatever with Dad hovering.

"Hey." He motions to the pale pink fabric twined between my fingers. "That looks cool. What is it?"

"A scarf." I stab the head scarf with my needle and pull the thread taut, unnerved by his interest. Why does he care? "You know I'm not off for another five hours, right?" Sure, I could *ignore* him for those five hours, but I've decided Beckett's presence is the social equivalent of black mold—unassuming, and it might kill you if you don't get rid of it.

Beckett places a twenty-dollar bill beside the register. "I'm here to bowl." He peers over the counter and cocks his head. "Nice overalls."

The comment oozes sarcasm, but I flash him a smile. "Thank you."

They're no ordinary overalls. I tailored and customized them. I believe—after many *Friends* reruns—the nineties ruined overalls for future generations. Which is a shame. I'm trying to rectify that, although I get an awful lot of weird looks for wearing overalls. Even in San Francisco, capital of the Weird.

"Just one game?" I ask, sliding the twenty off the countertop.

"Yep."

I ring Beckett up, careful not to touch his hand as I drop the coins into his palm.

Beckett sets up in lane seven, and yeah, he still *sucks*. Why is he spending money on something he clearly lacks the skills for? But I might have high standards. It's a miracle I wasn't born in this damn alley, that's how ingrained bowling is in our family.

Grandpa Ben opened Bigmouth's in the late sixties, christening it after the nickname my grandmother gave him for being a huge gossip. Benjamin "Bigmouth" O'Neill died when I was six months old, my grandma a year after him. Death came in threes for my family, because my mom died two years later.

The business was already going downhill when my dad took it on full-time. Through the years, we've cycled through landlords, iffy clauses, increased rent thanks to the tech boom, and now we're stuck with Jesset's eviction threats.

I fiddle with the Biba scarf, but spying on Beckett while I'm sewing is kind of hard, so I set the project aside. Inside my carpetbag purse is my latest library find, and I crack the spine, flipping idly through the pages. Much more suited for spying.

From the corner of my eye, Beckett flounders to knock

over pins. He's consistently crappy and doesn't manage a single strike. Which makes me wonder how he got into hustling. I make a mental note to ask about his bowling history later when we—I refuse to call it *hang out*—have our business meeting.

If you can call hustling a business.

Dad comes out from his office to watch Beckett bowl. Dad clearly still adores Beckett, and seeing them together acting chummy, talking, laughing? It sets off alarms, raises red flags, and broadcasts warning signals. S-O-freaking-S.

Beckett is giving my dad the wrong impression, instilling false hope that we're friends again. Dad was pretty devastated when we had our falling-out. He pushed me to forgive Beckett and mend our friendship, but it's not my fault he's unworthy of redemption.

I hide behind the library book when they both approach the register.

"Caroline, honey, why didn't you tell me you were doing a project with Beckett?"

I shoot Beckett a look. There's no way he told him.

Beckett says to Dad, "Our teacher asked us to spend break doing a research project on something unique to San Francisco."

Mr. Haust, my history teacher, assigned no such project. We're not even in the same class. Beckett's lying to my dad to give us a reason to spend time together. To get me out of work. I hate lying, and Beckett's lied me into a corner.

"What's your project on?"

"We're thinking of focusing on the city's criminal roots," Beckett adds.

"Fascinating," Dad says, then to me, "What're you still doing sitting back there?"

I glance around. "Back where? The counter? Because you told me to."

"School comes first."

Uneasily, I smile. "I didn't want to inconvenience you, Dad."

"Nonsense. Beckett's headed to the library. You should join him."

"What about—" I gesture to my work space helplessly. And here I thought I had a few more hours to compose myself before meeting with Beckett. "Who will do my job?"

"I'll need your help if things pick up, but an afternoon away might do you good."

When I don't move, they both stare, waiting. Sighing, I pack up the scarf and my book and sling my purse over my shoulder. "I have my phone, okay?"

Dad grins so wide, the gold in his molar fillings glints. Not only is he excited I'm interacting with someone in real life, but the fact that said person happens to be Beckett Porter is apparently too much joy for him to handle.

"I'll be fine. You two have fun."

I hug Dad and burrow my face against his chest, rolling my eyes. Yeah. Fun with Beckett. Not in this lifetime, or the next. That chapter in our shared history ended a year ago.

Beckett returns his bowling shoes and walks out with

me. He carries a beat-up bowling bag held together with electrical tape.

"Pretty smooth, huh?" he asks, pumping his eyebrows at me. Like he's challenging me *not* to laugh at his ridiculousness.

"You're way too pleased with yourself." A smile threatens my lips, so I look away and study the sidewalk. We're here to talk business, not joke around. "School project is the most basic lie in the book. Be happy my dad is super gullible and feels guilty for saddling me with work during spring break." I gamble a sideways look at him. "What're we even doing right now?"

"We need to talk over the plan," he says, patting down his pockets. After a moment, he pulls out a set of keys. "There's a lot you don't understand yet. You've got the talent, but hustling is an entirely different game."

Hustling. The word alone throws me. "Enlighten me," I say, the pulse of nerves making my hands shake. I cross my arms so Beckett can't see my weakness.

Beckett glances darkly at Bigmouth's closed doors. "Not here."

Wow, dramatic.

I tread behind Beckett as we walk along the street and stop at a parked junker near an expired meter. The car is a patchy blue, from the eighties by the condition. A Honda Accord. "Nice ride," I say sarcastically.

"You're just jealous I have one," Beckett fires back, rounding to the other side of his shitty little car.

He has a point. Having been held back in kindergarten, Beckett turned sixteen last year, before our fight. We couldn't wait until his provisional license period was over. City driving sucks, and parking is worse, but there's something to be said for the freedom of having your own car. Or so I've been told. I don't even have my learner's permit.

Beckett leans across the seat and unlocks the passenger door from the inside, popping it open. I duck into the Accord, which smells of coffee and something warm and spicy, like cinnamon breath mints. Not bad, but weird. Like this entire situation.

"Can this deathtrap make it up the hills?"

Beckett turns on the radio. His phone has a cassette player adapter plugged into the headphone jack, and he studies the screen before selecting a song. Father John Misty's "Hollywood Forever Cemetery Sings." I introduced him to the singer, and the fact that he still listens to him irks the hell out of me.

The car lurches as Beckett shifts into gear, and he flashes me a smile. "Let's find out, shall we?"

Oh my God, I'm going to die.

At least the music is appropriate.

"How have you never been to Dynamo's?" Beckett's accusation rivals Black Francis's hoarse scream in "Hey" on the Pixies' *Doolittle* album playing through the speakers.

The Accord chugs up a hill, and my knuckles whiten as I clutch the seat's edge. "Stop making it sound like I've broken a law. It's a *doughnut* place."

Beckett laughs. "That's where you are so, so wrong."

On Saturdays, street parking's the worst, but we find a spot a few blocks away.

Beckett lopes beside me, his stride longer than mine. When he's not looking, I study him. He's dressed nicer today than usual. Jeans without various stains. A long-sleeve with mismatched, chipped buttons. His loose curls become tousled in the wind.

The whole package is messy and categorically endearing; my heart thuds faster. I blame the uphill walk and misplaced hormones. Because even if Beckett Porter is mildly attractive, his looks no longer have any effect on me. Who cares if he's gotten marginally more handsome over the past year? He's still a pain in my ass. He still ruined our friendship.

We stand in line at the outdoor counter, and I am loath to admit the eclectic doughnut menu sounds tasty: Coconut Macadamia Nut, Hazelnut Lavender, Chocolate Rose, and more. I place an order for a plain coffee. Just to spite him.

"Black coffee?" Beckett scoffs. "Nope, you are not coming here just for black coffee."

"I'm not hungry," I insist, even as the sugary smell makes my mouth water against my will.

Beckett sighs and sways his head side to side. "You've always been an awful liar. We'll need to fix that." He pushes me aside and orders a Meyer Lemon Huckleberry, a Maple Bacon, and a second large coffee.

Typical Beckett. Acting like he knows everything about me. Maybe he knew everything about sophomore-year Chuck Wilson, but a lot can happen—and change—in a year. I'm *not* the same person. Sophomore-year Chuck preferred full-name Caroline until winter break, and she was far more trusting than I am now.

After getting our doughnuts and coffee, Beckett snags the last open table out on the garden patio. He takes a plastic knife and cuts the pastries in half, handing me one of each.

"These are the best in the city, and it's the ideal time of day to eat doughnuts. It'd be a crime if you didn't try them."

"A crime? Aren't you okay with those?"

"Ha-ha," he says. "Doughnuts are too sweet for breakfast, but most shops close or run out of the good stuff past one or two. Thus, early afternoon is key doughnut-consumption time."

"Right." I tentatively nibble into the first doughnut.

He wolfs his down in two bites.

"Don't choke."

Beckett points at me, chewing and swallowing. "Aw, Chuck, you care about my well-being."

"Nope. I don't know the Heimlich maneuver, and I don't have the morgue's number on speed dial."

Beckett howls with laughter, garnering glares from the other patrons, and my lips twitch with a grin. "I can't believe you've never been here," he says, eyes rolling back in his head as he finishes his second half. "Actually, I believe it considering you live at that bowling alley."

"I do not," I reply. "I go places."

"Yeah?" Beckett pushes his hair from his eyes. "Where?"

Copious estate sales. Berkeley for their thrift stores. That art-house movie theater in the Oakland Hills. The San Francisco Public Library. But I'm not defending myself to Beckett.

To change the subject, I say, "These aren't half bad."

"They're the best things on this planet."

"How could you tell?" I say. "You inhaled them."

Beckett smacks his lips. "I got a little mouth feel before I swallowed. Delicious."

"You're disgusting. Also, 'mouth feel'? *Really?*"

"I'm not disgusting. I'm rather charming." He leans back in his chair, self-satisfied. I can't help but smirk at the crumbled glaze clinging to his upper lip. Huh. Beckett has facial hair now? When did that happen?

"And humble."

"Yeah, well, I don't like to brag."

The smirk grows into a full-blown grin, and I hide my smile behind the rim of my mug. I will *not* smile for Beckett Porter. Despite the warmth in my chest, goose bumps line my arms. Like my central nervous system is running on overdrive.

"Can I ask you something?" Beckett's eyes flit from my lips to my eyes, and those goose bumps multiply.

"Sure," I say, trying to keep things light. "But we need to focus before all this sugar and caffeine puts me in a coma."

"I apologized for what happened at that party. Not immediately, but I apologized."

All my warmth and goose bumps disappear. Every tamped-down emotion that's lived inside my chest the past year bubbles to the surface. Today, with Beckett, has felt way too normal, too much like it was before we tore our friendship apart. I was right to be upset with him, wasn't I? Because I'm starting to second-guess myself, and it's making me cold-sweat through my T-shirt.

"Why'd you have to ruin our friendship over a mistake?" Beckett continues. "A shitty mistake, yeah, but I didn't mean to hurt you."

"Except you did." My voice cracks, and I hate myself. *Don't get upset*, I school myself. *Not in front of him*. I squeeze the chunk of doughnut so tight it turns to mush between my fingers. "You may have not started them, but the rumors about my mom—about me, my mental health— were your fault."

Beckett scratches his neck. "I didn't lie—"

"Fuck you." The words escape, more hostile than intended, but really I'm trying not to cry. I hate that he still has this effect on me. I scramble to gather my things. Why did I think I could do this? This was a mistake.

"Chuck." Beckett reaches for me, but I back away. "Leave if you want. I'm not holding you hostage. You're here because you want to hear me out. But first I'd like to clear the air."

After taking a deep breath, blinking to hide the rush of pain, the swirling mixture of resentment and sadness fades. Slightly. I drop back into my seat. "I need the money, but we don't need to dredge up the past to work together.

I just . . . I can't deal with what happened between us. Not right now."

"If not now, when? Chuck, I need some closure here. *Please*," Beckett says, his tone bordering on desperate. "After I apologized to you and your dad, you refused to acknowledge my existence." He picks at the sheet of wax paper that came with our doughnuts. Tears it to shreds. "Your dad accepted my apology, but you never did. Why can't you forgive me?"

My heart swoops with guilt, but the aftertaste is a familiar prickle of resentment. After what he did, I couldn't trust him. And if I couldn't trust him, we could never be friends again. What was the point in forgiving him if our friendship was over?

"I can't forgive you because I don't, and I'm not looking to ease your guilty conscience."

I thought saying those words would make me feel better. Slam the door shut on our situation for good, locking it up so tight that Beckett would never have a chance of breaking it down. But all I'm left feeling is hopeless. And kind of like an asshole. Thinking these things about Beckett is one thing. Saying them to his face is another.

Beckett stares at me, his brows scrunched together. Like he's trying to solve a difficult math problem. "Fine," he says after a moment. "But don't put all the blame on me. Okay?"

"Okay." I exhale slowly, glancing at my lap, at my fingers twisted and knotted together. Why does this hurt so much? I want to say something powerful, but all I say is,

"You were my *best* friend, Beckett. My only friend."

"And you were mine." He piles the slivers of wax paper into a miniature mountain, face downcast. "I'm so sorry. So fucking sorry." He lifts his eyes, and our gazes clash.

I study his face and wish I were better at reading him. A year ago, Beckett's face was like a well-loved book. Now I'm lost as to how to interpret the slant of his lips or the way his hands fidget.

When I say nothing, he offers a small smile. "So. You're still pissed."

I shrug with one shoulder. Am I still pissed? A mixture of things ache in my chest, and I remind myself to *breathe*. To not get overwhelmed. My emotions are like cotton, fuzzing up my head, diluting my thought processes, and I can't have that right now.

Beckett lifts both palms and makes a beckoning motion. "Come on, let it all out."

"What?"

"Get all the anger out. Wipe the slate clean." He squints, like he's preparing to be slapped.

The funny thing is, I'm not upset anymore. I'm just . . . done. We'll never get back to the way things were, so what's the point? Besides, do I even want to be his friend again if I'm hauling ass to Arizona?

I lean over the bistro table and flick his fingers. "Quit being dramatic."

Beckett lowers his hands. "I'm trying to set the record straight. Are we good?"

"Good?" I repeat.

"We don't have to be best friends again. Or even friends. But we should trust each other." His voice drops. "Hustling isn't for the faint of heart, Wilson."

"How do you propose we do this? Run some trust-fall exercises?" I joke, nerves exposed at that word—trust.

"No, but seriously," he replies. "If we're on the same page, if we can trust each other, then we can proceed. There's a small game tomorrow night." He pauses until I meet his eye. "What do you say?"

Tomorrow night? That's way too soon. Then again, we only have nine days left. My biggest fear is not being good enough to hustle, losing whatever money we bet. Swallowing hard, I say, "I'm rusty. Can we practice?"

Beckett's mouth upturns with a smile. "How about tonight? Bigmouth's after closing? You can practice, and we'll go over the mechanics of a hustle. How to play the other players. How to act."

"Fine. Tonight should work." Shifting in my seat, I ask, "What's in this for you? This can't all be for Willa's summer camp money."

"Camp's expensive, man," he says with an exaggerated shrug. "I'm never having kids."

"Like anyone would want to have kids with you," I mutter.

Beckett laughs, folding his arms behind his head. Lazily, like he's comfortable in this super-weird situation. He stretches his legs out, and beneath the table, his foot knocks into mine.

The brief contact is nice—all warm and familiar—and

I shift my legs out of reach. "If I agree to this, then you have to agree it's strictly business. We bowl, we hustle, and we go our separate ways. Deal?"

His smile flickers, a rare shift for his annoyingly sunny disposition. He scrubs his hand against his chin and says, "If that's what you want."

I ignore the depression of my ribs against my heart and hold out my hand. Trust is overrated. Who says I have to like Beckett to use him? Who needs trust when you have a mutually beneficial goal?

"I trust you," I lie, and we shake.

This was either the best decision I've ever made, or the worst.

I have a strong feeling it may be both.

Six

BECKETT AND I part ways with the plan to meet up tonight at Bigmouth's after closing. He offered to give me a ride, but I needed space. We just spent more time together in one day than we have in a year. Despite the rainy deluge, I walk to the Twenty-Fourth Street Mission BART. Once I'm sublevel, I lean against a column and wait for the Daly City train, which will drop me at the Glen Park station by Bigmouth's. The redbrick floors squeak as commuters hurry to and from their trains, the air musty with the sweet, earthy scent of fresh rain on concrete.

The rain plastered my hair to my skull, and normally I'd be freaking out over wearing my sparkly sequined platforms in the storm, but what's happening inside my chest is way more distressing.

All the physical distance between us can't keep Beckett's disappointment from lingering. But . . . I just can't let it go.

Pain lingers, and I'm used to resenting him—I'm not sure what my life would look like if I stopped.

After getting off at Glen Park, I walk the familiar path to Bigmouth's. The exterior bowling alley sign with its blue neon is reflected in the puddles, and I follow it to the door. Inside, I'm greeted by the uneven crash of pins echoing across the lanes. Nothing has changed in the last two hours, and it's painfully slow for a Saturday.

Dad waves me over from the register. "Wow, it must really be coming down out there."

A raindrop rolls down my nose. I brush it off with the back of my hand. "Cats and dogs."

"How'd your project go?"

"Oh, uh, fine? We still have a lot of work," I say, hating that Beckett's forced me into lying. "Sorry for bailing earlier."

Dad's grin is warm. Almost erases the ache in my chest. "No need to apologize. I'm real happy to see you hanging out with Beckett again. He's a great kid."

I doubt Dad would say that if he knew what we were really up to. "Dad, we're not friends again. You understand that, right?"

"Whatever you say, Caroline."

I've asked my dad to call me Chuck so many times I've lost count. He thinks it's not *feminine*. Doesn't grasp the concept that—shocker—I don't want to be called my mom's name. This is one battle I'll always lose, so I've given up.

"Thanks for letting me off the hook. If you'd like, I can close tonight and do inventory?"

"That'd be fantastic," Dad says, scooting out from behind the counter. Even though my clothes are soaked, he pulls me into a hug. "Thank you."

I rest my head on his shoulder. "Anytime."

The rest of the evening passes quickly. I spend ten minutes trying to dry my overalls with the hand dryer in the bathroom. Dinner consists of free nachos and a soda. We serve only three other groups of customers, and Dad leaves around eight.

When it's just me, I text Beckett that he can come by. He doesn't show up right away. All the customers are gone, but we're open until ten. I clean up the lanes. I spray bowling shoes with dual shots of disinfectant and Febreze. Inventory takes only fifteen minutes.

Half the lights are on timers and already winked out, leaving the alley in moody half darkness. In the silence, I can hear the rain pattering on the tin roof, sloshing against the windows. I underestimated how creepy it is to be alone this late in the bowling alley. The storm only amps up the creep factor. All those big mouths on the wall? I'm surprised this place hasn't shown up in my nightmares.

When Beckett knocks—three loud, booming taps—I jump like a freaking cartoon character. I locked up for security, so I hurry down the entry to let him in.

Rain smacks the cement, dribbling off the overhang as Beckett steps inside.

"What took you so long?" I shut the door behind him, flipping the latch. "It's late."

"Chill out. I thought you wanted me here after clos-ing." Shaking off the rainwater, he walks into the main part of the alley. Stubborn droplets cling to his curls. He plops down on a couch and unlaces his sodden sneakers. "I had to put Willa to bed, and there was an accident on the Bay Bridge."

"What were you doing on the bridge?" I gather two pairs of shoes from the cubbies behind the register.

"Uh," he replies, drawing it out, "we moved to Berkeley."

I hand him his shoes. "Since when?"

"After my dad left town and never came home."

I lower myself beside him. "Beckett, I had no idea." The guilt is thick. Beckett's dad must've left in the last year. The year when I ignored his existence.

"It's fine," he says, but it's not fine. Not at all.

"When did he leave?" I snap and unsnap the button on my overalls pocket.

Beckett exhales loudly. "About a week after that party, after our fight. I figured you knew? Heard from someone, or your dad?"

"Nope," I say, shaking my head. "It's not like I—"

"Cared?"

Ouch.

"I wasn't going to say that. But I didn't know. Honest."

"Would it have changed things?"

When I don't answer, Beckett leans forward to tie his shoelaces. We're close enough that I inhale the damp-ness of his clothes, the warmth of his skin, mixed with deodorant. The same deodorant he's always worn. My brain insists the Beckett sitting beside me is the same Beckett from sophomore year, just because he smells the same. Damn olfactory system. Swirling up all these old and bruising memories.

"I figured as much." Beckett drags his fingers through his hair. "Anyway, I couldn't deal. You were mad at me and my family was imploding and I didn't deal well. I let us fall apart too."

All the scrambled puzzle pieces slot into place. And as upsetting as this is, it makes sense. Why I saw him less and less at school. Why he got into a fight at the end of sophomore year. By junior year, he became a truant. I never let myself care—or show that I cared—why Beckett acted the way he did. Until now.

I chew on the inside of my cheek, wishing my heart would slow down or my mind would speed up and help me decide what to say. "I'm sorry about your dad," I eventually tell him. The other half of the sentence—*I should've been there*—stays unsaid.

"Me too." Beckett's smile is rueful. A lull of silence fills the air, and then he adds, "We moved toward the end of sophomore year, once it was clear my dad wasn't coming back."

"I'm sorry," I say again because the silence is too much.

"No worries. Enough sad shit." He clears the thickness from his throat and pulls his notebook from his backpack. "Let's get back on topic. The game tomorrow starts at ten at the Road."

"Ten? That's kind of late."

Beckett cocks a brow. "How old are you? It's spring break. Live a little."

"Excuse me for having a curfew." Technically, my weekend and holiday-break curfew is midnight. But I make it a habit to be folded between my comforter and sheets by ten p.m. every night.

"We'll figure it out." When he hops to his feet, it's like he leaves his sadness behind. "The Road's a bowling alley and pool hall in Oakland. Low-key, low stakes, and hopefully low stress. This is a good starter game because the players stick to this specific alley, and we won't run into them later in the week."

I flip through the notebook, my heart rate settling now we're talking business. Something straightforward without the taint of emotions. "What other games are we playing?"

"I'm still hitting up contacts about any games going on between now and next Sunday. Not all are announced in advance. With enough seed money, we should be able to flip a profit."

"I have two hundred to contribute." Doing so will drain my savings, but if we're doing this, we're doing this right.

Beckett bobs his head. "Excellent. I have three hundred to throw in. Five hundred is a decent starter. We can play a game tomorrow for cheap, like sixty a head. I was thinking this once we'd bowl as a team, so you can get a feel without too much pressure. The stakes are low, so if my sucky skills pull our score down, we won't lose much."

"Sure. That works." I study his notebook, then tap the

page listing different players. "How do you know these guys? And about hustling?"

"I don't know them, not personally. Back at the start of the school year, I was betting on games—I actually know a lot about bowling, thanks to you—and that's when I first saw people hustling. The good ones are subtle. Everything else I learned online."

"Why were you betting in the first place?"

Beckett checks out our selection of bowling balls, lifting them and testing their weight. "My mom was laid off last summer, and a little extra pocket change never killed anyone. Medicine, gas, and groceries don't pay for themselves."

My heart swoops—first with sympathy and then with curiosity. What the hell happened? Mrs. Porter used to be a pediatric nurse at St. Mary's Medical. Then again, Beckett's dad was still in the picture.

To busy myself from falling too deep into a well of guilt, I flip through the pages, full of countless bowling alley names and notes on their players. Never once do I read Bigmouth's name in the notebook, but I have to ask, "Does Bigmouth's ever do this?"

Beckett laughs and rubs his chin. "Nah. Your dad is too straitlaced to allow hustling."

True. My dad is old-fashioned and believes people should bowl because they love the sport, not because they prefer to get drunk and throw a ten-pound ball at pins for fun. But our lack of a liquor license wasn't Dad's idea—it was Grandpa Ben's. He was a recovering alcoholic and preferred not to be near booze twenty-four seven.

"First lesson," Beckett says, gently tugging the notebook from my hands. "Subtlety is key. An easy trick is appearing drunk. Drinking at bowling alleys is a given these days. If you appear tipsy and loose-handed with your cash, the players will view you as nonthreatening. I mean, you have the advantage of being a girl. I've never seen a female hustler."

Ah, sexism at its finest. "But won't that make me more noticeable? If I'm the only girl? What if people take pictures or something?" I slip off my platform heels and trade them for the bowling shoes.

Beckett pauses and squints at me. "Huh, okay, I hadn't thought of that. I know some more hard-core places require you to leave your cell phone at the door, but you raise a valid point."

I approach the nearest ball rack and hunt out my favorite, a twelve-pound Hammer Absolut Hook. The colors are funky, a rich purple marbled with black. I hoist the ball against my hip as I punch the override code into the console for a free game.

"What about wigs?" I set my ball in the return. Until now, Beckett's been running the show, and it's nice to contribute. "For me, obviously."

He laughs, tilting his head back. "Those creepy-as-fuck wigs in your bedroom? Those would be perfect!"

"Hey, they're not creepy—just the mannequin heads are. They're really nice wigs." I drag my fingers through what was once a pixie cut. My hair hangs in an unruly bob, short enough to disguise easily beneath a wig cap. "But what about you?"

"I doubt anyone will pay attention to me," Beckett says, "but maybe just a beanie to hide my hair?"

"Okay," I reply, satisfied. "What else can you tell me about hustling?" I'm surprised to realize I *wouldn't* rather be sleeping or chatting with Mila right now—and I'm not entirely sure how I feel about that.

"Hold up. Why don't you throw a few practice shots?"

I'm relieved, yet nervous at his suggestion. What if I suck? Last year I would've had no problem telling Beckett my fears. Now the admission that I'm anything but fearless feels too personal, too real. Too uncomfortably close to the truth.

"What?" I ask, shaking off my nerves and putting up my walls. "Afraid I'm not as good as you remembered?"

He grins, holding out his palms in innocence. "You said it, not me."

I resist the urge to stick my tongue out at him, instead picking up the ball and walking onto the platform. Every move I make feels like it's under some kind of Beckett microscope as he watches me from the sidelines. Not like his attention matters. Not like I *care* or anything.

With squared shoulders, I take my shot. The ball hammers down the lane, crashing into the headpin, and I swell with satisfaction. The other nine pins fall, rocketing and spiraling away. When my ball returns, I bowl another strike. And another, clearing the frames after the pinsetter resets them.

I can't bowl a perfect game, but it's undeniable—I'm pretty damn good.

Beckett lets out a low whistle. "Is it me, or have you gotten *better*?"

"I am impressive, aren't I?" My humor masks my insurmountable insecurity.

Rusty or not, I bowled well tonight, which wasn't a guarantee.

Beckett grabs his ball and shoots a sloppy frame. "What's really going to push you ahead is downplaying your skills. Showing an ineptitude for the game."

"Oh, is that what you're doing?" I joke, flicking my wrist to the nine remaining pins.

"I forgot how funny you are," he says dryly, abandoning the lane to grab something from his backpack. He holds up a money clip, then tosses it over. "So, strategy. There are little things, too, like dropping your money. We'll use this, fold a larger bill over the others, so when you drop it, it'll look like you have more than you're betting."

I twirl the money clip between my fingers. Plain brass with the initials *ACP* embossed onto one side. Adam-something-Porter. "This your dad's?"

"Yeah. I found it when we were moving." Beckett palms his neck. "Anyway. Keep it simple. You either act quiet and unassuming, or drunk and gregarious. Or distracting your opponents and getting *them* drunk also works."

I toss the money clip back. "People are sloppy when they're drunk. Got it."

Beckett catches and pockets the clip. "You'll have to be careful. You won't be bowling strikes, not unless you need to punch out to win."

"Punch out?"

"Bowl two strikes in the final frame," he clarifies, leaning against the ball return and kickstanding one leg behind him. "Most of your shots will be orchestrated. You want to be good but not too good. Try bowling a frame, but don't go for the strike pocket. Try for the pocket between pins two and four."

At the foul line, I take a calculated shot and aim between pins four and two. And I miss, my left hook winging out, so I only clip the fourth pin.

"My bad," I say, wincing as two pins clatter.

Beckett's laughter dissolves my threatening nerves. "That's why we're practicing. Bowling with the intention of not getting a strike isn't natural."

I follow Beckett's instructions and choreograph my throws. It takes practice, but after the fifth or sixth throw, I get the hang of it. Accounting for my left hook is essential, but as long as I keep that in mind and line up my shots, it's easy. With something external to focus on, Beckett and I work fine together. We're almost professional. Much more preferable to digging into our past.

After an hour I'm confident I can replicate these shots tomorrow night. And the night after.

I return my ball to the rack and stretch overhead, my arms aching from the repetition. "Anything else?"

Beckett tosses his ball at a newly set frame of pins. "Nah, I mean, we'll have to read the room. There's only so much planning we can do, but this is an excellent start. You feel ready?"

"As ready as I'll ever be." Flopping onto the couch, I kick off the bowling shoes. Pressed against the dull pinewood, my socked feet are wet from sweat and the rain. Curling my toes, I tuck my feet behind the legs of the seat, just in case they smell. I don't linger on why I'm concerned about Beckett smelling my feet; it's not like he hasn't before. I watch him bowl another terrible shot and add, "You're awful."

Beckett spins on his heel as his ball careens into the gutter. He flashes me a smile. "Thanks, but you don't have to be good to enjoy it. Maybe you forgot, but we had a blast bowling here every weekend. And I loved bowling with my dad before he split."

"Pun intended?" The inappropriate joke slips out.

His laugh surprises me.

Encouraged, I say, "Unfortunately, most of life can be summed up in poor bowling puns."

Beckett puts the ball away and joins me on the couch. He unlaces his shoes and slides them off, stretching out his legs. His socks are mismatched, his left big toe poking out of a hole. He sneezes loudly into the crook of his elbow.

"I think I'm allergic to something in here."

"Maybe you just lost your immunity to me," I tease, and he laughs. Except it's kind of the truth, since my cat sheds all over my clothes like it's his job. "Spending time and money on something you're bad at seems like a waste."

"Everyone's gotta have a passion." Beckett pauses to blow his nose with a tissue from his backpack, and I almost feel bad for inflicting him with cat dander. "Passion does not equal competence."

"Maybe not, but it makes things easier."

"You're clearly not passionate about bowling. But what about sewing? Or fashion?" He nods at my sequined platform shoes. "You have a unique sense of style."

"I sew because . . . it's therapeutic. I don't know." My skin flushes, like opening up is akin to tossing off a piece of clothing. "As for fashion, it isn't a proper passion or a life skill."

The real answer is that vintage clothes are proof that no matter how broken a piece is, how used up or out of style, someone will find the beauty. There's something so comforting about that.

"Says who?" Beckett scoffs, rubbing the tendons along his neck. "If you're right—which you're not—there wouldn't be design schools and fashion degrees."

Even if I love fashion—and I do—following in my mom's footsteps and attending fashion school carves at my heart. I'm not sure I'll be able to apply knowing I'm taking steps to fulfilling the dream she never got the chance to live.

The argument is a moot point, anyway. College is the hundred-dollar question with the even higher price tag. If I'm accepted. If I earn a scholarship. I hate situations that depend entirely on *ifs*. Which all hinges on a bigger if—if Bigmouth's pulls through.

"It's complicated." I scratch my nose, focusing on the tinny sound of rainfall striking the roof. Time to switch topics. Beckett isn't my friend—he's my business partner. That's all. "So, we're really doing this?"

Beckett shifts to face me, leaning his elbow onto his

thigh. "Yeah. Unless you're having second thoughts?"

I shake my head. "Nope," I say, even though I'm nervous.

"Good." Relief flickers in his eyes.

A tiny bit of tiredness seeps into my bloodstream. A relief. Hopefully I'll sleep tonight. "We should head out."

Beckett stuffs his feet into his loafers and pushes up from the couch. "Need a ride?" he offers, slinging his backpack over his shoulder.

We've been far too friendly tonight, but I also don't want to take BART or Muni. So I agree. Beckett helps me close up—tidying our lane, turning off the remaining lights—and after setting the alarm code, I follow him to his car.

Wordlessly, Beckett plugs his phone into the tape-deck auxiliary converter and holds it across the center console. The screen is unlocked, Spotify pulled up. The gesture is so small, and yet it says so much. Beckett and I used to trade music almost as often as we traded words.

The phone's heavy in my palm as I choose one of my more recent favorite bands. Manchester Orchestra plucks and reverberates against the Accord's speakers as Beckett takes me home.

SUNDAY, APRIL 22

DAYS UNTIL BIGMOUTH'S
EVICTION: 8

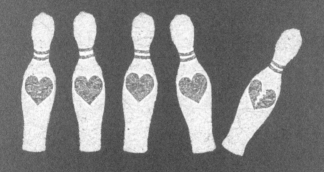

Seven

ALL I WANT to do is nervous-puke in my bathroom, but I pack my purse, along with a wig for tonight, and jog downstairs. Beckett's picking me up early to maintain our school project cover story; no idea how we'll kill time until the game at ten. Hopefully it'll be something that can keep my mind busy, because I'm dangerously close to freaking out.

I was banking on the house being empty, saving me from having to lie in person to my dad or Aunt Fiona, but no such luck. Dad's making a bologna sandwich in the kitchen. In his San Francisco Giants cap, poly-stained jersey paired with cargo shorts, he's so unassuming, but my chest clenches with nerves.

"You sure you don't need me at Bigmouth's?" I ask, swiping a banana from the fruit bowl, secretly hoping he does. Just so I have a logical reason to back out of tonight.

Dad squirts mustard onto rye bread, not even looking

up. The brim of his battered cap shields his face. "I'm sure. Fiona's covering while I have lunch, but Sundays are slow. Go have fun."

"We're working on a project, not hanging out."

Dad smooshes the two pieces of bread together. "It's okay, honey, if you forgive him."

"I don't—"

"I get it," he says, cutting me off. "The longer you hold on to something, the harder it is to let it go. Especially if it means admitting you might've been wrong."

I shake my head, flustered at his ability to voice the thoughts I refuse to acknowledge. "Jeez, Dad, whose side are you on?" When Beckett and I had our falling-out, I was surprised my dad didn't make TEAM BECKETT T-shirts.

"I'm on the side of your happiness, my darling daughter."

I roll my eyes.

"Speaking of"— Dad pauses, wiping his hands on his jeans—"I got the mail today." He slides a few envelopes across the counter.

One's from my bank; the other is a glossy trifold for FIDM. When I signed up for their tour at the start of the month, I entered my information as a prospective student. I didn't think they'd send me something in the mail. Who uses the postal service anymore?

"Thanks," I say, sliding the mail into my purse. Maybe Dad didn't see the envelope.

"Fashion school, huh?" Dad asks, dashing my hopes.

My stomach curls itself into one big cramp.

"I mean, maybe." My tongue sticks to the roof of my

mouth, the metallic of panic tainting my taste buds. Dad knows my heart lies with fashion, but I've never told him I was considering studying it at school. The implications, the fear, have kept me from taking my passion seriously. "Would that be okay?"

"Why wouldn't it be?" Setting his sandwich aside, Dad leans his elbows onto the kitchen island. "I think it's wonderful you share your mother's talents. That's a real special gift."

If I share Mom's talents, what else do we have in common? The thought leaves me heady with dread. I try brushing it off, but the unease lingers. "FIDM is super selective. I doubt I'll get in."

Dad picks up his plate and presses a kiss to my forehead. "Whatever you decide, I'm proud of you, Caroline."

I don't reply as he disappears into the den with his sandwich.

My body sags against the island counter. Of all days, why did we have to talk about FIDM before my first official hustle with Beckett? I'm left with nerves and sweat. Even though I already knew my mom studied design at CCA, I don't like thinking about it. Don't like looking too closely at how we overlap.

My mom had a commitment problem and never graduated from the California College of the Arts. Instead, she met my dad, and six months later they were married. But from what little Dad's told me over the years, she dreamed of owning a clothing store in the city, selling vintage threads alongside her own designs.

This hits close—too close—to the cordoned-off corners of my heart.

Fortunately, I can't dwell.

I've got bowlers to hustle.

Zipping up my army coat, I exit through the kitchen door. Beckett's parked on the opposite side of the rainy street.

"Hey," I say, dropping into the passenger seat. My heartbeat thuds out of rhythm, kicking up an unwanted racket. I never thought I'd be happy hanging out with Beckett again, but this is preferable to drowning in the negativity that is my headspace. I dump my belongings and untouched banana in the back, pulling out the mannequin head. "Check it out."

"Did you have to bring the wig *with* the head?"

"It keeps it from getting tangled," I insist, smoothing my fingers through the strands and returning the wig to the bag. But that's only one reason—I know how much the heads freak Beckett out.

"Creepy." He shudders comically. "You up to run errands?"

"Yeah, sure." Not like I have a choice.

"I have to grab a few things around the city before picking up dinner for my mom and Willa."

We both grow quiet for a moment. When I agreed to kill time before the hustle with Beckett, I figured I might be visiting the Porters' new house, but I didn't consider seeing his mom. I haven't seen Mrs. Porter in over a year, and the threat of an unwanted social situation makes me want to duck and roll out of the moving car. And yet I'm curious.

"You sure your mom won't mind?" I say.

"Nah, not at all. You know what? She still asks about you."

"Really?"

"Trust me, I don't understand the woman's fascination." Beckett winks at me. "You're pretty boring."

I ignore him the rest of the drive.

Beckett assures me he's only running a few basic errands. We stop by a specialty grocery store, a laundromat in Chinatown, Costco for a huge can of Folgers coffee, and a pet store for a box of small mice. Their nails scurry and scratch, and it takes all my willpower not to pop open the car door and release them into the wild.

Well, the wild of the Potrero Petco parking garage.

After wrapping up our errands, we drive over the Bay Bridge, classics playing on an oldies station and crackling through static. As we get closer to the East Bay, the rain picks up, sleeting down. I bundle my jacket into a ball and rest my head against the window, listening to the music and the pitter-patter of raindrops on glass.

Beckett stops at a Thai restaurant, and I wait in the car. He dashes through the shower and returns dripping, carrying two large to-go bags.

"Gotta love the unpredictability of this weather," he says with a rueful laugh, tossing his hair back and flicking water everywhere, including on me. "Here, I ordered extra. Fuel for tonight." He slides the warm bags onto my lap and settles into the driver's seat.

"Oh!" My hands start sweating, but maybe it's because of the food. "You didn't have to do that. I have a banana—"

"I got shrimp spring rolls, no cilantro." Beckett pulls onto a surface street, squinting as the rain flows like overturned buckets.

"You remembered," I say, staring at the to-go food. There goes my politeness theory. I glimpse my reflection in the side mirror, mortified at the blush coloring my cheeks.

"Your hatred of cilantro is *legendary*," he says. "Just you wait. I'll be ninety, senile, and I'll still remember how much Chuck Wilson hates cilantro."

"What? It's disgusting!" I pretend to gag. "The smell alone."

He laughs, glancing from the road and catching my gaze with his. Something strange and heated blossoms behind my sternum. Something like memories and the warm-flush glow of happiness. Despite digging in my heels, fighting this, my body likes being near him.

My brain, however, isn't as easily convinced.

But I can't deny that there's a comfort, a familiarity, that Beckett brings. He's a light shining on the shadowed parts of me I forgot existed.

We don't speak the rest of the drive, but I'm acutely aware of the Accord's cramped bucket seats and how Beckett's sleeve brushes mine when he adjusts the radio or heater.

The Porters live in an old, run-down part of Berkeley.

The house is a tiny single story with lots of ancient trees swathing the property in dark leaves. The grass is lush and springy under my feet, the pathway to the porch grown over by the lawn.

"We're renting," Beckett explains as he leads me to the front door. "It's cheaper than the city, and quieter. Closer to her caretaking gig too."

Despite the exterior, the house is downright charming. The entry hall has wooden floors, the walls painted a rustic blue. From the paintings to the tchotchkes on the shelves, everything is neat and tidy.

"Hey! I'm home." Beckett drops his keys into an abalone shell on a side table. "I brought company."

A small girl with lanky limbs and brown curls swings around the corner. "Are those my mice?" Willa asks her brother.

He presses his lips together and holds out the box. "Here's the sacrificial offering, m'lady."

"Wait, what are the mice for?" I ask, horrified.

"They're for Lester," Willa says. She breaks out in a grin when she notices me. "Chuck!"

"Hi, Willa." I crouch, and she tosses her arms around my neck. Willa wasn't even six years old when I last saw her. But somehow, in the past year, she's sprouted a foot, her hair wild tangles reaching her waist.

"Hey, do you want to watch me feed my snake?"

Beckett must see my horrified reaction. "Willa, chill-a, okay? Chuck just got here, and we brought Thai from Lucky House. Let's postpone the mice murder until *after* dinner."

Willa pouts. "Fine," she huffs, and disappears down a hallway.

"What kid has a pet snake?" I readjust the take-out bags in my arms.

"That's some big talk coming from the girl who collects mannequin heads."

I smack Beckett with a take-out bag, but he laughs. "Watch it! Willa wanted a cat, but that was a no-go."

"Oh right, you're allergic." I feign forgetting until just this moment. "Tell Willa she can come visit JP whenever she wants."

He tilts his head. "JP?"

"My cat."

"You got a cat? I thought you hated cats."

"No, I pretended to hate cats out of solidarity because your immune system can't handle them," I say. "I was really missing out."

"I can't believe you're a cat person now," he says in mock disgust, holding his hand to his heart. "Traitor."

We're stopped in the cramped hallway, and he steps even closer. I step backward, bumping into the wall. Beckett is standing so close I can see the faint dusting of freckles on the bridge of his nose. Smell that familiar scent of deodorant—spicy and warm. Feel his hand settle on my forearm. "What're you doing?" I ask, not sure if I'm asking him or myself. Because why am I still standing here?

Beckett plucks something off my jacket. He backs away, his thumb and forefinger pinched together. In them, a single white cat hair. "You're going to kill me, Chuck Wilson."

Flushed, I manage to say, "My master plan is working brilliantly, then."

He rolls his eyes, then takes off down the hall.

After my heart calms, I follow him into a brightly decorated kitchen.

Mrs. Porter is dressed in denim jeans and a loose white top. Her light brown hair is frizzy and piled on her head, and her face is youthfully lined. Her eyes are large and pale gray, free from the weight of makeup. The only thing missing from my mental images of the woman in front of me are the Minnie Mouse scrubs she always wore. When she smiles, it dazzles her face.

"Welcome home, kiddo," she says to Beckett, standing up from the small table. It's neat with a lacy white tablecloth, yellow-patterned plates, and water glasses. As if she was expecting company. "Chuck! So wonderful to see you!"

"Hey, Mrs. Porter." I give an awkward wave from my hip.

Mrs. Porter beams like a freaking lighthouse, clasping her hands beneath her chin. "It's so nice to see you, honey." To Beckett, she says, "See, I told you she'd come over to dinner if you asked nicely!"

Beckett palms the back of his neck and stares at the wall. He's embarrassed—the tips of his ears are turning bright red. Huh. I forgot how he blushes—light on the cheeks but fire-engine red when the blood hits his earlobes.

"Uh—" Confused, I look away from Beckett and smile at Mrs. Porter. "Nice to see you, too. Thanks for having me."

Mrs. Porter hurries across the kitchen and latches me into a tight hug. "Look at you! I knew you'd grow up to be beautiful. Didn't I tell you that, Beckett?"

"Mom, please stop," Beckett mutters, throwing me an apologetic glance before unloading the bags on the kitchen counter next to an old stovetop from the fifties. Its ancientness matches the large lime-green fridge.

Haltingly, Mrs. Porter's grip loosens, and I slide away. She brushes back a lock of my hair that's fallen across my cheek. "I'm so happy you're here. We've *missed* you."

Before I can reply, she lifts the takeout from my arms. I shrug off my damp jacket, heavy with rain, and hang it on the back of the closest chair.

Beckett smiles and turns to his mom, going over what he picked up. "I'll drop the dry cleaning in your room, okay?"

Mrs. Porter smiles. "Thank you."

Then we're alone.

I stare at an empty water glass on the table. "I hope it's okay Beckett invited me."

"Okay?" She laughs, moving to open the fridge. "This is great."

I manage a smile. "I appreciate it." Unable to stop fidgeting, I twist my fingers together. "Apparently I'm culpable for some future mouse murders. I handpicked those mice."

Mrs. Porter tosses her head back and laughs. "Willa loves that snake. God knows why."

Well. I'm officially out of small-talk topics.

Thankfully Beckett and Willa break the silence seconds later. They sit on either side of me, and Mrs. Porter pops open the containers and sets them in the center of the table before sitting.

"Chuck, how's junior year treating you?" Mrs. Porter asks, digging into her coconut curry.

I finish chewing a spring roll and swallow. "Not bad."

Mrs. Porter grins, and the corners of her mouth curve in parentheses. "I feel like it's been ages since I saw you last."

"A year," Beckett answers, studying his place mat.

"Right!" Mrs. Porter snaps her fingers. "That play with Beckett sophomore year. You two were so cute."

Beckett and I groan in unison. The play. Beckett starred in our tenth grade's spring production of *Grease*. It was hilarious because he lacks the swagger of any proper Danny Zuko. He's a great actor, but he can't sing to save his life. But I'm not groaning because it was embarrassing—the play was the night our friendship ended.

"Chuck wasn't in the play," he points out.

I glare at him. "Excuse me. I helped with the costumes."

"Only because you got turned down to play the role of Sandy." Beckett is so smug, and his gray eyes gleam with mischief. He's missed ragging on me.

I mouth *Fuck you* and shove down another spring roll. I'd be lying if I said I hadn't missed this, but that play is my sorest of spots.

97

"What're you up to these days?" Mrs. Porter asks, oblivious to our silent exchange.

"Other than school? I work at my dad's bowling alley on weekends."

"Oh right!" She studies my face, and I swear I catch the flash of a memory surfacing. "How's your dad? And your aunt?"

"They're good," I say, but I question whether or not this is the truth. Nervously, I double down on my lie and add, "Super good."

"Where's your mom?" Willa asks. "Did she leave like our dad?"

The table falls silent.

Beside me, Beckett stills. "You know what, Willa? Let's feed Lester now. I'm sure Chuck—"

I cut him off. "It's fine." But it's not. This question always hurts, no matter how many times I've answered it. "My mom passed away when I was young."

"What happened?"

"Willa, that's not polite dinner conversation." Turning to me with a worried expression, Mrs. Porter says, "I'm so sorry, Chuck."

Even though it happened fourteen years ago, and I've lived longer without her than I ever did with her, it's one of those wounds that refuses to heal.

Dad told me the truth about how my mom died during the winter break of sophomore year. Something he'd kept from me for almost thirteen years. He even omitted her cause of death in the obituary. No one likes hearing those stories. Except, they do. They thrive off them, knowing they're not that pathetic. To them, suicide is for the weak. How fucked up is *that*?

My eyes are wet, my breath hitching in my chest. I push away from the table. "Excuse me, uh, where's the bathroom?"

"Down the hall," Mrs. Porter says, eyes crinkled in motherly concern, which only makes me feel worse. "Are you feeling all right, honey?"

Beckett pops up. "Let me show you." He follows me, stopping in front of a closed door. "Hey, you okay?" He reaches for my arm.

And just like that, I'm back on a stranger's driveway, Beckett running after me and asking me *Are you okay?* "No, because I need to pee and you're blocking the door."

"Chuck," he whispers. "I'm sorry."

"Why?" It's hard keeping my voice level, and it grows louder, shaky. "Why are you sorry? Why do you still care?"

Beckett can't look me in the eye and steps aside, his hands clenched into fists at his sides. "I never—" He breaks off. "I'm trying to make up for the last year, okay?"

"Well, don't! I didn't ask for this!"

He tosses his hands up in the air. "What is wrong with you?"

The bathroom door is unblocked, and I push past him, shutting myself inside without answering.

Because excellent question. What the hell is wrong with me?

I perch on the edge of the tub, tears blurring my vision,

and I'm afraid to blink. To let them fall. Because I am not crying in Beckett Porter's bathroom. That'd be pathetic. Except that's exactly what I'm doing.

I slump forward and exhale a haggard, wet breath.

The emotion is overwhelming, the push of pain starting at my heart and spreading through my limbs. Tearing at my chest. This is why I was hesitant about teaming up with Beckett. We have too much history—he hurts me, so I hurt him right back. I already lost my best friend once, and I don't want to relive that pain.

The accidental heartbreak.

It was my idea to audition for *Grease*. After a rough winter, scraping through my first depressive episode—not to mention dealing with the truth that my mom died by suicide—I jumped at the opportunity for some fun. Spring was happening, more daylight, my depression was ebbing away. But I had an ulterior motive: my unrequited and secret crush on Beckett.

The previous August, Beckett's parents had invited me on their end-of-summer trip to the Santa Cruz Boardwalk, and my dad let me go with them. On the last day, Beckett and I split a funnel cake on the beach, and when I got powdered sugar on my nose, he leaned in and brushed it off with his thumb.

Sitting there, with our faces so close I could smell the sunscreen on his cheeks, I realized how badly I wanted him to kiss me.

But he never did.

So, *Grease*. I had this whole vision in my head—with

the two of us cast as the leads, we would kiss. And maybe, just maybe, if we kissed, he'd realize he liked me, too. But I didn't even get a supporting role, and Beckett landed the role of Danny.

Opposite him was Heidi Schilling. Blond with an amazing voice—a real-life Sandy. While I worked on costumes, Beckett ran lines and blocked scenes with Heidi. After rehearsals, though, he would peel away from the crowd and we'd hang out at Bigmouth's together, eating French fries and making new music playlists, proving he was still *mine*.

Since we swing danced every weekend at Golden Gate Park, I helped him practice his moves for the dance numbers. After the production of *Grease*, Heidi's parents held a wrap party with the cast and crew at their house, where Beckett promised to dance with me before the night was over. I was used to dancing among strangers at the park and wasn't eager to make a fool out of myself in front of my classmates, but I agreed.

My dad dropped us off, but we got separated. After failing at small talk with Heidi's parents, I searched for Beckett in the strange house. I was on the bottom floor when I peeked into the den, finding him along with most of the play's cast. Perched on the arm of the couch, with Heidi Schilling leaning up against him, Beckett was saying, "My friend's mom was bipolar, and she killed herself."

I swear, hearing those words was like someone *electrocuted* me. For a moment I went still. Everything—my blood, my heart, my brain. Then, as I thawed back to life, my fingers slipping around the unopened can of 7 Up in my hand, tears filled my eyes. I told Beckett that in confidence. *I trusted him.* And now he was throwing that away, why—to get close to some girl? To impress her in some twisted way? Or was this just casual gossip to him? That wasn't the Beckett I knew, but the Beck I knew wouldn't say those things either. I just couldn't make sense of the scene before me.

"Really? Whose mom?" Heidi pressed her Rydell High–sweatered boobs closer against Beckett's arm.

Before answering, Beckett glanced around the den. The second he spotted me, he pushed Heidi away and stumbled to his feet.

"Chuck—" he started saying, but I didn't want to hear it.

"Stop," I said, my voice quaking, my wobbly-kneed steps drawing me into the center of the room. He tried saying my name again, but I shook my head. "Just stop talking!"

Everyone stared, and four kids had their phones out. Probably eager to document our fight. The carpet swam, and my throat tightened until my eyesight turned blotchy. But all my words were caught in my throat, and I didn't know what to say.

Heidi's gaze darted between us. "O-oh," she drawled, mouth forming an O. "Holy shit, it's *Chuck's* mom, isn't it?"

There was no use denying it. I was one of the few kids with a dead mom, and Beckett and I were best friends. Easy enough to put two and two together. But I wasn't as concerned with Heidi, because my best friend had just broken my heart.

"What the fuck, Beck?" I demanded, bringing my fore-arm up to brush away my tears, but they'd already smeared my mascara. A line of watery black inked my skin.

"Wait. It's not what you think."

"God, I should've never trusted you," I said, my voice breaking. Vaguely conscious of our audience, I tried to play it off a disbelieving laugh. "You're an asshole. No, you're *worse* than an asshole. You're a shitty best friend."

Everything was hot and shivery, as if I were naked, like my bones were on the outside. A few kids tittered with uncomfortable laughter, and I wanted to scream.

One of the cast members muttered, "I wonder if she's as psycho as her mom."

There was no thinking, just action, as I hurled the soda can in Beckett's general direction, turned on my heel, and ran.

Beckett followed me through the house and out onto the driveway, calling after me. When he finally caught up, he grabbed my arm. "Chuck, stop it. You're acting crazy."

"Nice word choice." I wrenched out of his grasp like his touch was serrated. "I expect that from them"—I ges-tured toward the house—"but never from you."

"Shit, that's not what I meant!" He pulled at his curls, mussing them from their gelled pompadour. "It was an accident—" he was saying, but I couldn't listen to his excuses.

"An accident?" I interrupted. "Did you or did you not just tell Heidi fucking Schilling about my mom?"

"Technically," he began, holding out his palms, "yes,

but she was throwing around the word 'bipolar' like it was a bad thing, and I wanted her to realize it's not an adjective—"

I crossed my arms and hugged myself. "I don't care. My mom? Everything that happened? That's *not* your story to tell, Beck! I just—I *trusted* you."

"Chuck, c'mon," he said, reaching for me, his fingers grasping air.

I closed the gap between us and pushed him in the chest. Hard. "Stay away from me."

Beckett stumbled, his hands falling limp to his sides, his lips parted like he wanted to say more. His eyes were wet and soft, and he squeezed them shut. But before he could open them, I took off down the street. I didn't want to be there when he opened his eyes again.

And I wasn't. I ran ten blocks down the Divisadero, until my heart nearly gave out, and sank to the ground outside a closed coffee shop. Eventually, when I stopped sobbing, I called my dad. When he picked me up, concerned and confused, all I said was that I wasn't friends with Beckett anymore.

Until Thursday, that was the last conversation I'd had with Beckett Porter.

All this happened soon after I found out how my mom had died. Dad never told me the truth about Mom. I'm not sure if he was ashamed, or trying to protect me, but the truth eventually came out. After I slipped into my first depressive episode and didn't get out of bed for two weeks, he explained that she'd died by suicide—not a car accident. The next week, they shuttled me downtown, where my new therapist, Sarah, told me bipolar disorder is commonly seen in families. They don't know why, but it might be genetic, and Sarah said to keep an eye on me since I'd experienced a depressive episode.

Beckett knew, more than *anyone*, how much finding out about my mom changed things for me. How insecure I was—and still am—about my mental health. Never once did he question me when I asked to be called Chuck instead of Caroline. He was my best friend. He knew every little secret, and he was never supposed to tell.

Except Beckett told everyone. And it changed everything.

To make matters worse, the rumor mill did a number on our fight. A dozen different versions of that night existed. I slapped Beckett. I screamed myself hoarse. I broke one of Heidi Schilling's parents' favorite vases. Most people shied away, but a few made fun of me until the end of sophomore year. This asshole from my English class, Donnie Mathers, called me a *crazy bitch*, and I cried every morning in the shower for a month.

People were already used to dismissing me, because the only friend I'd ever needed was Beckett. But I lost him, too.

After wiping the snot from my nose with some toilet paper, I wash my hands. Splash lukewarm water on my face. It drips down my cheeks, pools in the curve of my lips, and trails down my neck. I challenge my reflection, the colorless girl.

You are not your mother's child.

When I'm positive the tears have dried up, I unlock the bathroom. The door across the hall hangs open, Beckett and Willa inside. Willa's bedroom from the looks of it. Tiny, with a twin bed in one corner, a closet showcasing a spill of clothing, and a chest underneath the window with a large terrarium on it. The box of mice sits on a desk on the far wall. Beckett catches my eye, and his expression is closed-off. For once, he's upset.

I used to think Beckett Porter was unflappable, but I might've discovered the one thing that pisses him off: me.

Eight

I'M A NERVOUS ball of tangled energy as we head to our first hustle. I flip through songs on my phone, disgusted by the sweaty smears my fingers leave on the screen. Beckett's been quiet since we left his house. Even though I have no desire to talk about tonight, his silence is unnerving. I can't tell if he's upset with me or annoyed or *what*. My imagination runs wild with the possibilities.

When we exit into Oakland off the freeway, Beckett clears his throat. "Hey, about what happened at the house," he starts, glancing at his GPS.

I groan and press my fingertips to my temples. "It's fine. Can we not talk about it? I don't want your apologies." I'm embarrassed. For all the walls I put up, it's way too easy to knock me down. But if Beckett wants to apologize, great. I just want to forget what happened outside the bathroom and get this night over with.

He turns on his blinker as we idle on Broadway. "I was going to ask if you're sure you wanna do this. Tonight might not be the best night to try out hustling if you're upset."

"I'm not upset," I say quickly. Too quickly, because I'm defensive as hell. "I'm fine, Beckett." Fan-fucking-tastic.

"And what makes you think I was apologizing? There's something seriously wrong with you."

"Yeah, well, there must be if I'm hanging out with you again."

The light's green and we turn onto Twenty-Seventh Street. He just sighs and drags his fingers through his curls. His wounded expression gives me way too much satisfaction.

Once Beckett gets over himself, we park and hash out our plan. Brisk and businesslike, we each do our best to check our emotions. We're experimenting with the techniques we went over last night. The biggest one is seeing how much the other players underestimate me as a girl, and a drunk girl at that.

I flip open the mirror in the car and use my thumb to smear my eyeliner, muss my hair. Then I tuck my hair into a wig cap and adjust the light-colored locks around my face. The curls hang past my shoulders, the side bang stiff against my forehead.

My mom was gorgeous and had these strawberry-blond curls you could never replicate, but she loved wigs. Wearing them. Dressing up. Pretending to be someone she wasn't. *Losing herself*, as Aunt Fee explained once.

"Whoa," he says with raised brows, taking me in. "You look weird as a blonde."

"Thanks." I bite back the sarcasm and adjust an errant curl. "But does it look natural? Or at least convincing?"

Beckett shuffles through his bowling bag, head bent and face obscured. "Yeah, definitely."

The only part of the plan I'm steadfastly against is Beckett's proposed cover story. He wants us to go in there as boyfriend and girlfriend.

"Trust me," he says for the third time as he recounts our buy-in money. "You'll seem less suspicious if you're my girlfriend. No one will question it."

"Trust me, it's not happening. Can't people platonically bowl together?" The malice in my eyes must scare Beckett, because he surrenders.

The Road is more dive bar than bowling alley. Even though we're on the outskirts of the nicer Lake Merritt neighborhood, it takes only a block or two for Oakland to go from beautiful to sketchy. The Road muddles somewhere in between.

The roof's flat and low, and the small parking lot is full of rusty cars and gleaming motorcycles. As we get out of the Accord, the wind nips, and there's an external buzz to the air. That or my nerves have officially seeped out of my skin and mixed with the elements.

When we reach the green-slated door blending in with the bland windowless building, Beckett pauses.

"You ready?" he asks.

My stomach pitches, growls. My heart beats so fiercely, the edges of my vision pulse. What happens if we lose? Or if we get caught? I wipe my palms on my thighs. "Yup. Let's do this."

Is my complete lack of confidence showing? I hope not, because Beckett opens the door.

The scent hits me first—sticky and nutty, beer and peanuts—and the worn carpet is ragged from decades of wear. Cigarette smoke clings to the wood paneling, and the felt on the billiard tables is ripped. A bar runs along an entire wall, and in the corner closest to us is a claw machine filled with—yeah, that's porn. A claw machine filled with porn DVDs.

It's easy to act intimidated or out of place, because I am all of those things, tenfold. I'm a seventeen-year-old girl in a seedy dive bar. It'll never be a struggle to look the part. I *am* the part.

Beckett presses his palm into the small of my back, a sensation that kick-starts me into consciousness.

"IDs?" the barkeeper demands.

Beckett smiles congenially. "We're here to bowl."

The barkeeper eyes us, mouth twisted in disbelief. Like anyone, let alone two teens, would come to this dump just to bowl. He walks over, brandishing a thick Sharpie, and slashes an X across Beckett's hand, then mine. "Uh-huh. Talk to Marky." With the pen, he points to a separate counter at the far end.

We thank him, walking past the barstools of inebriated patrons who are loud and choleric, or fast asleep on their stools. By the look of it, these people have been here since morning.

The alley itself has thirty lanes, but fewer than half are occupied. Everything's grimy as hell and has seen better days. Small groups of bowlers dot the lanes. A few nurse beer bottles while others focus on their game. We pay Marky, the cashier, for two games plus shoes.

Between us, we have around five hundred dollars. Not minus the twenty-five to play. If all goes as planned, we'll earn that back. Tonight, the betting is minor. Beckett told me you never play against the best, because if you beat them, you're done. No one else will play you. Between now and next Sunday, we're starting small and working our way up the ranks.

We settle at our lane, where I play my best fake drunk. Hard when I've never been drunk, but I've watched enough trashy reality television to put on a show. The mussed hair and makeup help. My nerves make me clumsy too.

The guys on the lanes to either side of us watch, so I flash the group of younger guys a smile, leaning forward to pull off my flats. I don't dare set my bare feet on the ground, though—the floor is damp, multicolored, and makes me want to vomit.

Which, hey, would do wonders for the drunk-girl act, wouldn't it?

"How're you doing?" Beckett asks, the drone of the local classic rock station pounding out of the mounted wall speakers.

"Nervous. Do I seem drunk?"

"Passable." He swaps his loafers for bowling shoes.

Beckett nods toward the lanes. "Okay, game time. You know what to do?"

I push away from the seats and wander over to inspect the ball rack. He programs the console as I pick out my ball from the rack of options. I test out the weight and shift my body; the ball's balanced in my grip. Bonus points for being bubblegum pink with glitter.

Beckett bowls, and it's comforting how truly horrible he is.

The setup is easy. After Beckett's second throw, I bowl sloppily. The pink ball hits a few pins. As we trade turns, I keep my play consistent with loose, random shots, but my ball spends quality time in the gutter. Beckett doesn't have to struggle to suck, but it's painful to throw bad shots; I'm glad we practiced choreographing.

The entire game, I'm loud and drunk and the absolute worst.

Toward the end of the game, I bowl a split. Then I convert it into a spare and clear the frame. It's no strike, but I act like I won the goddamn lottery. I may not have been a good enough actress to play Sandy in sophomore year, but I put on a convincing show tonight.

"Oh my God, did you see that? That's a strike, right?" I ask Beckett, who watches with thinly veiled amusement. I replay what he told me last night: *What's really going to push you ahead is downplaying your skills. Showing an ineptitude for the game.*

"A strike is when you knock down all ten at once. Real close, though," he says.

I stumble off the platform and lean against the plastic seats. "Nope, that was good. I'm *good*. You guys saw that, didn't you?" I ask, turning to the four men next to us.

The tallest man, with white-blond hair, cocks his head. "I saw it," he says.

"I can take anybody in this joint." The guy laughs, and I cut him off. "No, I'm dead serious. Anybody. I've got money! You're playing for money, right?"

His attention flickers between Beckett and me. "Yeah. I can show you some action."

Beckett's cue. "Caroline, I'm not so sure about that. These guys are serious players."

I try to not cringe at my full name. We figured it would fly better here.

"And I'm not?" I reply, turning fast and pretending to lose my balance; Beckett grabs my arm to steady me. Feigning drunken embarrassment, I reach for my purse and the money clip.

I peel off three twenties. "Sixty dollars," I say, shoving the cash at the guy.

"You're really not going to listen to me, huh?" Beckett mutters with a sigh, reaching for his own wallet. "Here, I'm in. Don't want her playing alone."

The guy squints in assessment. "Yeah, sure," he says, taking our money. "I'm Count."

I make a face at the grimy floor. Count? As in numbers, or does he moonlight as Dracula?

"Doubles then?" Count asks. "Me and Phil, against you and your girl?"

"I am *not* his girl," I point out, which garners laughter.

After that the men barely acknowledge me. Actually, that's a lie. One of the players' friends stares at my non-existent cleavage. Between my boldly patterned dress and honey-blond wig, I look like I tripped out of a seventies film.

The cash is tossed in plain sight, on the table we share between our coupled seats. As Beckett predicted, the owners of the Road don't show any concern for betting or illegal activities.

Beckett's first. He ties his hair back at the base of his neck, drying his hands over the blower, before approaching the foul line. He throws a creeper, a slow ball that takes a lifetime to reach the pocket. It knocks into the headpin and three pins clatter. His second shot is even worse.

Count bowls next and clears the frame with a strike that sends pins spinning.

My turn.

Beckett leans close and his hand lingers on my hip. "Knock over a max of three pins. Good luck."

"Will do." As I turn, his hand slides from my hip, sending confusing shivers down my spine.

On the platform, I gingerly slide my fingers into the ball's holes, my shellacked nails flashing. I tweak my left hook to sweep and fell three pins—the headpin, the third, and the sixth. A few others wobble, but my ball shoots into the gutter and the pinsetter resets my lane.

For my next shot, it's hard not to earn myself a spare and knock down the rest of the remaining pins. I receive four more points, leaving an open frame, which is decent enough. I can't let my score fall too low—or inch too high—in the beginning.

The night goes on like this. The men are drinking, getting sloppier and sloppier as each frame passes. Still feeling awkward from what happened at dinner, Beckett and I don't even bother with small talk. Preferable because being around him is stirring up feelings I'd rather bury.

When we've each bowled five frames, I pick my game up, imperceptibly. I upgrade my shots to include splits I convert into spares. Beckett tries hard, but he sucks. Admittedly, he puts on a good show.

My score has crept close to Phil's, but I'm behind Count. Only our joint score will matter. Beckett can bowl his sucky frames if I bag two strikes in the final frame. The friends are making side bets on who'll have the highest score between Count and Phil. They're not concerned about their friends losing to us.

Emboldened, I lean over the set of seats. "I'll bet you another forty dollars I can bowl a strike in the last frame."

"Caroline," Beckett says, jaw sharp.

Count overhears and lifts a pale eyebrow. "No offense, but you haven't bowled one all night."

I roll my eyes and grab my money. "This is for fun, right?" I slip out two twenties and dangle them above the pile of winnings. "You in?"

Count looks to Phil, who agrees. They each toss down two twenty-dollar bills. "Why the hell not?" To Beckett he adds, "I hope that's *her* money she's throwing away."

Annoyed by his sexist comment, I return to my lane and prepare for the final frame.

Beckett nods me over, his expression grim. "What're you doing? We aren't supposed to bet more."

"We're going to win." I eye the scoreboard with confidence. "They don't think I'm a threat. This is working." My giddiness would embarrass me if we weren't about to cash in.

Beckett's pissed. "We had a plan. In the future, *you do not deviate from the plan*, okay? It could get us into trouble."

"It's an extra forty dollars," I insist. "Besides, who made you boss?"

Beckett gives an annoyed shake of his head and shoots his last frame. He gets lucky, the first shot setting up an easy split, which he almost converts into a spare, but a single pin is left standing. He slumps into his seat and pulls the tie from his curls.

Count shoots his final frame, but at this point he's tipsy, and he doesn't bowl a second. Their lead has dwindled, but my palms still sweat as I do the mental math. I need to punch out to win. No room for error.

I approach the lane and grab my ball. Drop the charade. I draw my arm back, swinging it forward and releasing the ball. My follow-through isn't great, but I shoot a strike.

"Hell yeah!" Jumping in the air, I clap my hands together.

"Fuck," one friend says with a disbelieving laugh.

Count narrows his eyes. "Guess you got lucky."

I hold my fingers out over the blower to slick the sweat away. "Guess so."

Beckett leans forward in his seat, hands clasped tight.

My unease is a twisted and thorny knot in my chest as I set up my shot and take a second to settle my thoughts. Sure, being lucky is better than being good, but being both is *great*. I shoot another strike and ten more pins fall, electricity charging within me. Behind, swearing erupts, and after a beat I turn around.

I smile—easy when my insides are beaming—and run over to Beckett, who's no longer pissed. No, his face is stretched wide with a smile. And I can barely remember why I was so mad at him earlier tonight. In the high of the win, I don't push him away as he lifts me off my feet and spins me.

My heart palpitates when he whispers, "You did it, Chuck." His lips accidentally graze my jaw before he sets me down, and I'm flushed and tingly.

What is he doing?

What am *I* doing?

Why do I feel this way?

"What was that?" I ask, trying to keep my tone neutral while my head rings with alarm bells. The way his arms felt around my waist, the warmth of his lips on my jaw—it all felt *good*. And I'm freaking out.

"Um." Beckett shifts away from me and studies the sticky floor, his curls curtaining against his cheeks. "I'm just excited. That you won," he says, lifting his chin to meet my gaze.

My face is hot, and I wipe my sweaty palms off on my dress. "It's whatever. Just, uh, don't do it again."

"Two strikes, huh?" Count says loudly, his eyes darting suspiciously.

"Beginner's luck. The actual worst, am I right?" Beckett replies.

Innocent. Stay innocent. I pick up the glorious hunk of money off the table. The original two-hundred-and-forty pot, plus the eighty dollars in the side bet, totaling three hundred and twenty dollars. Minus what we bet and paid to play, that's a pure net profit of one hundred and seventy-five dollars.

This is a start. The start of guaranteeing my future in San Francisco.

Count's pale face spots with pinpricks of red. "If I find out you hustled us?"

"Hustle?" I repeat, as if the word is foreign, and tuck the winnings into my bra. "What's he talking about?"

Beckett places a hand on my shoulder. "Don't worry about it." To Count he adds, "You had us until the last frame."

"Fuck," Count swears again, and fists his hands. Phil chugs his beer. The nameless friends are amused more than anything else, exchanging money from separate side bets.

The money in my bra has a palpable weight. Money I won *illegally*.

"Maybe we'll see you guys around," Beckett tells Count.

"Nice to meet you," I add, and the guy who's been checking me out stops us. More specifically, he stops me. He's not bad-looking, but too old, college-age.

"Hey, I'm Matt," he says, and grins. "Have you ever been on a motorcycle?"

Is he trying to *flirt* with me? That's got to be the worst pickup line.

Beckett grunts, a noise somewhere between a laugh and disbelief. "Sorry, Matt, but—"

"Why don't you let Caroline answer for herself?" Matt hulks over Beckett, who's tall, but this guy is bigger. Wider, like he plays football or something.

Hearing my full name—my mother's name—is the verbal equivalent of having a bucket of ice water dumped on my head. "No," I say loudly. "Uh, no thank you." I grab Beckett's hand and drag him toward the door.

"This is why we should have a boyfriend-girlfriend act," he mutters. "Do you want to deal with creeps all week?"

My heart twists. A year ago, being Beckett's girlfriend was everything I wanted. I hate that it still hurts hearing those words thrown around casually. It's true that I don't want more run-ins with guys like Matt, but I can also tell it'll make Beckett happy. "Yeah, okay."

We're outside, and I focus on my adrenaline. It fills me like a shaken can of soda. Together we cross the parking lot, and Beckett tosses the bowling bag into the trunk.

I hop into the front seat of the Accord.

"Really? Fine?" he asks from the driver's seat.

I have no desire to dwell on rules or acts or anything other than the winnings I extract from my bra. "Yes, *fine*. Now, are you going to congratulate me or what?"

"You were damn impressive, Wilson." He holds up his hand for a high five and I slap his palm. It's safe to say that after tonight, our no-touching rule has officially been lifted.

As we leave the Road's parking lot, I release a bottled-up sigh. "Holy shit."

"I knew you could do it." He smacks the steering wheel. "I knew it."

"About the side bet—"

Beckett shakes his head. "Let's try sticking to the plan, okay? We're a team, and we need to be on the same page every second."

I nod and slip the curly blond wig off, securing it on the mannequin head. "Noted."

"I'm too wired to go home," Beckett says as he steers the car toward Lake Merritt. "Wanna check out the lake?"

"Uh." My body is buzzy and energetic, and oddly, I don't want to go home just yet. Spending *more* time with Beckett probably isn't advisable. And yet I find myself saying, "Sure. I'm already breaking curfew. Guess another hour can't hurt."

Something is shifting between us. What, I'm not quite sure. But despite what happened at his house earlier tonight, it's like we're on solid ground for the first time in a year. And I'd be lying if I said I wasn't the least bit curious to find out what this shift means.

At a red light, Beckett turns, wearing this beaming grin. "Great job tonight."

"Thanks." I can't contain my smile, and it's hard to stay mad at Beckett right now. He helped me win and get one step closer to saving Bigmouth's.

The happiness stretches my face, and my cheeks ache.

Nine

WHEN PEOPLE THINK of Oakland, they might imagine the violence of Fruitvale or the sporty coliseum, but certain areas are magnificent. Lake Merritt is a hidden gem of the East Bay, a tidal lagoon that was the first wildlife refuge in the United States.

Beckett parks on a side street near the water, and I grab my coat from the back seat.

The clock has officially ticked over into midnight, my curfew on weekends and holiday breaks, but the streets mill with people heading to and from bars, others leaving the many concert venues within walking distance. The fog hardly touches us here in the East Bay. The buildings are lower, more spread out, and as we near the lake, the sky is wide and cracked open, a constellation globe.

Moonlight reflects algae and trash on the shore, and my nostrils fill with a swampy smell. But brilliant little lights hang in the trees circling the water, and music pours from a house on the hill. A few people drunkenly walk about, but it's quieter than I'd expected.

"You doin' okay?" Beckett asks, tilting his chin as we cross the sidewalk and grass cushions our steps.

I grin and push my hair back. "Yeah, I am."

"You did awesome. The look on their faces?" He laughs, wildly and loudly. "Fucking priceless. We should've been doing this a long time ago," he says, and plunks down on a damp plot near the shore.

The slick strands of grass poke through my dress and tickle my ankles as I sit beside him.

"Impossible considering we stopped being friends until recently." I chew the inside of my cheek. Did I really tell him we're friends again? Then again, we kind of are. The realization isn't unwelcome, but scary. Friend territory is dangerous. The proverbial gateway drug of relationships.

Beckett looks at me sideways, hurt etching his features. "I've apologized, but you've never . . ."

"Never what?"

"Apologized for how *you* treated *me*," he says, dead serious. "I didn't mean to—"

"I know it was an accident," I say, cutting him off. "But I was still processing, so imagine how awful it was for me to hear you talking about it like it was no big deal."

Since I'd only recently found out the truth about my mom before our fight, I wasn't ready to share that information with strangers. My dad had avoided the truth for so long—dodging questions, letting me believe Mom died in a car accident—that when it all came spilling out, I didn't know how to cope.

Dad lies when he's trying to protect me. He lied then, and he's lying now. Shielding me from the reality that our family business is failing and we'll probably be leaving San Francisco in a few months. I hate being lied to. Like I'm not strong enough for the truth.

Beckett drops his chin to his chest. "I realize that now, and you know I'm sorry. I was *trying* to do a good thing. Heidi Schilling was calling one of our teachers bipolar because she was mean, like a negative adjective—and I just wanted her to *understand*."

I've wondered about his motivations and, once I'd calmed down, came to a similar conclusion. But hearing his side of the events clears up any lingering questions. A year ago I couldn't even say the word "bipolar" without panicking and my eyes misting. I wasn't ever ashamed . . . just afraid. I didn't want to look this thing—this big, scary thing—in the face. Not even with Beckett.

"Thank you," I say, embarrassed by my hoarse voice. "Last year it was all too new, too upsetting. I couldn't deal with—"

"Hey." Beckett nudges my foot with his. "You don't need to explain. I can't claim to understand what you were going through, but I know how much you were hurting. Honestly, I shouldn't have said anything, but I wanted Heidi to understand how powerful words are. You taught me that."

At this, the last bit of my animosity falls away. I wasn't

123

ready before, but maybe I am now. I can try forgiving.

"I'm sorry," I confess, the words foreign on my tongue. But they feel good, freeing. Like I'm leaving something heavy behind. "For not hearing you out. For ignoring you. For throwing a can of soda at you."

"Apology accepted," he says, that small smile lifting at the corners. A crack of laughter explodes from the house behind us, and he adds, "I have a scar. That was one heavy 7 Up." He ducks his head and pulls his curls aside. A tiny silver half-moon mars his temple.

Did I seriously hit him in the head? Yikes. I didn't think my aim was that good. "Shit. Sorry."

"Oh, it's fine. I've heard ladies dig scars," he jokes, and I roll my eyes.

Silence falls again, and while I feel better, forgiveness isn't a concept I'm familiar with. Being face-to-face with Beckett forces me to realize I might've made a mistake shutting him out the past year. I'm justified in my hurt, but I think I hurt Beckett more than I realized when I cut him out of my life.

Thankfully, the urge to cry has passed, but I blink several times just to make sure. "I wish you'd found a way to tell me sooner. That I would have *let* you tell me sooner."

He toys with the elastic on his wrist. Snaps it against his skin. "Sounds like we're both wishing for the same thing. Maybe instead of regretting the past, we should try to do better by each other in the future?"

"I'd . . . like that." I push my bangs from my eyes, the strands heavy with sweat from being trapped beneath the wig. The admission leaves my heart hammering, my stomach queasy. "So, how've you been the past year?" I ask jokingly. Instantly, I regret following up his kind and emotionally bare moment with some flimsy attempt at humor.

To my relief, Beckett laughs. "Other than my dad leaving and my mom losing her job, I guess I'm good?" His gaze follows the nervous fretting of my hands messing with my bangs before settling on my face. "I don't know. I've missed you."

My stomach warms, but I say, "Oh? Whenever I saw you at school, which was rare, it didn't seem like you missed me." I press him to really tell me the truth. Tell me what's happened in the past year—especially with school. Because suddenly, I want to know. Badly.

"Trust me, I missed you. And as for my less-than-stellar attendance record, that wasn't about you," Beckett explains, but adds lightly, "School and me don't get along."

"I've noticed. Are you really not doing the whole college thing?"

"C'mon, I'm not winning any attendance awards."

"I'll take that as a no. Why not?"

Beckett shrugs lopsidedly and twines his fingers through the grass, ripping blades free. "I don't have the money to pay for school or the grades for a scholarship. And being a truant doesn't sway in your favor."

"What's up with that? The truancy? The fighting? You're smarter than that." The more we talk, the calmer I become. The threat of tears fades completely, which is a damn relief because I've already cried once today. I can't cry again in front of Beckett. Even if we're opening up, crying feels like a weakness. And I'd really like Beckett to see me as strong.

His lips quirk in amusement. "Gee, thanks. But I blew it by sophomore year. Once your grades are *that* bad, there's no digging yourself out of an academic black hole. As for the fighting . . ."

"You're the most stoic person I know." I tuck my knees into my chest. "Someone must've seriously pissed you off if you threw a punch."

"Yeah." He focuses intently on ripping free strands of grass.

"Because of your dad leaving?"

Beckett takes a hitching breath. "Donnie Mathers was talking shit. About you. About that night."

"*Oh*," I say because words have officially failed me, and goose bumps flush over my skin.

Beckett stood up for me. Not only once, but twice—that I know of. He was suspended for that fight in May or June. So close to the end of the school year he didn't return until the start of this year. This was after he came to Bigmouth's and apologized to my dad while I locked myself in the bathroom, refusing to talk to him. After I ignored his calls and texts, his notes slipped into my backpack.

Wiping his hands off on his jeans, he glances at me. "I shouldn't have hit him, but he deserved it."

"Why?" I ask softly. "I was pretty awful to you." I was reactive; I pushed him away, hurt him because he hurt me. And my hurt defined so much of the past year. How I treated Beckett. How I viewed myself.

"You might've been done being my best friend," Beckett says, eyes meeting mine, "but I wasn't done being yours."

The tears prick at my eyes again, and we both fall silent. I tilt my head back. Stare at the cracked-open sky as his words press me into the earth. Unsure of how to respond to this comment, I say, "I don't know what I'll do if I have to leave here. Move to Arizona."

Beckett shifts, and the cadence of his breathing slows. "You'd be okay, you know. It'd suck and I'd personally hate it, but you'd be okay."

A smile tugs at the corners of my mouth. "Yeah? How come you sound so certain? I think I might combust the second I step foot outside of California."

"I know you pretty well. You're . . . tough. Even with a year missing in my encyclopedic knowledge of Chuck Wilson, I'm kind of an expert."

My smile grows. "You don't know everything about me."

Beckett cocks his head. "Oh really?" he says skeptically. "Tell me something I don't know."

I shift in the grass, contemplating my options. It'd be nice having Beckett understand why I was so emotional the night of the party, that I felt *romantically* betrayed, which is ridiculous because he was never mine. At least, not in that way. "I liked you. Last year."

No response.

Nervously, I glance at him. Maybe I shouldn't have said anything. He stares straight ahead, eyebrows knitted. "Beckett?"

Ladies and gentlemen, I've done it. I've stunned Beckett Porter into silence.

Beckett drags his hand across his mouth. "Wow. That's—"

Panic tightens my chest, and before he can tell me how unrealistic my crush was, I say it for him. "Ridiculous, huh? I wanted to clear the air, you know, get it all out there. Obviously, all those feelings are long dead." I press my eyes shut, cursing myself. Yes, clearing the air is a good way to start off a rekindled friendship, but maybe some secrets aren't worth sharing.

"Are you sure?" he asks, glancing sideways at me. "That they're dead? Because people are always saying not to mix business with pleasure." His tone is light, but it doesn't match the unreadable look in his eyes.

Swallowing down the small amount of pain that accompanies unreciprocated feelings—even dead ones—I say, "One hundred percent."

"One hundred percent," he repeats. "That's pretty damn sure." He gives me this funny grin before retraining his attention on the lake, his forearms folded over his knees.

I study Beckett's profile. The mess of his curls. The aquiline arch on his nose. The way his lips are slightly parted. No longer smiling, but not frowning either. His utter lack of a reaction is confusing. If anything, I expected laughter or surprise. Instead, I get indifference.

I'm over him. So why am I disappointed?

The music from the house party shifts from techno-pop

to indie. Calming and melodic. The grass is gross and damp, but I lie on my back and pillow my arms behind my head. "See, you don't know everything about me," I say, pushing my confusing feelings aside.

"Nope, I did not. You've got me there." Beckett lies down beside me, both of us staring up at the sky.

After a moment I say, "Can I ask you something?"

"Shoot."

"What happened with your mom's job?"

"The hospital laid her off, and she hasn't been able to find another full-time nursing gig." Beckett rests his hands on his stomach, fingers tapping against his ribs. "She's struggled since my dad left, so that hasn't helped. She still works, but as a caretaker for an old woman in Alameda. Odd hours, crappy pay. That's why I help out."

"Damn, I'm sorry."

"Don't be. A lot has happened. But you, my partner in crime, don't need to worry about it. I've got everything under control at home." Beckett's trying to be flip, but it doesn't work. "Speaking of, I'm sorry about dinner. Willa doesn't have the best grasp of social norms."

"Must run in the family," I joke, and he laughs. "And it's fine. She didn't know."

Beckett rips more grass, shredding the leaves. "You wanna talk about it?"

"No. I mean, you of all people know what happened. What else is there to say?"

I knot my fingers into the grass, grounding myself, and dirt shoves beneath my nails. The funny thing is, there's

129

a lot to talk about. To unpack. I'm not sure Beckett's the person to have this conversation with.

And yet I find myself saying, "I'm still afraid."

Beckett stills. "Of what?"

"Turning out like her. The past year, my dad and my aunt have *watched* me. They're afraid I'll have the same problems. Those kinds of disorders, they can be familial. The fact I've already been depressed—*clinically* depressed—means something isn't right. In my brain. All I can think about is, what else might be wrong, you know?"

The silence is heavy, and I can't stop staring at the sky. The stars are endless pockets of hope.

He clears his throat. "I thought maybe now that some time has passed, you were feeling better? About her?"

"I'm . . . getting there. But I don't want to end up like her," I whisper.

The thought of worsening mental health scares me—that I'll experience the other side of the coin with mania—but it's more than that. It's the thought that one day, my depressive episodes will become so bad that I'll stop getting out of bed. For good. That even if I have a happy life and a family that loves me, it won't be enough.

"You're nothing like your mom—not from what little you've told me about her," he says, but the words pass right through me. "Your depression hasn't gotten worse, has it?"

"No," I reply quickly. "I'm not . . . No. And it's not just the depression."

"Then what is it?"

"Sometimes more severe symptoms can manifest in

your late teens and early twenties. When I cut off my hair last summer, I second-guessed myself. Was I cutting it because I wanted short hair, or because I was making impulsive decisions? Little things like that."

I'm surprised how good it feels to talk about these things with someone other than a therapist. I don't talk to my dad about this stuff. When I was really suffering with my depression, Dad made sure I went to therapy. Now he thinks I'm all better and rarely checks in with me as a human. For whatever reason, Beckett still cares. He's here for me, even though I gave him every reason not to be.

"I think it's smart to recognize what you might be up against. But don't let fear stop you from living." The back of Beckett's hand brushes against mine. A zap of electricity bursts between us, and my heart stills briefly in my chest. Like it stops for a moment to catch its breath.

"For what it's worth," he adds, voice low, "I like your short hair."

I turn my head until my cheek is flush with the grass and immediately wish I hadn't. Because Beckett does the same and our noses nearly touch. We're close enough I could count the long lashes curling away from his gray eyes. The rings of steel, the variations of silver, rimming his pupils.

I force my mind to stay on topic—actually, I'm frantic for a *different* topic. It's like trying to locate a signal in a storm of static. I break the connection and fold both hands on my stomach. "So, partners in crime, huh?"

"Has a nice ring to it, doesn't it?" Beckett scratches his ear, smile strained.

"Yeah," I say, "it definitely does."

I've never missed curfew in my entire life. But this spring break is one of many firsts, and by the time Beckett pulls up to the curb down the street from the yellow house, it's past one in the morning. Before I go, I collect my belongings, the back of my dress still damp from the grass near the lake.

"What should I do with the winnings?" I tap the money clip against my leg.

Beckett's hand twists on the wheel. "Keep it. You don't have a little sister with no sense of boundaries. When the week's over we'll split everything. Sound good?"

"Yeah. You'll text me when you find out more about the other games?"

He hides a yawn and says, "For sure. I'm still digging around with my old betting contacts." He snaps the elastic on his wrist.

"Awesome." I push open the passenger-side door. "See you tomorrow?"

Beckett's expression is relaxed and sleepy. Calm. "Without a doubt. You're working, right?"

"Yep."

"Think your dad will let you off for another day of historical research?"

"Perhaps."

"Cool, cool." Beckett fiddles with the radio. "I'll try

stopping by. Rest up tonight, okay? This week will be a hurricane."

"Those are ominous parting words."

"Good night, Chuck," he says with a laugh.

"Night." I wave and slam the door shut, walking toward the house with my arms wrapped around myself.

If I leave San Francisco, it will be hard enough. But if we repair our friendship, it'll be downright *brutal*. And if this works? If we stay? Can Beckett and I return to what we had, given the chance? Is that what I want?

"Penny for your thoughts?"

I yelp, clutching my chest. The air is skunky and pungent. *Fiona.* "What the hell?" Squinting, I peer around the side of the house. Aunt Fiona huddles in the gated-off alleyway, sitting on this little stone bench in our miniature cactus garden.

"So, you and Beckett." The joint's cherry glows as she inhales. Aunt Fee adored Beckett, and like my dad, she was Team Beckett all the way. "What's going on with you two? You finally friends again?"

"Hardly." Something shifted tonight, but I don't quite have a label for it yet.

Aunt Fiona doesn't press, just draws a drag off her joint. I'm struck with the urge to tell her everything. About the back rent and the eviction. About how we're trying to turn five hundred dollars into ten thousand in seven days.

The urge passes and I stay silent, hoarding my lies. If Aunt Fiona found out what Beckett and I were up to, she wouldn't let me out of her sight.

Aunt Fee takes another hit from her joint before dropping it into an ashtray shaped like an octopus. "Come on, let's get you inside."

My arm linked with Fee's, we sneak in through the kitchen side door. My bones and muscles ache, and I smell like beer and cigarettes from the Road. And something mustier and greener—wet grass from the lake.

MONDAY, APRIL 23

DAYS UNTIL BIGMOUTH'S EVICTION: 7

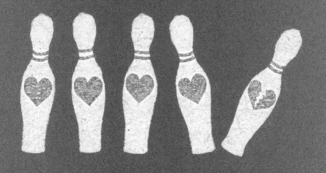

Ten

THE X ON my hand refuses to fade, despite my attempts at washing and scrubbing this morning. The skin's mottled pink, the inked lines a shade lighter than last night. It's a glaring distraction—and reminder—at work this morning.

On Mondays, a local bus of geriatrics makes the rounds, and Bigmouth's hosts several lanes of elderly bowlers. Today is no different. After I give the seniors their discounts, I watch them set up, curious why Beckett hasn't shown his annoying face yet.

An older customer pops two quarters into the jukebox and Bobby Darin wobbles to life through the ancient speakers. Bored, I lean my elbows on the counter, propping my chin up in my hand. I didn't bring any sewing, and my library book only has a chapter left. I assumed Beckett would be here to amuse me or get me out of work. I was wrong on both counts.

After last night I don't resent or hate him anymore. Actually, I've begun wondering if I ever really hated him in the first place. The end result is me sick with confusion and guilt. And beneath it all is the hope that we can be us again. The hope might be the scariest part.

Right before I break for lunch, my phone buzzes on the counter, inching across the surface with each vibration. At first I think it's Mila checking in, but Beckett's name appears.

BECKETT PORTER: When's your next break?

After a year of silence, it's still weird when his name graces the screen of my phone. Strange, but exciting.

ME: I'm due for my thirty. You around?

BECKETT PORTER: Awesome. Coffee's on me. Meet outside in five?

After checking on the geriatrics, I hurry down the hallway. I rap my knuckles on Dad's office door, and he calls, "Come in."

I ease the door open and lean inside. "Hey, Dad, can I take my thirty?"

Dad's reclining in his desk chair and pushes his glasses onto his balding head. When he smiles, his eyes crinkle. "Of course. Come give your old man a hug."

There are shadows beneath his eyes, and his fingers shake in that way, his tell of needing nicotine. Something about the narrow slope of his shoulders, the graying along his temples, sparks worry deep in my chest. Dad's fading before my eyes. A carbon copy of what he once was.

I wipe the sweat off my palms and cross the office.

When I hug Dad, I sneak a peek at whatever he's working on. The accounting books. An abundance of red, numerous negative signs, and next Monday's date—the day our lease ends—circled in ink on his calendar. Seven days. I wish I could tell him I'm trying to help. Trying to earn the money, because damn, he looks beaten. False hope is the worst thing in the world, and I keep it to myself. Besides, we've barely made any money yet.

"Have fun with Beckett?" Dad sets his glasses on the desk. He rubs his scalp, pulling at the rare strands of dark hair.

"Uh-huh."

"Caroline, I'm thrilled you're spending time with Beckett again," he says, "but Aunt Fiona said you were out late?"

I hesitate, but he doesn't call me out on missing curfew, so I guess Aunt Fee didn't completely rat on me. "We were just studying."

Dad nods slowly, relaxing in his chair. He folds his hands over the pooch of his stomach. "Right, but I've been thinking. If I move a few things around financially, we can find a way for you to return to therapy."

My eyebrows knit. Between my insistence that I was doing better—which was the truth—and the financial strain weekly therapy appointments put on Dad's bank account, I stopped sessions six months ago. Why now? What exactly is going on that we have money for therapy and not for Bigmouth's?

"Dad, it's not worth the money."

"That's not your decision to make," he says gruffly. "I've been meaning to bring this up for a while. You're going to be a senior next year, there are changes on the horizon, and I'd worry a hell of a lot less if I knew you had someone to talk to again."

Changes on the horizon? Does he mean Bigmouth's closing? *Arizona?*

"Fine." My stomach clenches; Dad's not asking, he's telling. But if I'm agreeing to this, I should at least benefit. "If I return to therapy, you'd be okay with me spending more time outside of the house and the bowling alley?"

"That's fair." Dad smiles. "You still have to make curfew, though."

"I'll e-mail the therapist," I promise. If weekly sessions mean more freedom while I work to save Bigmouth's, then I'm fine with it. But I'm still haunted by his comment about change—first on Thursday and now again today—and why he suddenly has money for my therapy. My gaze drops to the accounting books. "I was thinking, there's a lot of DIY improvements I can help you out with around here. Maybe during summer break?"

Dad slides some papers over the accounting books. "That's sweet, but I don't think it's necessary."

"Why not?" I challenge, all too aware I'm pushing, but I just want to see that he cares.

"Caroline—"

"*Dad,*" I cut him off. "I don't mind."

"We're not having this conversation," he says, and opens his laptop. Shutting me out. "Besides, business isn't great, and no amount of your DIY projects is going to change that."

I turn on my heel and storm out of the office. Dad calls after me, but I push forward. Hoping with enough distance, my anger might fade away. How is he okay with this? Why isn't he trying? Instead, he putters around in his stained clothes, mourning Bigmouth's before it's even dead.

I snatch my purse and jacket from the register and toss the service bell on the counter. In case anyone needs help, Dad will hear it from his office. Yeah, 80 percent of my job can be done by a small metal bell. How depressing.

Outside, I breathe in two lungfuls of clean, calming air. You'd never guess San Francisco is days away from May by the looks of the sky and the roiling, blustering wind. I tuck my jacket closer around my body. Dad might not want or accept my help, but he's getting it. I'm tougher than he is, and I'm not backing down. I'm going to earn the money for our back rent so Dad can keep Bigmouth's—and all the memories imprinted in its walls—and I can stay in San Francisco. End of story.

"Hey." Beckett jogs from the block where he parked. "You good to head out?"

"Yeah." I fall into step with him, and we cross the street. "Coffee?"

He tilts his chin toward Any Beans Necessary, the café I worked at last summer. "Are you okay? You look, um, angry?"

I loosen a sigh and give Beckett an abbreviated version of my talk with Dad. "It's just frustrating watching him roll over, you know?" I let him open the door, and the aroma of coffee is a slap in the face.

"Maybe he doesn't want to burden you," Beckett points out as we get in line.

As usual, Any Beans Necessary is packed to the gills. Spring break in San Francisco draws locals and tourists alike, and the line is one gigantic mass of people.

I cross my arms, unconvinced. "Maybe."

When it's my turn, I order a large coffee. Before I pay, Beckett nudges in front of me and orders the same, pulling dollar bills from his wallet.

"You didn't have to pay for me," I say as he crumples the receipt into his back pocket. My confession from last night still weighs on me, as well as Beckett's non-reaction. While he seems totally unaffected, him buying me stuff feels too *romantic* for my liking, which is very confusing for my current-day feelings.

"I know I didn't," he says with a wink, and grabs the drip coffee from the counter, pressing it into my palms. "Just accept the free coffee, Wilson."

Grumbling, I nod my thanks and we climb upstairs. Any Beans Necessary has a quieter and less hectic second story. The only couch is taken, and we settle at a bistro table.

Beckett wastes no time getting to the point of this coffee meeting, spreading the notebook out between us. "We should attend these three games. Tonight, Wednesday, and Thursday."

I study the notes and sip my coffee. "Not tomorrow?"

"Nah, my mom's working her caretaker gig, and Willa has a sleepover. I'm on Willa Watch as her chauffeur."

"Okay." I tap the sheet of paper. "What about Friday?"

At this he grimaces. "There's a game, but the buy-in is three thousand."

I balk and drop my jaw. "Like in dollars?"

Beckett snorts. "No, magical beans," he says, and I sigh my annoyance. "But if we win enough money at the games I mentioned, we won't have to risk it."

"Yeah, three thousand dollars is a little rich for my blood." I study the notebook. "Hey, who's this?" I tap my fingernail against the only name I've seen on multiple pages. *Wilkes.*

Beckett closes the notebook. "Someone we won't run into."

"Why? Who is he?"

He lowers his voice. "There's one guy who pulls the strings around San Francisco with illegal betting. A gambler with a nasty reputation. But these games are below him; don't worry about him."

"How come you know so much about this guy?" I prompt. "Or any of this, really. Betting on bowlers isn't like putting money on the ponies."

Beckett reaches his legs out beneath the table. "You wanna hear something wild?" He sips his coffee. "I'm pretty sure my dad was a hustler."

"Oh, come on." I give him a pointed look. "You can't expect me to believe that."

"The notebook?" He taps the composition notebook. "It was his."

"No way." I pick up the notebook and turn it over in my hands. "How'd you find out?"

"I've never seen him hustle or anything; at first it was just a hunch. But after he left town, I found the notebook in his study. Last summer I began checking out all the alleys he listed, trying to find him or someone who knew him."

I hand the notebook to Beckett. "And did you?"

"I found a few people who'd either been conned *by* him or conned *with* him." He thumbs the worn pages. "At first I was frustrated because I wasn't getting any information. That's why I started betting. People were more willing to talk on an even playing field. Winning was a nice upside."

I roll this information over in my head as it fills in the gaps of my knowledge. "Did anyone know what happened?"

Beckett squints. "Kind of? I heard, from several sources, that he *knew* Wilkes."

"Ah, the threads connect," I say, intrigued. "Go on."

"I don't know much, but my dad was in a lot of debt— possibly with Wilkes. Before he left, he was having money troubles, and I heard him talking about a guy named Wilkes on the phone. I didn't think much of it, not until he left."

"You're not trying to meet Wilkes, are you? Find out about your dad?"

"Hell no," Beckett says with a shake of his head.

"Everyone I've spoken with has warned me away from him. And you remember my dad—he was tough. If he felt the need to leave town, he must've been threatened. I have no desire to get involved in my dad's shit. Doesn't mean I don't hope he'll come home one day, though."

"Have you ever reached out to him?"

"Back when he first left, but he changed his number." His gray eyes are wide, hopeful. "But I should at least try, right?"

"Yeah. I doubt your dad actually wanted to leave you guys," I say, even if I have no idea if that's the truth or not. Mr. Porter wasn't always the most reliable dad. He struggled to hold down a full-time job, drank a lot. But he loved his kids.

Beckett gives me a tight smile before staring into his coffee mug. "Thanks."

After we drain our coffees, we go over tonight's game: the Dust Bowl in the Tenderloin District. But since the game's at midnight, I have to come up with a cover story. Aunt Fiona is really my only option, so I carefully construct a text message.

"Keep your lies simple," Beckett coaches. "Too many details make people suspicious. Simplicity is key."

"Here goes nothing." I read over my message once before hitting send.

ME: Hey, Beckett invited me to a party tonight. Can you cover me if I miss curfew?

I cross my fingers. Come on, Fiona, time to be the cool aunt.

AUNT FEE: Are you guys dating?! 👀 Tell me what's going on and I'll cover for you.

ME: We're going to a party together. Nothing more.

AUNT FEE: Fine. But if your "nothing more" turns into something more, I approve.

ME: Not happening.

AUNT FEE: Why not?! He was always cute. Does he still have great hair?

I reread the message, shaking my head in disbelief.

Beckett perks up. "What'd she say?"

"Nothing." I fumble trying to exit out of the message, but he spins the phone around.

A sly smile blooms across his face. The tips of his ears steadily turn pink. "Cute?"

I hold my hands up. "Hey, I didn't type that."

"Great hair?" he continues.

My cheeks prickle with heat. "What? You have nice hair. People notice these things." I rub my neck, skin hot underneath my palms.

It's not that I like Beckett. We're friends again, and just barely. Too much is on the line. Whatever spark I felt last night can be chalked up to faulty wiring. Okay, and some *possibly* unresolved feelings from before.

"Right, right." Beckett slides the phone back. "Are you one of those people, by chance?"

Embarrassingly, my face warms. I redirect the conversation by asking, "Hey, what conditioner do you use?" There's no doubt he's just teasing me, armed with my confession from last night, but it still makes me blush.

Beckett's eyes narrow. "What? No idea. It's a two-in-one thing." He leans across the table with a cocky grin. "What're you going to say?"

Ignoring him, I clutch my phone against my chest and type a reply.

> ME: Thanks for the unwanted opinion. Are you covering for me? Y/N?
>
> AUNT FEE: Yes, I got you. 👍
>
> AUNT FEE: Be safe and text when you get home, okay? Don't forget to have fun!

"We're good for tonight." I drop the phone in my purse, away from his curious gaze.

"The game could go late. Will that be enough?"

"I mean, it has to be. I have to look at the bigger picture. If I can't come up with the money . . ." I trail off, shaking my head. "Arizona isn't an option."

Beckett picks up his coffee and palms the mug, his gaze soft as it meets mine. "Why Arizona?"

"My dad's parents live down there," I explain, picking at my napkin. "I can't imagine not living here. This city is my *home*. I can't leave."

From its fraught history to the Gold Rush boom to the 1906 earthquake to the AIDs crisis, San Francisco's had a rough life. A city felled by earthquakes and scorched by fire. A city that built itself back up. A city so diverse, welcoming, and unique. Streets without judgment, nights without limits. I can't imagine living somewhere that isn't steeped in diversity like San Francisco. A city where I can be myself.

I might not know who Chuck Wilson is yet, but if I'm ever going to find her, it'll be here in San Francisco.

As if Beckett can read my mind, he says, "Then we're sure as hell finding a way for you to stay. I promise."

And damn it, I believe him.

Eleven

UNLIKE THE ROAD, the Dust Bowl is a proper bowling alley.

The building is red brick and ancient, with three stories of residential above; loud music pumps from the metal-barred windows. Beckett and I observe the building as we wait across the street for the sidewalk signal to change. I try my best not to act intimidated. This is my first solo game, and my nerves won't let me forget it.

I'm rarely out this late, and it never ceases to amaze me how this city stays awake when everyone else has long since gone to bed. The lights. The crowded seats at corner restaurants. The groupings of friends waiting for taxis or rideshares, stomping their feet to stay warm as they wait for the light to turn.

"You have any trouble with your dad?" Beckett asks, leaning against the streetlamp pole.

"Nope. He was out when I left, and Aunt Fiona's covering

me. We should be good." I wrap my arms around myself, wishing I'd worn something warmer than a flimsy caftan.

Back in the car, Beckett had me dab whiskey on my skin from an airplane-size bottle to help sell my drunken state—another facet of the hustle. Who knows if it'll work, but I smell *disgusting*.

"On a scale of one to ten, how happy is your aunt that you're hanging out with cute guys with amazing hair?" he asks, casting me a teasing grin.

I smack his arm. Now that we've cleared the air, it's frightening how comfortable we are with each other. How easy, how seamless, it's been to fall into our old dynamic. "Who said 'amazing'? You're so full of yourself."

His grin is wide, the tips of his ears pink. "I'm the right amount of full," he corrects me. "And admit it, my hair is amazing."

I eye his curls and the light turns. "Eh, it's okay."

Inside the Dust Bowl, the low ceiling is claustrophobic, and the bar's in a separate room guarded by a dour-looking bouncer. There are thirty-six lanes in the darkened alley. Weak overheads illuminate the building, but special bulbs give everything an electric glow. Black lights. Beckett smiles and his teeth are super white.

Unlike last night, I'm supposed to be Beckett's girlfriend. I know I agreed to this, but I didn't exactly consider how much *touching* would be involved. His hand pressing against my lower back as we pay the cashier. The outside of his thigh pressing into mine as we sit, scoping out the competition. Tucking the wig's hair behind my ear, promising to be right back, before he goes to chat up the other players.

All these small, very confusing actions.

We're stationed at lane seven. Half the people are here to drink and have a good time. The others are here to gamble. You can tell from their severe facial expressions, the discreet piles of money underneath beer coasters, and the overall air of hostility.

I bowl shitty, just like we planned. When I hit a spare, I loudly broadcast how I can take anyone in the bowling alley. Beckett pretends to be wary when the guys he's been chatting up agree to play me. No one questions our story. He was right. Simple lies work. No one gives me lingering glances, either.

Beckett joins me at our lane and says, "You'll be playing against Earl, Sandy, and Ace, those three at lane eight. Go introduce yourself. Get close enough for them to smell the alcohol, act drunk, got it?"

I raise a brow at their names. Did we stumble into a fifties movie? "Sure thing."

"Hey, guys," I say, careful to slur my words, and lean over the seats separating us. "I'm Caroline."

"Earl," says the oldest of the trio, a short man in his thirties with patchy black hair and a whitening goatee. From the way his face recoils, I'm betting he detects the whiskey soaked into my shirt, skin, and strands of the wig.

The other guy is in his late twenties and has a shaved head. "I'm Sandy. What's your name again?"

"Caroline." I smile and trip, clutching Sandy's shoulder for support. "Gosh, I am so sorry."

Sandy grins. "No problem, sweetheart."

I bite the inside of my cheek so whatever acidic response I'd love to lob at Sandy stays unspoken. I'm no one's sweetheart.

Ace is younger and gives me an appraising look. "Ace. Nice to meet you."

"Babe, you have the cash?" Beckett asks from our lane.

Babe? That's so unnecessary. I glare at him but pull the money clip from my bag. "One hundred sound fair?" With a twist of my wrist, I drop the clip in front of our opponents. "Oops!"

Beckett scoops up the cash. "Gotta be more careful."

After he tucks my one hundred dollars in the table's built-in cup holder, the other men do the same. Earl slides a coaster over the stash. The Dust Bowl isn't as ignorant about any illegal activities as the Road, but we're not letting that stop us.

The scoreboard screens hang side by side, and Beckett already programmed my name into the machine. Whoever ends with the highest score wins the whole pot. No team tonight. Just me, a green ball, and my left hook.

The guys offer to go first.

"Intimidation tactic," Beckett whispers, his arm loose around my waist. I focus on the game instead of his hand on my hip. The way the heat of his palm melts through the fabric like it's not even there.

Earl bowls a strike, Sandy a spare, and Ace another strike. "It's working."

Beckett surprises me by turning and leaning his forehead against mine. The toes of his loafers press against my bowling shoes, and this close up, his breath is cinnamon. His eyes find mine and lock on with an intensity that turns my stomach upside down.

Instinct tells me to move because—*hello*—his mouth is maybe two inches from mine, but I'm supposed to be Beckett's girlfriend. Besides, this isn't real; he's just pretending. I slide my hand up his arm, cupping the back of his neck. I really shouldn't like this. But holy shit, do I like this.

"Stay confident," he murmurs. "These guys are no better bowlers than Count and Phil. Just cockier with more cash. Keep your average higher than last time, but don't pull anything impressive. A seven-two split? Don't go for the spare."

I nod, and my nose bumps his.

"Now, I'm going to buy those gentlemen a beer." Beckett squeezes my arm before stepping away.

"With what ID?" Flushed, I try to focus. *What just happened?*

"My fake ID. I got you one too." He grins slyly. "Some bowling alleys might be twenty-one and over. I picked it up today; it's in my bag."

After I bowl my first turn, Beckett heads to the bar. The pins take a moment to reset, and I dip into the bowling bag and find the fake ID, wrinkling my nose at the picture. He used my yearbook photo from this year. They took them at the end of September, and I look painfully sixteen. I turned seventeen this February, but I doubt it matters—I don't look any older. I tuck the ID into my wallet anyway.

Beckett returns several frames later with the beers, his eyes flitting to the scoreboard. He's carrying five, one for each of us. He sips his and perches on the seats, talking to the guys as they bowl. They're wary of drinking, but when I force myself to take a gulp of the warm, foamy liquid, the three men sip their own.

But I don't swallow it. When they're not looking, I spit it back into the cup.

Like the Road, I increase my game by the sixth frame. By now Beckett's purchased a second round of beers, his dumped in a fake potted plant. The men pay little attention, and I'm having déjà vu from the Road.

Between turns, when my mind is at ease, I experience these shock-like moments of earlier when Beckett put his forehead to mine. How easy, natural, it felt. How *good* it felt. Of all the things I shouldn't be thinking about, it's earlier. But if you tell someone not to think of an elephant, what do they think about? An elephant.

Beckett's my elephant.

Later. I can unpack whatever the hell happened later. I take a convincing faux sip of my beer and eye the scoreboard. All three guys have a lead on me, but as I improve, they get sloppier. Ace is ten pins ahead of me. Sandy thirty. Earl forty.

During my seventh frame, I bowl a split, knocking over the pins and earning myself a spare. I need the lead.

I can't find myself in the same position as Saturday, where everything hinged on the final tenth frame.

"Getting lucky?" Ace calls.

Earl studies the scoreboard, then approaches the foul line.

I shrug and pretend to sip my beer, spilling droplets on my caftan. That beer better not stain.

Beckett turns his back to the guys, narrows his eyes at me, and subtly shakes his head. He wants me to hold off, but with four hundred dollars on the line, I'm not leaving anything to chance. And it's not like I bowled a strike. It was an easy spare.

"Third round?" Beckett offers as Earl bowls.

When Ace begins to say yes, Earl cuts him off. "Thanks, but we've had enough. Might want to watch out for your girl. She looks hammered."

"I'm fine," I protest, drunk-girl loud. For the first time, I wish I were drunk. It's a lightning-quick desire, one I tamp down just as fast as it appeared. I don't drink, ever. It's a pastime of my mom's I don't dare experience. I just wish I could escape from my mind—somehow. I can't stop replaying that moment. How, I'm pretty sure, Beckett smiled when I cupped the back of his neck. *Focus.*

Except I can't. If Beckett smiled, what did it mean? That he's a good actor? I already know how well he can sell a lie. For Beckett, this charade must be easy. He doesn't have any old and unresolved feelings that might complicate things. I can't let myself be fooled into thinking this is real.

Beckett pushes up from his seat and pulls me to him. His fingers loop around my wrist. "You good?"

"I'm nervous." This much is true. I shake free from his grip, thinking clearer now that we're not touching.

"Deep breaths. You got this in the bag. Try to not lose, okay?"

"Thanks. I was totally planning on losing," I say sarcastically. "You need to give better pep talks; you're shit at this."

Beckett's gray eyes narrow. "What did I do?"

Okay, so I'm not really mad about the pep talk. I'm nervous and confused, and pushing him away right now solves one of my problems. I grab the bottle of water from his bowling bag. "Forget it."

"Chuck—"

"You're distracting me, okay?"

Whatever annoyance was on his face disappears. "You find me distracting?" he teases, mouth curving into the cockiest of smiles. This right here is why my friendship with Beckett was always so confusing. He's always been an accidental flirt, and it's particularly grating tonight.

"That's not what I meant!" Blushing, I chug half the water bottle so I don't have to speak. Beckett keeps grinning, but he doesn't say anything else. Why is he so freaking annoying? I'm the one playing, not him. It's easy for him to joke around, act like tonight is no biggie.

The annoyance fuels me, and just to spite Beckett, I go for the strike. My left hook sweeps across the lane, smacking into the headpin. All ten pins spiral away, leaving an empty frame. Without their beers to distract them, all three men watched me throw that strike.

"Wow, that was lucky!" I say in faux surprise, not meeting Beckett's gaze as I sit beside him. The men murmur, but none approach or question me.

"Chuck," Beckett says in a low, warning tone.

Crossing my arms, I sit forward and pay attention to the game instead of indulging Beckett's disapproval. The hawkeyed men start paying me more attention, but I don't back down. I don't care if I'm not following Beckett's precious plan anymore.

When the men get up to bowl the tenth frame, they do far better than I anticipated. They still have a lead—troubling considering I've actually been playing well the last few frames. I need another strike. Bad.

Don't overthink it.

During my last frame, I throw the ball; five pins fall, revealing a split.

The men behind me howl with laughter.

Everyone thinks the toughest split to convert is a seven-ten. Yeah, that's a lie. The toughest is the one at the end of my lane, the Greek Church—pins four, six, seven, nine, and ten—resembling ancient religious architecture. I don't see the resemblance. Just one hell of a shot.

Beckett runs over. "This isn't good."

"No shit." The return spits out my ball, and I push him aside. I can't deal with him right now. "I've got this."

He holds up his hands and backs away.

After swallowing the dried spit in my throat, I make my move.

When I approach the foul line, my foot, clad in a cheap rental shoe, lurches forward onto the oiled lanes.

"Foul," Earl yells from the sidelines. "She crossed the line."

I turn to defend myself, but the world slips, ripped out from underneath me. The green ball bounces away, and all the air is knocked out of my body as my back hits the floor. I manage not to slam my skull against the platform. What the hell just happened? Stunned, I stare up at the ceiling. The rafters. A saggy Mylar balloon in the shape of a frog bobs near a light fixture.

Groaning, I curl onto my side and take huge gulps of air. My ears are ringing.

My shoes. They must've gotten oil on them.

Beckett slides to a stop beside me, and he peers down at me. "Are you okay?"

Eyes pricking with tears, I say, "I'm fine," and push up. I earned the five pins from my first shot, but there's an F marring the second box. I lost the game to Earl.

I limp off the pain, heading toward the shadowed corner. Beckett follows, yelling at the guys to wait. "Hey, are you hurt?"

We're near a bank of vending machines that sell everything from condoms to socks.

My lower back throbs, and my pride is shredded into insurmountable pieces. "No." But my eyes leak. Traitors.

Beckett steps forward to hug me, and I shove him away.

I can't stand his pity. "No one's watching us. Just. Stop."
I rub my back, wincing. "Damn it, I made a complete fool
out of myself. Did I really cross the foul line?"

"Yeah, barely." He folds his arms over his chest. "Nothing about this game is legal. It's bullshit they pulled the
foul card."

I lean against a vending machine full of Magnum condoms. "Shit. I can't believe I lost over a technicality."

Beckett hesitates before asking, "Did you really think
you could convert the Greek Church?"

I roll my eyes because the question is so ridiculous. "I
thought you believed in me."

He offers a smile, but my death glare kills it on contact.
"I believe in you, but you had less than a point-three percent chance of getting the spare."

"How'd you know that?"

Beckett rubs his chin. "I read up on different spares
online, their probabilities and statistics. It's a tough shot."

With the heels of my palms, I smear away my embarrassed tears. "Whatever. Can we go home?"

"What? You wanna quit?" His shoulders slump forward. "What happened to saving Bigmouth's? Staying in
San Francisco?"

"I don't know!" I'm shaking, the voice in my head
reminding me that I'm on the edge, that maybe I've lost
not only money, but control over myself. Because the logical part of me wants to stop, but it's so quiet, I can barely
hear it. "Maybe we should cut our losses? Give up?"

"If we leave," Beckett says, "if we cut our losses, then

you'll probably move to Arizona. I don't think that's a loss I can deal with, okay?"

"You'd be fine without me. Better off, even."

"No, I wouldn't," he insists with this air of finality, and leans one forearm against the display case, boxing me against the vending machine Then: "Double or nothing. What do you say?"

I shift, flushed over the lack of space between our bodies, at the heat of his voice. "What do you mean? With Earl?" My brain is still stuck on his earlier words. Will he really be that upset if I leave? Or is he just trying to motivate me? And why do I care so much if it's real?

Beckett pointedly looks over to the men, to the action. "You're good. That was a fluke."

"And what if I lose?"

"You won't. I believe in you." He steps back, closer to the lanes. "How's that for a pep talk?"

"You've made progress, but I don't know. . . ." My palms are slick with sweat, and the appeal of winning eats my fear of losing. I *need* this money. Staying in San Francisco, saving Bigmouth's—it's more important than my wounded pride and bruised back.

Beckett holds out his hand. "C'mon, it's now or never. Let's do this thing."

I place my hand in his, and he pulls me toward the hustle.

Twelve

BECKETT'S PEP TALK did the trick, resetting my confidence on-switch. My nerves haven't quieted, instead fueling a desire to walk away with all the money in the cup holder. To take that money and, over the next week, turn it into eight grand to guarantee I stay in San Francisco.

Earl's eager to make even more money off me, and he alone agrees to play me for double or nothing. Sandy and Ace sit the game out. Earl and I both toss an additional hundred into the pot. Earl saw me cry after the slip, storm off, and fight with Beckett. If he was ever worried about my proficiency as a bowler, he sure as hell isn't now. That very real mini breakdown made me a weak girl in his eyes. I'm using that to my advantage.

By the tenth and final frame, we're tied. When it's my turn, I *can* win. To play it safe, I—surprise, surprise—need to bag two strikes. This can't be easy on my nerves.

The first strike stuns the men into slack-jawed silence.

The second sends them into an uproar.

"You fucking bitch," Earl snarls, and the slur cuts through the music.

"Watch it!" Beckett hops to his feet.

I back away from the lane, heartbeat kicking up a storm.

My gaze darts to the exit—the door narrows, farther and farther, as my vision tunnels.

Dozens of eyes turn their attention to us, freezing a moment of time, and that's all we need. Beckett moves fast, grabbing the money out of the cup holder and shoving the thick wad of bills into his pocket.

As I reach for the bowling bag, Earl hops over the seats and traps both my forearms in a viselike grip. "You hustled us." He flips me, my spine pressed against his stomach, one arm tight across my shoulders and chest.

"Let her go," Beckett says lowly, calmly, but his eyes are large and worrisome.

Something sharp digs into my side, and I know it's a knife before I look down. A shiny switchblade that Earl presses into the flimsy material of my top. Not enough to really hurt, but hard enough to scare me. The metal pierces my ribs, somehow cold and hot, and I bite back my fear.

"I'll let her go when you give us our money." Earl spits on the ground; his breath yeasty from the beer. "I should've known something was up when she bowled that strike."

Beckett swears, his attention flitting from Earl and his knife to me. I force myself to stay calm, my frazzled mind fumbling to make sense of what to do. Sandy stays back, but when Ace sees the knife, he grabs his shit and runs. Smart guy.

My purse with the Mace is behind Beckett, but that's no use. *Think.* Earl's short, and my head should line up with his chin. I jerk a silent *no* when Beckett reaches for the money in his pocket. We're drawing quite the crowd and have only seconds until security or the sleepy bouncer breaks this up. Then all of us get caught. For hustling. For gambling. For underage drinking.

Before I think twice, I use Earl's tight grip to my favor. I brace against him and toss my head into what's hopefully his nose, or at least his mouth. Whatever I hit, it *hurts*, and I cry out. But he lets go, the blade clattering to the floor. Skull pounding, I kick the knife toward the lane. I grab Beckett's hand, and we run. People shout at us as we dash the length of the Dust Bowl, and Sandy dodges bystanders as he tries to catch up.

"Hurry!" My legs are shorter than Beckett's, but he's lagging, stunned. I tug hard on his hand, and we push outside. The icy night air slaps me in the face, cold against my sweat, and I keep running. Beckett comes to his senses, pace picking up as he digs his keys from his pocket.

Sandy isn't trailing us anymore. No one is, but we run the two blocks until we arrive at Beckett's Accord. We toss ourselves inside and lock the doors. Beckett hands me the wad of cash, slides the key into the ignition, and screeches from the street leading to the Dust Bowl.

We're silent except for the hush of our labored breathing in the car, which smells of whiskey and beer and sweat. I crank down the window and hang my head, taking huge gulps of fresh briny air.

"Fuck," Beckett says after a few minutes, the car speeding toward Hayes Valley. Lifting a shaky hand from the wheel, he drags his fingers through the matted curls clinging to his neck and face. "Are you okay? Did he hurt you?"

My limbs are softer than overcooked spaghetti, but I twist sideways to inspect my ribs. The caftan has a small slice in it, and it's spotted red. The knife barely got me, but enough to raise and pucker the skin along my ribs, drawing blood to the surface. My head aches, a dull thud at the base of my skull. The wig provided some protection, and the pain isn't too bad.

"I'm fine." But am I? My heart sings, hammering in my chest, and my hands shake harder than Beckett's. Fear. Adrenaline. Excitement. I feel it all at once, and it's overwhelming. I glance down at my feet and the cheap rental shoes. "Damn it, we left my shoes! They were my favorite pair."

Beckett laughs and offers me a wobbly smile. "We netted five hundred dollars tonight, Chuck. Five hundred fucking dollars. You can buy new shoes."

"Actually, I can't. They were vintage Finsk ballet flats. Irreplaceable."

"Do you want to go back for them?" he asks. "I bet Earl would love to have another chat about the ethics of bowling."

"Oh, shut up." I tuck my fingers beneath the wig and

pull it off. "Of course I don't want to go back. I'm just mourning the loss, okay?"

Our actual net is four hundred and eighty-five dollars, but added to what we've already won, we have just over a grand. A thousand dollars. I've had my doubts about this plan, but we're actually doing it. We're earning the money, slowly but surely, and my future in San Francisco no longer feels as precarious. Silly considering we barely have a fraction of what we need, but that's what hope does. It lifts you up when everything else is dragging you down, down, down.

I fold the bills into the money clip until I can add them to the stash at home. I haven't heard from Aunt Fiona all night and check my phone. A single text, sent thirty minutes ago.

AUNT FEE: Where the hell are you???

Shit. It's half past one.

I text Aunt Fee, telling her I'm almost home.

"Wouldn't it be safer to play fair?" I ask, putting my phone away. My body aware of every movement, sore from the fall. Outside the car, the city slides by in a blur of lights and fog.

"Sure, but what would be the fun of that?" Beckett jokes. Then he adds, "No, but really, since we're doing this short term, there's no harm in hustling. We'll net more money *and* guarantee our wins. But if we're gonna keep this up, you have to stick to the plan."

I wince, hoping he'd forget about my rebellious strike. "Yeah, yeah. I know. I was just . . ."

"Just what?"

I don't know how to explain myself. I was annoyed and frustrated and made an impulsive decision. Pretty much my MO at this point. Changing topics, I say, "Don't do this because you feel obligated to save Bigmouth's or something. I'm giving you an out. After tonight, I won't blame you if you want to take it."

"As much as I love Bigmouth's, I only care because it means keeping you in San Francisco. I'm as invested as you are."

My skin erupts in goose bumps at his words. "You want me to stay? Back at the alley, that wasn't just some pep-talk ploy?"

We slow to a stop as the traffic light changes to yellow, then red, and Beckett turns in my direction. The seat belt strains against his chest. "Of course I do. Believe it or not, I actually like having you around. I've missed this." He gestures to the space between us.

"Yeah?" The question slips out between my smiling lips before I can stop it. Before I can *think*. The look on his face intense and sincere. For the first time, I believe that he missed me.

"Yeah," he says, but really, he kind of breathes the word.

Against my will, my face turns hot and itchy.

Someone behind us honks, and Beckett swears, turning his attention back to the road.

"Um—" He flips his turn signal; we're close to my house. "You're really okay? I feel bad for underestimating them. What happened back there, that's on me."

"Yeah, I'm fine." I wave my hand dismissively, pretending like I'm not unnerved. "Don't worry about it."

Beckett bobs his head. "Good. What matters is you won, we got out unscathed, and you broke Earl's nose."

A strangled, surprised noise escapes my lips. "Seriously? I didn't look."

"His nose?" Beckett lifts his hands from the wheel to explode them away from his face, complete with sound effects. "A bloody fountain."

"Oh my God." I press my fingers to my mouth in disbelief. "Good to know those self-defense classes my dad made me take paid off."

Beckett idles near the stop sign at the base of the hill on my street. "Should I drop you here?"

The hill's grade is daunting, and every bone has ached since we began this hustling scheme, but I don't dare risk him driving closer. Tonight has been full of one mistake after another, and I don't need any more trouble.

"Yeah, here's good."

Beckett leans across the seat and hugs me tight. His body is warm through his T-shirt, smelling slightly of sweat and deodorant. *Bad idea*, my brain warns, but I loop my arms around his neck. The last time I hugged him was before he went onstage as Danny in *Grease*.

This hug is different, but we fit together all the same.

Clearing his throat, he pulls away. "I'm glad you're okay." He shifts to his side of the car. "Tonight was, um—"

"Intense?"

Beckett nods. "Talk to you later? I'll text you the details

for Wednesday's game if I can't make it to Bigmouth's tomorrow. I'm working, but I might swing by."

When I pop open the door, the late-night air—wet and dark—fills the car. It causes the hairs on the back of my neck to stand on end. "Sounds good."

He taps the steering wheel with the heel of his palm. "Night."

I lift my hand in a half wave and step onto the sidewalk. "Later," I say, my hand hovering in the air as he pulls a U-turn and putters down the street.

My toes hang over the edge of the curb, and I stand there for a breath, watching his taillights fade. Hayes Valley is infamously windy, and it whips my hair, my clothes, into a frenzy. When I can't see the Accord anymore, I turn and dig through my bag for my house key.

I sneak back into the house, texting Aunt Fiona that I'm home, and tiptoe upstairs. As I dump my belongings on my bed, my phone buzzes. But it's just Mila checking in, wondering what's going on with Bigmouth's and Beckett. I haven't had time to catch her up. So I fill her in on the past seventy-two hours.

What surprises me the most is when I tell Mila how it's nice having Beckett back in my life. I didn't anticipate this shift, but now that we've both said our piece and cleared the air, my resentment has faded. Sure, I'm still hurt and he still broke my trust, but the pain is less. Softer. Like it's a memory rather than a fresh wound.

After we log off, I check my e-mail—my eBay listings expired, and no one's bothered with the Etsy items. No surprise there. I plug my phone into its charger and get ready for bed. My bones scream with fatigue as I pull off the caftan. The inch-long jagged hole, courtesy of Earl's knife, is fixable, but I study myself in the full-length mirror, arching my arm over my head. The cut is puckered and red, a seam of fury across my ribs. Gingerly, I run my finger over the small wound, the reminder of what happened tonight. Of what was an act of bravery, or an act of thoughtlessness.

Is there even a difference?

Beckett might think I'm nothing like my mom, but lately I'm not so sure. I don't know what she was like before her illness took over, and that nestles fear into my core. What was the beginning of the end? Was it simple, like late nights, less sleep, less food?

What I'm doing—lying and gambling and sneaking around—makes me nervous. Because I'm happier tonight than I have been in a while. But isn't this impulsivity? Or am I simply happy because I've found a solution? I have no idea, and the unknown scares the shit out of me. All I do know is that the little pile of money is growing, and I'm eager to see what else I'm capable of. I've never really felt capable before, and I'm already addicted to this feeling.

Yet in the silent loneliness of my bedroom, worry sparks. Part of me loves this, the weirdness, the rush. But what will life be like once it's over? Beckett and I are friends again. Will that stay the same when we return to school next Monday?

What if I move to Arizona?

Tonight's thoughts brought to you by What If™.

I curl up on my bed, sleepless, staring at the fairy lights gleaming on the walls.

My mind drifts, shuffling through years and years of memories.

The time Beckett broke his ankle in the sixth grade on a school field trip. Folding pages in library books. Crying during Pixar movies. Our fingers linked every Sunday at Lindy at the Park as we danced. Singing "Summer Nights" on our school's auditorium stage. Studying the BART map on his phone, worry creased between his brows . . .

My phone buzzes across my comforter.

BECKETT PORTER: Look what I found! Maybe they're not as irreplaceable as you feared?

I click the accompanying link, pulling open a vintage online retailer selling a pair of Finsk ballet flats. Not the *exact* same style as the ones I left behind in the Dust Bowl, but I smile all the same. Maybe if we have leftover money, I can buy a replacement pair.

ME: Thank you ☺

After locking my phone, I roll onto my stomach and press my face into a pillow.

More than seven hundred and fifty miles separate San Francisco, California, and Arizona. Just the idea of that much space between me and Beckett makes my eyes grow hot with tears. I have no idea how I feel about Beckett. But I'd like a chance to trust my emotions instead of running screaming in the opposite direction. A chance to make things right—really right—between us.

TUESDAY, APRIL 24
DAYS UNTIL BIGMOUTH'S
EVICTION: 6

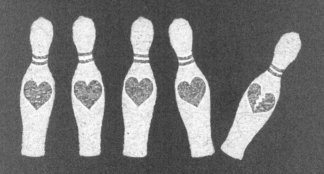

Thirteen

A BLISTER ACHES on the inner base of my right thumb, and I keep poking at it with my red-polished fingernail. This much back-to-back bowling has physical side effects. Not only the blister—I've barely slept. Unfortunately, my lack of sleep is reflected on my face. I'm paler than usual, with bags under my eyes. It's not a cute look.

Tuesdays aren't busy for Bigmouth's. We don't have the geriatrics from Monday, the knitting club stops by on Wednesdays, and Thursday's league night. Fridays can be busy. Same with Saturday nights. I wouldn't be surprised if a tumbleweed blew through here. However, that might be too *much* action for a Tuesday.

Since it's dead, I'm in the back, squaring off with a bunch of nasty bowling shoes. Before I get cleaning, I prop open the window so I don't pass out from all the chemicals. First the antifungal. Then a disinfectant that makes my eyes water. I top off the cleaning cocktail with a dousing of Febreze.

Collecting the shoes, I carry them out front to the register and slip behind the counter, organizing them in the cubbies. Someone behind me whistles tunelessly, and I glance over my shoulder, spotting Beckett as he heads in my direction.

I smile. Then panic. Because I most definitely look like a wreck. My red lipstick was a poor choice even if it's my signature color. Today it only stresses the other extremes. Lifeless pallor, crappy eye-makeup application, the cystic hormone pimple living on my chin. Ugh, why do I care? Why should I care what I look like in front of Beckett? I shouldn't care, but I do. Like, a *frightening* amount.

"Hey!" Beckett approaches the register with crates filled with Pepsi, Mountain Dew, and variety packs of Gatorade balanced on his hip. The clipboard slides precariously on top of the bottles, and he hoists the entire thing onto the counter. "I'd ask you to sign, but . . ." He trails off with a knowing grin.

"Come along." I shove the remaining shoes into the cubbies and lead him to Dad's office. Beckett's first delivery was only five days ago, but our dynamic is light-years different. Falling back into what we once had.

"What're you doing after work?" He flips the clipboard back and forth, the attached pen flying.

"Nothing really." I'll probably swap my dress for pajamas and binge *Antiques Roadshow* until I fall asleep, but even I know how boring that sounds. "You're watching Willa, right?"

"Unfortunately," he jokes. "You off at six?"

We stop at my dad's office. "Yep. Sooner if things stay dead."

"Come in," Dad calls, and we push inside. "Hey there, Porter. Need my autograph?"

Beckett presents the clipboard, and Dad loops his signature on the form. He glances between us. "How's your project going?"

As I say, "Not bad," Beckett says, "Terribly."

Backtracking, he adds, "What I meant is we could benefit from extra time." Beckett clutches the clipboard to his chest.

"I guess you can leave at four today," Dad says to me.

I glance at the wall clock—that's in an hour—and side-eye Beckett. Why is he smuggling me out of work when there isn't a game tonight? I swear, I can never get a read on the guy.

"You sure?"

"Yeah. I need to close early anyway."

"Why?" What's with Dad closing early lately? We're trying to make money and, you know, not shut down. This feels counterproductive.

"Okay, Caroline." Dad exhales and shuts his laptop. "If you must know, four months ago your aunt introduced me to her yoga instructor." Oh God, my dad is blushing. "Leigh and I hit it off, and things are starting to become serious. . . . I've been waiting for the best time to tell you."

I blink, my eyelids sliding over sandpaper eyeballs. "What? You've been seeing her for *four months* and you never told me? What the hell, Dad?"

Beckett keeps hugging the clipboard and takes a few exaggerated steps backward, but as he tries to leave the office, I clutch the hem of his shirt. Nice try. He's not leaving me here to endure this awkwardness alone.

"I wasn't going to say anything unless—"

"It got serious," I say, nodding stiffly. "Right. Okay."

I tuck my bottom lip between my teeth, biting hard. Dad hasn't dated much since Mom died. Sure, that was fourteen years ago, but there's something deeply unsettling about your parent dating. Especially when they lied about it for months.

The Wilson family has a serious problem with the truth.

Maybe it's different if your parents divorced, if you watched their former relationship dissolve in the acid of a split. Dad doesn't talk about Mom often, but he keeps their wedding photo on his bedside table. From what Aunt Fee has told me, Mom was Dad's tragic true love. He loves her. A love without an end. How do you move on from that?

Dad's few attempts at dating have never amounted to much, and I figured he was waiting until I left for college. But this is just plain odd. My dad, the greaseball in a bowling shirt, going out with a *yoga* instructor? And who goes out on a Tuesday? Who the hell is this woman to shut down Bigmouth's Bowl?

"Fine." I trip on the carpet as I back away and steady myself using the doorframe. "Have fun."

"Caroline," Dad says, his voice sharp. "Don't get weird on me."

"I'm great." I give him a fake smile. "Do you mind if I leave now? There's no one here, and this is Beckett's last delivery." I have no idea if that's true, but I can't be here anymore.

Dad glances at the clock, frowning. "I'm not sure."

"I e-mailed the therapist," I say, hoping this'll remind him of the leniency he promised. This is technically a lie because I forgot, but I *intend* to e-mail her. Eventually.

"That's fantastic, hon." Dad's genuinely pleased, eyes crinkling at the corners. Guilt stabs me in the stomach, but it vanishes when I remember all his lies. "I guess it's fine if you leave."

"Cool. See you tonight." I grab Beckett's arm and wheel him out the door.

"Um, are you okay?" Beckett asks.

"Mm-hmm, I'm peachy."

"So you claim." He thumps the clipboard against his thighs as he walks. "Think of it this way: the more time he spends with Yoga Leigh, the less likely he'll be wondering where you keep disappearing off to for the rest of spring break."

"Not a bad point." We reach the counter and the crates of drinks. "Do you need help with these?"

Beckett eyes them. "Storage closet?"

"Sure. It should be unlocked." I balance a crate on my hip and help Beckett put them away. "Do you know when Bigmouth's contract ends with Schulman's?"

"No, but they're generally yearlong contracts renewed in June. Why?"

My hope fades. I hoist the crate onto the shelf and say, "I thought if he was still getting deliveries, maybe he renewed his contract and knows something I don't."

Beckett slides the other crate onto the shelf. "Unless he renews this June, I have no idea. Sorry."

"I shouldn't be surprised." I nudge the storage room door shut. "My dad's given up on this place."

If Dad's been dating Yoga Leigh for the past few months, then he clearly isn't invested in saving Bigmouth's. His priorities lie elsewhere. The late nights, closing early, the phone calls he didn't want me to overhear . . . The realization stings.

I collect my belongings and toss the useless bell on the counter for our nonexistent clientele.

"This was my last stop, but I have to return the van to the warehouse. Wanna come with?" Beckett hooks his thumbs in his jean pockets. "I have a couple of hours until I need to pick up Willa."

When I glance around the lobby, my gaze lands heavy on one of the many framed photographs. Bigmouth's thirty-year anniversary. My mom posing beside the jukebox, her smile infectious. My parents kissing in front of the neon sign outside, the BIGMOUTH'S BOWL sign new and luminous.

I rake my fingers through my hair, nostrils flaring. "Yeah, let's get out of here."

I've never welcomed the similarities and parallels between me and my mom. They upset me on a cellular level. But there was always one small comfort. If Dad loved Mom, then he'd always love me. I want my dad to be happy. I really do. But why can't he be happy with someone more like Mom? If Dad wants normal and perfect, can he still love someone like me?

Fourteen

BECKETT INSISTS AN afternoon in Dolores Park will help me unwind, as he nicely put it at the warehouse, where I walked in anxious circles around him. Perched between the stately Spanish buildings of the Mission and the rainbow-splashed Castro, Dolores Park is one of my favorite places in the city.

Emerald-green grass slopes upward with strips of sidewalk breaking the lawn in a U-shape. Cement stairways lead to higher grounds, and tennis courts showcase barefooted and shirtless men lobbing a ball back and forth. For late April, it's sunnier than normal, which all of San Francisco seems to be taking advantage of.

The park is packed, and we find a spot on the outskirts of Hipster Hill. Beckett spreads out a blanket on the stubbly grass, and we sit. I tuck my legs to my chest and rest my chin on my kneecaps. Here, in the park, I'm infinitely calmer than I was at Bigmouth's. For a few hours, I don't want to think about Yoga Leigh, my dad, and his pathetic attempts to protect me.

I close my eyes for a moment and feel the breeze whistling through the air.

A Frisbee soars across the sky. On the other end of the park, kites fly. Sounds wholesome until you look closer and see two naked men constructing a Slip'n Slide down one hill. We even have a nudist that comes to the bowling alley. Dad lets him bowl as long as he's wearing his city-issued *sock* (yeah, disgusting), but here in Dolores Park, people bare all.

"You want your sewing?" Beckett asks, holding out the tote bag with my sewing kit.

"No thanks." I shift until my cheek rests against my knees comfortably. "You were right the other night, when you mentioned sewing being my passion."

"Yeah?" Beckett stretches his forearms back.

"I was supposed to go on a tour at FIDM, but I chickened out." I sigh heavily.

"What about Bigmouth's? You sure you don't want to enter the family business?"

"The bowling business is dying. At least the way my dad runs it. We don't have a liquor license. People bowl to get drunk and have fun, not hang out in a stale warehouse with a broken cigarette machine."

"Don't be so certain. Trends are cyclical. Maybe good old-fashioned bowling will make a comeback."

"Stranger things have happened."

Beckett pulls a water bottle out from his backpack and

181

takes a swig. "Like us hanging out again?" he asks, offering me the bottle.

"Exactly like us hanging out together." I grab the water bottle and take a sip before realizing I'm sharing germs with Beckett. "I guess it's weird. How things turned out. A week ago, I couldn't stand to look at you, let alone talk and hang out with you."

"Past tense," Beckett observes with a smug grin. He ditched his work uniform in the car and wears a plain blue shirt with fraying seams. It's frustrating how his T-shirt brings hidden elements of blue in his gray eyes to light.

"It's not funny! Last year . . . *sucked*."

"Hey, it sucked for me, too! I'm glad we've made it here, though." Beckett shifts on the blanket, and his shoulder brushes against mine. Maybe it's static electricity from our clothes, but something sparks and I feel the charge throughout my body.

Here. He means back to each other. I hang my head back, reveling at the weirdness of Beckett and me hanging out in our free time. Without the pretense of bowling, making money, or saving Bigmouth's. We're *us* again, two friends sharing a blanket and sitting beneath the San Franciscan sky. After my sleepless night yesterday, I'm more certain than ever that I want Beckett back, even if this ends, even if it all falls apart, even if I move to Arizona.

That want? It scares the shit out of me.

"You could've fooled me." I relax ever so slightly until my side presses solidly against his. "From my point of view, you moved on, made friends—"

"Not *friend* friends," he says. "*Superficial* friends. I wanted to seem like I was okay with losing you." He drops his voice to add, "I wasn't okay."

"And now?" I ask. "Are you okay?"

Beckett grins, squinting as the sun hits his eyes. "I'm sitting here with you, aren't I?"

"You are so cheesy," I deflect, unable to tame the happy flush his words ignited.

"Psh," he scoffs. "Like you don't love it."

I shift in the grass so I can face him. Because while I might enjoy the thrill of him saying those words, I have to remember that Beckett's like this with literally everyone. Friends. Strangers on the street. Checkout cashiers at the grocery store. An accidental flirt to the very end. "I don't," I say resolutely, lifting my chin.

"Mmm, see, this is where we disagree." Beckett's smile stretches even wider, and he casually rests his hand on my knee. "I think you're forgetting that I know an awful lot about you."

I stare at his hand, brows pinched. Then he *tickles* me.

Caught between surprise and laughter, I fall backward into the grass. "You asshole! I told you that in confidence."

I'm not ticklish like a normal person. My ribs or the bottom of my feet do nothing. But my knees are hypersensitive, something I made the mistake of telling Beckett years ago. So I take aim at his sides, tickling him back in revenge. It takes only a second of retaliation for him to abandon my knees, scooting a safe distance away from me.

"Truce?" he asks, his chest heaving from laughter and his curls mussed.

"Uh-huh." I push upright, picking grass from my hair. "Not funny! I'm never telling you anything ever again," I tease, leaning over and trying to smack his arm, but he catches my hand and curls my palm to his chest.

For a second I think it's a mistake. A midair collision of our two hands. That he'll let go. Instead, he presses my hand to his sternum. To the space above his heart. Warmth radiates between us, my fingers limp.

"You wanna know something?" he asks, his gaze tracking up from our hands and settling on my face.

"Sure." My voice is faint. The busyness of Dolores, and all I see is Beckett. All I smell is the warmth of his body and the cinnamon on his breath. All I feel is his hand pressing mine to his heart.

"You haven't laughed, not once, the past few days. I've missed that sound." His shirt is oh so soft, and there's the *thud thud thud* of his heart. Or is that my heart? "I just . . . wanted to hear you laugh."

Beckett loosens his grip on my wrist and laces his fingers through mine. Friends don't hold hands, right? We certainly didn't hold hands before. "After I tried apologizing, your dad told me to give you space until you came around. But I'm afraid I gave you too much space, and I lost you."

I look anywhere but at him. At the blanket, a *My Little Pony* beach towel I sincerely hope belongs to Willa. At the guy wandering between picnic blankets with a backpack selling edibles. Anywhere, everywhere, other than our intertwined hands.

Goose bumps ridge my skin, and I inhale sharply. "You didn't lose me, Beck. I'm right here."

The strange thing is, no part of me—not even my overactive and judgmental brain—wants to pull apart. My hand stays still. Locked with Beckett's. Twice the size of mine and pleasantly warm, especially now that the breeze is picking up, a whistling chill.

How did we get here? We're *holding hands*. The sensation of his skin against mine reminds me of our girlfriend-boyfriend hustling act. Reminds me of how Beckett's hands have affected me in ways I'm not proud of. How they lingered warm against the curve of my hips, the low indent of my back. Flexing in anger when I piss him off. Gripping me and spinning me off my feet in the bowling alley.

We're friends—faux dating on hustling nights—but today's a regular Tuesday. We're in public, sitting atop the grassy knoll of Dolores Park holding hands like it's the most natural thing in the world. I'm nervous, so nervous, but in an excited, hopeful way. The constant yarn ball of panic that's lived in my chest the last five days is unwinding.

My gaze flickers toward his mouth, and no matter how much I try backtracking, it's too late. My mind has already gone there, a place where I spent most of sophomore year. What would it be like to press my lips against Beckett's? It would be so easy to lean over and kiss him.

Shit. I can't be thinking this. Beckett and I are finally friends again—complicated, potentially non-platonic friends, but we can't be doing this. Maybe not ever, but especially not right now. We're partners in crime. If hustling is a business, that makes us partners.

And thou shalt not kiss thy hustling partner.

Fifteen

I RETURN HOME from the park before sunset with my body a confusing hormonal mindfuck, and I'm too muddled to dissect what happened, or didn't happen, until I sleep for a solid eight hours. Or ten. Or maybe I'll sleep an entire day to be safe.

I'm accosted by a strange scent the second I open the front door. Not Aunt Fiona's cooking. Worse. Ugh—the cologne Aunt Fee and I made the mistake of buying for Dad's birthday. I almost forgot about his date with Yoga Leigh. After slipping off my shoes, I follow the stench.

Dad stands in the hall by the mirror, rearranging his scant hair across his forehead. I blink in surprise. He's dressed in slacks and a button-down. Dad rarely wears anything other than his uniform of a stained bowling shirt and cargo shorts. Or basketball shorts if it's laundry day.

"Hey." I try to keep my tone neutral. "When's your date?"

"I'm leaving to pick up Leigh in five minutes." Dad

meets my reflection's gaze in the mirror. "How's that history project going?"

The way he phrases the question makes me wonder if he knows it's complete and utter bullshit. "Fine. New pants?"

"How'd you guess?"

I reach over and rip off the tag, and Dad's cheeks flush red.

There's something horrifying about watching your parents blush. I prefer to pretend my dad isn't human, thank you very much. Yet here he is, wearing new pants and sweating through his one fancy shirt. I hope for Yoga Leigh's sake he's wearing deodorant. Then again, she won't be able to smell his nervous flop-sweat or the stench of stale cigarettes over all that cologne.

Dad's phone sits on the hall table beneath the mirror, and it lights up, buzzing. In the mirror's reflection, I catch the name on the screen. JESSET CALLING shows on the display. He fumbles to send the call to voice mail.

"You're not going to get that?" The resentment I successfully tamped down earlier rises inside my chest once more. "It's got to be important if he's calling you late on a Tuesday."

Dad's reddening cheeks only get more inflamed. "I'll listen to the voice mail later. Leigh's expecting me."

"But what if there's something wrong at Bigmouth's? Maybe I should go check?" I'm practically begging for the truth. For Dad to show just an ounce of concern for our future. Instead, he's lying. He knows exactly why Art Jesset is calling his cell phone on a Tuesday night. And so do I.

With a swipe, Dad grabs his cell and shoves it in his

pants pocket. "Caroline, everything is fine. I'm sure Mr. Jesset wanted to talk over, ah, the new city parking meters."

"Parking meters. Right," I mutter, voice hollow.

"Well, come say goodbye," he says. "I'm nervous for my date."

I hug Dad, my arms tightening around his soft stomach as I endure a faceful of his horrid cologne. I squeeze him tight, even if I'm still pissed. Dad can't be too torn up over our financial woes if he's going out on dates. But he's not immune—I've seen the stress wearing on him, the worry playing across his face when he stares at the empty alley on a Saturday night. I just wish he was fighting to keep things the same. The way they're supposed to be.

Dad pats my shoulder and whistles as he saunters toward the garage.

With a sickening pulse of panic, I hurry into the kitchen, flexing my numb fingers. They haven't been my own since Dolores Park. Dad's laptop is on the table, and I shamelessly open it. After I punch in his password, I lower into the seat and sort through the tabs on his web browser. Nothing.

Then I load his e-mail and find an alert from some housing website—ten new listings in Surprise, Arizona.

Boxy little houses on dry lots. In plain subdivisions. Ordinary. Depressing. Ugly.

The exact opposite of this city.

I was right. Dad isn't fighting for Bigmouth's. He's looking at houses. In goddamn Surprise, Arizona. What kind of town name is that? Is it like, *Surprise, you live in the hottest, ugliest place in America*?

With a groan, I crumple forward onto the kitchen table.

I harbored a secret belief that Dad was also trying to solve our rent issue. Or that he had hope. At the very least, that he had a *plan*. But it's clear he doesn't even have that. I swallow hard, my throat itchy and tight.

"Whatcha doin'?"

I jump up from the kitchen table and find my aunt loitering in the doorway.

There's a chance she hasn't noticed, so I close Dad's laptop. "Nothing."

Aunt Fee purses her lips. "Doesn't look like nothing. Something wrong with your computer?"

"No," I say slowly. "I was . . ."

My aunt walks into the kitchen and hoists herself onto the counter. She's wearing a chunky knit fisherman's sweater and leggings. "Why were you grilling your dad about Bigmouth's?"

"You overheard that, did you?"

"What's been going on with you? Is it the boy?"

I snort. "What boy?"

Aunt Fiona grins. "The one with the hair?"

"Beckett's not the reason for anything. Ever," I say defensively.

She balances on the counter, her wet hair coiled into a bun on the top of her head. "You're an awful liar."

A flush seeps over my skin. "No, I'm not."

"Whatever it is, you can talk to me."

"About?" I sink back into the kitchen chair.

"About whatever you've been up to. Because you're up to something. An aunt is never wrong."

"That's not a saying." After a pause, I add, "My dad really hasn't said anything about Bigmouth's?"

Aunt Fee tilts her head in contemplation. "We rarely talk about it, but business isn't great. But what's new? I'm sure your dad would tell me if things took a turn for the worse."

Took a turn for the worse. A hospital patient knocking on death's door.

"Why're you suddenly concerned?"

"We lose Bigmouth's, we lose everything. We lose this house."

"Yeah, probably, but it's just a house," Aunt Fiona says with a sigh. "Wilsons are tough, kid. We'll make it."

Should I tell her about the housing listings? No. Aunt Fiona seems perfectly fine with the possibility of losing this house. She's not going to see what a shitty, dire situation I'm in. She's an adult—she has options. Her future isn't shackled to my dad's like mine.

My phone buzzes in my pocket, and I slide it out enough to read the text from Beckett.

"The boy?" Aunt Fee teases.

I shove my phone away and study the blister on my thumb, face aflame. "It's nothing."

"I'm glad you guys are hanging out again."

"It's not like that," I say, even though I just spent an hour in Dolores Park holding his hand, struggling to come up with logical reasons why I *shouldn't* kiss him.

My aunt hops off the counter. "Sure it isn't."

I roll my eyes, then leave the kitchen. I slip out my phone and read the message. Beckett only wants to talk about hustling. And it makes my heart sink.

BECKETT PORTER: Tomorrow's game is at a place called Four Horsemen Lanes in Alameda. 10pm. Big stakes. $300 buy-in. You down?

"Are you going out tonight?" Aunt Fiona asks, following me upstairs, and I hope she wasn't snooping over my shoulder.

"Not tonight. Tomorrow."

We're on the second-floor landing, and my aunt grabs my hand. "Please tell me what you're up to," she begs.

"I'm not up to anything!"

Lowering her voice, she asks, "You guys are being careful? If you need me to take you to Planned Parenthood—"

"Ugh, *God* no." I recoil and pull out of her grip, covering my reddened cheeks with my hands. Because now I'm thinking of the situations that would lead to me needing to go to Planned Parenthood. Super unhelpful when I'm trying to rein in any non-platonic thoughts toward Beckett. "We aren't dating. We're—"

"You're what?"

Beckett and I didn't talk about what happened. He hugged me before dropping me off, and now we're back to normal, texting about hustling. Whatever happened at Dolores Park is inconsequential. It was a blip, a mistake. Right?

I can't tell Aunt Fee what we're really up to. She's cool, but she's not *that* cool.

Swallowing the sticky, cotton-dry spit in my mouth, I lie. "The thing with Beckett . . . I like him. But it's all new and kind of precarious. I don't want to jinx it." As the words leave my lips, I know they're not a lie, as much as I want them to be. I like Beckett. Again. The feelings never truly went away. Sneaky bastards, feelings.

Aunt Fee can't control her chill to save her life. She nearly squeals in excitement. "Oh my God! I knew it! I always thought he had a crush on you, back in the day."

Yeah right. I shake my head. "What? No, he didn't."

"You sure?" She quirks a brow. "Whatever. Ah, I'm so excited for you!"

Fiona's totally off. Who knows what's going on between us, but back then? My crush was wholly unrequited. I have the angsty journal entries to prove it.

"Are you so excited you might cover for me tomorrow night?" I ask, grinning because my aunt's happiness is contagious. "I don't want Dad to know until I figure . . . everything out."

"What do you need?"

Tonight marks the first time in my young life that I'm happy my aunt is a hopeless romantic.

We put together a simple plan for my dad in case he gets curious. Aunt Fiona and I are going to a late movie. When she gets home, Dad should be asleep. If he isn't, Aunt Fee will cover for me and say I went to bed. My dad trusts his sister—why wouldn't he?—and I'm thankful she's willing to lie for me.

As we part ways, Aunt Fee pulls me into a hug. "The offer still stands."

"What?"

"Planned Parenthood. I know I'm not your mom, but I'm here if you need anything, okay?" She pulls back, both hands on my shoulders, a smile on her face.

"I'll, uh—thanks," I say haltingly, my cheeks flushing. Because that's apparently my go-to reaction whenever I think about Beckett and *anything* related to sex. Awesome, I'm twelve years old.

Up in my room, I stress clean the small piles of mess littered across the floor. Then I rearrange the bolts and scraps of fabric, fold clothes, and even brush the way-too-furry Jean Paul Gaultier.

My room is spotless, and I'm restless, so I settle in front of my laptop and open my iMessage app. A three-hundred-dollar game makes me sweat. Beckett's giving me the option to say no, but that'd be a huge haul. Or a big loss. From my last tally, we have over a thousand dollars. We've doubled our seed money. Impressive, but not enough.

> ME: Count me in. I have a cover for tomorrow night. I'm working until 6, but meet me at the Alameda Cinema Grill around 9. Long story, but we'll be good.
>
> BECKETT PORTER: Awesome. Remember to bring that kickass left hook and your finest trash talk. 🎳

A door creaks shut downstairs, a loud snap through this ancient house. Aunt Fiona busying herself with work, no doubt. Dragging her laptop to her work space in the garage, getting lost in words. While I appreciate our talk in the hallway, she was right—she's not my mom. She's great, *so great*, but she can't fill the jagged hole Mom left behind in the lining of my heart.

No one can. And it's such a lost feeling.

A feeling I'm far too familiar with.

The only days when I really miss my mom are on Mother's Day and the big family holidays. It's hard missing something you never really had to begin with. But every once in a while, I'll get this flash of longing. Not for who my mom was, but the person she could've become. For me. The role she could've had in my life. Right now I wish I had her beside me.

I cup my hands behind my neck, mind swirling. Curiosity gnaws at me, and I open my untouched Facebook account. Scrolling through Dad's profile makes me cringe— parents and social media are an awkward mix—but I find one person named Leigh on his friends list.

Leigh Sasaki works at Lotus Yoga, rarely posts on her Facebook, but her profile links to a blog. Snooping into Yoga Leigh's world isn't my finest moment, but who is she? The blog loads. Posts of health-conscious gluten-free recipes. A linked Instagram account, which is private. I scroll through her archived posts. More or less the same. Recipes. Posts on places she's traveled to—India, France, and Amsterdam to name a few.

One post catches my eye. From three years ago, titled "The Last Piece of the Puzzle." Leigh writes about putting her life back together after her divorce and how finally getting a correct diagnosis helped her immensely. Major depressive disorder. My hand stills on my mouse, the cursor hovering over the words.

For many, my mom included, a big facet of bipolar is depression. Leigh's diagnosis is close enough to hollow me out. After all, depression was my mom's downfall. Leigh is so candid on her blog. Coming from a family that adamantly ignored talking about mental health for the first fifteen years of my life, it's strange reading about someone's experiences so casually. Someone who, unlike my mom, is still around. Someone who survived.

Yoga Leigh's blog is public, but I can't help feeling like I've been snooping, reading words not meant for my eyes. The thing is, I know people with mental illness can be functional, happy members of society, but it's a hard concept to grasp when the only example I have is my mom. Why don't more people open up like Leigh? People talk so freely about issues with their physical health, so what's different about mental health?

Is everyone else as afraid as I am? Of being judged? Of losing control? Of failing at life?

I bookmark the blog post before shutting my laptop.

My head is full of noise, thoughts, questions. To quiet my mind, I grab the crumpled caftan from last night out of my hamper and spot clean the bloodstain in the bathroom sink using salt and cold water. Once the fabric has dried, I grab my sewing kit, settle among the various throw pillows on the floor, and begin mending the caftan. I lose myself in making perfect tiny stitches, one after another, centimeter by centimeter.

Until the damage is erased.

WEDNESDAY, APRIL 25

DAYS UNTIL BIGMOUTH'S EVICTION: 5

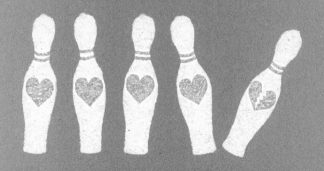

Sixteen

ALAMEDA IS A small island lodged in the San Francisco Bay between the city and Oakland, a short jaunt over the Bay Bridge. The next night, Aunt Fiona drops me off at the Cinema Grill—our proposed cover story.

"Have fun," Aunt Fee says, unlocking the door. "But not too much fun."

I fidget and try smiling, but it's tentative. My nerves buzz and rebound. "Thanks, Fee."

"If Beckett can't drop you off, call me, okay? And text me when he drops you off."

I palm my thermos of coffee and nod.

My aunt winks.

Beckett's car pulls alongside the curb opposite us, in front of the theater. I side-hug Fiona, inhaling her scent of perfume and marijuana. Then I hurry out of Aunt Fee's Bug and duck into Beckett's car.

The Accord is warm and welcoming.

"Hug me," I demand, because Aunt Fiona is definitely watching this.

Beckett doesn't even hesitate, his hands sliding around my waist, and I throw my arms around his neck. My face rests in the slope of his neck, and his fingers brush the exposed skin from my dress's open back. I press my eyes shut, allowing myself to enjoy the facade. Just for a moment.

When we part, I clear my throat, busying myself with clipping the seat belt. "Sorry about that. My aunt thinks we're, like, dating now, and she was probably spying on us."

"Oh!" Beckett watches Aunt Fee's Bug pull into traffic. "Um, why does she think that?"

"I had to come up with a better cover story."

"And was this your idea or . . . ?"

"Fiona assumed," I say. "So far it's working great. She didn't even ask me where we're going. I used your advice. Kept it simple when I lied."

Beckett shifts the car out of park and smiles. "Let me know if you want me to come over for a family dinner to help sell the deception."

"Yeah, not happening. I asked Fiona not to tell my dad. He'd be way too happy about it."

Beckett says nothing, just sways his head side to side like I amuse him.

We drive to the Four Horsemen and cram the Accord into a small parking lot. I skip the disguise because we'll have to leave our phones by the door. Still, the usual prep ensues—me smudging my makeup and the unholy baptism of airplane-bottle whiskey. When we're done, twenty minutes remain until the game begins.

After we lock up the Accord and cross the street, I take in the bowling alley. The multistoried building hulks, intimidating. A neon art graphic displays four horse heads and nothing else. Not even a name, only the daunting stallions. We've come a long way since the seediness of the Road.

"Now," Beckett says, critical eyes assessing the alley, "the Four Horsemen is notorious for gambling. More intense than the Dust Bowl, but less dodgy. Tonight will be more of a straight-up game with subtle hustling. As long as you keep it together and follow the usual pattern, tonight should be no different from the others."

I nod stiffly, but the tension melts when Beckett catches his hand over mine.

Is this part of the act, or is this real?

Shaking my head, I dislodge my desires.

The first floor of the building is a trendy bar and restaurant, but we follow the neon arrows pointing us downstairs to the bowling alley.

A bouncer at the door stops us and holds up one large palm. "Private game tonight," he says, taking in our age.

"I'm friends with Nic," Beckett says, jaw set and all confidence.

The bouncer huffs and opens the door wide enough for us to slip inside.

"Wow."

Beckett was right about this place being better known for its illegal activities. The lanes are sleek and dark, crowded by groups of two or four. No music, only fervent whispers. There's a card table near the entrance with another bouncer wearing black. The only items on the table are a lockbox, a pile of poker chips, and an off-white mail bin.

Yeah, this place is something else.

"We pay up front," Beckett whispers.

I take out the money clip and count three hundred dollars, handing it to the glowering man on the other side of the table. In exchange, he slides a single poker chip across the table.

"Phones," the man barks, and we surrender our devices. He drops them into the mail bin.

Beckett presses the chip into my palm. "The chip ensures you're a player *and* represents your buy-in. So don't lose it. As far as game play, the setup is different."

"How so?" I trace the embossed number twelve with my thumb.

"Players challenge one another. It makes things more interesting. You can play—accept or challenge—as many opponents as you'd like. Not that I'd recommend playing every person here. Let's see." He counts the players under his breath, and I do the same. Nine others linger among the lanes.

"Why can't I play them all, if they accept my challenge? We'd net over two thousand dollars."

Beckett glances at me. "Doesn't work that way. Once

you're out, you're out. You give your chip to the winner. And you can only challenge someone for as many chips as you have. Make sense?"

I tuck the chip into the small pocket I sewed into my dress. "Why is it so complicated?"

"Because it's a lot of money and people get shitty around that much cash. Rules keep people in line. If you can pull in anything over a grand, that would be killer."

No pressure or anything. "Okay. Don't lose the chip. Beat the players. Take all their money. Easy."

He laughs, and it unleashes a flush starting at my neck that warms my face.

We settle at lane twelve, and Beckett chats up my future opponents. One guy stands out. He's tall, in his late twenties, with a look I can only describe as "meth mod"—skinny as hell, leathery tan skin, dressed in blue silk, a yellow tie, and slim-fitting high-water gray pants. An eye-catching ensemble, but the guy is shinier than the synthetic oil on the lanes.

The guy straddles the gutters and in a booming voice announces the rules, a lengthier version of what Beckett told me.

"That's Nic." Beckett slides into the seat beside me. "I met him betting; he tipped me off about Wilkes and my dad."

Nic announces, "Players! You have fifteen minutes to warm up, challenge an opponent, and play. Anybody got questions?"

No one speaks up. They respect Nic's authority.

"Holy shit, look." I nudge Beckett to the men closest to

us. They're snorting cocaine, and the fine white powder dusts their facial hair. Sticks to their fingers. White motes dance in the air.

My skin erupts in goose bumps. Or hives. It's too dark to tell. But I know one thing for certain. I am so exquisitely out of my league. No bowling pun intended.

"Ignore them," Beckett says, dropping his voice to just above a whisper. "You okay?"

I press my palm to my fluttering stomach. "Aces."

After showing off my faux drunken stupor, I shoot a few shitty frames during the allotted practice time. The atmosphere differs from the other games; these are *serious* players. They're doing coke and who knows what else, shooting strikes, and fingering those poker chips, analyzing the competition with sharp, greedy eyes.

Won't they be able to see through my charade? And what will happen if they do? These men will not take kindly to being bested by me.

While I'm practicing, the bouncer holds up someone's phone. "Whose is this?" he calls, clearly annoyed. "Been ringing for the last few minutes."

"Shit." Beckett jumps up. "That's mine."

The bouncer hands him the phone. "Go outside, answer it, and then put it on silent. Got it?"

"Sure thing." To me, he says, "I'll be right back."

I throw a few more shots as I wait for Beckett.

He's only gone a minute, and when he returns, I ask, "Who was it?"

Beckett presses his lips together, then takes a deep breath. "My mom let me off Willa Watch, but Eugenia—the woman she takes care of—needs her tonight. I'm so sorry."

"Uh, for what?"

He hangs his head back for a second and sighs. "She wants me to come home to watch Willa. I have to go home."

"Wait, what?" I ask, confused. "You're leaving?"

"I wish I could stay." And the pain on Beckett's face shows how much. He checks the time—five minutes until the game begins. "Walk me to my car?"

I grab my purse, and Beckett takes his bowling bag. We hurry up the stairs and through the crowded bar.

"Chuck, I'm so sorry," Beckett says once we're on street level.

Even though my stomach dips at the thought of being down there alone, all by myself, I think I've got this under control. "It's okay. I'll be okay."

"Are you sure? My mom—" He cuts off with an annoyed sigh when we reach the Accord. At this situation, at his life, I'm not sure. "She can't turn down a night's pay."

"Trust me, I understand." We're both leaning against the Accord's bumper, and I nudge his shoulder with mine. "Don't worry about me."

Beckett exhales, his annoyance fading into a smile. "Yeah, I know. You've got this." He pushes away from the bumper and stands in front of me, placing either hand on my shoulders. Then his hands slide to my forearms, fingers gliding over my goose bumps, erasing them with a single touch. "You don't need me to be great."

"Oh, I'm well aware," I say, alarmed at how nice his touch feels. "I'm pretty great on my own."

"Yes, yes you are." Beckett steps even closer and cups my face with his palm. "But just so you know, I won't ditch you again. Promise."

"It's okay." I find myself tilting my cheek into his hand. "You should get going." My voice lacks any conviction. There's not as much space between our bodies as I once thought, my knee between his legs. The way his gaze settles on my lips sets my nerves on fire.

I can't stop looking at those lips. Maybe I'm sleep deprived? Yeah, *that's* the reason I'm woozy and warm. I force my gaze north. To those gunmetal-gray eyes.

What the hell happened? I liked it better when I resented Beckett Porter. That emotion was safe. What I'm feeling right now is dangerous. When we were friends, he never touched me like this. Every signal Beckett's thrown at me tonight makes me hope he has some dangerous feelings of his own. But I'm too damn scared to find out the truth. I need *more* from him.

"You're going to kick ass," he says roughly, breaking the moment. He traces my jaw with his thumb, the tips of his ears mottled red. "If I can get Willa to sleep, I'll try sneaking back out before the game's over. But if not, can Fiona pick you up?"

When I nod, it's more bobblehead than anything else. "Yeah."

Beckett squeezes my hand and steps to the Accord. Without the warmth of his body in front of mine, the air is cold. "Good luck," he says, and adds with a small grin, "Not like you need it."

The game starts in a minute. After debating whether to stay out here with a boy I'm aching to touch, I pivot on my heel and return to the Four Horsemen. I'm dizzy and drunk and sober as I hurry to my lane.

Nic strolls past the players in his fantastical getup. "Where's Beckett?" he asks.

"Family shit," I say, my heart a rapid, wild, untamed creature in my chest. "Everything okay?"

"Yeah, yeah." Nic shakes his head, unfazed yet frazzled. "Best of luck."

Most of the players know one another, and it takes a minute until someone wanders my way.

"Hey," a man calls. It's generous to assume he's in his sixties, arms wide and burly, inked with faded tattoos and weathered muscles. A curved handlebar mustache obscures his lips. He's clad in a stained tank top and baggy jeans, and I recognize him as one of the men snorting coke.

How are his hands so steady?

I manage a loose-lipped smile. "Hi."

"Down to play?" he calls, hocking a loogie into a cup. I must agree, because he returns a second later with his ball. "Rufus," the man introduces himself, and programs the game console.

I pop my knuckles. "Caroline."

Rufus adds my name to the roster, and from his body language, it's clear I'm not intimidating. Rufus thought this challenge would be an easy win. I love being under-estimated.

Rufus is good, but I'm better, and my score rises with each passing frame. In the tenth, I bag two strikes, push-ing me ahead. I squeal with delight and pretend to act astonished at my luck in case anyone is watching. Rufus snarls, but snaps his chip on the console and walks out of the Four Horsemen.

Our game ended earlier than the rest, and I casually observe the players while awaiting the next challenge. The usual lot. Either ancient with beer bellies, or sleek and sleazy. I flip Rufus's chip between my fingers before pocketing it. A few games end and the losers retreat to the back or storm out in anger.

The man playing on lane one catches and holds my attention. He's my dad's age, midforties, and his shoes make him stand out. The man is bowling with cowboy boots on. Not authentic horseshit-clad boots. These are expensive Italian leather, polished to reflect the lights shining on us. Cowboy Boots's jeans are pressed, crease-free. His shirt is a button-down with perfect cuffs, and his dark hair is gelled. An ascot is tied like a colorful noose around his neck. When he turns from the lane, I gag at the chest hair escaping the low-buttoned shirt.

Cowboy Boots appraises me with a critical eye.

I return to lane twelve on unsteady feet. The men around here don't notice me until I'm wiping the lanes with them. That Cowboy Boots noticed me makes all the hairs on my arm stand on end.

Players are challenging one another again, but no one's approached me yet. Will I have to make the challenge? I eye the remaining players. The closest man is finishing up a game.

"Hey." I wave my hand in the air. "Wanna play?"

My confidence wavers, but I can't leave yet. I'm relieved when the guy laughs and agrees. He doesn't bother telling me his name, but he's on lane eleven.

"Only one chip," he says, and the game is on.

Lane Eleven isn't worried about me even though I won against my first opponent, and we get playing. Between frames I try not to think about what almost happened outside. Definitely *not* friend or friend-adjacent behavior. As for my feelings? They careened off the "just friends" cliff in Dolores Park.

Cowboy Boots clacks over in those impractical shoes and watches as I finish off Lane Eleven, winning by twenty pins. As I collect Lane Eleven's chip, I assess the crowd. I need to get out of here soon. But I'm stalling, hoping Beckett will return.

Cowboy Boots saunters down the alley, and his scrutinizing gaze churns the bile in my stomach. What if *he* challenges *me*? Am I allowed to turn a game down?

"Hey," he calls out. "That was one hell of a game."

I flex my hands over the air vent on the ball return, trying to slick away the sweat. "I know."

Cowboy Boots laughs, perching on a seat by my lane. "You're Caroline, right?"

My body is full of buzzy energy, but I keep calm. I

swallow the hardened lump in my throat and meet his gaze. "Do I know you?" I ask, even though we've certainly never met.

"I'm Ray," he says, smiling charismatically. "My friend says you've been looking for some action."

"Isn't that why we're all here?"

He laughs, scrubbing his chin with his palm. "Fair point. Say, if you're interested, I'm looking for someone to play in the Bay Area Bowling League this Saturday."

I squint in confusion. "Okay?"

Hopping to his feet, Ray reaches into his pocket and pulls out a piece of paper. "I was watching you play, and you surprised me. You're good. I've seen it all. You put on a helluva act. Real convincing. Real *profitable*."

My stomach clenches. Does he know I'm hustling? If so, he's not too torn up morally. I take the flyer. "Thanks. I'll think about it." Yeah, not happening.

"Grand prize is twenty-five," says Ray. "Five hundred buy-in. It's a closed game, so I ask for a small cut of five grand for working out the logistics. My number's there, on the back. You hit me up if you're interested, okay?"

Wait. *Twenty-five thousand dollars?* For one game of bowling? No matter how tempting his offer is, Beckett's in charge of choosing our games. I fold the flyer in half, my fingers worrying across the crease. Someone hollers down the lanes, and Ray tilts his head.

"Good luck," he adds before strolling away.

As mysteriously as Ray and his cowboy boots appeared, he's gone.

I unfold the flyer and stare at that grand prize money. All those zeros. The flyer explains that the pricey game is a yearly tournament held for players willing to put up the buy-in. Why did Ray think I'd be anywhere near competent enough to play with these people? I mean, I'm good and all, but that's with the advantage of being underestimated. Of lying. But if I were good enough? I could guarantee Bigmouth's rent for *months* with that prize money.

I stuff the flyer into my purse as another player walks up and challenges me to play two chips. I drive my interaction with Ray from my mind and focus. This'll be my last game. After we begin, it's clear this guy's game is razor sharp. I struggle to keep up. Finessing my game, I bowl hard.

The tenth frame is my final hope. I ready myself and shoot. A split. I inhale a cleansing breath and go for the spare. All the oxygen whooshes out of my lungs as the pins firecracker apart, slamming into the gutter and back wall.

"Damn," someone says appraisingly from the crowd.

I don't turn around and instead take full advantage of the bonus frame. I put spin on the ball, and it glides beautifully down the lane, fast and slick, colliding with the headpin, a satisfying *crack*.

My eyes flash to the scoreboard. I won. By two pins.

"Hell yes," I shout, and jump off the platform.

Someone puts their hands on me, and I jerk away. "Hey, watch it—"

"Chuck!"

Beckett. I launch myself at him and wrap my arms

around him, breath labored like I ran a marathon. "You did good," he whispers into my hair, breath hot against my ear. "I caught the last frame."

The loser angrily drops two chips onto the center console, and Beckett lets me go to hand over my prize. "How'd you do?"

If I count my buy-in chip, I have five.

Beckett's face cracks with a grin as he sees the chips in my cupped palms. "Whoa, nice."

"Let's cash these in." I want to jump around and celebrate, but I keep a neutral expression as I bring my chips to the bouncer. "How's Willa? You slip her some Benadryl so you could sneak out?"

"Very funny. She sleeps like the dead, but I feel shitty for leaving her home alone."

"We'll hurry," I promise, tapping my foot as the bouncer cashes out the chips.

"Guess you didn't really need me here," he says, nodding to the money the bouncer shuffles into an envelope.

When I laugh, it's low and desperate. "Maybe not, but it's better when you're here."

"Oh, *really*?" Beckett's grin is cocky as hell.

I shove his shoulder and take the envelope from the bouncer—along with my phone—and count the contents. One thousand two hundred net. Holy shit.

We hurry upstairs and out onto the street. Now free from the scrutiny of the men downstairs, Beckett lets out a wild whoop and wraps me in a crushing hug underneath the flickering neon sign. The envelope of cash is pressed between us. I inhale the fresh air tainted by the muck of the Four Horsemen and a nearby dumpster, head dizzy.

"We can do this." Beckett's voice is filled with untouchable hope.

I lean back, all too aware of how our bodies align—chests, hip bones, kneecaps. "Did you doubt me beforehand?"

He shrugs affably. "We both knew this was a gamble. Now it's a gamble with a profit."

I waggle the fat envelope. "Hell yeah it's profitable."

"The power's going to your head," he jokes, his hand lingering on the divot of my waist.

"Hey, you created this monster." I point to my chest with the envelope. "Now you're responsible for me." He's right, the glory—and money—might be going to my head. I'm unsteady with too many emotions and too much power. I fold the envelope and tuck it into my purse.

"I'm okay with that." Beckett smiles sheepishly.

I'm acutely aware of how close we are. It'd be so easy—just lean in and finally figure out what Beckett tastes like. Probably like cinnamon. A crowd of bowlers exit the bar, eyeing us as they light their cigarettes, but I'm so focused on Beckett that I don't care. I'm still afraid, so afraid, but I'm equally impatient.

I lift onto my toes and slide my fingers through his curls. He lifts a brow, eyes crinkled in confusion. I rest my palm on the nape of his neck, draw him closer. And

I do what I wanted to do—what I thought we were going to do—out by the Accord before the game. I lean in to kiss him. But before our lips meet, Beckett grips my wrist, halting me in my tracks.

"What're you doing?" There's a thickness to his voice.

"I'm—" My breath catches. Face burning, I scramble for an excuse. Something, *anything*, to make this less humiliating. "I'm selling the act. They're all watching."

For the briefest of moments, his hold on my wrist loosens, and his head ducks closer, igniting me with hope.

Until he says, "Sorry," and drops his hands from my waist. "I can't."

Embarrassment burns through my veins. My eyes prick with tears and I start toward the car.

"Chuck!" Beckett jogs to catch up with me. "I'm sorry, but—"

I nearly trip over a curb, but I don't slow down. "You know what? It was a bad idea. Just forget it."

Stopped in front of the car now, Beckett rolls his shoulders forward, like he's fighting his own emotions. I don't dare feel sorry for him. Because I'm too busy being crushed, deep into the earth, from his rejection.

Once we're in the Accord, I turn on the radio to drown out any awkward silence.

Beckett cranks the heat, turns down the radio, and steers us toward the Bay Bridge. The Bay Lights ripple and wink against the night. "About what happened—"

"Please? Can we not talk about that right now?" I say, my voice a pathetic whisper.

"Okay." His jaw is set, eyes focused on the road, but he turns up the radio.

The thirty-minute car ride is peak awkwardness, and I fold into myself. Dying to get away from him and what I just did.

Beckett barely pulls to a stop at the base of my street, and I throw open the door. Before I can dash out of the car, he grabs my forearm. "Wait. Please?"

I need to get out of this car. More important, I need to get far, far away from him. But the soft, desperate tone of his voice stalls me. "What? I'm fine. It was an act, okay? I'm only upset because . . . our cover was probably blown."

One by one, his fingers unfurl from around my arm. "Right. The cover." Beckett studies my face, but I don't betray any hint of emotion. "I just don't want you thinking that I don't care about you. We've been friends . . ."

My hearing goes fuzzy after that. Because there it is. The reason why he doesn't want to kiss me. Why he *never* wanted to kiss me. I'm his friend. That's it—just a friend. Last year I always worried, always wondered, if that's how he saw me.

Now I have my answer. Was his recent behavior really that different? Or have I just gone too long without any real-life contact outside of my dad and Fiona to know what's normal and what's not? Without saying goodbye, I climb out of the car and shut the door behind me.

I run up the hill to the yellow house, my body full of conflicted and confusing feelings. I'm nauseated with the embarrassment of it all. For once, I put myself out there, and look where it got me. The crushing blow is all too familiar to what I felt last year.

Aunt Fiona's at the kitchen table when I walk inside.

"Whoa," she says, taking in my wild-eyed appearance, her spoon dripping milk into the cereal bowl. "Are you okay?"

"Boys are assholes." The anger comes more naturally than the bruised hurt spreading throughout my body.

My aunt laughs. "Have truer words ever been spoken? C'mere."

All I want to do is scream into a pillow, but I join Aunt Fee in the kitchen. She pours me a bowl of cereal, covers me in a chenille blanket from the couch. "Spill. What happened?"

"I messed up," I whisper into my cereal bowl. "This stuff with Beckett is . . . really confusing."

Settled across from me, Fee asks, "You wanna talk about it?"

Luckily, I avoided going into detail about our fake relationship earlier. Now I edit out anything incriminating about our hustling, using a party cover story, and give her some background before venting. "I'm so socially incompetent; I totally misread his signals."

"Maybe not! Let me get this straight. You're at this party," Aunt Fiona says, and my mind is so jumbled I almost correct her, "and you tried kissing him?"

Setting the bowl aside, I drop my forehead to the table. "Yes. It was humiliating! It was impulsive, but I did it anyway." That would make an excellent title for my future memoir. *Chuck Wilson: It Was Impulsive, but I Did It Anyway.*

"You're so dramatic. Sit up," Fiona demands. I comply, but pout at her. "Okay, were you guys alone?"

I shake my head. "No. There were a lot of people around. Kind of watching?"

Steepling her fingers beneath her chin like an armchair therapist, she asks, "Did you ever think he didn't want a bunch of strangers watching you kiss?"

"Beckett wouldn't care." He's blissfully unaware and doesn't care what other people think about him. He's always been my exact opposite in that regard.

"How do you know? Did he say he didn't want to kiss you?"

"I mean, not in those *exact* words." Staring at the milk in the cereal bowl, at the faded marshmallows, I sigh. "When he dropped me off, he told me he cared about me. As a friend."

"Chuck, look at me."

I lift my chin and look my aunt in the eye. Her braid is frizzing, draped over one shoulder, and her green eyes are kind. "What?"

"You're awesome, okay? I might be biased because you're my niece and I love you, but you are certifiably awesome. If Beckett doesn't have feelings for you, it's his loss. But do you want to lose him as a friend—again— over this?"

I worry my bottom lip between my teeth. "No."

"Then talk to him. As a species, boys are dense.

Teenage boys are even denser. Try telling him how this made you feel. You won't be able to move forward—with friendship or otherwise—if you ignore what happened." Aunt Fee shrugs. "That's my take. Feel free to ignore it."

"Thank you." After dumping my cereal in the sink, I hug my aunt, resting my chin on her shoulder.

Sure, sometimes Aunt Fee gets it wrong (the tampon incident still haunts me to this day), but she helps more than she knows. Fiona put her life on hold for us. For me. In moments like these, when she talks me down, I wonder how I'll ever be able to repay her.

"I love you, Fee."

"Love you too, kid," she says, and hugs me even tighter.

Upstairs in my bedroom, I curl up on my bed beside Jean Paul and let myself cry. Aunt Fiona helped calm me down and see the situation more clearly, but I'm still overflowing with emotions. There's no worse feeling than offering up all the insecure parts of yourself, only to be rejected.

Lying there, I replay the moment over and over again. Fresh and more painful each time I mentally roll back the night. I can't always give in to my impulses, no matter how persuasive they seem in the moment. And trust me, they were pretty damn persuasive. Intoxicating, almost. Thinking before speaking or acting has never been my forte.

Nothing's changed, and I can't believe I thought otherwise.

Why did I think Beckett would ever want me?

I'm unkissable. I've never kissed anyone before! I don't

know what I was thinking, putting myself out there. I didn't think he'd turn me down. I really didn't think—at all. You want to know how many attractive and redeeming qualities I have? Zero. I talk too loud and too fast. My brain is several layers of fucked up and complicated. Not to mention my frizzy hair, and I'm short—and not in a cute and delicate way.

Beckett can do way better than me.

My old therapist, Sarah, used to call this negative self-talk.

Fine by me.

I deserve every ugly word.

THURSDAY, APRIL 26

DAYS UNTIL BIGMOUTH'S
EVICTION: 4

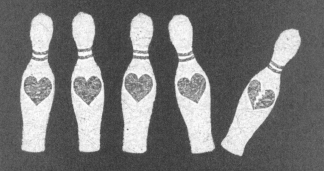

Seventeen

I HAVE AN emotional hangover.

Stuck between hating myself and hating Beckett, I'm entirely unpleasant to be around. Dad commented several times about my grouchiness before he left to have lunch with Yoga Leigh. I told him I was on my period and that was the end of that. No more questions asked. Now he and the yogi are at Greens Restaurant, a fancy vegetarian place across town. Things seem serious between them, and it leaves me equally nervous and nauseated. My blog snooping the other night humanized Leigh, but that doesn't mean I'm okay with the situation.

Beckett's texted several times, but I don't open my messaging app. I'm not ready yet, not prepared to relive last night in writing.

Slouched against the counter, I scroll through Instagram with one hand, the other propping up my chin.

The bell above the door jangles, but I'm in the middle

of reading one of Mila's most recent posts on her personal Instagram. I know social media is all about algorithms and manipulating your brain chemistry to rely on likes and upvotes, but man, that doesn't stop it from making me feel like crap. Mila's life is literally picture perfect.

Footsteps echo throughout the entry, but Dad's not around, and no longer caring about appearing unprofessional, I keep my eyes glued to my phone. No one is here bowling, and whoever walked in probably just wants to use our bathroom or something.

When the person clears their throat, my gaze flits up. Beckett. For some reason, my heart lifts in happiness over seeing him again. Must be muscle memory, because I'm not happy. No, I'm conflicted. Extremely and emotionally conflicted. But I force a frown and say, "What're you doing here?"

Beckett strolls up to the register. "Hey . . ." His backpack is slung over one shoulder, and he's carrying a plastic bag from CVS. "Um, are you due for a break?"

"Nope." I return my attention to my Instagram feed, tapping a random photo twice to like it. I'm acting petulant and immature, but I don't have the energy to deal with him right now. We're friends, which is great, and I wholly intend on trying to maintain our friendship. But last night was one of the most embarrassing moments of my life. Ideally, I want to ignore any unnecessary one-on-one time until our hustles are over. Then, when I know if I'll be staying in the city, I'll figure out how to save our friendship.

Turns out Beckett has other plans.

In my peripheral vision, I see him lean against the counter. Closer to me. The air smells of his deodorant and the rain clinging to his jacket.

"Okay," he says, drawing out the word. "Is there any chance you can help me with something?"

"Beckett," I say with a sigh. "I'm working."

"There's no one here." He spreads his arms out to encompass the empty alley. "Besides, I can't dye my hair on my own. I mean, I could, but it'd probably end poorly. I know how much you like my hair, so yeah, I figured—"

I squint at him, and my iciness slips. "Wait, what're you prattling on about?"

Beckett grabs something from the CVS bag and sets it on the counter. A box of hair dye. *Blue* hair dye. "We should work on my disguise for tonight's game."

"You want me to dye your hair?"

"Yup."

Glancing between the box of semipermanent hair dye and Beckett's confusingly hopeful face, I nod. "Fine." I pocket my phone, snatch the box of hair dye off the counter, and lead Beckett to the handicapped bathroom down the hall from Dad's office.

Beckett trails me, and I push open the door. The single stall is small, barely large enough for two people, but it has its own counter and sink. He slips inside and dumps the CVS bag on the counter. A pack of alligator clips tumbles out, along with a cheap travel blow-dryer.

We're quiet as we set up. Beckett fetches the stool from

225

behind the register and gets situated while I study the box of hair dye. I've never dyed someone's hair before. Doesn't seem too complicated. And if I end up burning Beckett's scalp? Oh well.

The tiniest bit of guilt slithers into my chest as I prep the "Blue Jeans" hair dye. Beckett's not to blame for not kissing me. I'd probably be *more* upset if he kissed me but didn't have feelings for me. At least this way, we're kind of honest with each other. We can move past this. Eventually. When I'm not as upset. That day is not today, however.

After sectioning off his hair with the alligator clips, I snap on the rubber gloves that came with the hair dye and dip my fingers into the plastic bowl of dark-blue cream. "Okay, here goes nothing," I mutter, smearing the dye into Beckett's curls. He shifts as I massage the dye closer to his scalp, trying to get his roots. The heat of his body, the weight of his head, stirs up the desperate yearning I've failed to bury. His eyes are closed—totally surrendered to me—and I'm embarrassed by how much I still want him.

Every breath, every movement, is louder than gunfire.

I should've put on music.

After a few agonizing minutes, Beckett clears his throat and asks, "How's it going?"

"Good," I say, grimacing at my squeaky, nervous voice. After I check to make sure the section is fully covered, I unclip the next. I squirt out more dye from the tube and a small drop lands on the counter. Shit. I might need to bleach the counter before Dad gets back.

The hair dye smells like blueberries, and under any other circumstance, this might be kind of fun. And in another world? Almost romantic. Lightning cracks outside. The small window in the bathroom is rectangular, high up on the wall. Temperamental rain patters against the pane.

As I work my way through his hair, I'm glad there isn't a mirror in the bathroom—Beckett can't see my pained facial expression if he were to open his eyes. I like him, which is the *worst idea ever*. What's even the point of crushes? More important, how can I make it go away?

"Ouch. You're pulling kind of hard," Beckett says in alarm. "On my hair?"

"Oh, sorry." That was actually an accident. I grimace and try to be more careful. After unclipping the third and final section of hair and coating the curls in hair dye, the job is done. I strip off the gloves, toss them in the bowl, and wash up. The dye needs to sit for another five minutes.

"Hey, so, I've been meaning to tell you something."

I dry my hands with a paper towel, standing behind Beckett so I don't have to look him in the face. "Okay?"

"I already saved up enough money for Willa's summer camp."

"What?" My heart aches. Does this mean he's done hustling? But why would I be dyeing his hair if he was quitting? "When?"

Beckett tugs at the elastic on his wrist. "Like three months ago; I sold some of my comics. But that's beside the point—"

"Wait, three months ago?" I interrupt. "Then why—"

"This was never about the money, Chuck." He moves to run his fingers through his hair but drops them before he covers his hands in blue dye. "All of this was for you. I just wanted to help *you*."

"Okay . . . but why'd you lie?" Suddenly nervous, I chew on the inside of my cheek.

"I figured being up front wouldn't go over well," he explains. "Not until we talked things out. So I lied."

My mouth tightens, and embarrassingly, my eyes burn. I wish I were infuriated by this—I hate being lied to. But I'm not mad. Beckett's right. I would've been even more hesitant if I'd known he wanted to do this only to help me. He really is a good friend and undoubtedly one of the best people I know. We'll never be more than just friends. And if that's all I can have, I'll take it.

"You really did all this because you missed me?"

"No, I did this because I was done missing you," Beckett says, and his voice cracks. "I gave you a year. I got that job at Schulman's because of you, Chuck. I needed a job, yeah, but I needed *you* more. I thought . . . if I worked for Schulman's, you'd see me every week and you'd realize you missed me, too."

"Oh." I lean my back against the counter because I don't trust my legs to hold me upright. "And the hustling?"

"Last week, after we overheard your dad and that landlord guy, you said you might have to leave San Francisco. I needed a way to make it right—make *us* right—and if I could do that while helping you stay in the city, then I had to try. I had my dad's notebook, my old betting contacts. . . ." Beckett trails off with a shrug, twisting in the seat to look at me. His eyes are shiny and hopeful.

The alarm on my phone goes off—the five minutes are up.

"Chuck?" he prompts, drawing his brows closer.

"I need to focus on your hair." Partially a lie, but I need time to collect my thoughts. Wrangle my emotions. I don't know what to make of his confession, but for now I instruct Beckett to lean over the sink. I turn on the tap, and he ducks beneath the stream of lukewarm water. I already ditched my gloves, so with bare hands I rinse the blue dye until the water runs clear. My cuticles gain a blue hue.

With a fistful of paper towels, I dry the excess water from his curls, and Beckett straightens. His wet hair is too dark to tell if the dye took. But he has this rumpled, apprehensive look about him that makes me light-headed. Then again, we're trapped in a small room with chemicals, so it's probably that.

"One second." I turn away to plug in the hair dryer and turn it on, blasting his hair and creating too much noise for us to talk.

"How's it look?" he asks once it's dry.

Beckett's hair is naturally brown, but now it's taken on a dusky denim wash. Each curl is inky blue, and under the fluorescent bathroom lights, it looks good. Kind of hot, actually. His eyes are bluer too.

My face warms, and I look away, handing him my phone. "Here, see for yourself."

Beckett uses the camera on my phone to check out his new look. "Oh God, I thought it would be subtle. I look like a homeless clown."

I crack a grin as my nerves from earlier pitter-patter. "Blue is a good look for you. I think you should keep it. Forever."

He tosses the phone back and runs his fingers through the blue curls. "Shut up, Wilson."

Beckett helps me clean up, bagging all the hair-dyeing tools.

"I might not act like it, but I appreciate all your help. I really do," I tell him as I wipe down the bathroom counter.

"Um, you're welcome? Are you . . . are you still good for tonight?" Beckett digs a beanie out of his backpack, leaning against the bathroom's doorframe.

"Why wouldn't I be?" I toss the paper towels into the trash and force a smile that doubles as a grimace.

With an annoyed sigh, he pulls the beanie on over his hair. "C'mon, are we really going to do this? Avoid talking about last night? Avoid talking about, well, everything?"

"Ideally, yes." I move to pass him out of the bathroom, but he shifts, blocking my exit.

Beckett crosses his arms, a surprisingly defensive move for him. "Well, I need to talk about it, okay?" When I don't reply, he says, "Outside the Four Horsemen—"

"You should've just kissed me." I'm trying for flippant—because apparently humor is my only defense mechanism.

Unsure whether he buys it, I add, "It's not like it's a big deal or anything."

"Maybe not for you," he mutters, scuffing the toe of his loafer against the linoleum.

"What?"

"Nothing. Just forget about it." Beckett steps out of the doorway. "I'll see you tonight, I guess," he says before disappearing down the hallway.

"No, what did you say?" I ask, following him into the lobby. When he doesn't reply, the tightness in my chest becomes unbearable. I reach out and grab his sleeve, my fingers brushing up against his wrist. *"Beck?"*

Maybe it's the nickname or my desperation, but he finally says, "I'm not like you, okay? It's harder for me to, um, platonically hang out with you. You got over your feelings. I didn't."

Wait a second—does Beckett like me? No. Wait. *What?*

Beckett's watching me so carefully and softly, waiting for my response.

"Uh . . ." My palms start sweating.

Beneath his breath, he says, "Fuck it," and palms the back of his neck. "I like you, okay? I've liked you for a while. There. I said it."

The silence of Bigmouth's Bowl becomes uproarious: the faint static from the jukebox; the rhythmic swoosh of the fan in the corner; the tick of the wall clock. Seconds slide by, my mind working in overdrive. But none of the words rebounding around seem *right*, and I have no idea what to say.

"Back at Lake Merritt, I almost told you," he continues, "but you were so adamant—one hundred percent sure—that your feelings were gone. But then you tried kissing me as part of our cover—"

"My feelings aren't gone," I blurt out, shoving my sweaty palms from sight. "But I didn't lie—I thought I was over you. I'm not. And it isn't easy for me, either. Hanging out with you platonically."

"Yeah?" His ears tinge red, barely visible from beneath the beanie. "We should try hanging out non-platonically sometime. To compare and contrast."

My smile is hesitant but hopeful, and my body's rocking full-on goose bumps. "What exactly is non-platonic hanging out?"

"A date," he answers quickly. "I'd really love it if you'd go on a date. With me. If that wasn't clear—"

"Yes." This time, I'm glad I spoke before I thought. I didn't have the time to second-guess myself.

Beckett's smile liquifies me. "How about tomorrow night?"

"Okay, yeah." I'm nodding and smiling, pleasantly confused. "Tomorrow."

Tonight we have a game, possibly our last, and tomorrow's Friday, the maybe-game with super-high stakes. But regardless of our bowling plans, we have a date. I've never even been on a proper date. Now I have one—with Beckett.

"What'd you have in mind?" I ask, resisting the urge to lean over and kiss him. It's truly unfair for someone to have that kissable of a mouth. Not that I'd know from experience, but his lips look *very* kissable.

"You'll have to wait and see." Beckett's smile is so sweet and genuine, it makes my chest flutter, palpitate. Wild blue strands sneak out from the fold of his beanie. The smile lights up his face as he backs down the hallway, nearly tripping on the linoleum. "Okay, I'm making myself leave now—I don't want to leave—because I have to pick Willa up from school. But I'll see you tonight?"

"I'll be the girl with the creepy mannequin head and wig."

Beckett bites his lower lip before fondly shaking his head and slipping outside.

"Did that really happen?" I ask out loud, my voice lofted in disbelief.

That. Really. Happened.

Unable to shake the grin on my face, I return to the handicapped bathroom to finish cleaning up. Standing there, inhaling bleach and hair dye, my smile fades. In the moment, I allowed myself to forget the only reason Beckett and I are back on speaking terms: saving Bigmouth's. We'll have our first date, but who knows if I'll be around long enough for us to have a second.

Eighteen

THE CLOCK JUST ticked over into midnight, and Beckett should be here soon.

As I wait for him to text, I grab the fattened money clip from its hiding spot in my bookshelf and weigh the heft of our winnings in my palm. Eventually, I'll have to tell my dad some version of the truth. Since Beckett and I have done pretty well the past few days, I stayed up last night and settled on a cover for where I got the money.

Dad's not exactly technologically savvy—he can use Facebook and that's about it—so I'm going to tell him I started a GoFundMe. There's no chance Dad'll turn away money that he thinks the community raised to save Bigmouth's. Maybe I'm getting ahead of myself. We don't even have the money yet. I'm worrying too much, and little stress hives bud to the surface of my skin.

Focus, Chuck.

I tuck the money clip into my bag with tonight's

peroxide-blond wig, grabbing a bobby pin for my bangs to keep them out of my eyes. These little motions of beauty prep remind me that tomorrow I'll be prepping for something much different.

A date with Beckett.

The date doesn't feel any more real than it did earlier today. The words are foreign. It still feels like an elaborate hoax. But the date's *real,* and I'm scared how happy that thought makes me. For once in our friendship, I'm trying not to box Beckett out. I want to find out what my feelings for him are capable of.

When I dip into my purse for my lipstick, I unearth a folded piece of paper fused to a melted piece of gum. It's not until I unfold it that I recognize the flyer from the Four Horsemen. The font is pure Microsoft Word cheesiness. BAY AREA BOWLING LEAGUE is arched across the top of the page with clip-art decorations, and the prize money is listed at the bottom. Twenty-five thousand dollars.

Winning that much money could go a *long* way toward securing Bigmouth's future in this city. Even if I gave half to Beckett, it'd mean more than two months of rent. Or it could mean renovations and a liquor license. A resuscitation. A second chance. My phone buzzes on my comforter, and I tuck the flyer beneath the tissue box on my bedside table.

BECKETT PORTER: I'm parked down the street!

Exhaling my nerves, I switch off my bedroom lights. I have two options. The rickety fire escape outside my window or sneaking downstairs. I creak open my door and listen keenly, like JP when he hears birds outside the attic window. The hallway's lamp is on, and a low hum—a podcast or a TV show—drones.

Fire escape it is.

I've never used the fire escape to sneak out. Never had a reason to.

I remove the screen and hide it in my closet. *Impulsive*, my brain accuses, but I push that thought away as I swing one leg over the ledge, foot reaching out in the darkness. The metal is slick from the rain, but once I'm steady, I wiggle my other leg out and climb through the window.

A tiny bit of vertigo strikes as I shimmy my way down the fire escape. Luckily, both Dad's and Aunt Fiona's rooms are on the other side of the house. The escape passes the guest bedroom on the second floor; the lights are out. I reach the bottom, jump the last step, and land on the cement. I nearly drop to my knees and kiss the ground.

San Francisco doesn't disappoint tonight, and its consistency is comforting. The rain returns, ominous and swirling, and I flip up my hood. I sprint through the rain and darkness, along the sidewalk, until the red octagonal stop sign appears. Two headlights blear out of the night, low to the ground, belonging to Beckett's junkier-than-hell Accord.

Inside, the heater's blasting, and I uncurl my frigid fingers in front of the vents. "Hey there."

"Hey," he says, offering up a crooked grin.

We exchange awkward smiles, and even though I'm freezing, my face is hot.

Beckett's blue curls are frizzing out from beneath the fold of his beanie. It's oddly satisfying. I mean, his hair is still amazing, but at least it's not immune to Mother Nature. The car groans as he shifts out of park and pulls a tight U-turn. His left leg bounces with energy, and he taps the steering wheel tunelessly as he drives.

"You look nice. Not to say you haven't looked nice other nights. You always do. Look nice, that is . . ." He trails off and focuses pointedly on the road. We pass beneath a streetlamp, which illuminates his face for a second—eyebrows scrunched, ears red, teeth indenting into his bottom lip.

Let the record show that nervous Beckett is quite possibly the cutest thing. Ever.

"Thanks." I laugh because Beckett's *bumbling*, which is such a novelty. My palms are all sweaty, and I press them between my thighs. "So, where's Double Decker?"

Around dinner, Beckett texted me the name and details for tonight's game, since we were distracted earlier at Bigmouth's. Nic, the friend Beckett introduced me to the other night, is the manager and opens the doors for illegal gambling after midnight.

"South San Francisco. Outside of Brisbane." He checks the GPS. "Should only take us thirty minutes."

"Cool." I spot the coffees in the center console cup holders. "Ooh, is one for me?"

"Yep. My hustler needs to be on her game tonight."

Hearing him say those words, laced with a tinge of

fondness, throws me. Not in a bad way, but more because I'm not at all bothered by him saying it. Which is very unusual for me. What's weirder? I like it. Beckett asked me out this afternoon, but my brain is still struggling to grasp the concept of these feelings being *requited*. I focus on my coffee because it's past midnight, and the aroma is strong enough to burn my eyelids wide open.

We drive in silence to Double Decker, the warmth of our bodies filling the car. A weird nighttime radio talk show plays—*Al's Anomalies*—and the host, Al, interviews callers about alien abductions.

Despite its name, Double Decker is a low building in Orange Park. We're close enough to the San Francisco International Airport that the sky seems to shake with each and every takeoff. We get ready in the car, following our usual routine. Beckett removes his beanie and slicks back his curls.

I'm gut-punched at how good he looks. The blue suits him.

"Check it out," Beckett says. He pulls the ugliest jacket I've seen in my life out of a duffel bag. Geometric shapes in blue, pink, orange, yellow, and green decorate the nylon monstrosity; there's a zipper *and* snap buttons. When he tugs it on over his T-shirt, the jacket hangs awkwardly from his narrow frame, at least three sizes too large.

I laugh, clapping my palms over my mouth. "Oh my God, where did you find that?"

"In a box of my dad's old things. I think it's from the eighties or nineties."

"Your dad has horrible taste." I poke his shoulder, where the fabric puckers up. "Ugh, it has hanger nipples."

Beckett snorts, popping the collar. "What?"

"The little bumps? Hanger nipples? They're from being on the hanger for too long."

"You're so weird," he says with a laugh, and puts on a pair of thick plastic-rimmed glasses. "How do I look?"

"Do you really want me to answer that question?"

"I look ridiculous," he says, "but I don't look like myself, do I?"

Well, he's got me there. But I don't mind his disguise. He looks like a dork, but an adorable dork I wouldn't mind kissing. Not one bit.

After I put on my wig, we're ready.

I leave my hood up as we approach Double Decker to protect the wig, but let the raindrops spatter against my face, smear my eyeliner, and hang in droplets from my eyelashes.

I'm stunned by how different the alleys are. The Four Horsemen was hard-core, but the atmosphere here is under wraps. Not a stray dollar in sight. The men are subdued, but twitchy. Antsy.

Beckett flags Nic over, but before he reaches us, I ask, "You sure Nic's cool?"

He spreads his arms wide open. "Nic's responsible for this *entire* game. Trust me, he doesn't give a shit."

The air is heavy with weed and beer and drugstore cologne.

I wave as Nic skids to a stop beside us, reserved, even

if Beckett claims he's cool. He sports tight white jeans and a checkered jacket. Nic glances over and squints as if he's struggling to place me. Last night he saw me without a wig. Shrugging, he says, "Caroline, right? You won big last night. Nice job."

"Thanks."

"Sweet jacket, Beckett." He gives us a double thumbs-up and darts toward another player calling his name.

Beckett and I dissolve in laughter, leaning into each other, and it's the most *us* I've felt in a year. But then he takes my hands, enveloping them with his, reminding me some things are very, very different.

Once we catch our breath, he says, "No need to pay ahead of time. Let's set up at lane three and get bowling. Nic tipped me off on who you should play against."

I eye the rows of bowlers, tongue tucked against my cheek as I assess the potential competition. "Who?"

Beckett slyly points out four men huddled together at lane six. "Them."

"All four?"

"The buy-in is kinda steep; Nic said a grand. But if you win? Four thousand dollars. This could be big, Chuck. Nic and I are buddies. We can trust him. He said those guys have been drinking and are getting worse with the hour."

Can we trust Nic? I shake the question away, because, dude, *four thousand dollars*. That's more money than I can wrap my head around. We'd be closer to our goal.

I empty the coffee, not tasting the liquid. "Four thousand dollars?"

Beckett's eyes glimmer. "Four thousand *fucking* dollars."

I'm sweating caffeine and misplaced confidence, Bacardi and perspiration sliding down my arms. Double Decker is humid, the dank warmth and rain carried in with every player, heating the room like a putrid sauna. To say it's nasty is an understatement, but despite being uncomfortable, I'm doing pretty well on the lanes.

Beckett nurses a beer—one he bought when supplying drinks for the guys I'm playing against—and watches from the hard plastic benches. My opponents are Tick, Andy, Brue, and Sal. They're well over fifty and have decades of bowling experience over me, but Nic was right tipping off Beckett. They were drunk before Beckett bought them beers and totally believed my drunk-girl act. Their play is sloppy, which helps, but they're erratic, unpredictable.

I'm not sure who these four men are, or how they can part with a grand each, but I've learned not to ask questions. They're more concerned about losing their money to one another over side bets, and by the fifth frame, I'm sure they've forgotten about my existence.

Fine by me.

I'm a few pins behind the others but play hard. I didn't leave a wide pin gap on purpose because we're playing for too much money to leave my fate to the tenth frame. I can't take the stress of losing a grand—or winning four thousand—on two shots. When we approach the final frames, my stomach is in knots.

Sensing my anxiety, Beckett gives me an amused look. "You okay?"

I pointedly eye the cup of money stashed in an empty beer cup between our lanes. "That depends on your definition of okay."

"C'mere." He nods to the seats, and I plunk down beside him. After a beat, he drapes his arm over my shoulders. The boyfriend-girlfriend facade has gotten weirder now that we're going on a date. My skin pricks pleasantly at the thought.

"How do we know they're not hustling us?" One of the guys actually *drops* his ball as he walks up to the foul line. You'd think they'd care more with so much money on the line. Hence my suspicion.

"Nah, no way," Beckett says confidently. "I trust Nic. Just play your hardest, okay?"

"I always do."

Beckett tilts his head until it rests against mine and his ridiculous glasses bump my nose. His shampoo wafts, something spicy and fresh, with a hint of the blueberry hair dye. His smile is warm and encouraging. "Relax. We've got this. *You've* got this."

The guy Sal finishes his frame, and then it's my turn. Ninth frame. I extricate myself from Beckett's embrace and he squeezes my hand, a Morse code of support. At the foul line, I roll my shoulders and set up the shot. From the second my ball leaves my fingertips, I know it's a strike.

I feel it, the energy stretching between me and the pins, shrinking in distance as the ball barrels toward the head-pin. The sound of my ball smacking the pins is so satisfying it makes my bones tingle. I hang my head back, grinning to the ceiling, and turn on my heel.

The guys watch the reset drop ten fresh pins, confusion and anger tainting their expressions.

"The hell was that?" Tick barks across his lane, straddling the return as he lifts his fifteen-pounder.

My smile drops into a mask of innocence. "Can you believe it? A strike. What're the odds?"

Tick's too drunk to hold eye contact. He grunts and wobbles toward the lanes. They're not hustling us. They're really *that* careless. I slick my synthetic hair back and join Beckett as the men bowl their final frame. I don't pay attention to their game; I only have eyes for the scoreboard. My meager lead sparks anger between the friends, rumblings about *how did this happen*, and *you better bowl a strike* between turns.

For once, I don't have to punch out during my final frame. The other men played so poorly, and I've already won. But I've lost all modesty, and I add flair into my final frame. Brilliant and perfect strikes earn twenty extra points.

Beckett does an awful job trying to hide his smile as he takes the winnings. "Better luck next time, fellas," he says, aware there'll never be a next time.

I got what I came for. Four grand. I can't comprehend the amount. I bowled for an hour and earned more money than I've had in my entire life. I'm struck with the odd desire to count every bill. Four thousand fucking dollars. Unbelievable.

Beckett wraps an arm around my waist, steering me out of Double Decker.

"Nicely done," he whispers against my ear.

I laugh and exhale in one breath. Everyone watches as we leave, and the heaviness of their gazes lifts as we reach the sidewalk. I am weightless, buoyant.

"I can't believe it." I shake my head and unravel myself from Beckett. With my freed hands, I pull off my wig and drag my fingers through my real hair. "Four *thousand* dollars."

"I've had fun this week." Beckett unlocks the Accord. "But it's good this hustle has an expiration date."

"Why's that?"

"Bowling's a small community." He shrugs off the awful jacket, tosses it in the back seat, and puts the glasses in the cup holder. "Word will get out about some girl with a left hook kicking the asses of the Bay Area's best action bowlers."

"You make me sound *cool.* I'm just bowling. And lying."

Beckett eyes me and laughs. "Fine. Be humble."

"Hey, do you know the details for tomorrow's game yet?"

"I was thinking in there. . . . Let's skip it. We've earned, what, six grand total? If you take all of it, that's almost enough for Bigmouth's back rent. You'd be two grand short, but six grand would still be impressive."

"What? You can't be serious. I'm not taking your share."

244

"I'm totally serious. The money would be nice, sure, but not as nice as keeping you in San Francisco."

"No way. You deserve twenty-five—if not fifty—percent. We'll win a couple thousand more, right?"

With tonight's winnings, he's right—rent is within reach. Dad can't be completely broke and can hopefully make up the deficit. But why stop now? Whatever reservations I had about Friday's game have melted away. I won big tonight, and I can do it again.

Beckett drags his fingers through his hair, the blue curls still frizzy from the weather. "Like I said, people are gonna talk, if they haven't already. That's why this kind of game only works in one area for so long. If we hustle Friday night, we've hustled the top. We'll be done. For good."

"Friday's our last game," I point out. "Let's go out with a bang. See how much money we can win."

"I don't know, Chuck," he murmurs, and rubs his chin, not thoughtfully but anxiously. "It's risky. We could lose most of our winnings. And we have a lot to lose."

"How about this? I'll sleep on it," I say, even though I've already decided that I'm in tomorrow tonight. *All in.* But I'm sure Beckett would feel better if I at least pretended to wrestle with this decision.

Beckett hesitates, but nods. "Yeah, okay. Just let me know before our date. We can't have the game interfering."

Beckett says these words carefully. *Our date.*

When I'm with him, the panic in my brain dampens, and I just *live.* I can't walk away from any of it now. Not from Beckett. Not from one last hustle. I don't want to. Undiluted happiness, fiery with adrenaline, fills my veins. And for the first time, I'm aware I'm alive.

This feeling? Knowing you're alive?

It's rare. Addictive.

I hold on tight.

FRIDAY, APRIL 27
DAYS UNTIL BIGMOUTH'S
EVICTION: 3

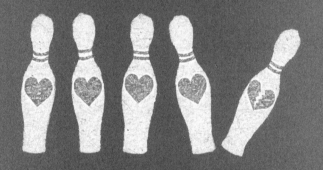

Nineteen

IN THE MORNING before work, I'm a mess of nerves. Dad's already left for Bigmouth's, and Aunt Fee is holed up in the garage—her pseudo work space—writing an article. Dad's going out with Yoga Leigh. Again. Tonight. So there's that. Not to mention the secret date Beck's springing on me, and the high-buy-in game afterward.

Upstairs in my bathroom, I clamp the straightening iron over my bangs, turning my wrist and flattening them with the slightest bend. My bedroom is a hurricane of clothing options. Beckett refuses to tell me what we're doing tonight; therefore, I have no idea how to dress.

After singeing my bangs into submission, I fix my winged eyeliner with a cotton swab. Technically, my date isn't for another eleven hours. But still. It occupies my mind with fierce, pit-stain-inducing persistence.

I'm not regretting saying yes to Beckett, not at all, but

it's alarming how badly I need this date to be success-ful. After this spring break, no longer will my loner picnic bench in the quad bring me any joy. Eating alone. Walk-ing to classes alone. *Everything* alone. When Monday rolls around and we're at school, I don't want to lose him.

In my head, my life *before* made logical sense—avoid reckless situations and you won't end up like your mom. But the past week? I've felt alive. Like I'm glowing from the inside out. No heavy cloak of depression, and any stress or anxiety has been purely situational. I have my best friend back, and maybe something more.

Maybe not all recklessness is bad.

But I force myself to remain wary of my happiness. Because I don't know what it means. I spent the last year alone and relatively unhappy. Not depressed, but blandly content with my life. All this happiness and hope—all at once—makes me nervous. Is it a sign? A step closer to losing control? Or are things just working in my favor for once in my life?

I layer on more deodorant and return to my bedroom, picking through the piles layering my floor. When did I get so many clothes? Ugh. No one human needs this many dresses. In the end I go with a carefully curated outfit. Boatneck white top, circa 1980. Tight black pedal push-ers. Red-accented yellow vintage satin bomber jacket, imported from Japan and discovered at an estate sale. Vintage leather baby-doll pumps.

No idea if this will be appropriate for whatever Beckett has in store, but I like the way I feel in these clothes. I like the sleek, elongating lines of the capri pants and the way the boatneck top showcases my collarbones. The way the heels give me the slightest edge of height and the red accents in the jacket match my lipstick.

I grab the tube of lipstick and retrace my lips. Layering on the red like armor. The thought that tonight I might *finally* kiss Beckett skyrockets my nerves. But they're good nerves—anxious, excited, and hopeful all at once. Smiling at my reflection, I cap the lipstick and head downstairs.

I don't get far, nearly tripping over a box on the landing. There's no shipping label on it, but a piece of paper is taped to the front. I kneel down and heft the box onto my hip, taking it back to my bedroom.

I read the note, brows drawn.

> *Caroline,*
> *I was cleaning some boxes out of the*
> *storage locker and came across this.*
> *Thought you might like to have it.*
> *Love,*
> *Dad*

The box drops from my hands and lands sideways on the bedroom floor.

No, no, no. This is *bad*. This is so bad! Dad doesn't clean the house, let alone our junky storage locker. I nudge the box with my foot, like it's a dead body or something. Dread lances my rapidly beating heart, and my hearing goes fuzzy. Dad must be cleaning out the storage locker to prepare for our move to Arizona.

The box taunts me, so I flop onto my butt and rip the note off. Glower at it. Ball it up and toss it into my trash can. I peel back the folds of the cardboard and sneeze as the box exhales dust. On the very top is a sketchbook. It's old, the pages yellowed. At the bottom right-hand corner, in bubbly print, is *Property of C. O'Neill.*

Seeing Mom's handwriting does something funny to my chest. The longer I stare at those letters, the more my eyes well up. Her handwriting looks so *happy*. My throat tightens as the first tear crests my eyelid and drops onto my cheek. Crying is the absolute worst, but no one is up here to see me. My perfect winged eyeliner is no doubt running down my cheeks. I flip open the notebook to find Mom's design sketches filling the pages.

With the notebook set aside, I dig into the box's contents. It's full of clothing. I drape the first item across my lap, my vision all blurry. A multicolored beaded dress. I rub the nubbins of the beads between my fingers. I had no idea my dad held on to this stuff.

All of it—Mom's design sketches, works in progress, finished pieces—it's beautiful.

Growing up, my life was devoid of my mom, and since finding out the truth, I considered it a relief. Between my depression, big emotions, and swings into irritability, I didn't want any other reminders of what could be. I only have the wigs because one day at the storage locker, I saw them and begged my dad for them.

They're cool, but I just wanted something that belonged to her.

That was before. Before I learned what really happened. Before I got afraid.

On some level, I understand my mom. More than I'd care to. I understand that sometimes, the world becomes too heavy. I wish I'd been enough, that Dad had been enough, to keep her here.

Such a pointless want. I shouldn't even be allowed this want, because it's all my fault. I'm the reason she went off her mood stabilizers—*me*. She wanted to get pregnant and have a kid so bad. I guess her psychiatrist warned her against going off her medication or waiting until she could transition onto something equally effective but safe for conception. Mom didn't wait. She cold-turkeyed her meds when the stick turned blue.

After a rough pregnancy, she fell into an awful postpartum depression.

Three years later, she was dead.

I clench my molars, my nails digging into my thighs, but the tears come faster now. They're hot, stinging as the saline hits my cracked lips. *No.* No, unraveling is not an option. Aching, I sit there for a moment. Until I steel myself and the tears fade.

Today isn't the time to wallow over Mom. Wallowing leads to depression, and a depressive episode would really throw a wrench into our date and the game tonight. My head's all cloudy, and I take a few deep diaphragm breaths.

Dad is no doubt waiting for me at Bigmouth's, and with

all my plans tonight, I can't afford to piss him off by being late. I force myself to my feet. Sniffling, I shove the contents of the box back inside. Before going downstairs, I duck into the bathroom to fix my makeup.

Embarrassment floods as I stare at my reflection. I can't be crying over old scars. This is why I avoid my mom. She's the gaping wound on my heart. And if these wounds won't heal, then I need to prevent any infection from spreading. Eyes red but makeup fixed, I pick up the box, and it's as if it weighs a hundred pounds.

I know what I need to do. I hurry downstairs, the box held to my chest.

"Chuck, what the hell?" Fiona asks, looking up from her laptop as I burst into the garage without knocking. "I'm working—are you *okay*?"

I dump the box into the trash can. "Fine. I'm fine," I say, smiling my fakest smile. No longer holding that box already makes me feel better. Lighter. Like I can really leave this pain behind.

Aunt Fiona glances from me to the trash can, green eyes narrowed. "Sure you—"

"I said I'm fine." Maybe if I say it enough times, I'll believe it. "Just cleaning out some junk."

My aunt swivels around in her desk chair. Her eyeglasses are propped on her head, nearly getting lost in her loose bun. "You off to work?"

"Uh-huh. Afterward I'm going out with Beckett." Even I can't hide the smile creeping into my voice.

"Like a date-date?"

"So it seems."

"I'm glad he came to his senses," Fiona says musingly. "Good. Have you kissed him yet?"

My chest flurries with nerves and I cross the garage. "I'm late for work."

"Sorry for being invested in your romantic well-being," she calls after me.

I lean against the doorframe. "You really need a new girlfriend. It's pathetic that you're this invested in your niece's love life."

Aunt Fiona laughs and rotates the chair back to face her laptop. "You're telling me. Have fun tonight!"

I smile, my heart several shades of conflicted and confused. As I move to shut the door, my gaze lands on the trash bins on the other side of Fiona's yellow VW Bug. For just a moment, I hesitate. But I can't deal with my mom and our darkened past. Not today. Maybe not ever.

I shut the door and leave the box of memories behind in the trash.

Where they can't hurt me.

Behind the register, I sew and listen to loud music that crackles my eardrums in the best way. The metallic chiffon Alice of California dress edges on the more eccentric side of vintage fashion, but it's an intricate task that will keep me busy. Keep my mind busy. A previous owner, or time, destroyed the inner sheath lining, and I'm using silk panels from Goodwill as a replacement.

I lose myself in the calm of the needle piercing in and

out of the fabric, the tight pull of thread. The day's been slow, but I've effectively shoved finding that box far into the recesses of my mind. Focusing on better, if not equally nauseating, topics. Like my date. Fiona's disembodied voice flits through my mind: *Have you kissed him yet?*

I tug the thread too tight until it snaps.

"Damn." I stick the needle between my teeth and tie the loose ends. I fish around for a spool of thin white thread and unwind a length, tossing the broken end in the trash.

The song playing on my phone ends, and in the two-second lull between tracks, I hear footsteps approaching. The shuffle of loafers on linoleum is unmistakable. He's early.

"Hey," Beckett says as he reaches the register.

"Hi." I set the needle aside and tug down my head-phones. Covertly, I peer around him for whatever first-date surprise he may have carted in. Balloons. A horse-drawn carriage. A bowling alley full of roses. But the only thing Beckett Porter brought was himself. And trust me, there's nothing disappointing about that.

For a moment we just smile at each other.

He's all messy handsomeness tonight. Jeans and a white-and-blue pin-striped shirt billowing around his sinewy frame. A gray suit blazer on top, cuffed. A knowing smile. He must've spent the last twenty-four hours washing his hair, because the blue dye has faded from his curls.

Beckett looks good. Like *ridiculously good*. My heart pounds, the swish of my blood through my veins loud in my ears. A tug of longing strikes across my heart and tugs behind my belly button. I'm nervous as hell, but this is Beckett we're talking about. Not a stranger. Goofy, cocky, sweet Beckett Porter. Nothing to be afraid of.

It's only five, and I'm not off until eight. Since only two lanes are taken, and Dad's fiddling with the sock dispenser—fielding more customer interaction than normal—I could sneak out early.

Beckett palms the counter and peers at my sewing project. "What're you working on?"

"Oh, uh, a dress."

He tucks his hands in his back pockets, a move that's awkwardly adorable. "Cool, cool."

"You know I'm not off for three hours, right?" I'm honestly worried Beckett might sit and wait until I'm free. Not that I *mind* him sitting within my eye line for three hours, but there's zero chance I'd get any work done. Then again, I rarely do much when I'm here, so what's the difference?

He winks and turns to my dad, who is working on sketchy rewiring with the sock vending machine. "Hey, Mr. Wilson."

Dad shimmies backward from behind the machine, dust clinging to his hair. He studies Beckett's street clothes. "You off work today?"

"Yes, sir."

Suck-up. I wait for him to give the usual line about our nonexistent school project.

Instead, Beck says, "Cool if Chuck leaves work early . . . for our date?"

I make a weird noise and choke on the spit in my throat.

No one expresses concern.

Dad huffs as he pulls himself upright, and he's beaming when he looks at us. "Well, well," he says, "look at the Wilson family. Putting themselves out there."

I'm going to die in this bowling alley. "Dad—"

"I *knew* something was going on between you two."

I almost laugh. Almost. But I'm too busy with the dying thing.

Dad continues. "All the sneaking around. There is no school project, is there?"

I widen my eyes at Beckett. This is on him, since it was his lie.

"No, sir. I was nervous about spending time with Chuck, and she *was* helping me with a project."

Dad levels a stare between us. Doing his best to be intimidating. Failing greatly. "What do you have planned for tonight?"

A light blush colors Beckett's ears. "Actually, I was hoping to surprise Chuck."

Dad motions for Beckett to come over, and he does, rocking on his heels. Dad pumps his eyebrows, and Beck cozies up to my dad, whispering our date plans into his ear. Yeah, all this embarrassment might be the end of me.

Unable to watch this any longer, I drop my face into my palms.

"Caroline," Dad calls, and I peek through my fingers. "You're officially off the clock."

Relieved that the super-awkward interaction is over,

I slide off the stool without questioning him. "Great! Thanks, Dad."

Quickly, I repack my sewing kit and fold the Alice of California dress into my tote bag. I round the counter, saying to Beckett, "Considering I had zero hints about what we're doing, I hope I dressed appropriately."

The outfit was kick-ass this morning. Now it's either too much, or too little, and I'm too confused to tell the difference, because I can't read Beckett's face to save my life.

Beckett's smile unravels slowly, and the weight of his gaze makes my chest hot.

"Is this okay?" I ask. "I have a change of clothes—"

"It's perfect." He motions for my bag, and I hand it over.

"Home by one," Dad hollers after us, giving me a goofy thumbs-up when Beckett's not looking.

"Wow, he must really like you," I tell Beckett once we're outside. "My curfew is normally midnight."

"Don't act so surprised. You're clearly aware of how charming I am."

I roll my eyes before saying, "About tonight. We should play. I understand your concerns, but you deserve your cut. We've got this."

Beckett smiles, swinging my tote against his legs, but his brows pucker. "You sure? The buy-in . . . It's a lot of money. A huge gamble. Is it really worth the risk?"

The Accord's parked on the other side of the street, the paint slick and shining after being washed for the first time this decade.

"When did you get conservative with this scheme? Yes,

it's a lot of money to play, and it's even more to win. We'll earn that money tonight. The more we win, the greater the chances I'll stay in San Francisco."

When we reach the car, Beckett stops and wraps his hand around mine. "If you're sure, I'll let Nic know we're in. Enough shoptalk. For now, can we focus on you and me?"

Shaking off the flush Beckett's skin-on-skin contact gives me, I draw a huge smile. "I suppose." I tilt my head back to look into his cloudy eyes. "Where are we going?"

"We," he says, unlocking the Accord, "are going on the best date of our lives."

I drop into my seat, nerves and happy energy bundled into one. "Oh yeah? You might want to keep my expectations low."

Beckett hops into the driver's seat. "Why's that?"

"If I'm expecting a crappy high school date, whatever you've planned will wow me. Now I'm expecting a hot-air balloon and a secret concert no one's ever heard of."

"Our date is way better than that. Set your expectations to the highest, Chuck, because you will not be disappointed."

I cover my mouth with my hand. My smile is so wide my teeth brush against my fingers, and I face the window so Beckett can't see my happiness displayed, raw and vulnerable.

Twenty

"TONIGHT'S DATE IS broken into thirds," Beckett explains as we park on Twentieth Street, "and if you're not having fun, tell me and we'll move on. But I'm ninety percent certain you'll approve of this evening's activities."

"What happened to your confidence?" I tease, studying the scenery outside the window. We're in a residential neighborhood. Interesting. I haven't been able to guess what our plans are tonight.

"Oh, I'm confident, but I'm hedging my bets. You're more judgmental than most people."

"Am not." As I grab my bag, I remember the gift I brought for Beckett. "Oh, I almost forgot! This is for you." I hand Beckett a bottle of allergy medicine.

"Thanks?"

"You're always sneezing around me—"

"Because you're a traitor and adopted a cat," he tells me. "Me and my rhinitis haven't forgotten."

"If you don't want it, I'll take it back."

Beckett holds the bottle out of reach. "Nondrowsy?"

"Duh."

He pops an allergy pill and sets the bottle in the cup holder. "Thanks."

I bite my lip as my mouth upturns with a grin.

Beckett leans into the back seat for his bag and two large pieces of cardboard.

I eye the cardboard. Each piece is about two feet by four feet in size. "Are we hitting up a recycling center?"

He maneuvers the cardboard out of the car. "Patience."

The cold air is a front. No longer raining, the sky is soft with clouds dissipating into a lingering fog. Fisting my hands together, I slide my sleeves over them and follow Beckett onto the sidewalk. Dolores Park is a jewel in the distance, but we head in the opposite direction, into a stretch of neighborhood gaining in elevation.

"We're in for a walk," Beckett says apologetically. "Parking where we're headed can be a problem."

"That's fine. At least it's a nice evening." The sun hasn't set yet, and it slides in the sky like an oozing drop of lava. We walk along Douglass Street, and Beckett gestures to a detour mounting up the hill. The Douglass Stairs, cement and nothing special. But the greenery escapes, growing over the metal and cracking the cement.

San Francisco has a way of wrapping the city up in nature. Softening traffic jams with the parrots of Telegraph Hill. Quieting city-life noises with the bison in Golden Gate

Park. Comforting the street crime with the wilds of Glen Canyon Park.

We could do nothing, just walk this city, and it'd be the best night of my life, as long as Beckett was by my side.

He seems to have a destination in mind, though. What around here would be date-worthy? Sure, it's beautiful. It's April in San Francisco and *everywhere* is beautiful. But to my knowledge, there's nothing here.

As we top the Douglass Stairs, my calves aching, we enter a cluster of California buckeyes that create a green canopy above our heads, dotted with red berries. We're both out of breath from the walk, and for once I don't know what to say to Beckett. Until a few days ago, I always had something to say. Something witty or angry or jagged around the edges. But that was *before*.

Now there's unspoken pressure. Expectations. When we walk, electricity charges and bounces between our bodies.

I glance at Beckett, noticing how the wind billows his formal dress shirt away from his torso, and the loose threads on his jacket. I could sew those and patch the holes in his button-down. The way his curls keep escaping from behind his ears endears him to me.

Beck catches me watching him and smiles. No snarky remark, no teasing.

This is uncharted territory.

"Here we are," he proclaims.

Up ahead, a sign reads SEWARD MINI PARK. The name sounds familiar, but I've never been here. Never knew there was anything to see. In front of us are two cement slides curving into the earth. Scattered bits of cardboard and junk decorate the mini park, and the sign advises that the park closes at sunset.

He passes me a square of cardboard. "For you."

"Aw, you shouldn't have," I joke, turning the piece over. "Seriously, what's this for?"

"It's to ride on."

"You want to slide down those things?" I study the slides. These aren't kiddie slides. No safe, brightly colored plastic or wood chips at the end. They're slick cement, hazed with graffiti.

Beckett's smile wavers for a fraction of a second. "We can skip this. I thought it'd be cool."

"No! It *is* cool. I had no idea this was here." I bend the cardboard between my palms and inch closer to the edge, to the juxtaposition of cement and greenery.

Beckett unzips his backpack and tosses over a can of cooking spray.

I snatch it out of the air and turn the can around in my hands. "Okay, now I'm actually confused."

"To oil the cardboard. It's all about the aerodynamics."

"Of course it is," I say dryly. I drop the cardboard at my feet and shake the Pam cooking spray. After I hose down my square, I hold the can out.

"Thanks." Beckett's fingers brush mine, and my nerves zip with excitement. He must feel it too, because he looks up and grins. This slow and knowing and promising grin.

Beckett and I have shared endless experiences together

over the years, from sneaking into our first-ever R-rated movie together to concerts to the darker moments, like my depression in sophomore year or the breast cancer scare his mom had when we were in middle school.

But we've never done *this*.

Once the cardboard is oiled, Beckett says, "I've only been here once before."

"And what about it screamed 'great date idea'?" I tease, approaching the slides with my cardboard in hand.

"Hey." He pretends to be affronted. "Planning a first date is hard, but I stand by my choices. A lot of thought went into tonight."

I glance over my shoulder at him. "Oh really?"

"So much thought," he confirms. "This date? You? It's all I've been thinking about since yesterday afternoon."

I blush and look away, although I don't know why I'm still trying to hide my emotions. Old habits, I guess. "This is a *great* date idea, Beck."

We share a smile before positioning ourselves on our makeshift sleds. The slides run beside each other with a short barrier in between, curving serpentine down the hill.

A thrill of adrenaline courses through my body and my heart thuds painfully.

"On three." Beckett tucks his knees to his chest and grips each wall of the slide. The edges of his sneakers barely fit on the cardboard. I do the same, glad I didn't wear a skirt or dress. "One, two—"

I push off before he gets to three—the anticipation too anxiety-inducing—and hold my arms against my body as the oiled cardboard soars downhill. Beside me, Beckett laughs and throws his hands in the air, body swaying and curving with each turn of the slide.

The ride looked long from the top, but it snaps by in a second. Over before I comprehend the thrill. I reach level ground a few seconds before Beckett, slowing to a stop. His laughter is contagious. My body heaves with it, and my cheeks ache from smiling.

When I turn to Beckett and his radiating happiness, my chest swells with warmth.

He hops to his feet, holds out his hand, and pulls me upright. His hair is disheveled from the wind, and my fingertips trace his ears as I tuck away a curl. He's so damn confident, but his ears? A bright and traitorous red. I try to catch my breath, but I can't. Not when he's looking at me like *that*.

Like he sees every hidden part of me. And he wouldn't dare change a thing.

Even though my desire to kiss Beckett Porter has officially usurped all my other desires—save Bigmouth's, stay in San Francisco, get into FIDM, never step foot in Arizona—I'm nervous again. Afraid of the intensity of my own feelings. Which, for the record, are pretty intense right now.

"Let's go again," I say, because as afraid as I am, I can't lose this feeling. The addictive hope of before, the excitement of possibilities. All the unknown, unexplored, and unimaginable.

Our fingers laced and palms cupped, we race to the top.

Stage one ends with us smelling vaguely of cooking oil and sweat. I'm buoyant with Beckett-infused happiness, an incalculable feeling I want to bottle and put on my bookshelf. Beckett and I progress onto stage two, leaving the Seward slides behind. This may be my first-ever first date, but I already know tonight is something special.

We toss our cardboard sleds in a recycling bin and head back to the Accord, the space between our bodies narrowing. Little, purposeful movements bringing us closer. The way I lean against him as we walk. The way his fingers brush mine.

"Hungry?" Beckett asks, uncuffing the sleeves of his coat and rolling them to his wrists.

The wind is turning cold and bitter now that the sun is gone. I zip my jacket, but the satin fabric does little for insulation. "I could eat."

He checks his phone, thumb scrolling along the glowing screen. The artificial light bounces off the sharp planes of his face. "You sure about tonight? The hustle, I mean?"

So much for no shoptalk. Our shoulders bump against each other. "I haven't changed my mind, and I'm not going to. We can double our winnings. I'm not passing that up."

Beckett doesn't question me again. "I just heard from Nic. He said the game is being held at Miracle Alley at eleven. Can your aunt cover for you?"

"I'll text her, but it shouldn't be a problem."

We return to the car, and Beckett drives, not telling me where we're having dinner or what stage two entails. His phone is hooked up to the stereo, and Grouplove's debut album booms through the speakers. Beckett discovered the band when we were in the eighth grade, but I was the one who convinced my dad to accompany us to their show at the Fox Theater in Oakland.

Beckett takes us down Twenty-Third into Union Square. The traffic gridlocks as we turn onto Mission, and we park in a garage off Bartlett. The sun's officially dropped from the sky, taking with it any remnants of warmth. San Francisco is quirky. It's one reason why I love it. The city has microclimates, meaning it'll be cloudy and fifty degrees in one neighborhood and in another, a few miles away, it'll be sixty-five and sunny.

I'm cold, but I don't care. The air is fresh, and I draw close to Beckett as he leads me to Twenty-Second Street and back to Mission. The streets are flooded with people. Getting off work. Waiting for their Ubers. Going on dates.

The city is alive, and I'm alive in it. A part of it.

Loving a place isn't like loving a person. San Francisco is wildly expensive, and yeah, you occasionally find hypodermic needles on the sidewalk, but it's a living, breathing love story. For some, San Francisco is a one-night stand. For others, it's their soul mate.

And there's no question which one San Francisco is to me—this city is *my* soul mate.

I must've stopped because Beckett holds his hand out toward me. "What're you doing?" he asks, and threads his fingers through mine. There's that heat, the undeniable spark when he touches me. Even when it's as innocent as interlacing fingers.

"Admiring this city," I say, squeezing his hand. Beautiful even though we're in front of a plain building called Bonita's Trading Co. and across the street is a Chase Bank. The fog drifts, thick and cloying, coating the buildings.

Loving a city—being an intrinsic part of a *place*—always seemed safer than ever relying on another person. But the past week, I've slowly come to terms with the fact that relying on other people isn't a weakness.

We huddle beneath the building's overhang, the ocean of people pushing past us.

"You really love San Francisco, don't you?" Beckett says fondly.

"Did you know," I say, "it's a crime *not* to leave your heart in San Francisco?"

"Is that a fact?" His laugh is low, appreciative. "You're so freaking weird. I love it."

The warmth flooding my body erases any lingering cold. "I'm glad you find me so amusing, because I was being totally sincere."

"Trust me, I'm aware." He grins in this overwhelmingly charming way. "Now, c'mon, no more dillydallying. We have a reservation in *three* minutes."

"Really?" The formality surprises me, and I laugh. I mean, Beckett's not the most organized person I've ever met. He's the Patron Saint of Cute Messes. "A reservation?"

"Um, yeah?" He cups the back of his neck with his free hand. "Can you blame me for trying to do this right? Not

269

like I'm *not* confident in your hustling skills, but there's a chance you'll leave the city—"

"Hey, don't say that." His nervous rambling is adorable, but my heart stings at the unneeded reminder of what's at stake. Leaving San Francisco has been on my mind constantly all week; I want one night where I can pretend like it might not happen. "I don't even want to think about leaving the city. Or you. Now let's go eat."

His demeanor softens. "Sorry. I'm nervous?"

"Is that a question? Because if so, I'm nervous too?"

Beckett smiles and shakes his head. "The restaurant is up here." He leads me by the hand, and we stop at the Foreign Cinema.

First impressions? Fancy as fuck.

He opens the door for me, following me into the restaurant. It's bustling, loud, and we wait by the bar while the hostess checks on our table. The restaurant is one large room, the ceilings two stories high. It's rustic, but the really fancy Napa Wine Country type of rustic. As in, not rustic at all.

"Whoa," I say, because that's all I keep thinking. If I wasn't so hungry, I'd probably be embarrassed because we're obviously the only teenagers here without their parents. "Just whoa."

He laughs and says, "Yeah?"

I tilt my head to look at him. "Thank you for this. It's beyond awesome."

The hostess returns and grabs our menus. "Follow me."

"It's about to get more awesome," Beckett says, glancing over his shoulder as we follow the hostess.

We're led to a covered outdoor patio set up like a large alleyway. The white brick walls on either side create a narrow dining space. Above our heads are strings of lights. Heaters hang from the walls, but freestanding lamps are lined up between every other table. What literally stops me in my tracks is the movie screen, where *The Princess Bride* is playing.

Beckett grabs my arm so I'm not left behind.

The hostess seats us at a cozy table. "Here you are," she says, laying down our menus. "Your server will be with you shortly."

I hang my purse on the back of my seat and sit down. "Beckett. This is like a legitimate date."

He plays with a loose strand on his jacket, wrapping the string tightly around his finger. "Do you like it?"

"Are you kidding? I love it."

We exchange supercharged nervous smiles.

Fidgety, I tuck my hair behind my ears, hoping I'm not too messy after our cement sliding. To do something with my hands, I open my menu. My initial impression was correct. This place is fancy and expensive. I scan the items and their prices. Bar none, this is the nicest restaurant I've ever been to.

I worry my lip between my bottom teeth and seek the cheapest menu items.

As if he can read my mind, he says, "I've got dinner."

The fact Beckett knows me that well isn't unnerving. It's comforting. "You don't have to."

"You've been staring at the prices for a full minute." He laughs and relaxes back in his seat. "Seriously, I've got it. I chose the restaurant."

"You sure?" Before our fight, we'd split any check if we ate out. Totally equal. Other than him buying me coffee, he's never done this. Another mark in the "Yes, this is 100 percent a real date" column.

Beckett leans forward and rests his elbows on the table. "Plus, I asked you out. Social etiquette says I should pay. Next time, when you ask me out, it's all you."

"Deal," I say with a grin. My stomach warms at the words "next time."

"There's a reason all my clothes are falling apart," he adds. "What money I don't use to help out around the house is pack-rat saved in my bank account. I can't remember the last time I bought a brand-new shirt."

"Huh. I always thought that was a stylistic choice."

"It's fifty-fifty," he admits, and we both laugh.

Our laughter fades, replaced by content silence as we look into each other's eyes, and I let everything about this moment in. I *like* him. A frightening amount. Again. And I shouldn't like him, but I do.

Considering I live my entire life carefully, safely, opening up just seems unnatural. People hurt each other even if they care for each other. My mom taught me that. What's dawning on me, though, is the fact that I'm already not like my mom. I don't know much about her, but she was wild. Impulsive. Heavy and depressive. She hurt people, maybe not intentionally, but she hurt me. She hurt Dad. I don't think I'm like that. Because I really, really don't want to hurt Beckett.

I don't want to be untouchable anymore.

Beckett nudges my foot. "Hey," he says softly. "Where'd you go?"

I shake my head and unfold the cloth napkin over my lap. "Oh, it's nothing." If I'm going to enjoy myself, I need to stop worrying. Get out of my head. So I say, "This place is really beautiful. Bonus points for *The Princess Bride*."

"Is it still your second-favorite movie? When I saw they were screening it this month, it was a sign."

"Yep." Over the past week, it's like I've taken all my old Beckett knowledge out of storage. Blown the dust off and reacquainted myself. "And it's your third favorite, right behind *Ferris Bueller's Day Off*."

"My top five have stayed locked in over the years."

I may not have an encyclopedic knowledge of Beckett Porter, but I'm pretty damn close.

"Oh my God," I say, pointing to an item on the menu. "They have *coffee-rubbed steak*. I think I need to eat that."

"As you wish," Beckett quotes, and I can't stop smiling. A server stops by our table, and we order.

"I've been thinking about something you said," he says, occasionally glancing at the epic love story of Buttercup and Westley.

"Yeah? I say a lot of things."

"That night we practiced at Bigmouth's, you said sewing wasn't a proper passion. Then at Dolores Park, you said you'd go to fashion school if you could, but it's complicated. What's the complication?"

I swirl my coffee around in the mug, focusing on the mixture of cream and brew so I have a second to think. "Fashion has always been a hobby. I'm not sure how to turn a hobby into a career. Plus, my mom went to fashion school, and it's too weird."

"What's too weird?"

"Following in her footsteps."

"Oh, come on," he says. "There's nothing bad about sharing common interests with your mom. It isn't a *sign*."

My mouth twitches. "Whatever."

He shakes his head. "For what it's worth, I think you should follow what you're passionate about."

I switch the conversation on him. "What about you? There are junior colleges in Berkeley. Even with your grades, you could get in and stay close to your mom and Willa."

Now it's Beckett's turn to deflect. "We're talking about your future as a prolific fashion designer. I don't know what this has to do with my—"

"You're smart, Beck! Just because you and high school don't get along doesn't mean you're doomed for eternity."

"I never said I was doomed."

"I believe the term 'black hole' was used when we last talked about school."

Beckett leans back until the chair balances on two legs, a smug smile playing on his lips. "We still have all of senior year to figure college out."

"Technically," I say, pointing at him with my coffee stir

stick, "we have nine months. A lot of applications are due in January."

"Between now and January, I'll look into junior colleges and attend school regularly if you apply to a school with a fashion program." He tips his seat forward until he's steady and holds his palm across the table. "Deal?"

Beckett might be right, but my entire life I've aimed to be practical and levelheaded. "I don't know," I hedge. Is this really a leap I want to take? Especially if I don't know what the future holds?

"Do you *want* to study fashion?"

"Well, sure—"

"Then you have no reason not to try." He waggles his fingers at me. "Deal?"

Relenting, I shake his hand. "Fine. Deal." I suppose it isn't too late to pursue the Fashion Institute of Design and Merchandising. Agreeing to apply thrills me. I can't deny that it's becoming clearer and clearer that nothing's gained from playing life safe.

We watch *The Princess Bride* as we wait for our food, but I barely pay attention because Beckett holds my hand, his thumb tracing the ridges of my knuckles. I'm ravenous by the time our food arrives. While we eat, I'm grinning because tonight is perfect.

"I'm never eating uncaffeinated beef ever again." I seriously regret my choice to wear tight pants.

Beckett's cleaned his rack of lamb to the bone, but that's far from surprising. He inhales food. "I can't move. Can we stay here forever?"

I laugh, but it sounds kind of appealing. "What about stage three?"

"Stage three is big," he says, struggling to sit upright in his chair. "The best stage, if I say so myself."

"The best stage, huh? Tonight's already been pretty great. You really think you can top this?"

Beckett grins. "Oh, I can definitely top this."

"I admire your confidence."

Even though I'm nearly tempted to get dessert, he reminds me that to complete stage three in time before the last hustle, we need to actually hustle. For most of dinner, I forgot about the game. But it's late and I'm hit with a heavy dose of reality. One more night. I check my phone. A little over an hour until we need to be at Miracle Lanes, which twists my gut with anxiety.

After Beckett pays and I thank him for dinner, he takes my hand and leads me out of Foreign Cinema, and we retrace our steps to the parking garage. San Francisco's perpetually fall weather has me shivering, so he shrugs off his blazer and drapes it over my shoulders. Purposefully, I slow my steps the closer we get to the garage because—*holy romantic moment*—will he kiss me already?

The fog. The softness of our clasped hands. His jacket, still warm from his body. It can't get any better than this.

"C'mon, stage three awaits," he says with a grin, tugging me toward the Accord.

The disappointment barely touches me, and we hurry to the car.

Beckett turns the heater on full blast. "The first two stages were a success, yeah?"

Despite agonizing over the lack of kissing, I grin. "Surprisingly successful."

"Why 'surprisingly'?"

I twist my lips to the side, thinking. "I didn't know what to expect from tonight. From you," I admit. "I still don't. You know how to keep a girl on her toes."

"Is that good or bad?"

I glance at Beckett's face, at the unusual handsomeness it captures as we drive, streetlamps illuminating his features. "Good. I'm pretty sure it's good," I say.

"The date isn't over yet. Maybe I can convince you to make up your mind? I mean, I enjoy a challenge."

"Wait, are you saying I'm challenging? *Me?*" I feign innocence.

We're stopped at a light and Beckett comically clutches his chest. "You have no idea. You keep me awake at night, Chuck Mae Wilson."

My stomach flutters, and I experience a brief moment of falling. Like when you're dreaming and step off an invisible ledge, stomach plummeting to your toes. The night shifts us even closer, and I don't fight the fall.

Twenty-One

I IMAGINE A map of San Francisco and the wild lines of our date stretching from one side of the city to the other. The oldies station is on, and Roy Orbison's voice is undeniably romantic. I'm so caught up in listening to "Only the Lonely" and mouthing the lyrics that I don't notice we're winding on familiar streets. Streets I walk along five days a week from the nearest Muni. Soon our high school crests into view, and we cruise into the small teachers' lot.

"What are we doing?" I ask, unable to mask the reluctance in my voice.

Beckett pulls the key out of the ignition and spins the chain around his finger. "Have a little faith in me."

Narrowing my eyes, I peer out the window. "I have faith in you, but the *high school*?"

He hops out of the car without answering. With no other option, I follow.

The campus is haunting at night, especially during

spring break. Beckett leads me toward one of the back buildings. He's moving swiftly, his long legs double the stride of my own, and I jog to keep up.

"Are we trespassing?" God, I'm wearing a *yellow* jacket. Bright yellow, like a traffic sign. I pull Beckett's coat closer and button it up. "This is illegal."

Beckett stops so abruptly I smack into his back. He turns and squeezes my fidgety hand. "Oh, *now* you're concerned with breaking the law?"

I restrain myself from rolling my eyes. "You know what I mean."

"Are you coming with me or not? Trust me, this is a victimless crime, and I'll make it worth your while."

Maybe my nerves are date related, not lawbreaking related. I release a relenting sigh. "Let's go before someone sees us."

"That's the spirit. Follow me."

And I do, onto the shadowed sidewalk, along the pruned mow strips, passing the boxy planters. The moon is a slice in the sky, the buildings near indistinguishable. All the other lights are out. I follow Beckett to a closed door behind a larger building. The auditorium. Does our school have nighttime security during spring break? I gnaw my bottom lip as he fiddles with the lock. To my surprise, the door opens.

At least we're not breaking. Just entering. Illegal, but not as damning.

"How'd you do that?"

Beckett grins and holds up a small silver key. "I still have an in with the drama club."

Auditoriums and theaters have a particular smell. The shut-in aroma of hot dust burning on light fixtures, the plastic scent of props, fresh paint from set designs, and an undercurrent of body odor. The door we entered leads into the pitch-black backstage. I still work behind the scenes on costumes, but rarely show up for the performances anymore.

Unsurely, I walk backstage, my arms folded across my chest. "What're we doing here?"

"Be patient. I swear it'll all make sense." His expression softens, and he holds out both hands. I place mine in Beckett's. "I have a theory that the best way to exorcise a negative memory is to replace it with a pleasant one."

"Is that so?" I lace my fingers through his, linking us together. "And your point is . . . ?"

"I can't take you back to Heidi Schilling's house, to that party—where everything changed—but this theater is second-best."

I don't know what he's up to, but I'm curious to find out. "Fair enough. How do you plan to exorcise the negative memory?"

Beckett nods toward the stage, and our footfalls echo as we walk to the center.

"One moment, please," he says, rooting around in his backpack for his phone. He taps the screen, humming beneath his breath. Then music plays. Tucking his phone speaker-side up in his pants pocket, he offers his right hand. "If memory serves, I promised you a dance a year ago. I always keep my promises."

"Beckett." I laugh, shaking my head. "That's sweet, but I haven't danced in . . . forever."

"Neither have I!" He waggles his fingers. "C'mon, this is a limited-time offer."

My laughter fades as I relent, placing my hand in his.

The song playing isn't classical, not suitable for swing dancing, but Beckett clumsily shifts us into the opening steps. Even though it's been over a year since I last danced, it's effortless with him leading.

Step, step, rock, step, step.

We're both terribly out of practice, tripping over each other in the dark, like the past year never happened.

Rock, step, triple-step, rock.

Beckett hugs his arm around my waist and slows his feet until we're no longer moving. My head rests against his chest; his heart rapidly pounds against my cheekbone. My insides are all crashing yearning and nerves, and I press my eyes closed. Listening to his heart.

After a moment, Beckett says, "About the other night . . ."

"Hmm?" We barely move, our feet shuffling uselessly along the stage. I open my eyes, blinking into the darkness.

"Outside the Four Horsemen. I didn't want to kiss you like that, okay? Standing next to a nasty dumpster with a bunch of strangers watching?" He shakes his head. "This—you—means too much. That's what I wanted to say, afterward in the car. But you took off."

Oh. My heart simultaneously swells and aches. I swallow, my throat tight. "You've put some thought into this,"

I say. I'm overflowing with nerves. Not bad nerves, just *holy-shit-is-this-finally-happening* nerves.

"Do you remember that school field trip to the MOMA?" he asks, holding me tighter.

"Yeah, of course." Where's he going with this? We broke away from the class and wandered around the museum until our history teacher tracked us down. We both got lunchtime detention. "What about it?" I tilt my head back to peer up at him, eyebrows raised.

"That trip? That's when I realized I liked you. As more than a friend."

I take a half step back, his arms still looped around my waist. "Hold up. That was in the *eighth grade*."

"Trust me, I'm well aware of how long ago that was," he says, his gaze searching mine in the dark.

If Beckett's liked me since we were thirteen, all my unrequited crush angst was apparently requited. But what's really got my mind whirling is that he's liked me *since* the eighth grade. Like he's held on to that desire for more than three years.

I manage to ask, "Why didn't you ever say anything?"

Beckett's soft laughter reverberates in the theater. "You never said anything either! I was scared you'd reject me. We were best friends. I didn't want to jeopardize that."

"Then what changed? I mean, we're friends again." No longer sway-dancing, we're rooted to the center of the stage.

He's quiet for a moment. "A few things changed. This time around, I don't have as much to lose. You might leave.

I wanted my shot, one chance to lay it all on the line. I don't want to waste any more time with you."

My heart somehow softens and turns frenetic all at once. I step closer, my hands finding his waist. "I don't want to waste any more time either."

"One other thing changed too. As close as we used to be, I always felt like you kept distance between us. A buffer." He gestures to the literal *half foot* of space between us, and I nod. He's right—I used to keep Beckett an emotional arm's length away. Like that *tiny* bit of distance would keep me from getting hurt. Which obviously didn't work. "Because of that distance, I could never figure out how you felt about me. I was so scared you'd never see me as more than your goofy best friend. Then you tried to kiss me three days ago."

I laugh in embarrassment. "You didn't buy my excuse, did you?"

Beckett's face is full of shadows, and I can barely make out the shape of his eyes. His nose. His mouth. "In the moment, I almost did. But you'd never get that upset if you didn't care."

I reach my arms up around his neck. "I care. A lot."

He traces my jaw with his thumb as he shifts closer. "Chuck—"

Far away, a door slams.

"Shit," we say in unison, and ricochet apart. Beckett fumbles to turn the music off as he pulls me deeper into the shadows and behind the thick velvet curtains. A beam of light sweeps across the stage. The dust tickles my nose, and I hold back a sneeze.

"Who's there?" the security guard yells, his words echoing throughout the auditorium. He strolls up and down each aisle, taking his sweet time.

"Let's wait him out," Beckett suggests, voice hushed.

"I don't know." I check my phone. "We need to go. We'll be late," I whisper, watching the guard from the corner of my eye as he investigates the disturbance.

"For what?"

"The game? It's almost eleven."

"Or we could skip? Enjoy the rest of our date?"

The security guard finally moves on, the door clattering shut, and silence buzzes.

"Sorry, Beck. This game is so huge. Like I said earlier, if I bring in more money than just the back rent, my dad will have to let us stay." I catch his hand in mine, hang on tight. "For what it's worth, this was the best date I've ever been on."

"Thanks, but isn't this the *only* date you've ever been on?"

I playfully shove him. "Well, yeah, but that doesn't mean it's any less spectacular."

"Spectacular?" He whistles, smiles. "All right, I can live with that."

"Don't let it go to your head."

"Too late," he says, reaching out and tucking my hair behind my ear. "I should've told you this when I picked you up, but I was even *more* nervous then and wasn't thinking straight. You look so beautiful tonight, Chuck."

"Thank you." My face heats, and I bite my lip to keep from smiling too much.

"Don't let it go to your head," he whispers, and leans down.

The warmth of his lips against my cheek lasts only a second, but I press my eyes shut and revel in it. Before I can fully wrap my head around what just happened, he pulls away and takes my hand, and we retrace our steps through the dark. We're in the clear, but we hurry across campus and to the Accord.

The security guard might've ruined the moment, but I now know an undeniable fact: Beckett wants to kiss me.

After all of this, if I move to Arizona, there's no doubt I'll leave my heart behind.

Not just with San Francisco, but with Beckett Porter.

Twenty-Two

MIRACLE LANES IS an average building, painted a uniform navy blue, with one wall of windows covered in graffiti. The colorful street art masks the building's insides. Beckett and I are in an unsavory stretch of San Francisco known as Sixth Street in SoMa. As a girl with six grand in her purse, it's an alarming place to be.

Beckett snags street parking close by, and we shift to the back seat for our pregame ritual. I'm playing a tournament, and even though they're taking phones at the door, I brought a wig. The last in my collection, a chic black bob, isn't too different from my own hair, but I could never, in a million years, make my hair this sleek.

"You ready to do this?" Beck adjusts his jacket, which I reluctantly returned.

"Yeah, I'm ready."

I don't know how many people will be playing tonight, but with a buy-in as steep as three grand, if I win, I'll walk away with a pretty huge chunk of cash. We need this. As is, I don't have the full eight grand in back rent; I'm two grand short. That's not counting Beckett's cut, which he deserves. But clearing the back rent will only do so much. We need more time to turn things around—renovations, a liquor license, digital scorecards. The more I earn, the more easily we can clear our debt and have extra money for the next few months to get a profit rolling.

We walk across the street, which smells of urine, and Beckett grabs my hand as we pass a CityTeam methadone clinic. Lights glow from behind the graffiti-coated windows, and in arched, bold writing is MIRACLE LANES. A clump of men stand beneath a striped awning, oozing smoke from cigarettes, vapor from pens. Beckett nods to a few of them; I keep my eyes in front of me. Bodies shove and brush past, but he wraps a protective arm around my waist and steers me into the thick of the chaos.

The bowling alley is sublevel below a bar, similar to the Four Horsemen. We use our fake IDs at the entrance, then head downstairs, where we have to forfeit our phones. It's dirty and loud down here, but there's a serious undercurrent among the players.

"What now?" The large digital clock hanging on the wall tells me it's past eleven, but no one's playing yet.

"Thank God!" Someone rushes over, and it takes a moment to place him. Nic. "You guys are late." I want to point out we're only two minutes late, but Nic doesn't give us the chance to talk. "Beckett, you're at lane six. Girlie, you're at lane four."

Beckett's face knots in confusion. "Chuck's playing, not me."

"If you're not playin', then you gotta wait upstairs in the bar." Nic glances at me and scratches his head as if the wig is throwing him off again, but he's too high to figure out what's different. Tonight he's wearing a white top and black pants with suspenders. His billowy patchwork coat is too big, the cuffs pushed over his elbows.

"Says who?" Beckett scans the lanes for an authority figure.

"Boss man," Nic replies shortly. Then he says to me, "You know the rules? Players face off against one another. Then the final four winners play, yadda yadda. Winner winner, chicken dinner."

Beckett drags his fingers through his hair. "Okay, I'll wait upstairs. Chuck, do you have your buy-in?"

I unclasp my purse and root around for Beckett's money clip, peeling free the three thousand to play. A week of handling large sums of money still hasn't normalized it; I hand over the cash before I can doubt myself. After I pass the money to Nic, he darts away. I stay rooted to the floor, attention turned to Beckett. "You're leaving me down here?"

"I'm not *leaving* you. I'll just be right upstairs," he says, wrapping me in a hug. "If you're having second thoughts . . ."

I lean into him, just for a second. Breathe him in. Listen to the drum of his heartbeat. The date might be over, but whatever's blossomed between us is still here. "No second thoughts."

The lights flicker, and Nic's voice crackles over the speakers, disembodied and eerie. "If you have yet to pay, see me, Nic, your emcee for the night. If you're not playing, get off the lanes. Otherwise, find your lane, grab your ball, and challenge the player to your right. The game begins in three minutes."

Beckett and I step apart as the other players settle at their lanes. "I've got this," I tell him with a grin.

"Good luck." He returns my smile before retreating upstairs.

I push my shoulders back and locate lane four. I program my console, entering in my name. Tonight I'm full-name Caroline as usual. According to Nic's instructions, I'll play the person to my right. If I win, then we shift down the lanes.

Even if this is a tournament, surprise and being underestimated will work in my favor.

My first match with lane three is an easy win, and the victory bolsters my confidence in a way that's not conducive to this situation. But the confidence is earned. I'm doing *well*. Better than well. It's safe to say I'm kicking some serious ass. Once everyone is done with the first round, the lights flicker.

Over the speakers, Nic drawls, "Losers, you don't have to go home, but you can't stay here. Winners, everyone shift lanes to your right and reprogram the console. Wash, rinse, repeat."

I hoist my ball and rest the weight on my hip, watching the losers peel off. In the corner, a few men exchange cash. *Side bets.* One player even hands Nic a wad of bills before funneling upstairs to the bar with the others. Interesting. A side bet would mean an even bigger haul if I win.

My next opponent is a man named Koichi, who bowls well. But I'm better. If I beat him and the remaining player from the second game, I'll be bringing home *thousands*. Thousands of dollars I can use to clear our back rent, secure our future rent—the options are endless and hopeful.

As the game wears on, Koichi and I jockey for the top score. I bowl my hardest with each frame, and ultimately I beat him. I punch out in the last frame, which wasn't necessary, but what's the point in playing it safe anymore? Beckett's overly cautious. This is my last hustle. I bowl a 260, my best game to date.

Koichi accepts his fate without a fight. "Good game," he says with a respectful nod.

Emboldened by my win, I motion Nic over as Koichi packs up.

"You're taking side bets, right?" I ask Nic, reaching for my purse.

Nic tilts his head in contemplation, pulls a hit from his vape pen. "What're you thinking?"

Three grand remains in my bag, wrapped around the money clip. Oh God, I hope I'm making the right call. But I have a good gut feeling about tonight. "Two grand on me winning this entire thing?"

A stream of nicotine vapor hits me in the face as he cracks open a smile. "You got yourself a deal."

Swallowing my doubt, I hand over the two grand and hurry back to my lane to size up my last opponent.

The man standing between me and my money. Standing between me and San Francisco. Standing between me and whatever the hell I have with Beckett.

The man holds out his hand. "Donegan," he says, brisk and businesslike.

"Caroline." We shake hands and start playing.

When I shoot my first frame, it's no holds barred. All I want is to defeat Donegan. Because if I fail, the foundation and the fabric of the Wilson family—the walls, the lanes, the pins of Bigmouth's Bowl—will disappear. Donegan's going down.

Except it becomes clear—fast—that my game isn't as steady as Donegan's. He doesn't sweat shooting strikes every frame, and I only manage a strike every other turn. My score falls further and further behind. My heart rate rises higher and higher, threatening to flatline and take me out.

Time blurs together, and I fall into a kind of daze—a mash-up of heart palpitations, blistering hands, and fevered nerves. Then it's the tenth frame. My saving grace this past week.

I bowl first, but before stepping to the foul line, I do the math. If I punch out and Donegan doesn't, I'll win. Not great odds, but I take them and shoot. The ball turns and turns, the noise like gunfire, and it hits the headpin slightly off. A seven-ten split, also known as Bed Posts. After the Greek Church–split fiasco, I approach with caution. If I earn this spare, I can bowl a second frame and shoot a strike in the bonus.

Donegan might screw up. I really hope Donegan screws up.

I've converted a seven-ten split before. Okay, it was once, but it happened. I step up to the lane and use the arrows on the lane to adjust my shot, exhaling a whistling breath between my lips. Pull my arm back. And release.

My ball and my beautiful left hook wing too far to the left, hitting the tenpin.

The seventh remains standing like a middle finger.

Like a *fuck you*.

For a moment I stand there, rooted to the polished floors.

Donegan punches out, bowling two flawless—I imagine, I don't watch—strikes beside me. Everything rushes back. Color. Noises. Reality. I cover my mouth with both hands to hold back whatever struggles inside. A scream. A sob. A swear. My pain contains multitudes, and it claws at my seams for freedom. The world crushes on top of me, and my kneecaps slam to the floor.

The ironic part is I should be *lighter*.

I'm five thousand dollars lighter than I was this morning.

Twenty-Three

WHAT HAPPENS AFTERWARD is muddled.

Somehow, I get to my feet, kneecaps aching.

Nic awards Donegan his winnings.

All I'm awarded? A handshake. A sympathetic smile. A *better luck next time.*

Except there will be no next time. I pack up my belongings, agitated panic filling every scrap of white space inside my body. The bowling alley is large, cavernous, Nic's and Donegan's laughter rebounding against the walls. It grates, makes me shrink smaller into myself. Doesn't matter if they're laughing at me or not. Just the noise of their happiness hammers in my endless dread.

This wasn't how this night was supposed to go.

What the hell do I tell Beckett?

All that's left in my purse is a thousand dollars. Not enough to make the smallest dent in our back rent. Not nearly enough to split with Beckett. *Damn it.* How could

I lose? We were so close to winning big. Reluctantly, I drag my feet upstairs and pause in the bathroom hallway beside the staircase.

I lost. I'm moving to Arizona. I'm a failure.

A fucking failure.

On the other side of the bar, Beckett leans against the wall, scrolling on his phone. He doesn't see me yet. Soft curls frame his face, and his lips are pulled into this charming half smile.

He believed in me, and I let him down. Beckett didn't want to play this game—he warned me against it—but I insisted. This mess is all mine.

All. My. Fault.

The bar's busy, the pulsation of bodies making me nauseous. All the noise makes me want to claw my skin off. Before I really know what I'm doing, I pivot on my heel and sprint down the hallway. Past the bathrooms. Out of the emergency exit. The exit spills into a back alleyway; misty fog glooms the air, thick with rain, and my breath escapes in harsh gasps. My lungs refuse to expand. They ache, sharp pains shooting to my ribs. My hands are reddened and blistered, and my soul is crushed. Beyond crushed—it's empty. Lifeless.

Rocking back on my heels, I bring my fist to my mouth and bite down.

SoMa is only a mile, maybe two, from home.

Distantly, I know walking home by myself is risky. I remember Dad once telling me SoMa has a crime rate more than 50 percent higher than the rest of the country. It's late, past midnight. My mind is mixed somewhere between not truly believing I'm putting myself in danger and simply not caring.

All I care about? The overwhelming need to be gone. Turning off my phone because Beckett will no doubt try calling and texting, I begin walking, tripping a bit as I pick up my pace to a run. Along Folsom Street. Up Tenth. Cut across Fell Street and beneath the Highway 101 overpass. My mind goes blissfully silent as I move. My shins aching. My heart broken.

By the time I hike the hill to the yellow house, it's one in the morning. Weird, inappropriate laughter bubbles in my chest. How the hell did I make my extended-date curfew? Still, I'm thankful all the lights are off. I'm about as mentally astute as the soupy fog. Nowhere calm enough to face Fiona.

Inside the sleeping house, Jean Paul Gaultier is eating dry kibble from his fish-shaped bowl in the kitchen. I scratch his bony head before tiptoeing upstairs. In my bedroom, I rip off the rain-soaked black wig and dump my purse on my bed.

I'm sure Beckett wants to know what happened. Where I went. But I can't bring myself to turn my phone back on. I can't tell him I ruined everything. Like, I *know* I'm a fuckup. A mess. But Beckett never saw that part of me. He saw competent and funny and beautiful. I don't want him to find out how wrong he was.

I sink to the bed and bury my face in my hands. All the tears wet my palms and cheeks.

All that money—I had it. It was *mine*. And now it's gone. In freaking Donegan's and Nic's pockets. God! What is wrong with me? Why didn't I just listen to Beckett and stay in the auditorium, dancing and kissing? I dig my fingers into my hair and pull against the roots, pressing my lips together to keep the crying muffled.

I grab my box of tissues off the bedside table, knocking a piece of paper to the ground in the process. Blowing my nose with one hand, I lean down and snatch the paper off the floor. Hope hits me somewhere between my heart and my stomach.

The Bay Area Bowling League Championship.

The twenty-five-thousand-dollar prize.

More than we need, but excess money isn't what I'm worried about right now.

This is it. My answer.

That guy in the cowboy boots, Ray, said he'd take a five-grand cut, so if I play tomorrow, I'll walk away with what I could've won tonight. *Should have* won tonight. The longer I mull over this plan, the better I feel. Not entirely hopeful, but I'm no longer leaded with dread. The championship is held at none other than Billy Goat Bowl. At least I know where it is. I flip the flyer over, and a phone number is written along the bottom. Before I lose my courage, I grab my phone and power it on.

Sure enough, Beckett's texted me half a dozen times.

I'll read them later. Once I have a plan.

ME: This is Caroline from the Four Horsemen. Still need a player tomorrow?

As I wait for Ray's response, I mop up the tears lingering on my cheeks and school myself to calm down. Maybe this isn't as bad as I first thought. Betting—and losing—five thousand dollars was, okay, *impulsive*, but maybe this doesn't have to be the end. Because it can't be the end. I can't give up. I can't lose this house or this city. Or Beckett.

Just as my mind begins to slide back into that dark place, my phone buzzes.

14155550196: Why? You offering?

ME: Yeah. $500 to play?

14155550196: See you tomorrow. Arrive early. I'll be waiting outside.

I exhale slowly and slide off the bed. Toss my phone between my hands. How do I tell Beckett? *What* do I tell Beckett? He's going to hate me, he probably already hates me, I hate myself, God this night is the worst—

A loud tapping jars me from my negative thought hurricane.

I turn around, and Beckett's crouching outside my bedroom on the fire escape, his fist held up like he was knocking. He catches my gaze and jerks his head to the side, like he wants in. *Shit.* Even if my heart brightens at seeing him, the feeling doesn't seem mutual. He looks pissed.

I pad across my bedroom and wiggle the window open.

"Be quiet," I warn, stepping aside. "Everyone's asleep."

Beckett tumbles through the window and miraculously lands on his feet. Silently, like a cat. He's soaked from the temperamental rain. "What the hell happened? I tried calling you," he whisper-yells, pulling me into a hug.

Shocked, I relax against him for a second. Wrap my arms around his waist. "Sorry—"

Then Beckett lets me go and takes a step back. Like he doesn't want to be near me anymore. "I'm glad you're okay and not in a fucking ditch somewhere, but what the hell? Why'd you just leave?" His voice cracks on the last word.

"Beck, I'm sorry, but it's complicated." I cross my arms over my stomach, bending at the waist. "I—uh, I lost. Like all the money."

Beckett's staring at me with his brows raised. "That's it? That's why you left?" He tosses his hands in the air. "Sure, that *sucks*, but you don't just leave like that! How'd you get home?"

"I ran."

"You ran? Two miles in the rain? At *midnight*?"

"Yeah." My bottom lip quivers.

"Goddammit, Chuck." He paces away from me.

"I'm fine!"

Beckett gives me this look, and his voice turns soft. "Are you?"

I hate that look—like I'm not competent, like I'm broken—so I grab the flyer off my bed. "I have a plan, okay?"

With a sigh, he takes the flyer, studying the information. "What is this?" Quickly, I tell him what happened at the Four Horsemen when he was with Willa. "You didn't text him already, did you?"

"Yeah. It's all set for tomorrow. Why?"

Beckett shoves the flyer at my chest. "You just agreed to work with Ray Wilkes."

"What are you talking about?"

"The guy I warned you about? His first name is Ray. He was wearing cowboy boots, right?"

"Maybe."

"Chuck!"

"Okay, yeah, it's the same guy." I sink to the floor and pull my knees to my chest. Annoyance replaces my heavy sadness. I've found an alternate option. Who cares if it's for Wilkes? It's just a game. The fact that it's for the mysterious and theoretically dangerous Wilkes doesn't dissuade me. Not entirely sure what that says about me. Not entirely sure I care.

Beckett sits beside me, our backs to the wall beneath the window. When I reach for his hand, he pulls away. "Let's rewind. What happened at Miracle Lanes?"

I explain what happened after Beckett left for the bar. It's easier talking this way—shoulder to shoulder and staring straight ahead.

After I'm done, one moment passes and another. Then, "You can't do this. Wilkes isn't a good guy."

"What other choice do I have?" I say, face downcast as I pull a loose thread from my capri pants. "Don't you want me to stay?"

"Low blow, Chuck," he mutters, drawing his hand across his mouth. "Of course I want you to stay, but that doesn't mean—"

"We didn't think this through. Even if I hadn't lost it all, eight grand would only clear the back rent. That's it. If we're going to have a fighting chance, the more months we have secured the better."

Beckett sighs, then leans his head against the wall with a *thunk*. "And what? Twenty grand will erase Bigmouth's problems?"

"Ten grand—you still get half. And no, probably not, but it's a start."

"C'mon, don't do this. How much money is left?"

My laugh is humorless. "Like a grand? It's not much. Not enough to matter."

"You know tomorrow could be dangerous, right? Wilkes *is* dangerous."

"It's in a public place, for a legit association. What's so dangerous about that? It's probably safer than the other games I've played."

"Do you think Wilkes will allow you to play one game for him and walk away?"

"I don't see why not."

"Because he's a liar, Chuck. People are pawns to him." Beckett drags his fingers through his damp curls. "Somehow my dad got involved with him, and look what happened! I'm not getting involved with someone like him."

"Then don't." The words are harsher than I intended, but I'm too wired, anxious, and *desperate* to care. "I'll go. You don't need to be involved."

He stares at his hands and says softly, "I know what you're doing."

"I'm not doing anything."

"You're shutting me out. Just like you shut me out sophomore year."

"What're you talking about?"

"Instead of having a rational conversation with me, you ran away." Beckett shakes his head in disbelief. "You're scared."

"No," I say, trying to laugh off his comment, but the sound stays trapped in my throat. "You're clearly the one who is scared in this situation."

"Not of Wilkes. Of this." He gestures to the inches between us that might as well be a valley. "You like me. I like you. And you're freaking out. You're taking a disagreement and blowing it out of proportion."

"That's ridiculous." My face is hot from his accusations. "I'm not afraid of us. If I were afraid, why would I be trying to stay in the city? That's why I'm playing tomorrow!"

Beckett's wrong, right? Maybe I was afraid before, but I'm not anymore. At least I don't think I am. *Whatever.* It's unfair for him talk with such authority. Like he knows me better than I know myself.

"You lied and you're shutting me out. And it sucks, okay? It fucking sucks." He twists to face me, pale gray eyes wide and desperate. "The thing is, if this were about *anything* else, I wouldn't fight you. But playing for Wilkes? I can't get behind that. Wilkes is bad news, and I don't want you getting hurt. Not after Earl."

"Wilkes isn't going to hurt me, okay? I'm not weak; I've got this." I push up from the floor and onto wobbly legs.

Beckett stands but leans his body against the wall. He looks so defeated. Wet curls hang limp to his shoulders, the whites of his eyes turning red with exhaustion. His jaw sets as he grinds his teeth. "You're not seeing the big picture anymore. You're being careless, and honestly, I'm worried about you. The past week? It worked because we did it together, because we had each other's backs. But if you want to risk it, go for it. I can't stop you."

"No, you can't stop me. Glad we can agree on that." I unlatch the window and open it. The rain patters down outside, hitting the metal of the fire escape hard. "Don't waste your energy worrying about me. I'm fine."

Something shifts in his eyes. "Chuck—"

"If you're not going to support me, then I don't want you here." Beckett just stares at me, mouth parted like the words are slow to surface. I walk over and shove his shoulder. "Leave."

"Stop it," he says, but his arms hang uselessly by his sides.

"Leave!" Tears pushing at my eyelids, I shove him in the chest. He doesn't even stumble. "Please, just leave me alone!"

Footsteps sound in the hallway, electrifying my already frayed nerves. I can't have Dad or Fiona finding Beckett in my bedroom. They'd ground me, and I'd never be able to play tomorrow if that happened.

"Leave," I whisper, widening my eyes at him in a silent plea. "Just go."

Beckett glances at my closed bedroom door before shaking his head and ducking outside. I shut the window quietly and stand in the center of my bedroom, holding my breath. The footsteps retreat.

Rattled, I collapse on my bed, curl onto my side. I grab a pillow, press it over my face, and scream. The gravity of what I did to Beckett slams onto my shoulders, and my tears soak into my comforter. What is wrong with me?

He's *gone*.

Who knows if he'll ever come back.

I wasn't thinking. My body moved of its own accord, all this dark and hyper energy making the decisions. An energy I don't understand, accompanied by an irritable anger I've never felt before. What *was* that? Since our date ended, I've slowly been unraveling, and I need it to stop. Stop before I fall apart completely. I thought I could do this and be safe—reined in and stable—but I'm not so sure anymore.

You're fine, my brain whispers. But what if it's just trying to trick me?

I blink at my blurry tears, struggling over a fractured breath. The simple act of breathing, of living, makes my lungs ache. With shaky hands, I wipe the tears from my eyes, unsure if they're from exhaustion or anger. Or both.

Standing next to the claw machine filled with porn in the seedy bowling alley where I first learned to hustle, I acknowledged it'd never be a struggle to look intimidated or out of place. In the past week, I found my groove, I found confidence. But I'm back in that moment: a scared little girl.

I'm completely and totally in over my head, but too—what, stubborn?—to back down. With no one to talk to, to help me unravel my options, untangle my questions, talk me down from the mounting self-hatred, I grab my purse and slip downstairs, releasing myself into the endless night.

SATURDAY, APRIL 28
DAYS UNTIL BIGMOUTH'S
EVICTION: 2

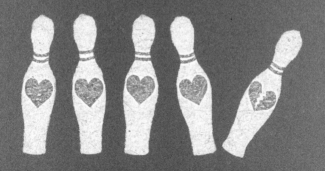

Twenty-Four

MY FELLOW NIGHTTIME transients give me weird looks and second glances on the 14-Mission bus, which is saying something. Being a Friday night—well, a Saturday morning—the owl bus is full of partiers, a few homeless curled onto the seats, and a woman smacking overturned cans tunelessly for tips.

Tonight it was the all-nighter bus or forking over a small fortune for a taxi—the decision made itself.

Since I forgot a jacket, I'm shivering, my teeth clacking and clenching. It's past three in the morning. I jog my usual, well-worn path from the Muni stop to the front doors of Bigmouth's Bowl. I have my key, and I know all the alarm codes by heart. Soundlessly, I slip into Bigmouth's because, for once, I *need* to be here.

They're just lanes slicked with synthetic oil and smelly used shoes and an ancient jukebox, but they're the building blocks of everything I know to be true. The heart and soul of the Wilson family. Even if it isn't *my* heart or soul, the ache pulls at my chest. Because I didn't always used to hate it here. Maybe I've never really hated it. Maybe I shut Bigmouth's out. If I hate it, it won't hurt if it closes.

Who would the Wilsons be if Bigmouth's closed? The house would be gone. We'd be gone. Everything Grandpa Ben worked for, the last lingering of the O'Neills—gone. *Where* would we be?

In Surprise, Arizona.

In the entry, I study the photographs on the walls with my phone's flashlight. My grandfather and grandmother at Bigmouth's grand opening. My mom, an only child, sitting at the snack counter with a book. Jump forward a few decades. My mom and dad. Mom thrived here—it was in her blood. Or that's what my dad tells me, on the rare occasion he's had two beers, which loosens his tongue when it comes to all things Mom. How she loved Bigmouth's, how she loved her father's passion.

Mom always lit up when a camera lens landed on her. The camera didn't steal her soul, but it masked her pain. She was beautiful. Her curly strawberry-blond hair, wide toothy smile, the gap between her front teeth. Impeccably dressed, perched on the same vinyl stool where I spend most of my free time.

When you lose a parent young, it's hard to remember life with them. My mom died when I was three years old, and I'd like to say I have one memory of her. A hand reaching out, a kiss on my forehead, maternal love bathing me like sunlight, but that would be a lie. I don't know my mother at all. All I have is her defective brain chemistry, a handful of stories, pictures, but I don't—and never will—have *her*.

People who know about my mom give me this pitying look. I can see behind their eyes, into their brains—they're wondering how a mother could kill herself when her daughter was still learning to speak full sentences, say her own name. A toddler who could run with confidence and count her numbers? But all those looks, all those unasked questions, aren't as bad as the ones that fill my mind when I can't get out of bed.

If I wasn't enough for my mom, then how the hell am I supposed to be enough for myself?

I press my palm to another photograph of my mom standing in the center of one lane, mouth parted in laughter. The glass is cold beneath my fingers. Am I like her? Will I turn out like her? When she was my age, did she have any inkling, any idea, she'd become so miserable she'd die before she was thirty?

Mouth twisting, I turn the beam of light away from the photographs. What am I looking for? Beckett acted like I have a choice, a decision to make, when I'd already made it. Maybe I'm stubborn, but I can't accept leaving San Francisco. Leaving him.

Embarking on this journey wasn't the smartest or safest thing I've ever done, but what kind of person walks away when they're this close to their goal? To reaching their endgame? Who gives up at this point? I have nothing else to lose and everything to gain. I only wish Beckett would see it my way.

No matter how upset I got earlier, I don't blame him.

Even *if* I'm shutting him out, maybe the distance is good. Once I know for certain if I'm staying in San Francisco or going to Arizona, I'll try to reconcile things with Beckett. But he was right—I'm afraid of what I felt tonight.

I love this city.

I might even love a boy.

And I don't want to leave them.

Once the sun is up and I'm back home, I head into battle with our shitty coffee maker.

The machine is always on the fritz. I'm resisting the urge to drop-kick it into the alley outside when there's a light patter of feet down the stairs. I haven't spoken to Aunt Fee since before my date with Beckett, and I brace myself for the onslaught of questions. Questions I'm not entirely sure how to answer after everything went south. Because if my aunt is anything, it's tactless. And nosy. And way too invested in whatever potential relationship is blooming between me and Beckett with the Hair.

The coffee maker finally gurgles to life and starts brewing, and I turn around, catching sight of a dark-haired head that doesn't belong to Aunt Fiona. The woman is shorter and older than Aunt Fee, wearing a light green T-shirt. Without a bra.

With a shriek, I clutch at the ties of my bathrobe. "Who the hell are you?"

The woman's cheeks turn pink. "I'm, um . . ." She

pauses, as if she's forgotten her name. "Leigh. You must be Caroline."

Oh. My. God. *Yoga* Leigh? In my kitchen *at eight in the morning. Without a bra on.* In my panic, I didn't recognize her from my blog snooping. Mostly because I never expected to find her in my kitchen, free-boobing it. My entire stomach threatens to revolt, and I hold back a dry heave.

"Chuck," I say through gritted teeth. "I go by Chuck."

Dad pounds down the stairs, swinging into the kitchen. His robe is tied tight around his body, and his thin hair is mussed. The balding man's version of bedhead. Or sex hair. "Caroline! You're awake."

The coffee maker wheezes. I check the floor beneath me. Nope. I'm not sinking through the hardwood in horror. Yet. Did Dad have a woman stay the night? And not any woman. Yoga Leigh. Perfect Yoga Leigh with her perfect swingy lob haircut and perfectly yoga-toned legs.

The three of us stare at one another, like an unarmed standoff.

The coffee isn't done, but I grab a mug off the shelf and pour the cup to the brim, leaving the carafe empty on the burner. I scald my tongue and the roof of my mouth as I sip and move to circumvent the kitchen island, stepping far away from Dad and Yoga Leigh. They huddle next to the refrigerator, both flushed in embarrassment.

This can't be my life.

Then Dad has the gall to ask, "Hey, hon, how was your date with Beckett?"

I stop at the base of the stairs. "It was great," I say, "but obviously not as great as yours."

This leaves them in enough stunned silence for me to rush up the stairs, enough time for guilt to sucker punch me in the face for acting like a jackass. I don't go to my bedroom. The only rooms in our house with locks are the bathrooms, so I barge right into Aunt Fiona's.

Aunt Fee is tangled in her checkered flannel sheets, one leg dangling off the mattress. After setting the coffee on her dresser, I rip the comforter off. *She's* responsible for this.

"Wake up," I whisper-shout, jostling my aunt.

Fiona rolls onto her back with a groan and blinks at me. "What's going on?" She struggles upright, propping herself on her elbows. "Hey, how'd your date with Beckett go?"

Oh my God. Do they all just sit around and talk about my pathetic love life?

"It's complicated, but more important, Dad's in the kitchen with Yoga Leigh."

The information takes a second to process through Aunt Fiona's sleepy brain. Then her eyes brighten, and she swings her legs over the side of the bed. "Holy shit. Really?"

I hate how upset I am, how my hands shake and my throat is scratchy and thick. This morning, I thought I could have a better handle on my wild emotions from last night. But seeing Dad and Yoga Leigh threw me off-balance once more. "Stop acting like this is a good thing."

"No offense, but your mom died fourteen years ago, and your dad is lonely as fuck. Did you ever think about what'll happen when you leave for college? I'm not sticking around forever either. He needs someone other than us, kid."

Digging my teeth into my bottom lip, I blink rapidly. "But she's so . . ."

"So what?"

Normal. Zen. Well adjusted. "She's not Mom."

"I'm sorry. I realize your dad having a woman spend the night isn't an ideal situation," she admits with a grimace, "but this is good. For the whole family."

In every daydream, every fantasy, I go to college in San Francisco, but I don't live at home. Wishful thinking, considering our financial situation, but I'd stay in the dorms. I never thought what Dad would do alone in the yellow house. Especially if Fiona left. Dad needs *someone*.

I clear the thickness in my throat. "Whatever. I'll be out this afternoon, and I need you to cover for me if things run late. No saying no. That," I say, pointing to the kitchen beneath the floorboards, "is all your fault."

Aunt Fee scrubs her face with her palms, then looks up at me with tired eyes. "Your dad knows about you and Beckett. Why the sneaking around?"

"Just cover for me, okay? Please?"

"Fine. But we're all going out to dinner at six thirty. I'll text you the address."

I have no idea how long the game will take. But if agreeing keeps Fiona silent until then, I'll have to hedge my bets. "Sure. Yeah. I'll be there."

Leaving Aunt Fee, I head upstairs and check the time.

I have six hours until I need to be at Billy Goat Bowl. My bedroom is still a mess from my pre-date outfit anxiety—how was that just yesterday?—and sadness tugs, but I ignore it. I put on some music and focus on cleaning up my room.

When someone knocks on my door thirty minutes later, I really hope it's Aunt Fiona.

"Hey, Caroline," Dad says, edging into the room. "You have a minute?"

"Nope." I'm sitting on my bed folding a bunch of T-shirts. "Kinda busy here," I mutter, holding up a T-shirt as proof. "Why aren't you at work?"

Dad shuffles into my room, stepping around the hazardous piles of clothes. "I'm going in late. Leigh's still here and—"

I snort. "Shocking."

"What's that?"

I glance up, and his brows are so close together they practically merge into one. Staring at my dad, at his sad face and balding head and soft stomach and hands on his hips, sets something off inside me. I just *break*.

"You're always either going into work late or leaving early. Kind of shitty, don't you think? Especially when we're two days away from getting evicted."

All the color is wiped from Dad's face. "How do you know about that? Did Jesset talk to you?"

"Does it matter?" I shove the pile of T-shirts aside. "What gives, Dad? We have a good life, and you're giving it all away! For what? A yoga instructor? For some cheap house in Arizona? What's so wrong with what we have?" My voice raises, all crackly and emotional. "Why aren't you fighting for us?"

Dad shifts toward me, but I shake my head. Resigned, he says, "This situation is complicated, Caroline. And I don't appreciate you speaking this way to me. I'm the one in charge, you hear me?"

I roll my eyes. "You might be in charge, but you're not doing shit. Setting a real great example, Dad."

"Watch it!" Anger flares in his normally docile eyes. "I don't have time to talk about this. Leigh's down-stairs. Tonight, after dinner, we're talking. Got it? This behavior—" He breaks off with a shake of his head. "I don't know what's gotten into you."

A toxic kind of anger fills my heart. "What's gotten into me? *Really?* I'm trying! I am trying to do something about the shitty situation you've clearly given up on."

Dad just watches me, confused. Disappointed. "You're grounded," he says after a second. "Don't come into work. Stay home and clean up this goddamn mess before school on Monday. But you better change your attitude before dinner. Leigh was so excited to meet you, and you're act-ing like a spoiled brat." And with that, he turns on his heel and storms out of my bedroom. Slams the door after him.

I really hate myself sometimes.

Twenty-Five

THE HOUSE EMPTIES by noon. Dad officially off to Bigmouth's with Yoga Leigh. Aunt Fiona took her car, headed to San Jose to meet up with some old college friends. I thought my fight with Dad would rattle me, but if anything, it's made me bolder. Dad's given up. Moved on. I'm all I have left.

Aunt Fiona texted me the address of the restaurant where I'm supposed to meet her, Dad, and Yoga Leigh at six thirty. I replied with a smiley face. There's a fifty-fifty chance I'll be done in time to make it. And right now I can't worry about missing some faux family dinner.

My phone is a graveyard of messages. Unread texts from Beckett. WhatsApp alerts from Mila, who I've seriously neglected the last week. Instagram notifications. All of it is overwhelming, so instead of reading them, I finish cleaning my room—reorganizing the wigs on their mannequin heads on top of my bookshelf—and I take a scalding-hot shower.

No disguises today, and the yellow silk James Galanos hanging on my dress form calls to me. I pull it over my head after showering; it's boxy since I haven't altered the waistline, and I use a thick band of black fabric to cinch it. I keep everything else simple—black tights, black flats, army jacket, and I smooth my hair into a nubby ponytail at the base of my neck.

When it's time to leave, I check my wallet. The paltry thousand dollars is secured in Beckett's money clip. Half will go for my buy-in at Billy Goat Bowl. My hands shake as I put it back into my purse, along with my Mace, the flyer, and my favorite red lipstick. My entire body is weak from too little food and too much fear.

God, I need confidence, need to find my fight and vigor from last night.

I pad downstairs and feed Jean Paul Gaultier some wet cat food. Guilt stabs when I realize I've forgotten to feed him the past few days. Not that he's hurting—he has quite the tummy—and he has dry food. But he turns into a bundle of purrs when I crack open the can.

As I clean up, something outside the kitchen window catches my eye.

Well, someone.

Beckett Porter paces the sidewalk outside my house. Hands stuffed in his corduroy jacket pockets, head ducked, he walks up and down the sidewalk. Elation hits, quickly followed by dread. Of course he showed up. Beckett won't miss his last opportunity to talk me out of playing today. Or yell at me. Express his concern and disappointment.

Ugh. Too bad there's no other way out of the house.

I don't want to face him, but I have to.

Shrugging on my jacket, I give JP a scratch on the back and head outside. Behind me, the old house groans good-bye. To get to Billy Goat Bowl, I can take my usual BART route I ride to work, then walk the extra few blocks to the other bowling alley. Even if it's hard, I *have* to ignore Beckett and keep moving if I want to get there on time.

"Chuck," Beckett says, walking over to the stoop. "Hey, um, about last night—"

"You made it pretty clear you were done," I mutter, hurrying down the steps and pushing past him.

"Wait." He trails me along the sidewalk. "If you read *any* of my messages last night, then you'd know I'm in this with you. All in."

My eyes burn with the promise of tears. I want to believe him, believe those words, but I can't help wondering if he's trying to stall me. Just long enough so he can change my mind. "Go home." I power walk, dodging pedestrians, and he follows me down the hill.

Beckett reaches out and manages to catch my wrist. "I'm not here to stop you. I'm coming. Please, just stop for a second." He's a good liar, but the way his voice breaks? You can't fake that.

I stop and turn on my heel. Now that we're close enough for me to see him properly, I study his eyes. As awful and bloodshot as mine. Beckett slides his hand to cover mine, comforting as ever. Damn it. Goose bumps and warmth flush my body.

"Did you think I would let you do this alone?" he asks. "Last night, I was upset, and I'm sorry."

With each passing second, my resolve melts and crumbles. He's really not here to change my mind; he's here to support me. But I can't let him do that.

"I'm sorry. I don't want to drag you into this. More into it, I mean." I shift on my feet, the relief that he doesn't hate me threatening to buckle my knees. "You can still go home. I'm doing this, and I'm going to kick ass."

"One more time with confidence," he jokes, mouth upturning in a small smile.

Even though it's clear what Beckett's intentions are, it's still hard to reconcile. He should be furious with me. But he's not, and I don't dare question him any further. I crumple against his chest and he hugs me close.

I press my face against his cotton T-shirt. Maybe Beckett is my confidence, because that contact fills something inside my chest. His presence and touch make me capable of anything. Everything.

"You aren't mad?"

Beckett shrugs simply, lightly. His arms are tight around my waist. I don't want him to let me go. "I wasn't ever mad. I just don't want you getting hurt. But if you want me to leave, say the word." When I don't say anything, he steps back, and his mouth quirks with a smile. "Excellent. Let's do this."

"At least I don't have to ride BART anymore."

"Glad you appreciate what I bring to the table."

I nudge him, and we get walking. The Accord is parked illegally near the stop sign. "Don't get me wrong, I'm glad you're here. But I didn't want to force you into this."

"You're not forcing me to do anything. We're partners in crime until the very end," Beckett says, taking the flyer Wilkes gave me and typing the address into his phone. "It should only take us fifteen or twenty minutes to drive there. Let's grab coffee first."

"I didn't sleep. No way in hell I'm turning down coffee." My entire body sighs in relief as I climb into the Accord.

"I didn't sleep much either," he admits. "Hey, what I was trying to say earlier was that I was wrong last night. I shouldn't have accused you of—"

"You were right," I cut him off, surprising myself. But during my sleepless night, I thought. A lot. Beckett's words echoed throughout my head and burrowed beneath the barbed surface of my heart. *I know what you're doing. . . . You're shutting me out.* Last night turned into so many complicated layers of messed up, I don't know where to begin. But the weight in my heart made me realize Beckett was right.

If I win today and guarantee Bigmouth's rent for the next few months, will Dad even be happy? Will he still upend everything and move us to Arizona? If he does, I'll have to say goodbye to Beckett. So yeah. Maybe I fell into old ways. Pushing him away so it won't hurt as bad if we leave. But I care too much about Beckett to keep hurting him. If he's all in, then I'm all in too. Whatever that means.

"Right about what?" he asks.

"I was shutting you out."

"Whoa." Beck glances from the road, steel eyes full of

wonder. "Did you just admit to being in the wrong?"

"Watch it," I mutter, pulling my feet up onto the seat, compacting into myself. I tuck my knees to my chest—an attempt to hold myself together—my feet balanced on the edge until I'm folded up. Because, yeah, this conversation is making me uncomfortable fast. Vulnerability and me? We're not friends. "You keep saying you don't want me getting hurt. But the physical hurt doesn't scare me. The cut Earl gave me? It's nearly healed. The emotional hurt, though? I . . . don't want to lose you again."

"You know I'd never hurt you, right? I'm so sorry I ever did anything that made you think otherwise."

I turn, pressing my cheek to my kneecaps. "I know," I say quietly. "Thank you."

Trust me, if I've learned one thing this past week, it's that I hurt myself way more than others hurt me.

Beckett reaches over and squeezes my hand twice. Lucky doesn't describe having him beside me. Even if I talked myself into believing I could do this alone, that was a lie. Beckett's my backbone, my courage, my comfort. My partner in crime. The one person I should have never denied, never rejected. Because he's always there for me, no matter how many chances and opportunities I've given him to turn his back on me.

Those type of people? They're rare.

I promise myself I'll never turn my back on Beckett again.

Billy Goat Bowl is every bit of hipster nonsense I suspected, located a mile from Bigmouth's Bowl and near its namesake, Billy Goat Hill. The building is a rustic two stories, resembling a rural barn with its simple exterior decor. We haven't even gone inside yet and I already hate the place. Hate it for helping play a hand in Bigmouth's demise, hate it for how it represents everything that's changing in my city.

Parked on the street, Beckett and I sip from our to-go cups from Any Beans Necessary. The windows are rolled down and the day's springlike weather filters in.

Beckett has the flyer spread out on his lap. "Did you read the fine print on here?"

"Yeah, why?"

"Says during weekends the bowling alley is twenty-one and over."

I empty the cup, set it aside, and yank my purse onto my lap. "Good thing you got me this, huh?" I fish out the fake ID I've had to use only once this week. "Think they'll buy it? You couldn't find a picture of me that *wasn't* my yearbook photo?"

Beckett grins at my cheesy photo. "Hey, these aren't cheap, and it's a convincing fake. Got it from the same guy who made mine, and I've never been caught. Besides, you only need ID to get in the door."

I return it to my wallet, hiding my Castelli High School student ID behind my Clipper card. My fingers tremble with an undercurrent of nerves. Earlier, I felt like a doomed mess. But with Beckett here, this feels normal. Maybe even exciting.

"Let's do this thing," I say, and we get out of the car.

Even though everything is confusing, Beckett holds my hand as we walk toward Billy Goat Bowl. I regret not kissing him last night—I regret *a lot* of things about last night—so I squeeze his hand even tighter. I hope we haven't missed our moment.

Linked together, we approach the building, my eyes alert.

Wilkes lurks, sitting in Billy Goat Bowl's shadowed outdoor patio.

Before we get closer, I tug Beckett to a stop and say, "Thanks for being here."

"Hey, if we go down, we both go down together. Deal?"

I squeeze his hand. "Deal."

Ray Wilkes gets up and strolls toward us, a burning cigarette dangling between his fingers. "Caroline, you showed."

I pull my hand free from Beckett's and cross my arms over my chest. "I said I'd be here, didn't I?"

Wilkes assesses me. "Yes, yes you did." He's dressed in a tight-fitting T-shirt and a sports coat, jeans chalked white in some areas with starch, and his damn cowboy boots. His gaze slides toward Beckett. "Who's this?"

I glance to Beckett as he takes in Ray Wilkes. His jaw is squared, fists tight at his sides. "Beckett," he says, "Porter."

If Wilkes recognizes his last name, it doesn't play on his face. He just motions for us to follow as he sits at a small bistro table, the top littered with cigarette ashes and smashed filters.

"Okay, kids. The plan's simple. Go inside and sign up. My buddy was registered to hold the spot open, but he called out sick, so they'll have an opening. Show them this card; they don't allow non-league players." Wilkes slides a membership card across the table. An ID number with no name or photo. On the other side is an unreadable signature scrawled in ink. Nothing else. "The buy-in to play is five hundred dollars. Got it?"

I pick up the card, nodding. Easy enough. "And where will you be? You're not playing?"

"I was banned from BABL games, but not from spectating. I'll be in the crowd."

Who the hell gets banned from a bowling league? "Anything else?"

Wilkes crushes his cigarette beneath the heel of his boot, lights a fresh one. "The game's bracketed and you bowl until the last player's standing. Giancarlo is the BABL champion; he'll undoubtedly make the finals. If you beat him, then you get your cut of the winnings. Their only requirement is for the winner to be there to receive the cash prize. Questions?"

"Yeah. Why are you doing this?" I ask, tapping the membership card against my leg; the thin plastic plucks at my leggings.

"It's tradition." He spins a gold wedding band around his ring finger. "Several years ago Giancarlo took something of mine, so I make a habit of taking something of his."

Wilkes has a complicated personal life I'm not touching with a ten-foot pole. "Okay then," I reply. "Is that it?"

"Yup." After a drag of his cigarette, he adds, "Good luck, Caroline."

Beckett and I walk into Billy Goat Bowl and I shudder. Something about that guy is off. "I'm starting to think this might be a bad idea."

Beckett laughs. "Oh, this is *definitely* a bad idea," he says, tucking me affectionately against his side as we walk. "But today's gonna be great."

"I really hope so," I say with a smile, lifting my chin higher as we reach the door.

We show the bouncer our IDs, and he doesn't double take or ask us a dozen questions about our astrology signs, zip codes, or addresses. The bowling alley is relatively small, only ten lanes lofted onto a platform, with a bar, a viewing lounge, and a restaurant.

A banner above the bar proclaims WELCOME BAY AREA BOWLING LEAGUE.

To the right of the bar is a cardboard table, and a sign hangs in front, instructing players to sign up. I cross the room and approach the table. The woman fielding sign-ups is cheerful, all smiles. Her stick-on name tag reads HELLO, MY NAME IS DANA!

"Hi," I say, my voice uncertain, lacking conviction. "I was hoping to play in today's tournament if you had any openings?"

Dana clucks her tongue. "Well, aren't you cute? But I'm sorry, we have a full roster today, honey."

I clear my throat and stand taller, pissed off by her dismissiveness. "You sure? Can you double-check?"

With a sigh, Dana opens her laptop. "Oh, lookie here," she says after a moment. "We had a last-minute call-out. Do you have your membership card?"

I hand the card over. "Buy-in's five hundred, right?"

"Yes." She takes down the member ID number. "Cash only, unless you arranged otherwise earlier."

I hand over the money. All that's left is five hundred dollars. It's laughable. We're right back where we started.

Dana slides the money off the table, counts out the amount, and puts it away in a lockbox. "Perfect. We've got ourselves a player. Last name?"

"Wilson."

"Okay, Ms. Wilson, the setup is simple." She speaks fast, like she's rehearsed this speech. "Today players are in five groups of ten. You're randomly assigned a group, and each is numbered off, one through five. The winner of each advances to the semifinals. The top scores from that game advance to the finals. Understood?"

With a bowling alley this small, it makes sense they'd have to split the players up. "Yeah."

"Fantastic." Dana reaches forward to stamp my hand. The rubber leaves behind a simple image of two criss-crossing bowling pins. "You're in group three. We'll call your number over the PA system, so until then, have some food, drink, and enjoy yourself!"

The tournament is supposed to start in five minutes. Hand in hand, Beckett and I wade through the crowd into the back of the large building and sink into an abandoned pair of velvet armchairs. My nerves are restless, excitable things. On one hand, I'm calmed by Beckett and our conversation earlier. On the other, I'm playing over all the different ways this day might go south.

I lost last night, and I might lose again. But I don't have much to lose, not anymore, and somehow that makes this situation more bearable. If I lose the five hundred today, nothing will change. I'll be in the exact same position I'm in now. But if I win? Well, that'll change everything.

"How're you feeling?" Beckett relaxes into the chair. The thing that used to annoy me the most about him—his complete inability to become truly annoyed or put off—is one of my favorite things about him now. Because I'm on the verge of freaking out, but his sense of calmness is contagious.

"Nervous." Both for the game and the fact I'll be in major trouble later.

I've spent enough time at Bigmouth's to know it can take a group of ten players up to an hour to finish. The tournament begins at two, meaning it could be close to eight or nine at night when things wrap up. I'll text Fiona if I'm going to be late, but there's a huge chance I won't make dinner at all. Not that I care. Dad already grounded me. I have zero intention of playing the role of the dutiful daughter so he can show me off to Leigh.

Billy Goat Bowl is as threatening as chicken noodle soup, but it's overwhelming. No other word for it. There are several players bowling test runs at the lanes. Even though a sign reads NO SMOKING, the smeared scent of weed and tobacco drifts. Dozens of voices rise, trying to drown out the others.

The accidental crash of beer bottles on cement floors.

The *boom, boom, boom* of bowling balls against innocent pins.

Classical music pours overhead, an off-putting contrast.

Everything rides on this. But it's just another game. A game I can win.

Twenty-Six

WE WATCH THE first group of players face off from our seats in the back, the lanes on a raised platform and visible throughout the alley. Billy Goat Bowl has high ceilings and a small second-story loft; the vaulted ceiling peaks, with glass-topped panels exposing the spring-day sky. Sunny with a hint of cottony fog. On the wall to the right is a gigantic digital scoreboard with brackets and last names that narrow until one winner remains.

Beckett grabs waters from the bar, and I chug mine as if it were filled with alcohol, or some magical elixir to give me the talent to win. We don't talk much, but the silence is comforting. Beckett solidly beside me, occasionally touching or squeezing my hand. After forty-five minutes, group one wraps up and the winner stalks outside for a cigarette. Group two wastes no time getting things rolling. Wilkes's drifted in and out of Billy's, always sticking to the walls, the thick crowds.

"Hey, Beck," I say, grateful we found this little corner of seclusion. "Did everyone else bring their own shoes?" Each lane has a ball return with bowling balls—and racks with extras—but I can't figure out where people are getting their shoes from.

"Don't worry, I've gotcha covered." Beckett hoists his bowling bag onto his lap and unzips it. "On both fronts." He lifts out a twelve-pound Hammer Absolut Hook from the bag. Black and purple.

I suppress a laugh. "Did you steal my bowling ball from Bigmouth's?"

"I borrowed it," he insists, and sets it back into the bag before pulling out a pair of shoes.

I wrinkle my nose. "Please don't tell me you 'borrowed' shoes, too, because I clean those, and I don't do a good job."

"Nope. Brand-new." He dangles blue-and-white bowling shoes with red laces from his fingers. They're retro and vintage-inspired—in other words, perfect.

I place my palm over my heart. "Aw, I'm touched. You bought me bowling shoes?" I joke, but my heart swoops over this small, yet weirdly sweet, gesture.

Beckett grins, and I bet his ears are reddening. "It's kind of weird you don't have a pair. Your family owns a bowling alley."

I snort. "Yeah, but for how long?"

He drops the shoes on the floor. "C'mon, wishful thinking today."

"You're right. Thanks for the shoes." I slide off my flats, pulling on extra socks over my tights-clad feet. I slip on the bowling shoes and wiggle my toes. "How'd you know my size?"

Beckett taps his head. "Steel trap," he says. "You mentioned your shoe size like four times this week at the other bowling alleys."

We both sit there, staring and smiling at each other.

I can't stop kicking myself over wasting the perfect opportunity last night to kiss him. I should've stayed in the auditorium. Never played at Miracle Lanes. Because now we're on the brink of uncertainty and there's a huge chance this will fail and I'll be carted off to Arizona, the land of cacti and car handles so hot they scald you on contact.

I lean closer. "Beckett—"

A lithe figure dressed in blue slides to a stop in front of our seats. Nic's powder-blue suit is one size too small for him. "Beckett Porter and the spitfire!"

I must be sleep-deprived, because I can't help noting that'd make an awesome band name. Except why does Beckett get top billing?

"Nic Manzione," Beckett says with a half smile. "What're you doing here?"

Nic grins toothily. "Wilkes asked me to help out with the, er, logistics today."

"You work with Wilkes?" Beckett asks, drawing back.

"I don't have much of an option," Nic explains, shrugging. "I owe him money. I like my kneecaps where they are, ya know?"

"That's rough." Beckett gives me an alarmed look

before dragging his hand over his jaw, thinking. "Hey, can I ask you something?"

"Shoot."

"Do you know where my dad went?" he asks, and the sincerity hurts my heart. "You said Wilkes ran him out of town, but is there anything else you can tell me?"

"Sorry, man, I don't know where he went." Nic throws his hands up in an exaggerated shrug. "Your dad hustled around the Bay, made and lost a lotta money, made a mess out of himself, yeah? Wilkes cleaned up his mess. Told him he'd get punished if he kept hustling, told him to get the hell out of the city. Probably smart of him to leave."

Beckett studies the floor. "He's a smart guy."

"Life, right?" Nic mutters without an ounce of empathy.

"Yeah." Beckett's dull voice is humorless when he laughs. *Life.*

"Later," he says to Beckett, and to me, "Can't wait to watch ya play, spitfire." He bounds back into the crowd.

Beckett collapses into the seat. "Ugh, I'm pathetic. Nic's not the one I need to talk to."

"Are you going to try and find your dad?"

"Yeah," he says, "I think so. I've waited long enough."

We don't have the chance to unpack that decision because the music cuts from overhead.

"Calling all members of group three! Time to play!"

I grab the ball from Beckett's bag and stand up. "Any parting words?"

"Go kick some ass."

"Thanks for believing in me." Hoisting the ball onto

332

my hip, I wrap Beckett in a one-armed hug. "Seriously, thank you. I mean it."

"Always," he says, and I know he means that, too.

Even though I know no one's really paying attention, it feels as if everyone inside Billy Goat Bowl is watching me approach the lanes. Sweat trickles down the back of my neck, along my spine, and the satin dress clings to my skin. I settle at the lane to the far left. Down the line are my direct opponents. We're all waiting for someone to make the first move.

I skip the formalities, the niceties, and I don't ask to bowl first.

Instead, I let my first shot loose because the game is on.

There's validation in league bowling.

Most of the games I've played have been hustles. I've lied, conned, and cloaked my talent in giggling, fanciful wigs, and airplane-size bottles of whiskey. Today there's no show. Today I play my best. Every shot, every frame, and every breath of air shares the singular purpose of winning. And I do.

Group three is a decent collection of players, ranging in skill and ability, and yet I beat them all during our round. Halfway through the game, I suspect I might win. By the eighth frame, I know it with certainty. My pin lead isn't strong, but it's enough to crown me the winner of my round.

My last name appears on the huge bracketed scoreboard, which infuses me with confidence. I'm *winning*.

Later, I'll join the other winners in the semifinals. Beckett's been watching from the back, and grins like mad when I walk over. I won't have to play for another hour, maybe an hour and a half by the way the games have been moving.

After I set the ball down in Beckett's bowling bag, I flex my fingers and groan. My hands are cramping painfully, the kind of cramp that has worked its way into my forearm and neck.

"You did it!" Beckett lifts his hand for a high five, and I wince as our palms smack together.

"Don't celebrate just yet," I warn. "I have two more games to survive if I'm gonna win this thing."

"You're doing great." He motions for me to sit. "You've guaranteed a spot on the semifinals."

"What time is it?"

He checks his phone. "Almost six. Why?"

"Oh. Well. I'm supposed to be at dinner with everyone at six thirty," I explain, regretting not texting Aunt Fiona sooner or just bailing when she invited me. Not like she gave me a choice. I'll talk to my dad tomorrow. When I have the money. No one will care how much I lied if I bring them the back rent.

"It won't be a big deal if you miss dinner, will it?"

"Let's hope not. There's no way I'm making it in time. Not if I want to win." I still text Aunt Fiona and tell her I'm running late because my BART train malfunctioned, and I'll be there as soon as I can—but not to wait for me.

Even though it means forfeiting our seats, Beckett and I gather our belongings and explore the rest of Billy Goat

Bowl. Mainly looking for food, because I'm starved. The restaurant is serving quick and easy food like sandwiches, fries, and wraps. I show them my stamped hand and get a free meal. I go with a falafel wrap, eating it as we walk a loop around the bowling alley.

Now that I'm here, I understand why Billy Goat Bowl so easily knocked Bigmouth's into the red. For one, they serve falafel. Bigmouth's serves nachos with fake cheese pumped from a concession dispenser circa 1980. Even if it's hipster central, everything here is curated, nicely decorated. Whoever owns this place put a lot of time and money into the design and the upkeep. I can't hate them for that.

The food helped fuel me, but I suggest, "Coffee?"

The restaurant offers fair-trade coffee in kitschy yellow mugs for *four* dollars, but Beckett spots a table near the entrance serving free instant coffee for the players. We fill Styrofoam cups full of crappy instant coffee. I'm savoring every moment, being here with Beckett. I don't let myself take it for granted.

"Wanna check out upstairs?" He gestures with his cup to the small spiral staircase leading to the loft overlooking the lanes. We follow the staircase, and it's less crowded upstairs, with a few couches and a pool table.

"Look at his," he says, and pushes open a door that's nearly invisible, painted to blend into the wall. An emergency exit leads out to a narrow platform, a small set of metal stairs leading to the roof. I hesitate, but he says, "C'mon," and I climb.

The building is only two stories, and we're not that high up, but we can still see the arc of the city, a slice of the bay. Beckett walks to the edge of the roof, sitting down with his legs hanging free. I settle beside him, leaning into his shoulder.

"It's nice out. Finally feels like spring." By spring, I mean the fog isn't as dense, the smallest scraps of sunlight pushing through the clouds. The air is refreshing after being downstairs.

"How're you holding up?"

"Good," I say through a mouthful of grainy coffee. "I guess. You?"

Beckett shrugs beside me. "Me? I'm fine. A little in awe of all the ass you're kicking."

"The game isn't over yet. I could fuck it up."

"You won't fuck it up," Beck says. "Confidence, Wilson."

I hang my head back, staring at the sky. The sun's teasing its departure. "I'll be confident when Bigmouth's is safe and I can stay in San Francisco."

What I want to say? *I'll be confident when I know I'm not going to have to leave you.* But vulnerability takes baby steps.

"You've done everything you can. If nothing else, feel good about that."

"I do," I say hesitantly, "but it makes me nervous."

"What can I do to make you stop worrying about"—he pauses and taps my temple—"what's going on in there?"

"A lobotomy's not appropriate, is it? Too extreme?"

"Oh, come on," he says, voice rising. "You're the strongest person I've ever met. I get it—you think you're damaged or a ticking time bomb, or *whatever*. But that's not you, Chuck. For once, I wish you could see what I see every day. Strength, so much strength. Beauty. Resilience."

Eyes welling, I wipe at the tears with my forearm. I've never described myself, or my mental stability, as strong, but hearing it from Beckett's mouth gives it an air of authenticity. Like maybe, no matter how tonight ends, there's a thread of strength woven in my mental tapestry.

I hide my smile—my tears, all the wild emotions—and turn toward Beckett as he wraps his arm around me. I set my coffee aside and palm his face with both hands. How did I ever think Beckett's eyes were steel? They're fog. San Franciscan fog.

We meet somewhere in the middle, and the kiss is inevitable.

First, the slight bump of our noses until I turn my face and press my lips to his.

Beckett makes this throaty noise and tangles his fingers through my hair. When his lips part, I shiver, but I hold him close. I should be nervous, unsure of what to do with my tongue or my hands, but my thoughts and worries melt away. Instead, I kiss Beckett boldly, his mouth warm against mine. He tastes like instant coffee and cinnamon. Right now it's the best taste. I wish I could taste it forever.

The gentle kiss spins a cocoon around us until it turns into something more urgent. The kisses slice me open, raw and vulnerable. A heat bundles behind my heart and sends tingles the length of my spine. A sensation so thrilling and calming and increasingly addictive. I shift closer, knocking over the dregs of my coffee, and slide my palms against his chest. Beckett's breath hitches. His T-shirt is thin, and I push beneath the fabric, feeling for his bones. The heat of his skin.

Eventually, regretfully, the kiss winds down. I don't want to stop exploring our two-person-only world, but Beckett cradles my face, his breathing sharp and ragged.

"Can you promise me something?" he asks.

My eyes are shut, our heads tilted together. "What?"

"If this plan doesn't work and you move to Arizona, can we . . . can we still be us?"

I don't know what we are or what the future may hold, but I say, "Of course," and Beckett kisses me again. His lips feather against mine, softly chapped and eager. Truthfully, I'd agree to grand larceny if it meant he would keep kissing me. But I like the idea of having him by my side, no matter what.

"I should probably go back down there." The words are the unfortunate truth. I can't miss out on my game, even if every cell inside me is begging me to shut up.

"Yeah. Probably." He sighs and pulls me to my feet.

Beckett's curls are mussed, his lips swollen, and his chest rises and falls rapidly. Rising to my tiptoes, I kiss him again, just once more.

For luck.

When we part, I take Beckett's hand, and we descend back into the competition.

Twenty-Seven

THE FINAL PLAYERS are assigned a lane. I'm lane ten. We're still setting up, and I've already wavered between doubt and self-confidence—both extremes on the spectrum.

This is it. We can walk away with enough money to make the past week worth something. Worth the small scar on my rib cage, worth the countless lies, worth the late nights. What Beckett and I have done? It's one of those *don't do this at home, kids!* kind of deals. But I wouldn't trade a second of this week for normalcy.

Beckett snags one of the last open seats near the lanes. Even though this huge foolish part of me wants to say "fuck it," and go make out in his car, I'll keep playing. Because I think I can win the entire thing. A trickling rush and a pump of caffeine pushes through my veins from that cup of coffee, and the high of our kiss gives me the rush I need to win.

I focus on the other players, searching out tells, tics,

and faults. Anything to give me the upper hand. Lanes one through nine are a mixture of players—drunk and sober, young and old—but they're all seriously good.

I won my first match—and if I blot last night from my memory, I've kicked ass all week—but I still suffer a nauseous thrill. I pretend this is any other game and snip away my surroundings. Hipster Billy Goat Bowl. Dizzying red lights. A large group of professional bowlers, older and more experienced, watching my every move. Wilkes, lurking out in the crowd.

Each player bowls in order of lane number, and lane one starts us off.

Between frames, I hang out with Beckett. He supplies me with fresh cups of coffee and tends to my battle wounds. One blister ruptured, and he applies a Band-Aid. We don't talk much. It's too difficult with the music, the number of people, and how everything echoes off the glass ceiling. His presence is comforting, supportive, and I was a fool for almost doing this without him.

I'm not worried when we each bowl our tenth frame, because I did better than half the players. The huge scoreboard displays those advancing into the finals. Since I don't know anyone's names, I watch the losers peel off until four remain: me, an elderly woman, a guy in his early twenties, and a player with a right hook—who, I overhear, is the infamous Giancarlo.

We're given a short break.

"How are you?" Beckett asks as I slump onto the arm of his chair.

"Fine. I'm nervous." I side-eye the other players. "They're *good*, Beck."

"Maybe, but you've got this in the bag," he says, and I believe him. Part of me *knows* I'll be the last player standing when the pins are down and the final scores are tallied. I can feel it.

I glance at the clock above the entrance. It's eight. I've officially missed dinner. I have no idea if Aunt Fee bought my bullshit story about the train breaking down, and I'm too afraid to check my phone and find out.

The finals begin, and we bowl in descending order this time. The lights and music and stench of bodies give me a headache. I don't let my pounding head alter my game. After all, I might miss this. I'll miss the hustling, the thrill, the money.

Except my playing hard isn't paying off. My skill is sloppy, my shots uneven. I manage a strike early on, but by my fourth frame, I'm only knocking down maybe five pins a turn. Soon, I'm left with splits I don't clear and open frames; my score reflects how poorly I've begun playing. How am I bowling worse than everyone else?

Any remaining confidence evaporates.

After the fifth frame, I hurry over to Beckett. The anxiety is too much. It's brimming. Overflowing. "I can't do this!"

He furrows his brows. "What do you mean?"

"I'm bombing! I'm too fucking nervous and it's showing. If I pick things up, maybe I can pull through. But I'm not going to win, not if I'm playing like this." Dragging my

341

fingers through my hair, I try to shake off the anxiety, but it clings. "I'm thirsty. I'll be back."

I grab my purse and beeline for the bar before Beckett replies.

I fully intended to order a 7 Up, but my eyes stray to the chalkboard menu. The list of fancy alcoholic drinks. Other than an ill-advised beer at a party freshman year, I've never drunk before. Drinking leads to looser inhibitions, a lack of control, which might lead to something much, much worse. And yet. What if it takes the edge off? Everyone else is drinking and bowling just fine. Actually, they're playing *better* than fine.

The bartender raps his knuckles against the bar. "What can I get you? First drink is free if you're playing."

I show him my stamp in exchange for Billy Goat Bowl's signature drink.

The vodka-and-ginger-liqueur concoction is poured in—no joke—a mason jar.

The jar's chilled, and I sip the odorless liquid as I weave through the crowd to the lanes. It burns like acid and has a tang. After another long sip, I don't mind the way my throat aches.

"What are you doing?" Beckett hisses when I reach him. "What happened to no drinking?"

"I'm about to lose—again—and I can't let that happen. I need to relax." I hate how Beckett's watching me, like he's disappointed. But then the liquid settles in my stomach and calms my nerves with a comforting, deft touch. "It's one drink."

"Fine. Take it easy, okay?" he says, eyeing me nervously.

"Here, hold this for me," I tell him.

"Sure." He looks like he wants to say more, but he holds on to the drink, slouching in the chair. "You're up."

With my liquid courage, I convince myself to bowl better. On the sixth frame, I bowl a split. But it's not enough. By the tenth frame, I've taken four more gulping sips of my vodka until the mason jar is empty, but I don't think it's helping. Regardless, I focus. If I get a strike, I'll punch out and win. If I did the math right. Debatable because my head is fuzzy.

Twenty grand. So. Close.

I recenter and compose myself. Time to do this. The tenth-frame punch-out. I've done it before, and I'll do it again. Nothing is different about this game. I am not nervous. I am not dizzy. I am not covered in Band-Aids, stiff and sore.

My toes are perpendicular to the foul line, and I tunnel myself away. Eye the headpin, arch my arm back, and draw my hand forward. Release the ball. Pure silence as it arcs through the air, the slam as it hits the oiled lanes, and the crash of ten pins as they spin into submission. The soundtrack of victory.

The shot? A strike so brilliant even I'm impressed. Textbook perfection. People whoop, clap, and laugh in astonishment. Grinning, I glance at Beckett, who must be over his disappointment as he gives me the dorkiest double thumbs-up. I look past him and into the crowd, searching for Wilkes or Nic, when I catch sight of dark hair held back with a bandanna.

Aunt Fiona is wading through the cluster of onlookers. And behind her? My dad.

Twenty-Eight

FOR A SECOND I stand there, unable to think, unable to move.

"Hey, Wilson," another player shouts, and I turn my back to my approaching guardians. "What're you waiting for? It's still your turn!"

Right. The bonus frame. I move toward the ball return, but a hand wrenches me around.

"Caroline Mae Wilson," Dad growls. He literally growls the words as he pulls me down from the platform. Dressed fancy in his date khakis and a blazer I've never seen before, Dad stands out. Ironic, considering these are his people. "What the hell are you doing?"

Aunt Fee hovers behind him, mouth pinched tight.

"Bowling?" I'm not trying to be a smart-ass, I swear. But what else am I supposed to say? My vision swims. From the impending nervous breakdown or the vodka,

I'm not sure. Laughter bubbles, even if this situation isn't anywhere near funny.

"Mr. Wilson," Beckett says, stepping closer and into our family circle, "this is all my fault."

"Shut it, Porter." Dad's grip tightens as he yanks me farther away from the lanes. The players look on curiously, but they have a game to play. To win. Dad drags me to the sitting area where Beckett left our bags.

"Dad," I plead. "Come on—"

Dad levels his gaze at me. He sniffs, nostrils flaring. "Have you been drinking? Goddammit, Caroline! Come on, we're going home. Get your stuff."

"If Caroline leaves, she'll be disqualified," someone says, and I struggle out of Dad's hold, searching for the voice. Wilkes steps out of the crowd, Nic a shadow behind him.

Does that mean I won?

I lift onto my toes to glimpse the scoreboard, but Dad holds me down.

"Who are you?" Dad glances to Aunt Fee, who shrugs, just as confused as he is.

"That's Wilkes," I say, my words heavy, suddenly too tired to explain.

Wilkes gives me a withering glance. "Caroline and I have a deal. She's playing for me. If she wins, she gets to keep most of the winnings. But that can't happen if she leaves. So why don't you let her—"

Dad turns to Wilkes, and even in my stupor, it's clear his patience is wearing thin. "Don't you dare tell me what to do with my daughter."

Wilkes doesn't flinch. Despite the snarl in Dad's voice, he's not intimidating to someone like Ray Wilkes. "Mr. Wilson, if Caroline isn't present when the winner is announced, she can't collect her winnings. After my cut, she'll win twenty grand. That'd go pretty far in saving your little bowling alley, don't you think?"

"Look, I don't know what the hell you're talking about, but this is a family matter and we're leaving." To Beckett, Dad says, "Porter, get yourself home. I'll deal with you later. Take BART if you've been drinking."

"I haven't, sir." He shrinks beneath Dad's gaze. "Can I talk to Chuck for a moment?"

Dad wraps his arm around my shoulders. "Nope. Not tonight."

"Dad, wait," I beg, fighting through the mental haze. "Just until the winner is announced! The game's almost over. Aunt Fee, can you make him stop?"

My aunt shakes her head.

That's when I know I've fucked up big time. Not even Aunt Fiona can help me now.

Beckett hands over my purse, his face full of regret. He mouths, *I'm sorry*. My cheeks are hot, eyes burning. I want to cry.

Then the overheard PA crackles. "Ladies and gents, the winner of the Bay Area Bowling's Tournament is . . . Giancarlo Russo on lane four!"

The bowling alley erupts in cheers and applause.

No. I didn't throw my last frame, but I still foolishly hoped I would somehow come out on top.

I tear from Dad's grip and stagger up the platform, Wilkes following, for a better view of the scoreboard. Because they must've read it wrong. But no. I came in fourth. Dead last. My stomach drops to my knees.

I lost.

Wilkes grabs my forearm. "What the fuck, Caroline?"

"What? I didn't lose on purpose." I struggle to pull free, but his grip tightens. Tears spring to my eyes. I lost, Wilkes's hurting me, and I'm in over my head.

"Like hell you didn't. You skipped out on your last frame!" Wilkes's up in my face—cheeks ruddy, breath fast and rancid—and a zip of terror strikes me.

"Let me go!" I say, trying again to twist free. But it's no use. Wilkes's bigger, stronger.

And that's when my dad punches Ray Wilkes in the face.

The man drops to the floor with a *thud.*

"Oh shit," someone yells from the crowd, and another person calls for help.

"Jack," Aunt Fiona says to her brother, shaking his shoulder. Dad swears, staggers a few steps back, and cradles his hand. "Let's go before someone calls the cops. We've got Chuck drinking and you punching people! What the hell happened to this family?"

Valid question.

We gather our belongings and strongarm our way through the crowd. Beckett follows us outside onto the sidewalk. The briny nighttime air sobers me up fast, but my head still swims. I look over my shoulder and into Billy

348

Goat Bowl, where an employee attends to Wilkes while everyone watches. Nic's nowhere to be seen. It's over. Everything is truly over. And I lost.

Dad's steering me away, his good hand pressed to the small of my back. Maybe he feels bad for me because he relents, letting me say goodbye to Beckett.

I wrap my arms around Beckett's neck and hug him tight.

"I'm so sorry," he whispers. "This is my fault."

"Shut up." I hold him tighter, crying into the crook of his neck. "I don't want to leave."

Beckett presses his lips to my cheek. He knows what I really mean.

I've failed Bigmouth's. Failed Dad. Failed *everyone*. And now I'll have to leave San Francisco. And Beckett. Not right now, but soon, and I can't stomach the thought.

Tears blur my vision as Dad hauls me off Beckett, pushing me toward his car. His sedan is parked in a loading zone. He pops open the back door and I stumble inside. Aunt Fiona shoves my bags in after me and shuts the door, sitting up front with Dad. No one speaks the entire car ride home.

This erratic behavior? It was irresponsible. I put myself—and others—at risk because of my carelessness.

You are not your mother's child.

But for the first time, the words don't work.

I press my eyes shut and let the tears roll down my cheeks.

SUNDAY, APRIL 29

DAYS UNTIL BIGMOUTH'S EVICTION: 1

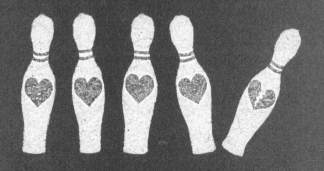

Twenty-Nine

DAD LETS ME sleep until morning.

When the sunlight reaching through the curtains becomes too bright to ignore, I roll onto my back and stare at the ceiling. My head throbs, my eyes swollen from crying. I'm still wearing my silk dress and tights. Dad confiscated my phone and laptop last night before pouring me into bed.

I'm kind of shocked he did—I'm rarely in trouble, and I hoped Dad would be blundering, out of his element. Turns out, I underestimated him. Without my phone and laptop, I have no way to contact Beckett. No way to ask if he got home okay or if he's also in trouble. Dad better not have called Beckett's mom. Nothing that went wrong was his fault.

I push upright and swing my legs over the edge of my bed, head spinning. Someone left a glass of water and two aspirin. Aunt Fee, probably. I pop the pills and guzzle the water. Then I peel off my dress and roll my tights down my legs, kicking them off. I really need a shower, but I pull on pajamas and a sweater.

Down in the kitchen, Aunt Fee's making acai berry pancakes and Dad's reading the paper. If I didn't know any better, it'd be like any other Sunday morning.

"Hey," I say groggily.

Dad and Fee glance from me to each other. They share a knowing look—the not-so-casual lifting of eyebrows and volleying of unspoken words.

Dad clears his throat, but Aunt Fiona suggests, "Why don't we have breakfast in the den?"

I agree, and my aunt serves up pancakes, filling a cup with honeyed tea.

We shift into the other room. Me on the couch with a blanket, a stack of pancakes, and tea. Dad's pacing around the small space, expression unreadable. Aunt Fiona settles in the velvet armchair beside me, the bags under her eyes reflecting my guilt.

I did this. I did this to my family.

"Do you like the tea?" Aunt Fiona asks nervously. "The honey's from a local—"

"Fiona," Dad says, exasperated. "Stay on topic."

Clearly, we're all on edge.

My stomach's too hollow for food. I sip my tea so I have something to do, something to occupy my mouth other than words. It's hot enough to burn my tongue. Good, though.

"What the hell were you thinking?" Dad goes right for it.

"I'm not sure where to start," I say. "How did you guys know where I was?"

"We found you because we tracked your phone, genius," Aunt Fee interjects.

Of course they did. I laugh at my failure to be properly sneaky, and even my aunt joins in. The most basic mistake in the book. But when Dad glares at us, we both shut up.

"What happened last night, Caroline?" he asks, clasping both hands behind his head. "Who was that man? Whose money were you gambling with—and why? I just don't understand why you'd do something like this. Is this what you were talking about the other day? Trying to save Bigmouth's?"

Another sip of tea tasteless on my burnt tongue. A second to collect myself and I explain. I tell Dad and Aunt Fiona everything. The truth. I only tell one lie. In this version, I approached Beckett—they don't need to know it was his idea. I insist Beckett never put me in danger, and most of the mistakes were of my own making. Which is the honest truth.

At some point, I start crying. The tears pour. Because I'm clearly unhinged. Normal teenagers don't do this. They don't put themselves in danger. Is this what mania is? I drank. I never drink. Mom loved drinking.

I'm starting to lose track of where Mom ends and I begin.

Tea spills as I set the mug on the coffee table and fold my arms over my tucked-in knees. "I'm sorry," I say between hiccuping sobs. "I wanted to save Bigmouth's

355

and stay in San Francisco. I wasn't trying to be reckless. I only drank because I was nervous about losing. It was just one drink, I swear. I thought it'd help take the edge off. Help me focus and win."

Dad looks away as if he can't stand the sight of me.

Aunt Fiona remains silent.

"I've been so careful," I whisper to myself, "to not end up like her."

Dad pauses his pacing. "Like who?" he asks, a crease of confusion forming between his brows.

Snot drips down my chin. "Mom."

Aunt Fiona takes a sharp inhalation.

"What do you mean, Caroline?" He sits beside me, and the cushion dips toward him.

"Please don't call me Caroline. I'm not Mom. I thought I wasn't. But maybe I am? What I did—I wasn't thinking. I fucked up, Dad. I tried so hard to keep myself in line, I didn't notice when I swung out of control."

Except that's not the truth. Not entirely. On some level, I knew what I was doing wasn't right. That it was risky, illegal. But that didn't stop me, because it was fun. Thrilling. I felt so alive. The opposite of depression—I didn't want to give that up. And I hate that about myself, that I didn't care enough about my safety to stop.

Dad wraps his arm around me. "Chuck," he says, and the nickname sounds like a truce, "you would be lucky to turn out like your mother."

I lean against him, my tears soaking into his shirt. "What do you mean? Mom was—"

356

"Your mom suffered. She suffered for many years, and my biggest failure was not being able to save her from her depression." Dad pauses and takes a shaky breath, wiping at his own tears. "Your mom isn't someone to fear. She was a vibrant, talented, and loving woman. She loved you so much."

Dad's voice cracks.

I crack.

Clearing his throat, he continues. "Your mother was the love of my life, and sometimes she experienced *too* much. She lived in the extremes, and after you were born, when she told me she was taking her medication, I believed her."

"Why'd she lie?" I manage to ask between my tears.

"I don't know, and trust me, I've thought about it a lot. Too much. Guess she thought she didn't need it." Dad's gaze drops to the floor, forehead creased. "And I was so stressed, with a new baby and taking over her dad's business, that I never looked too close. For a long time, I told myself I couldn't control her. But it was never about control—it was about caring. I cared, so much, but somewhere down the line, I stopped showing her how much. That's why . . . I didn't want to tell you the truth about her death."

"Jack." Aunt Fiona's bottom lip trembles, and she tucks it between her teeth. "It wasn't your fault."

Sniffing loudly, Dad sits back. "Oh, I know. But back then?" He shakes his head sadly, eyes watery and bloodshot. "I'm so sorry, Chuck, for lying to you about your mom. I didn't know how to handle my grief and my guilt—"

"Don't feel guilty. If anything, it's my fault. She stopped her meds because of me."

Dad swears, pulling me closer. I curl up against him, crying so hard my chest aches. The literal bones hurt as my shoulders roll forward with each and every sob. "What happened with your mom is not your fault," he says, rocking me back and forth. "It's no one's fault, not your mom's, not mine, not yours. It's the same as any other illness. Cancer or pneumonia or a heart attack.

"I'm more educated now, but when you were younger, I never wanted you to think your mom left you *willingly*. I never wanted you to think she had a choice, that she made a decision to leave us. She loved you. She loved you more than anything. But she was sick. I was supposed to be her support system, and I failed. And I'm sure as hell not failing you. We haven't done right by your mom, or you, by ignoring these topics, no matter how hard they are. No matter how painful. We'll talk more from now on, okay?"

I shift away and wipe my eyes. What he's saying right now? It's everything I never knew I needed from him. I'm too choked up to speak, but I manage a nod.

Dad's smile is tentative. "You deserve to know more about your mother. She was such a wonderful person, so funny and talented. I hope you understand that her illness doesn't make her someone you should *ever* be afraid of."

"I know." Or at least I'm beginning to know. I blow my nose and sink back into the cushions. My chest is light, my head woozy with emotional overhaul. "I'm sorry about last night."

Dad swipes at his tears, but he can't hide the shake of his hands. Normally, I'd think he needed a cigarette, but these trembles come from deep within. "You were trying to do a good thing, and you got off track. Despite it all, you amaze me. I don't condone what you did—far from it—but the lengths you went to save Bigmouth's break my heart."

"I didn't do it just for you," I admit with a sniff, and ball the tissue up in my hand. "I don't want to leave San Francisco. You always said if we didn't have the business anymore, we'd move to Arizona to be with Grandma and Grandpa. I saw the housing listings for Surprise, Arizona, on your laptop. Why the hell is there a town called Surprise—"

Dad cuts me off. "You weren't supposed to see that. I didn't want you getting upset before you had all the information. Jesset and I had an agreement. If I paid partial rent, we could stay. A month or two ago, I told him I was looking to close up shop, but I needed time to get everything squared away. I didn't want to drop this bomb on you, Chuck, and I wanted to secure a new job first. When Jesset moved up the timeline—"

"The conversation last week," I say, the murky questions in my head becoming clearer now. "That's what you two were talking about?"

"He found a new tenant, and since I owed over a month of rent, he had legal grounds to evict. I doubt we're in any trouble as long as I clear the rest of what I owe him. But we have to be out by June. That's when the new tenant moves in."

My breath hitches, stuck on the question I've avoided for so long, but I need to know the answer. "So . . . we're not leaving the city? We're not going to Arizona?"

"No." Dad shakes his head. "We'll find a way to stay in San Francisco."

Sitting up a bit straighter, I ask, "Why'd you lie, though? Why didn't you just tell us what was going on?"

Dad swallows, hesitates as his eyes dart around the room. "I shouldn't have hidden the truth, but you're at the end of junior year, school's going well, you're doing well—I didn't want to throw a cog in your progress. I knew you'd take the news of Bigmouth's closing hard. And you, my darling daughter, would've tried to find a solution." He breaks off with a laugh. "I called that one. Anyway, I panicked when Jesset moved up the deadline on me. I was supposed to have until September. And I guess I was ashamed."

"You could've told us," Aunt Fiona says gently. "Bigmouth's closing isn't a failure. If anything, it was a long time coming."

"Yeah," I say, agreeing even though I see where Dad's coming from. He was doing what he always does: trying to save me hurt and pain and anxiety. "It's okay, Dad."

"Thanks." He sniffs. "Arizona was my backup plan," he admits, sagging against the couch cushions. "Until I met Leigh."

"What does Leigh have to do with this?"

Dad blows his nose. "Months ago, when business really took a hit, I began looking at housing in Arizona. But it wasn't until after I'd been dating Leigh for a month or so that I realized I didn't want to leave. San Francisco was always your mom's city—not mine. Your mom's ghost is *everywhere*. Curled up with a new release at the Booksmith. Buying banana cream tartlets at Miette. Sunbathing at Dolores. It's always been hard for me.

"Leigh's experienced her fair share of grief and recommended a therapist. We only met a handful of times, but he helped me come to terms with our situation. I always viewed Bigmouth's as my last link to the city. With your mom gone, the business gone, I didn't think I belonged here anymore. But this city is my home now too."

The tears are drying on my cheeks and my breath is slowly returning to normal. I'd never thought of the situation that way. Like Dad might be running from his ghosts. "What does that mean for us? What're we going to do?"

"Well, Arizona's off the table," he replies. "For now. I can't promise I'll *always* stay in this city, but no matter what, we'll talk things over as a family. San Francisco means so much to you, and we'll figure something out. It won't be easy, but we'll find our way. As for Bigmouth's . . ."

"We can still save it," I say, blowing my nose. "Maybe we can set up a fundraiser or something? I can help renovate; I was serious about those DIY projects."

Dad smiles a sad smile. "No, honey. It's too late for that. Even if you got the back rent, I barely have enough for next month. It's just too expensive. I never wanted to renovate Bigmouth's because that's how it was when I met your mom. That's how your grandfather ran it, and it thrived.

I don't have it in me to strip it bare and renovate it, just to make a profit. I don't think your mom or grandfather would've wanted that."

The past week, I told myself if Bigmouth's closed, we'd be out of San Francisco before the Fourth of July. But staying? My heart floods with tentative hope.

"Even before Jesset threatened to evict us," Dad continues, "I had been sending my résumé out. Looking at my options. Nothing's forever, and sometimes you need to say goodbye to move forward. The Wilson family has been treading water for some time now, and I'm ready to take a step into the future."

"What are you going to tell Jesset?" Aunt Fiona asks, ever the pragmatist.

Dad wipes his hand over his eyes. "That we'll be out by June." His smile is sorrowful, but his eyes have this shiny hope to them. "As for us, well, think of this as the next chapter. Not saying goodbye but moving forward. And we'll do it together. Sound good?" He nudges me.

"Yeah. I'm sorry." I smear away any leftover tears.

Dad forces a smile. Now that all the truth is out there, he seems lighter. "We'll talk more tonight, okay?" He pushes up from the couch and adds, "I hate doing this to you, but you're grounded for the rest of the school year and all of summer. You have to return to weekly therapy appointments, and if you ever get near a drop of alcohol again, we'll be having a much different conversation. Understood?"

I nod. It's a lenient sentence considering all the shit I've done. "Yes."

Dad squeezes my shoulder. "I love you. So damn much."

Aunt Fiona leans over to hug me. "I'm glad you're safe," she whispers. "And like your dad said, we'll figure everything out. Wilsons are tough."

I can't help thinking I'm only half Wilson. Half of me is my mom, an O'Neill, whatever that's worth. If it's strength, or weakness, or something else entirely. But the unknown isn't as scary as it used to be.

I take a deep breath and ask Dad, "Can you tell me about when you met Mom?"

Thirty

AUNT FIONA KNOCKS on my bedroom door later that evening.

Dad's at Bigmouth's, releasing me from work duty for the final hours of spring break. He's meeting with Jesset tomorrow to discuss a payment plan for the back rent and eviction. I'm under my aunt's watch until he gets home.

"Come in," I call from my bed, breaking the staring contest I'm having with the wall. Without my phone and laptop, I'm dying a slow death. I haven't heard from Beckett, and I have no idea if he's tried reaching out. I miss him on a fundamental, cellular level.

My aunt nudges the door open, carrying a smooshed box to her chest.

"Hey, kid," she says, setting the box down at the foot of my bed.

I hoist myself upright, crisscrossing my legs. "What's that?"

Aunt Fee perches on the edge of my mattress. "Thought you might regret throwing this out."

The box. Mom's box.

With everything going on this week, it was easy to pretend like I didn't break down. Didn't toss the box of memories in the trash. This tiny, shy part of me sighs with relief. Throwing away the box was a mistake. An easy, temporary fix to an insurmountable problem.

"Thanks, Fee." I slide the box across the comforter and hug it to my stomach. Inhale the scent of mothballs, cardboard, and something faint. Like perfume. I don't know what I'll do with Mom's clothes or her unfinished designs, but they don't belong in the trash. If anything, *I* belong in the trash for what I did.

"How're you holding up?" Aunt Fiona asks.

"Not well." I frown, playing with the flaps of the cardboard box. "I need to talk to Beckett. Monday seems so far away."

"It's *tomorrow*. One sleep away."

"Stop being logical. He doesn't even know we're not moving to Arizona." My voice seismically cracks. "He could've driven over here. But he hasn't. . . . You sure Dad didn't call Beck's mom?"

"I convinced him not to. Beckett did nothing wrong, other than egg you on." She tosses a throw pillow between her hands, green eyes slanted with mischief. "Considering he's like, in love with you, I can't fault him for going along with your plan."

"Fiona! He's not—" My face heats up, my words twisting and stumbling. "Just no. Stop it."

"Ignorance isn't a good look for you," my aunt quips, then tosses the pillow at my face.

The pillow bounces off my head and lands in my lap. "Shut up. Can we just check on him? Swing by his house?"

While I want to update Beckett on the Arizona situation, my biggest fear is a selfish one. What if Beckett's ignoring me? What if thinking I'm moving to Arizona made him reevaluate if I was worth it? What if, after *everything* we've been through, he wants nothing to do with me?

"No way, kid." Aunt Fee shifts, tucking one leg beneath her. "You're in deep shit."

"Exactly! Dad's *already* mad. I'm *already* grounded." I scoot the box of Mom's designs aside and grasp Aunt Fee's hand. "Please? One quick trip into Berkeley. Dad will never know if we're fast." It's past five in the evening. He won't be home until he closes for the night, eight on Sundays.

Aunt Fiona flops onto her back and groans. "Chuck, I can't. Your dad would kill me."

"I need to see him." Because the ping-ponging irrational fears filling me up from head to toe are unbearable. "Please, Fiona."

Something about my tone causes Aunt Fee to relent. "You really like him, huh?"

"I really do." My voice is a shredded whisper. "So much. I hate it."

Hefting the greatest sigh known to humankind, she stands up. Hand cocked on her hip, she says, "All right. Let's go."

"Seriously?" I scramble off the bed, wasting no time in choosing an outfit. I haven't done laundry in over a week, and the pickings are slim.

On her way out of my room, Fiona adds, "We're just doing a drive-by, okay?"

I nod, displacing Jean Paul Gaultier as I tug a sweater on my floor out from beneath him. The cat glares at me, slinking off and jumping onto my bed. The sweater has cat hair on it, smells like patchouli and thrift store, but it'll do. "Gimme two minutes, okay?"

"Two minutes. But hurry up before I change my mind."

I cross my room and shut the door, forcing my aunt into the stairwell. Alone, I strip off my pajamas, tug the sweater over my head, and pull on thick leggings. In the bathroom, I brush my teeth and swish mouthwash. No amount of cosmetics can make me look healthy and well rested. The exhaustion is wrinkled into my skin, full of lifeless pallor. I rub on tinted moisturizer and layer my lips in red. Good enough.

Yesterday's brief springlike day is long gone, so I grab my army jacket to protect me from the rain. Downstairs, I follow Aunt Fiona into the garage and her VW Bug. I don't have Beckett's address, so I work off memory, directing her the best I can across the glittering Bay Bridge and into Berkeley.

When Aunt Fiona turns onto Beckett's street, I hold my breath. The Bug rolls to a stop outside his house. The battered Accord is in the driveway.

"That's his car!" I exhale so hard my lungs threaten to collapse. "Can I go inside? Please? Just for a few minutes?"

"That wasn't the deal. He's clearly fine."

"C'mon, once Dad gets home I'm grounded for good! I need to talk to him before we're back in school, Fee. Please."

Even I hear how pathetic I sound.

So must my aunt, because she motions toward the house. "Go on. But don't take too long, you hear me? I'll honk when it's time to go."

All my bravado drains as I step out of the Bug, the rain pattering on my hood. I walk down the slicked driveway, past Beckett's Accord, and to the front door. I push the bell and wait.

Mrs. Porter opens the door. "Hi, Chuck," she says, widening the gap. "Come on in! Is Beckett expecting you?"

I twist my hands around the cuffs of my jacket and wipe my shoes off on the doormat. "Oh, uh, not exactly."

Beckett's mom just smiles. "He's in his room. Down the hall to the left."

"Thanks, Mrs. Porter."

I take off down the hallway. The bedroom door on the left is closed, and I hesitate before knocking. No one answers. After trying the knob, I ease open the door. A few inches at a time. Huh. Beckett's room. I spent a lot of time at his old house, but I've never seen his new bedroom. The floor lamp in the corner is switched on, casting the room in a faint artificial glow.

Everything about Beckett's room is dark. Short and nubby black carpet. The closet's closed, the accordion door shut tight. An unmade bed with chevron-printed sheets and a navy-blue comforter. It's not messy, but it's not neat, either. A laundry hamper overflows in the corner. The spines on the bookshelf are organized by color. Snow globes, old-fashioned insulators, and shallow decorated dishes filled with loose change crowd the shelves. His desk is piled with papers, notebooks, and dozens of pens and Sharpies.

I step farther into the room. A framed photo sits on his dresser, and I pick it up. Enclosed in red plastic is a picture of me and Beckett from last year. Beckett's dressed in tight jeans, his shorter yet wild curls slicked back. Face flushed, his prop leather jacket tied around his waist. I'm pulled to his side, wide-eyed and camera shy. Hard to believe a few hours later our friendship dissolved over a misplaced family secret that shouldn't have ever been a secret and a few unfortunate words. Harder to believe Beckett kept—and *framed*—this picture.

"Chuck?" Beckett stands in the doorway. He's dressed in checkered pajama pants and a long-sleeved shirt, but his curls are wet, and he holds a bath towel in one hand. "What're you doing here?"

"Hey." Relief whooshes over me, but it's double-edged. Is he even happy to see me? "I was, uh, worried about you. But you're fine, so I should probably go."

Beckett eases the bedroom door closed and tosses the towel onto his desk chair. "You overthink *every-thing*, don't you?" In two strides he crosses the room and wraps me up in a hug. He clutches me to his chest, the framed photograph caught between our bodies. Wet curls drip onto my skin; he smells strongly of his spicy body wash.

"Chuck, listen to me. I want you in my future. Even if you're leaving for Arizona, we can make it work. In whatever capacity. As friends. As bowling buddies. As your boyfriend. *Whatever.* I wanna be around you. Is that okay?"

"Yeah, definitely, but—"

Before I can explain about Arizona, his mouth catches mine and we're falling onto his bed.

The sheets smell like him.

This kiss is different from the first. It's slow, careful, oddly intense. Appreciative.

When Beckett pulls away, I shake my head, tug his lips back onto mine. Soak him in. Because any minute now, I'll have to leave. And leaving Beckett will be painful even if it won't be for long. Shit, I almost forgot about Aunt Fiona. I don't think she honked, but then again, I'm not really paying attention to the outside world right now.

Beckett's body presses mine into the mattress like the world's greatest weighted gravity blanket. His thumbs press against my hip bones as he tilts me closer. I hate that Beckett and I could've been doing this a long time ago. Better late than never, though.

When we part, it takes all my willpower not to kiss him again. He shifts off me and flops onto his back. He doesn't say anything, just laughs softly in this disbelieving kind of way.

"Good thing I'm staying in the city." I roll onto my side and rest my head on his chest. "Because we should keep doing that. Like daily."

Beckett pushes to his elbow. "Wait, you're staying? Why didn't you lead with that?"

"I tried, but you cut me off. Not like I'm complaining." Beckett's ears are red. Like stop-sign red, and the sight of those red ears makes me swell with satisfaction. My willpower sucks, and I kiss him again because I'm pretty damn sure I'm in love with him, I'm not leaving San Francisco, and somehow, my life feels like it might be okay.

"You're really staying?" he asks between kisses.

"Yup, no Arizona. And I have Yoga Leigh to thank."

"What?"

"It's complicated."

"I don't care why or how, but I'm so glad you're staying." Beckett drops his forehead to mine. "You make me so happy."

"Yeah?" I blink back tears. "You make me so happy too."

The way we are with each other is different from what it was a year ago, but Beckett always made me happy. Our hands wind together. At the foot of the bed, the framed photograph lies faceup.

"Sorry I didn't reach out earlier. I tried texting—"

"My dad took my phone and laptop away. I'm majorly grounded."

Beckett laughs. "I figured. My mom was working so I had to stay here with Willa, but if I didn't hear from you by tonight, I was going to drive into the city. Even if your dad probably wouldn't let me inside, I'd find a way. Climb up that fire escape again."

"What? No carrier pigeon?"

"They're very picky birds. They hate the rain."

I laugh and hug him tight. "Oh really?"

"Yeah," he murmurs into my hair. "Hey, if you're grounded, how're you here right now?"

"I convinced Aunt Fiona to jailbreak me; she's waiting outside. I doubt we have much longer, though." I tell the abbreviated version of what went down this morning. "I'm sorry I can't stay longer."

As if I summoned her, the Bug's horn sounds outside.

I push off the bed. "I should go."

"Stay." Beckett holds on to my waist. "I'll drive you home."

So. Tempting. But I slide out of his embrace. "Do you want me grounded all of senior year?"

"Fine," he says, but he's smiling. "Wait! I found something." Holding up one finger, he grabs his phone off the desk and taps at the screen before handing it over.

Pulled up on the small screen is an article from the *SF Chronicle* posted two hours ago. KINGPIN KNOCKED DOWN: MAJOR ARREST MADE BY LOCAL POLICE.

I scroll, reading in earnest.

Ray Wilkes was arrested last night at Billy Goat Bowl when a physical altercation alerted police to his whereabouts. An unnamed man punched Mr. Wilkes, which prompted an onlooker to call the police. When approached by law enforcement, Mr. Wilkes ran. Unaware the man they were chasing was a wanted felon, the officers caught up with Mr. Wilkes several blocks later and arrested him. The officers were shocked that a simple fight led to the arrest of a man who has evaded police capture since the nineties. Mr. Wilkes is notorious in the Bay Area for the trafficking of narcotics and running several illegal gambling operations at local businesses without the proprietors' knowledge or permission. During his decades-long crime spree, Mr. Wilkes has racked up a long list of charges, and he's due in court by the end of next month.

"Holy shit," I say with a broken laugh. "I can't believe my dad accidentally led to his arrest. I mean, that's *perfect*."

Beckett takes the phone, grinning. "Right? I figured my dad can come home now."

I grab his hand and squeeze. "You should try to find him."

Beckett's smile is hopeful. "Even if it was a complete disaster, I'm glad we did this."

"Me too."

"I am sorry it didn't work out and we couldn't save Bigmouth's."

"That reminds me"—I pause to grab my bag off the

floor—"this belongs to you." Inside are Beckett's money clip and the last of our winnings.

"But half of this is yours."

I could use the extra cash, but I don't *need* it anymore. Not like they do. "Seriously," I say, and press the money clip into his palm, "it's yours. We were in that Wilkes mess because of me. Take the money." Aunt Fiona honks again, and I wince. "Okay, I really need to go."

Beckett relents and folds his fingers around the money clip. "See you tomorrow at school?" he asks, pulling me in for another kiss, lips hovering on mine.

"God, that sounds weird. *School*."

"We'll have each other."

The words make me smile and float, nearly lifting me off my toes. "Yeah?"

Beck nods. "We survived the last week. Surely we can handle the rest of high school?"

"We can definitely try," I say, surprising myself with optimism.

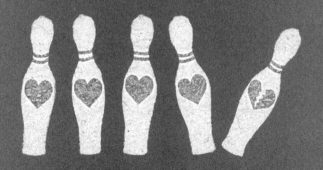

Epilogue

FOR THE FIRST time in decades, the lanes at Bigmouth's Bowl are packed.

The ancient disco lights flash and dance across the pinewood. Our weekly customers are here: the geriatrics, the knitting club, and the bowling league. Everyone has shown up to say goodbye to Bigmouth's. Even Marty, the guy who bowled Bigmouth's last perfect game, showed up with his buddies.

Everyone who has touched our lives, or has been touched by Bigmouth's, showed up to give our strange little bowling alley a proper send-off. My old boss, the owner of Any Beans Necessary. Dad's buddies from the bar. Pete, our former employee. Strangers who saw the open doors, the flashing lights, and wandered inside. Mila, too. She made it to San Francisco during her summer break in the States; we get along even better in person.

Then there are the vultures. The other Bay Area bowling

alley owners we contacted because, to raise money to pay off the back rent to Jesset, we're selling off anything not nailed to the floor. And if it's nailed, we're lenient. Dad owns all the equipment, and it's expensive. The local bowling alley owners flit around the party and pick our bones clean. Pinball machine junkies crowd in the corner, considering our broken machines for renovation.

Almost every lane has a bowler stationed on the platform, or a group of red-faced partiers into their fourth beer. Yes, my dad smuggled some of his own beer into Bigmouth's. The air is full of nacho cheese aroma, Febreze, and that fibrous cancer smell from when we ripped up the carpet in Dad's office. The party was Dad's idea, but the sale was mine.

The equipment. The decorations. The trophies.

All gone come tomorrow morning.

Castelli High School had their finals this week, and the upcoming week is strictly formalities, the cleaning out of lockers and collecting of library books. Then I'll be free for the summer. Or as free as I can be. I'm still grounded until September. Dad insists I find another job now that Bigmouth's will be no more. Beckett and I both put in applications to Any Beans Necessary last weekend—our plan to spend the summer together.

When Beckett and I walked onto the quad together, holding hands, no one looked twice. This was such a big deal to us, but no one at school cared. Dad cared, though, and his pure adoration of Beckett came in handy when he convinced my dad to lift my grounding for prom. We spent the night on a yacht the school rented. Dancing, laughing, and kissing. There was so much kissing.

"There you are." Beckett dashes out of the way as a few kids run down the hall, holding a hot dog in a crinkled paper napkin above the crowd. He lost me earlier when we went to get food, and I returned to packing. Because some of these items? I don't want them auctioned off.

Plus, Beckett's dad is here with Willa and his mom, and I don't want to intrude on their family time. Beckett spent weeks tracking his dad down. He came home to Berkeley a few days ago.

"Hey." I ease a photograph off the wall and set it in the cardboard box, place a fold of newspaper down, and move on to the next frame.

"You aren't going to show off your mad skills?" He juts his chin toward the lanes before digging into his hot dog.

"Nah. Not today."

I crouch, study a picture of my mother. It's safe to say the past month gave me the time and space to untangle my emotions surrounding Bigmouth's, my fear of my father losing his purpose, and my worries over my brain's stability.

I finally went back to therapy with Sarah, and I let everything out. Every emotion—big or small—that I've kept bottled inside. During our first session back, I told Sarah about how scared I was of ending up like my mom. Dead before thirty. But Sarah helped me remember that I'm not my mental health, and there's no shame in being Caroline Wilson. That's a message I have to enforce daily.

When you fear something so long, it becomes habitual. And bad habits are hard to break.

I even agreed to see a psychiatrist. The psychiatrist diagnosed me after our first session—bipolar not otherwise specified, which means I exhibit some diagnostic symptoms. They might get worse, but maybe not. With my family history, it's better safe than sorry. But the psychiatrist explained that bipolar disorder is a *spectrum*, whereas pop culture and news cycles tend to focus on the extremes, driving home that stigma even further.

My case isn't extreme, but that's no guarantee for the future. My diagnosis can worsen if I stay careless. I have to be diligent and take care of myself. Between my new medication and weekly therapy sessions, I feel better than I have in a long time. And instead of shunning my mom, I've embraced all that we have in common.

I'm back to living carefully and consciously but not cautiously.

I've even adopted a new mantra, a new set of calming words for when I'm overwhelmed.

I am my mother's daughter—and proud of it.

As for bowling, I haven't picked up a ball since the disaster at Billy Goat Bowl. Instead, I traded hustling for a more practical future—I'm working on my FIDM application. I'm also applying to FIDM's National Scholarship Competition to secure tuition for my first year and using my mom's designs as inspiration for my project. I'm even wearing one of her finished designs tonight. I spent the last two weeks sewing it. A sleeveless off-white sundress with a hand-beaded belt, the gauzy white material light and summery.

Beckett crumples up his hot dog wrapper and hoists me to my feet. "You tried," he whispers into my ear, nuzzling my neck. I revel in his spicy scent, insta-comfort. "That's way more than anyone else would do."

I turn into Beck and wrap my arms around him. His thin T-shirt sticks to his chest with a light sheen of sweat and my fingers make fists with the fabric. Now that he has someone to stitch those broken seams, Beckett's shirts no longer have holes and all the buttons match. He's still the Patron Saint of Cute Messes, and I wouldn't trade that for the world. He's real. Anyone can appear put-together and normal, but there's something damn nice about a person who's comfortable displaying their stains rather than hiding them.

Beckett kisses my forehead. "I get this is hard, but we knew this day would come."

I loosen a sigh. "Yeah, but it's weird. And tomorrow—"

"I'll be here tomorrow, too."

As if one change isn't enough, tomorrow the movers are carting away the rest of our lives. We can't stay in our yellow Victorian house on the hill. It was silly to ever humor the idea we'd have the house without Bigmouth's, but I'd harbored a secret hope. The bank wants to foreclose on the house, so Dad found us a tiny apartment near Golden Gate Park. No Hayes Valley, lush hills, and colorful houses, but we're still in San Francisco.

We're staying in the city of my heart, and I'm grateful. I really am.

But something else is missing. There's an Aunt Fiona–shaped hole. My aunt's moving up north after Dad and I settle at our new apartment. She snagged a job writing articles of substance for the *Seattle Times* and leaves California for Washington tomorrow night. The Bug is packed, the rest of her belongings already on their way to the Pacific Northwest. Also in Seattle? The girlfriend she met online and started dating last month.

Now she'll have her own relationship to obsess over. Not mine and Beckett's.

Beckett and I lean against the wall, our shoes slipping on the red-and-white-checkered linoleum floor. It's peeling up around the corners, one of the next things to go. The new tenant is renovating the building, and they'll take or trash whatever we leave behind. Which is why we're trying to make the most out of this final night.

Dust tickles my nose, and my fingertips are smudged with newspaper ink. We watch the owner of Billy Goat Bowl, of all places, eye our ball returns. It's not like we're selling everything. We're keeping the jukebox, the photographs I'm packing, my vinyl stool, and the broken neon sign, the last of which will go into garage storage at our apartment.

I pick up the latest addition to our wall of photographs, the frame cheap, encasing a newspaper article from the *San Francisco Chronicle* last month. The headline reads OWNER OF SOON-TO-CLOSE VINTAGE BOWLING ALLEY GETS ONE FINAL STRIKE and includes a very dorky photograph of Dad in front of Bigmouth's.

When Dad found out his sucker punch to Ray Wilkes's face led to his arrest and several videos surfaced online of the fight, Dad spoke with the police. He wasn't fined or given jail time. The police looked the other way, since Wilkes manhandled me and hailed Dad as a local hero for helping them catch the criminal.

The trial's set for late summer, but things aren't looking good for Wilkes. We later found out Nic called the cops. I don't know if he'd been worried for Wilkes's safety, or if he was trying to get him arrested; he's disappeared. Good for Nic.

Beckett pulls the framed newspaper article from my hands and sets it in the box with the others. After helping me pack the rest of the photographs, he says, "You realize you don't work here anymore, right? Relax and have some fun."

I laugh shortly. "I can't believe I'm saying this, but I'll miss this place."

"Me too."

Beckett holds out his hand, and I grasp it. We stash the box of photographs behind the counter and zigzag our way to the crowd of people. Friends. Strangers. Former employees. It's a different atmosphere than I'm used to at Bigmouth's.

Dad's tipsy, laughing at Aunt Fee as she tries to bowl. Their happiness is warm and swelling. Even with the little red stickers on half the sellable items. It's a new beginning, right?

We left my favorite ball at the league tournament, so Beckett brings me a close second, an Ebonite, from the racks. The couple that owns Double Decker already claimed our impressive stock of bowling balls, but they're not picking them up until tomorrow morning.

"You know you want to." Beckett holds the marbled orange-and-blue ball out like a tantalizing piece of candy, but I hesitate.

I went to illegal lengths to save Bigmouth's and failed epically. But we're all going to be okay. Dad's already got a job lined up working for BART, and Yoga Leigh is becoming a permanent feature. Tonight she's with Dad, wearing stretchy pants and a flowery top, drinking a beer.

Yoga Leigh's not as flawless and Zen as I typecast her to be. I watch as she attempts to bowl one-handed, her cup of beer in the other. The ball wings into the gutter, beer splattering on her top. She tosses her head back and laughs. No. Not perfect. Leigh's smart, owns her own yoga studio, and bought us a new coffee maker. It's taken some getting used to, but I don't hate her.

I eventually fessed up to reading Leigh's blog, and she's been supportive. In a strange way, she's helped me work through these complicated feelings about my mom. Not everyone falls prey to the darkness inside their minds. And even if they do, it's not their fault. I think, more than anything, I needed someone to show me that. To be an example. No stereotypes of mental illness on TV, no sensationalized stories in the news, just people taking care of themselves and thriving in the process.

Turning away from my family, I slide my fingers into the holes and grip the orange-and-blue Ebonite. The ball is heavier than I normally play with, but my muscles appreciate the strain. Lane fifteen is empty, and Beckett follows me, carrying a ball of his own. He still sucks, but he loves it, and that's what matters. Loving something even when you make a fool out of yourself.

Kind of like my relationship with Beckett.

"One strike," he teases as he sets up at lane fifteen, "then I'll stop harassing you."

I scoff, pretending to be offended. "A strike is easy. Let's see *you* throw a strike."

Beck laughs and makes a wily attempt at knocking down all ten pins. He misses, of course. "Your turn."

I cast him a rueful glance, then approach the foul line. How odd. Bowling when there aren't piles of money on the table, men with switchblades, or shady deals with strangers. It's almost anticlimactic. Because I'd be lying if I said I didn't enjoy my stint breaking the law. There's a certain rush to it. But I hated how it felt to be drunk. I hated the disappointment reflected in my father's eyes. I hated Wilkes's anger and being indebted to him. Just because a bad situation turns out okay doesn't mean you want to repeat history.

My hustling days are definitely over.

I hold my shoulders back, take three quick steps, and toss the ball. My muscles sigh as I release, and the ball rolls down the lane. I smile when it crashes with the headpin.

My strike pops up on the leaderboard. A beautiful X to signify my score. I flex my toes in my flats and hold my hand out to Beckett. "Hey, let's go outside."

Even though we have a week of school left, summer

looms, and with it comes the rest of my grounding. Who knows how often I'll see Beckett. Unless we both land jobs as baristas, we'll spend most of our summer apart. The thought ruins me.

Dad's busy with Aunt Fee and Yoga Leigh, so I link my hand with Beckett's and we weave through the crowd. Mila waves from the snack bar and I hold up one finger, telling her I'll circle back in a minute so we can hang out. The crowd presses against us, and I'm eager to slip out the emergency exit, where the back alley is dark and cool. We step outside and shut the door behind us. June is right around the corner, not yet summer. No longer spring. Something in between.

I push Beckett up against the brick wall of Bigmouth's and kiss him.

Because there's nothing quite like kissing Beckett Porter.

It's a rush, not dissimilar to the rush of winning thousands of dollars, knowing we have each other.

Bigmouth's Bowl won't be here tomorrow morning, but it will never be truly gone. Beck's right. I tried saving a cause that was beyond saving. Not for noble reasons. I wanted this. I wanted to stay in my hilly city, kiss a boy with amazing hair, and hold on tight to our fragile memories.

San Francisco is brimming with forgotten hearts, but mine will forever be pressed within its gray skies, rust with the paint on the Golden Gate Bridge, and soar like the Powell-Hyde cable cars. Tomorrow morning Bigmouth's Bowl will be closed. That's okay, because we'll still be here—the girl with a San Franciscan heart and the boy with morning-fog eyes.

Author's Note

Chuck's story, while it shares many parallels with my own mental-health journey, is fictional. But like Chuck, I come from a family where mental health was never discussed—until it was almost too late. In middle school, I fell into a serious depression that included suicidal ideation. By high school, I received a diagnosis on the bipolar disorder spectrum.

When my peers learned of my diagnosis, I wasn't treated with empathy. Like Chuck, I was called a "crazy bitch" on more than one occasion during high school. My mental health became gossip fodder, and as a result, I became deeply ashamed. The narrative—*my* narrative—changed. No longer did I have a medical diagnosis. No, I had a label. One that came jam-packed with enough stigmas to last me a lifetime.

Stigmas and stereotypes cause serious damage when it comes to mental health. As Chuck mentions in the last chapter, bipolar is a spectrum. But you'd never know that from media coverage to characters in books and movies. Bipolar is often romanticized, dramatized, and characterized—all highs, all the time. But what's important to remember is everyone's journey is different, and no one's experience is a monolith.

At times Chuck uses incorrect language, with terms

like "crazy" and "normal" in reference to herself and others. Through her fear and misinformation, she experiences disordered thinking. But in the end she manages to self-correct and learn. Not only about herself, but about her mother. While Chuck's guilt over her mother's death is very realistic, it shows her misinformation. When someone dies by suicide, it's *never* anyone's fault.

Symptoms of bipolar disorder, like all health conditions, can vary greatly by individual. If you're experiencing symptoms of bipolar, it's imperative to seek help from a medical professional. On the next page, I've included resources and information for mental health and suicide prevention.

According to NAMI, one in five children ages thirteen to eighteen will be diagnosed with a serious mental disorder. So, if you're that one in five—just like I was—you're not alone. I see you, and *trust* me when I say that life gets so much better. And if you're not that one in five? Be kind and empathetic to your peers. You never know how your support and understanding will impact their lives in the long run.

Resources

SAMHSA: Substance Abuse and Mental Health Services Administration
https://www.samhsa.gov
Suicide Prevention Hotline—1-800-662-HELP (4357)

NAMI: National Alliance of Mental Illness
https://www.nami.org

AFSP: American Foundation for Suicide Prevention
https://afsp.org/

DBSA: Depression and Bipolar Support Alliance
https://www.dbsalliance.org/

Psychology Today Therapist Database
https://www.psychologytoday.com/us/therapists

BPHope: Hope and Harmony for People with Bipolar
https://www.bphope.com/

Acknowledgments

First and foremost, thank you to my agent, Jennie Kendrick. Jennie, we've been through literary hell together and back! Between our mutual love of Seth Cohen and our adoration for all things San Francisco, I knew we'd make an unstoppable team. (I hereby promise to include all the Jennie Bait in my projects to come.) I can't imagine taking this wild publishing ride with anyone but you. You saw the potential in this book and fought like hell to find it a home. Thank you for being such an amazing agent—and friend.

The biggest thanks I can muster go to my editor, Jessi Smith. This book only exists today because of you and your boundless enthusiasm. Your keen insight, understanding, and compassion for Chuck brought this quirky little book to the next level; you gave my book the heart it sorely lacked. I don't think I can ever thank you enough. But, since I have to start somewhere: thank you, thank you, thank you.

Additional thanks to my entire team at Simon & Schuster/Pulse and my publisher, Mara Anastas. I feel incredibly lucky to be published with the very imprint I read as a teenager. Special thanks to Tiara Iandiorio for a cover so gorgeous that I turned it into my next tattoo.

Thank you to the wonderful ladies at Red Fox Literary. It's an honor to be a foxie. Hugs to RFL:OGJS—you all are a talented bunch of badass lady authors.

Over countless drafts and three years, this book has had many readers. But I began forming my writing family when I entered Pitch Wars in 2016. Thank you to Emily Martin for believing in my writing from day one. Many thanks to Jeanmarie Anaya—you were this book's very first champion, and I cannot thank you enough. Endless thank-yous and gratitude to Laura Lashley, Rachel Griffin, Mary Dunbar, Clay Harmon, Ian Barnes, and Heather Ezell. A special thank-you to Rachel Lynn Solomon for the endless well of publishing advice and guidance.

I'd be remiss if I didn't acknowledge some of this book's earliest readers. (I apologize for those awful first drafts you read! Yikes!) Rachel Simon, your positivity and enthusiasm for my writing makes my heart glow—thank you, friend. To Erin Cotter, for being a truly fantastic friend and critique partner; I can't wait to explore Seattle with you. To Andrea Contos, Austin and Emily, Molly Cluff, Julia Miller, and Lindsey Ouimet. Thank you to AMM for the guidance, support, and community.

Thank you to my family. Mom and Dad—your support and love know no bounds. Thank you for creating a home that encouraged reading and for making sure new books were never in short supply. Thank you to my sisters— Jessie, your enthusiasm for my writing means more than you know. (Also, thanks for letting me borrow your term of "hanger nipples" in this book!)

To my therapist, Heather Stone, for helping me reach a place of acceptance with my mental health and encouraging me to write my experiences with authority and authenticity. Thank you to Erin Byrn, for the friendship and workout sessions and laughter—I admire and miss you. To Sadie Blach, for always letting my scream my anxieties into your Twitter DMs.

Endless thanks and chin scrubs to Sofiya, the world's best and fluffiest cat. Your quiet disdain and ability to shed like no other inspired Chuck's cat, Jean Paul Gaultier.

Finally, thank you to Steve—my best friend and partner in crime. I would have never made it to this point without you. Since our very first date, you've listened to me go on about books, querying, and ALL my writing-related anxiety. And you're still listening, to this day. You've helped celebrate my wins and commiserated my losses. From Magic the Gathering tournaments to endless pots of coffee to hiking the Redwoods, you've helped me become the truest, happiest version of myself. And for that, I cannot thank you enough.